Make My Wish Come True

Katie Price is one of the UK's top celebrities. She was formerly the glamour model Jordan and is now a bestselling author and successful businesswoman. Katie is patron of The Vision Charity and currently lives in Sussex with her husband and five children.

Also available by Katie Price

Fiction
Angel
Angel Uncovered
Paradise
Crystal
Sapphire
The Comeback Girl
In the Name of Love
Santa Baby
He's the One

Non-Fiction
Being Jordan
Jordan: A Whole New World
Jordan: Pushed to the Limit
Standing Out
You Only Live Once
Love, Lipstick and Lies

Katie Price x

Make My Wish Come True

arrow books

1 3 5 7 9 10 8 6 4 2

Arrow Books
20 Vauxhall Bridge Road
London SW1V 2SA

Arrow Books is part of the Penguin Random House group of companies
whose addresses can be found at global.penguinrandomhouse.com.

Penguin
Random House
UK

First published as a hardback in the UK by Century in 2014
First published in paperback by Arrow Books in 2015

www.randomhouse.co.uk

A CIP catalogue record for this book is
available from the British Library.

ISBN 9780099598947

Typeset in Baskerville MT Std by SX Composing DTP Ltd, Rayleigh
Printed and bound by CPI Group (UK) Ltd, Croydon CR0 4YY

MIX
Paper from
responsible sources
FSC® C018179

Penguin Random House is committed to a sustainable future
for our business, our readers and our planet. This book is
made from Forest Stewardship Council® certified paper.

Then

As sunlight streamed through the kitchen window, Storm Saunders paused midway through basting the turkey and allowed the warmth to wash over her. She couldn't remember the last time the sun had put in an appearance on Christmas morning – perhaps it was the sign of a perfect day ahead for them.

It was only mid-morning but she had been up for hours, wrapping last-minute gifts, putting finishing touches to the tree, preparing the lunch and hastily getting rid of the mince pie left for Santa – all before her younger brother Bailey and sister Lexie got up.

Still, it had been worth it. The kids had loved the second-hand toys and games she had saved for, and her mother Sally had been impressed with the perfume set. As for Storm, her brother and sister had treated her to a lovely new pair of woolly gloves that were soft as snow. Spotting them on the worktop, she absentmindedly stroked them. She always felt the cold and was touched the kids had remembered that. After she had pushed the turkey back into the oven, she flicked on the kettle and reached on top of the breadbin for her bumper edition of *Vida!* magazine. Peering at the kitchen clock, she saw there was just enough time for her to catch up on some celebrity gossip. Bliss!

'Enjoying a well-earned rest, love?' said Sally, walking into the kitchen.

'Something like that,' replied Storm, unable to tear her eyes from the magazine. 'I've got about twenty minutes before I have to put the spuds on.'

'Why don't you let me do that?' her mother suggested. 'Go out and play with Bailey and Lexie. They're dying to show off the new scooter that you bought them.'

Storm looked up from her magazine in surprise. Usually Sally didn't get out of bed until lunchtime. Perhaps the sun outside really was a promise of change.

'If you're sure?' Storm grinned, eager for the chance to spend some time with the kids. 'I'll take them to the park for an hour.'

'Don't rush back,' Sally replied, shooing Storm away as she reached for the apron hanging behind the kitchen door. 'I can manage here.'

Storm walked along the hallway's threadbare floral carpet, calling to her brother and sister, 'Kids, get your coats on. We're going to the park.' Hearing the sudden scramble of Bailey and Lexie running down the stairs, she couldn't help smiling. Christmas really could be a magical time of year.

Reaching for their hands, Storm shouted goodbye to her mother and together the three of them walked out into the cold morning air. They were halfway down the road when Storm realised she'd forgotten her gloves. 'You guys wait here for just two seconds and I'll be right back,' she told them, racing towards the house.

But passing the kitchen window, Storm stood rooted to the spot as she took in the sight of Sally adding a very generous measure of whisky to her cup of tea. Storm's eyes brimmed with tears as she watched her mother sip her drink and smile. To any bystander this would just look like a busy mum enjoying a drink on Christmas morning. But Storm knew the truth of it – since her father Alan had passed away four years ago, her mother had become an alcoholic, constantly looking for ways to sneak a drink whenever she could.

Looking at her mother now, filling her mug with more whisky, Storm felt like kicking herself. How could she have been so stupid as to hope for a happy Christmas? Leaving the gloves, she stuffed her hands in her pockets as she ran back towards the kids, she realised that for her there was no such thing.

Chapter One

Storm raced into her flat and began tearing off her clothes before the door had even banged shut.

As a journalist for Brighton's *Daily Post* she'd spent the past three hours covering what could only be described as the world's most boring planning meeting, and was now running seriously late for her one and only swanky Christmas party.

'Can you get me a wine?' she shouted to Dermot, her boyfriend. 'I'm gagging! The meeting ran over.'

'You're the one who looks like you've been run over,' a voice bantered from the living room.

Storm spun round and saw her friend Carly, taking the piss as always. Perched on the battered IKEA sofa, smiling her trademark toothy grin, she waved a bottle of supermarket champagne in the air. The best medicine! Dumping her bag on the floor, Storm realised one of the reasons why she and Carly were best mates.

'You're a mind reader, I've had a shitty day,' she complained to her friend.

'I'd ask you to tell me all about it, but before he went out Dermot said you were covering some council thing. I think the details might kill the party spirit.'

Fair point. Watching her friend fill her glass, Storm admired Carly's outfit. At a little over five foot Carly was sensitive about her height, but she was an absolute stunner. Tonight she was dressed in a black and coral shift dress, skyscraper black heels and a chunky metal necklace. With her long blonde hair effortlessly piled on top of her head and secured with diamante pins, she looked gorgeous.

'Do you ever have an off day?' Storm asked, hugging her friend.

'Can't afford too, babe, image is everything!' As a stylist Carly never walked out of the door looking less than one hundred per cent perfect. Luckily for Storm, Carly's job meant that she could usually lend her cash-strapped pal a bit of bling, and had even been known to 'lose' the odd designer dress Storm's way. Tonight, one of Carly's clients had invited her to the biggest party in town and Storm was her plus one.

Just as well. Being a journalist for the local rag wasn't exactly what you'd call glamorous. In fact, weekly planning meetings, neighbourhood watch groups and prize marrow contests were not at all what Storm had imagined when she'd left college seven years ago with dreams of becoming a showbiz journalist. Back then she'd imagined she'd be hanging out at Cameron Diaz's birthday party one day and shopping for Jimmy Choos with Cat Deeley the next.

Instead, despite hundreds of applications to magazines and newspapers across the UK, Storm had landed a job as a reporter for Brighton's *Daily Post*. The salary was so lean, the only designer lining her wardrobe was George at Asda – talk about a reality check.

She was well aware of how she measured up against her glamorous friend. Her hands were covered in biro and as for the unflattering purple blouse she'd thrown on that morning, she had a horrible feeling it reeked of stale garlic thanks to last night's takeaway. She kicked herself – she should have squirted on that extra bit of perfume before leaving the office.

As Storm reached for a glass and took her first grateful glug, the sound of the doorbell killed her party vibe.

'What now?' she grumbled, hurrying down the stairs.

Opening the door, she came face to face with Sally, who was clutching a pair of straightening irons as if her life depended on it. 'You left these behind when you styled my hair last week.' Her mother smiled and kissed Storm on the cheek. 'I thought you might need them for tonight.'

'Oh, you're a lifesaver, I'd forgotten all about them,' she said gratefully.

'No problem. Do you need any help getting ready?'

'Not really, Sal, but why don't you come on up for a cuppa and say hi to Carly?'

As Storm shut the front door she saw a cloud briefly pass over her mother's face. It wasn't lost on Storm how much Sally wanted to be called Mum, but even though she'd been clean almost nine years now Storm still found it difficult to forgive her for everything she'd put her children through.

Nobody had been happier than Storm when her mother had finally admitted she had a drink problem and went to Alcoholics Anonymous. Now she had sorted herself out and built a new life for herself away from drink. She worked part-time at a nearby supermarket and had made many friends while working on the checkout there. She liked to play bingo on nights out with them. But these days she insisted family came first.

'I've got to be there for my kids,' Sally always said.

Storm knew her mother meant well, but now that Storm had reached the age of twenty-five this show of maternal devotion was too little, too late. As far as Storm was concerned, Sally was never going to be anything more than a kind, well-meaning relative she had to keep an eye on. Nearing the top of the stairs, Storm was grateful to see Carly was already boiling the kettle. Storm could have kissed her – her bestie was always one step ahead when it came to Sally.

'Thought I heard voices. How are you, Sal? I haven't seen you for ages.'

As Carly gave Sally a warm hug, Storm wished she could be more like her friend, who seemed to find it easy to act naturally in every circumstance.

'Oh, Carly, it's wonderful to see you, love. You look fab.'

Graciously, Carly did a little twirl in the kitchen, showing off her new dress.

'Do you mind if I leave you both to it? I've got to ransack my wardrobe for something clean to wear,' Storm told them.

Carly grinned, handing her a carrier bag. 'You need to

chill, babe, it's all taken care of. Now, get your arse in gear and get that on so we can enjoy a girlie night out.'

Reaching inside the bag, Storm gasped as she pulled out a midnight blue mini-dress studded with crystals. It was obviously designer and God knows how much it cost. More than she'd make in a year, if not two. Turning the soft material over in her hands, she smiled in delight. 'It's gorgeous, thanks.'

Carly poured herself another glass of champagne, and shrugged. 'No biggie. Just don't spill anything on it, that one is not on permanent loan!'

Emerging from the shower with her wet hair wrapped in a towel, Storm quickly did her make-up. When she wasn't wearing a suit, she stuck to her uniform of skinny jeans, jumpers and a slick of lip gloss. But tonight she had a feeling her usual mango lip butter wouldn't cut it.

Considering the contents of her make-up bag, Storm decided to go for a classic smoky eye with lots of sultry black kohl and a nude lip gloss to give her a super sexy pout. After blow drying her long hair she reached for the dress, teaming it with a pair of tan stilettos and a matching clutch. Storm felt like a different person. Peering at her reflection in the full-length mirror, she hardly recognised herself. There was no denying the dress was a brilliant fit. It showed off her long, slender legs and hugged her in all the right places, but it was so short it barely covered her arse! Feeling self-conscious, she tugged it down.

'You sure I don't look mutton in this?'

'Don't be stupid,' said Carly firmly. 'Storm, quite

honestly, if I had your legs I probably wouldn't even bother wearing a skirt at all.'

'Carly's right, Stormy. You look beautiful. A far cry from when you were a teen and barely knew one end of a mascara wand from the other,' Sally teased her.

Yes, because make-up was the last thing I had time for when I was so busy taking care of you and being mum to your other two kids, Storm thought furiously.

She had never forgotten how, when she was still coping with the shock of her dad's death, she'd been cruelly teased by the kids at school. Tall and skinny, with pale skin and thick black hair, she'd become a target for the bullies. But over the years Storm had blossomed and was now a knockout with her high cheekbones, taut stomach, clear porcelain skin and deep green eyes. As for the long black hair she'd always hated, it now hung in natural face-framing waves, highlighting her perfect features.

Outside Carly hailed two cabs, one to take Sally home and another for Storm and herself. By half-past nine the two women had reached the seafront restaurant and were more than ready for a good time.

Nico's had opened a month ago and already had an achingly long waiting list. The celebrity chef, known for his brooding Italian good looks, not to mention his Latin temper, was famed for cooking up hip fusion food with a Mediterranean twist. With a primetime TV show and Michelin-starred restaurants in London, Hampshire and now Brighton, Nico had been catapulted into A-list stardom over the last year. When Carly had insisted Storm should join her at his Christmas party, she didn't even need to check her diary to see if she was free – she was there! When she'd pressed her mate for details of who exactly was on the guest list, Carly had reeled off an impressive list of names that included several actors, reality stars and TV presenters, as well as a string of premiership footballers and WAGs.

Spotting a stack of paps waiting by the red carpet, Storm clambered out of the cab with as much grace as possible in what she felt could only be described as a pussy pelmet. Linking her arm through Carly's, she felt a stab of excitement as they sashayed up the red carpet together.

'How posh is this?' Storm exclaimed.

The restaurant looked stunning. The huge white sash windows were lit with gold hurricane lamps and matching candles. At the entrance stood two enormous pillars, decked in billowing gold drapes. As for the red carpet itself, understated was not the look the party planners had gone for, as a glittering gold yarn with the restaurant's name was woven into the luxe red pile. The whole place screamed glamour – and the security guards dressed in black suits and crisp white shirts added an extra frisson to the general excitement of it all.

Watching the latest TV star glide up the carpet towards the paps, Storm felt a flash of irritation. A journalist just out of her teens stuck a microphone into the star's face and asked which designer she was wearing. How had a young reporter got so lucky?

Sensing trouble, Carly quickly pulled Storm towards the restaurant's entrance and gave their names to the girl in charge of the guest list.

'Have a night off,' whispered Carly. 'You're beautiful, talented, and one day you'll get your big break without sleeping your way to the top like that skank probably did!'

Typical Carly. She always knew just what to say to cheer her up. Storm was seriously impressed to find that inside the restaurant had even more of the wow factor. Greeted by a waiter dressed in black tie, she grabbed a glass of champagne and took a sip. Bliss! Usually the only Christmas do she managed was the office party, where everyone indulged in overcooked turkey and a slab of Arctic Roll at the local pub. Her editor Ron always guzzled way too much whisky and tried to pull Lucy from advertising.

Now Storm drank it all in. Here were the rich and famous, dressed from head to toe in couture. As they sipped free-flowing champagne and feasted on delicate canapés, the sultry voice of Emeli Sandé pumped through the sound system. In one corner stood a huge Christmas tree, lavishly decorated in gold and black, and in another a small gold and black stage had been set up for superstar singers to perform on later. Peering around the corner, Storm was delighted to see a group of elves inside a massive gingerbread house, helping guests make their very own delicious miniature versions – this party really was the bollocks!

'Thanks so much for inviting me, babe.'

'Any time!' Carly smiled as she scanned the room, looking for anyone she might know – it didn't take long.

Weaving her way through the crowds with Storm following close behind, she patted the shoulder of a man dressed in skinny black jeans and a fitted blazer. He whipped around and his face broke into an excited smile as he saw Carly. 'OMG, you look fab!' he said, air kissing her on both cheeks before she introduced him to Storm.

'That dress looks like it was made for you – damn, girl, you look fierce.'

Storm smiled. Jez was clearly a sweetheart. She'd heard all about him from Carly, as they often worked together when she styled magazine shoots, but Storm had never had the pleasure of meeting him until now. She knew Jez was a hairdresser, gay, married to Rufus and total BFFs with Brighton royalty Angel Summer and Liberty Evans, the Hollywood actress who flitted between the States and the south coast with her artist fiancé Cory Richardson.

'Thanks! You're totally rocking that Tom Ford,' Storm replied.

'Oh, I'd like to do more than rock Tom Ford,' sighed Jez theatrically. 'With those brooding eyes, he is *gorgeous*!'

'And what am I . . . chopped liver!' mocked the good-looking man standing next to him.

Jez smiled fondly at his husband Rufus. 'Darling, you know I only have eyes for you, but Tom's on my allowed list! Besides, I said I'd totes forgive you an indiscretion with Michael Fassbender. But enough about me. What do you do, Storm?'

'Oh, Storm's a news—' cut in Carly.

'Don't say it!' she interrupted, putting a hand in front of Carly's face. 'Tonight I'm anything but a local newspaper hack. I'm having a night off, like you said.'

'Ooh, be an air stewardess!' exclaimed Jez. 'With those

legs you could easily pass for a trolley dolly, doling out chicken or fish in first class.'

Storm giggled. 'Knowing my luck, I'd end up dropping it in their laps so often I'd be bumped straight back to economy, but it's definitely different.'

'And what about you?' Jez turned to Carly. 'The spray tan you had earlier really sets off that divine little coral number. Wearing it for anyone in particular tonight?'

'Pah! I'm off men, remember?'

'Darling, can I be honest? I know you caught your ex with his hand in the cookie jar, but they're not all the same, I promise.'

That's putting it mildly, thought Storm. A year ago, Carly had been loved up and planning the wedding of the century to Paul, a music promoter. With his open, friendly face and thinning hair, Paul wasn't the best-looking bloke Storm had ever seen but he adored Carly.

They'd been together five years when he'd proposed on a beach in the Maldives with a whopping two-carat diamond engagement ring. And although Storm would never admit this in a million years, from the moment Paul had slipped that ring on her finger, Carly became a bit of a Bridezilla. In fact, she got so wound up about everything that she made herself ill and fainted at work. Jez sent her home, making her promise she'd do nothing more than put her feet up for the rest of the day.

But when Carly walked through the door, she found Paul with another woman in their bed. Poor Carly was broken-hearted. To add insult to injury, Paul then threw her out of the flat he owned, telling her that the slapper he'd been screwing was moving in instead. Bastard! Storm could have killed him.

Thanks to Jez, who had once dated an estate agent, Carly found a gorgeous new flat overlooking the sea. After selling the ring, she had enough money for a deposit and could rebuild her life.

Now she was doing much better, but Storm knew her friend was still fragile. She hadn't been on a date since the split.

'Listen, I know the hottest straight man with seriously ripped abs,' continued Jez.

Rufus rolled his eyes. 'Don't ask how he knows that.'

'Yes, well, I might have tried to show him the error of his ways by convincing him he was wasted as a heterosexual, but he wasn't having it. Anyway, you know what they say . . . when you fall off a horse, you have to get right back on. And I think he'd be the perfect stud to get you back in the saddle!'

'Yeah, come on, live a little. We're at a party, there must be someone here you fancy,' Storm coaxed her friend.

'Thanks, guys, but no.'

Storm reached for a canapé from a passing waiter's tray and took a hungry bite. 'If you don't get some action soon, you're in danger of becoming a virgin again, and you know how bad it was popping your cherry first time around!'

'Cheers for that, but seriously I'm in no mood to find Mr Right or even Mr Right Now.'

'What about Mrs Right? Jez twinkled. 'If you fancy a complete change of scene, I know a gorgeous American lesbian who insists on a Brazilian, if you know what I mean.'

'We all know what you mean!' laughed Carly. 'And, no, leave me alone, all of you! I don't want a man, or a woman, or even a Rampant Rabbit! All I want is another drink.'

With that, Carly left her pals to gossip and went in search of more champagne.

By half-past ten the party was in full swing. Scanning the now crowded restaurant, Storm caught sight of Carly by the Christmas tree, being chatted up by a very handsome man. Tall, mixed-race, with broad shoulders and dressed in designer jeans and a navy V-neck jumper, he was gorgeous. Storm looked again. Hang on. That was only Dillon Adams, Chelsea's newest player. Way to go, Carly!

Storm smiled. It was about time Carly listened to her. She couldn't avoid men for ever. And this one was seriously hot – maybe Carly was in for a little Christmas bonus. God knows, she deserved it. But taking a closer look, Storm realised Dillon wasn't chatting Carly up. Instead he seemed to be having a go at her. With his face bent over hers and a mean look in his eyes, Dillon appeared menacing. As for Carly, she looked defeated with her eyes cast down and her mouth set in a grim line. Storm knew tears would start flowing any minute.

Tosser! Who the fuck did this two-bit footballer think he was, upsetting her friend? She drained her drink, banged down the empty glass on the nearest table and threw her shoulders back, ready to give the scumbag a piece of her mind. She didn't see the man heading towards her, carrying a very large glass of red wine. As Storm stepped straight into his path they collided, wine spilling all over his pristine white shirt.

'*Per l'amor di Dio!* Try looking where you're going,' the man snarled.

Storm was horrified. 'I'm so, so sorry. Let me help clean you up.'

Reaching into her clutch for the packet of tissues she always carried, she feebly started patting at the stranger's chest. But it was no use, she was only making the stain worse. Aghast, she looked up into his seething eyes. What she saw took her breath away – he was fit! Taller than her, with olive skin and black hair that was greying at the temples, he was seriously her type.

'Just leave it,' the stranger hissed, gripping her wrist.

His touch sent a jolt of electricity through Storm. Looking into his chocolate brown eyes, she knew he'd felt it too. Dropping her hand as if it had scalded him he stepped back, their eyes still locked. As Storm's pulse raced the man eventually looked away, breaking the spell. His fierce expression softened.

Taking a deep breath, he looked down at his shiny Italian loafers before returning his gaze to Storm. 'I'm sorry. I overreacted, it's just a shirt, and I shouldn't have lost my temper like that . . .?'

'This is Storm, she's an air stewardess,' chimed in Jez, who had very suddenly appeared at his new friend's side. Elbowing Storm out of the way, he thrust his hand towards the stranger and babbled on. 'She's just as clumsy in first class, so she's back in economy from next week. Let me just say, hand on heart, Nico, those lobster canapés were to die for.'

Storm looked again at the man quietly steaming in front of her. Of course – Nico Alvise! Some showbiz journalist she would make if she couldn't even recognise the man throwing the party. Storm wanted the ground to swallow her up there and then. Had she really just slopped wine all over the hottest chef in the country?

Must have been those razor-sharp cheekbones that distracted me, she thought as she ran her eyes appreciatively over his face and what appeared to be some very solid pecs. Shit! What was the matter with her? She had a boyfriend at home!

As Jez prattled on Storm saw a smartly dressed young woman scurry over to Nico to hand him a fresh white shirt. He murmured his thanks and turned back to Storm, bending down to kiss her cheek.

'My apologies again for losing my temper. Please enjoy the rest of the party. *Ciao, bella.*'

Speechless, Storm watched him walk away, already unbuttoning his sodden shirt. Jez nudged her sharply in the ribs.

'What a silver fox! He's even better in real life than he is on the telly. What I wouldn't give . . .'

'Adding him to your list, are you?' she laughed.

'I'm tempted. He's like a younger George Clooney, and you know Clooney never goes out of style.'

'Forget it. My husband wouldn't have time to get through his existing list, never mind start adding to it,' Rufus added, joining them.

'That's what you think. I'm a young man in my prime,

I'll have you know,' protested Jez. As he kissed Rufus firmly on the lips, Storm was finally able to rescue her friend.

It didn't take long to find her. Sitting alone at the bar in a black velvet tub chair, Carly was steadily working her way through another glass of champagne. It looked like she was definitely drinking to forget, Storm thought, as she slid into the chair next to hers.

'Everything all right?'

'Yeah, fine,' Carly slurred.

Storm grimaced. 'Don't give me that, babe. You know I can see right through your bullshit. How do you know Dillon Adams and why was he giving you grief?'

'No reason,' muttered Carly, pretending Storm didn't know her better than she knew herself.

Wordlessly Storm waited. She reached for another glass of champagne. She knew Carly would talk eventually. 'I've done something really stupid,' her friend admitted.

'What? Convinced a bitchy client to buy a mini-dress when they've got legs like tree trunks?' Storm teased her.

Carly shook her head. Putting her hand over her eyes, she started weeping.

'If only it were that simple.'

For the second time that night, Storm reached into her clutch for a tissue. This time she pressed it into her best friend's hand and put her arm around Carly's heaving shoulders.

'Bollocks!' Carly sniffed back tears. 'It took me hours to do my make-up tonight.'

'Yeah, and you'll have to go to the loos and spend hours doing it all over again unless you want to look like Marilyn

18

Manson.' Storm smiled. 'Now tell me what is going on?'

'Promise me you won't tell anyone?'

'Do you really have to ask that?' Storm fired back.

The girls had been through hell and high water together over the years and had been the keeper of more of each other's secrets than either of them cared to remember.

'You know I worked on a shoot for that football magazine the other week?' Carly sighed.

Storm nodded. Carly often styled models for the covers of glossy monthlies, but when a friend of hers fell ill at the last minute, she'd agreed to step in and style a handful of premiership players for a football mag.

'Yeah, you said it went really well.'

'It was brilliant. Afterwards one of the players wanted to talk to me about helping his sister find an outfit for her twenty-first birthday party, so we went to Nobu together and afterwards to The Sanderson for cocktails.'

'And?'

Carly didn't miss a beat. 'It was fab. I had the sea bass and one too many dirty Martinis.'

At the mention of food, Storm looked fleetingly around her. Everybody was now busy devouring the blinis which were being handed out. Storm's tummy grumbled appreciatively. The two canapés she'd eaten earlier hadn't touched the sides. Especially as all she'd had time for at lunch was a bag of Quavers and a can of Diet Coke. Now she was starving and predictably the booze was going straight to her head.

'But what about the outfit?' she urged.

Carly shifted uncomfortably in her chair. She'd forgotten

why Storm was such a good journalist. She was like a dog with a bone and always managed to get people to talk, not satisfied until she'd heard every last detail.

'That's the thing, we never actually got around to deciding on an outfit.' Carly laughed. 'I mean, we discussed it obviously, but after The Sanderson he was a bit tired, and so was I, so we . . .'

Storm squealed and clapped her hands in delight. 'You shagged him, didn't you? No wonder you didn't want to meet anyone tonight. Come on, I want all the gory details, and I mean *all*. Who is he? Are you going to see him again?'

Taking another sip of champagne, Carly drummed her fingers on the chair's armrest and avoided meeting her friend's eye.

Storm was confused. This was brilliant news. No wonder Carly didn't want to pull if she'd already met someone. So why the secrecy? This was something to celebrate! There was no reason for her suddenly to start being weird unless . . .

'He's married, isn't he?' Storm asked quietly.

Nodding her head, Carly slumped back in her chair. Storm did her best to hide her shock. Carly was the last person in the world she would have expected to do this. Storm thought back to all the late nights she'd shared with Carly drinking tequila after Paul had betrayed her. She'd lost count of all the conversations they'd had then, insisting they'd never sleep with a married man. That it was a total deal breaker. That you should always think about the wife or girlfriend at home waiting for her man.

'Please don't look at me like that, Storm, I didn't set out

to do this. I feel terrible about it.'

'So what happened?' she asked gently.

Carly didn't answer for what felt like an age. 'I don't know. I don't know if it was because I hadn't been touched in what felt like for ever, because I was lonely, because I wanted to feel loved and special for a change, because I was sick of being on my own . . . or even just because it felt like a good idea at the time.'

'Who is he?'

'I'd rather not say.'

'You've come this far, you might as well tell me everything.'

Carly hesitated then she said, 'Aston Booth.'

Storm flinched. Aston Booth wasn't just married, he had three kids and another on the way. Like Dillon, he played for Chelsea and England. Together with his wife Tanya he was always in the press, plugging his charity that helped disadvantaged kids across the world. Storm had thought he was different from a lot of footballers. He seemed a kind, decent, devoted family man, still madly in love with his childhood sweetheart. While other players were constantly in the press after bedding lap dancers, Aston never was. In fact, Storm was sure he had been in the papers the other day, talking about how he couldn't wait to be a dad again. Apparently he wanted a football team all of his own.

There could very well be a football team out there with his name already on it, thought Storm wryly. She suddenly felt nauseous and wasn't entirely sure it was down to lack of food. As for Carly, she looked beaten. Storm knew kicking her while she was down wasn't the answer. She'd suffered enough for one night.

'So how was he?' she asked, lightening the mood.

'OK,' Carly replied. 'Not brilliant, but definitely not the worst. He seemed a bit out of practice, shall we say?'

Storm giggled. 'And was it weird, being with someone else?'

Carly shrugged. 'Yeah, but it was nice. I took a photo of us together . . . look.'

Fishing out her phone, Carly showed her friend a selfie of her with Aston, who seemed completely absorbed in kissing Carly's neck. They looked like a typical couple, young and in love.

'Afterwards wasn't great,' Carly admitted as she put her phone away. 'He couldn't get out of the hotel quick enough. I thought he might at least stick around for breakfast.'

Storm said nothing. What else was Carly expecting? Hearts and flowers? He had a wife and kids to get back to, for God's sake.

'So what did his team mate want?'

'To warn me off going to the press.'

'As if you'd do something like that!' exclaimed Storm, loyal to the core. 'That is totally out of order, branding you as some cheap slut who needs to sell her soul for a couple of quid.'

It was not OK for some lowlife footballer to diss her best friend. Cheeky bastard!

'That's what I said, but Dillon told me there'd be trouble if I even thought about it. He said he'd make sure my career ended in tatters if I talked to the papers.'

Storm shook with rage as she scanned the room looking

for Dillon. He'd gone too far and she was about to tell him just how much of a tosser she thought he was. But he seemed to have disappeared. Getting to her feet, Storm suddenly sobered up. She realised it might be a blessing in disguise if he'd gone home after all. That wanker had ruined enough of their night. It was time to draw a line under all this.

'Let's party,' she said, reaching for Carly's hand.

The rest of the night passed in a blur as the girls drank too much champagne and ate too little. Thankfully, Storm didn't see Nico for the rest of the night and they both danced like mad as the DJ played hit after hit.

But if anyone was really going for it it was Jez, who prided himself on an outrageous Dirty Dancing routine.

With his pelvic thrusts and perfectly timed moves, he gathered quite a crowd of onlookers, including Storm and Carly who joined Rufus to show their support.

'What's got into him?' Carly asked.

'He filled in for one of the hairdressers on *Strictly* the other week,' Rufus explained. 'Since then he's convinced he's Craig Revel Horwood.'

'He looks more like Darcey Bussell, with that woman over there trying to pick him up,' Carly laughed.

Amazed, Storm saw a large woman try to lift Jez off the floor. Obviously pissed, it looked like she was trying to reinvent Patrick Swayze's famous move, but Jez was having none of it.

'Get off me!' he hissed, shaking himself free.

Back in solo performance, he was keen to step things

up a gear. It didn't take long. He soon had his audience's full attention as he grabbed hold of a counter-height table packed with drinks and began bumping and grinding against it as if his life depended on it. As the crowd whooped and cheered, he executed some further ambitious moves that included the splits and an eye-watering high kick.

Sadly for him, disaster struck when one turn too many brought the table and drinks crashing to the floor. Jez was lying on the ground, his blazer and skinny jeans soaked in champagne. Rufus rushed to his aid, leaving Storm, Carly and the crowd howling with laughter.

As Rufus pulled the table off Jez, he got to his feet and hobbled towards the girls. 'It's not bloody funny! I could have drowned in all that booze, you witches. In fact, it's a miracle I'm alive at all.'

'You've survived, but your street cred definitely hasn't,' Carly giggled.

Still shaking with laughter, they watched Jez limp towards a taxi. Deciding nothing was going to top that, the girls called it a night.

Chapter Two

The following morning Storm woke to find that drummers had moved into her brain. Gasping for water, she reached for the glass she always kept on her nightstand and gulped down the liquid gratefully.

'Oh, God! My mouth feels as dry as a pair of grubby Havaianas,' she groaned.

'So just how scuttered were you last night?' murmured Dermot, snaking his hand around her waist.

'You don't want to know.'

Leaning against the headboard, Storm reflected on the night before. On the whole, it had been brilliant. She and Carly had partied hard, and the place had been wall-to-wall with celebs. Star-struck at first, Storm had felt shy, but after a few glasses of champagne she'd loosened up. She'd spent a lot of time talking to a couple of the *Made in Chelsea* girls, who turned out to be really sweet. It was exactly the sort of event she'd have expected to cover if she'd ever made it as a showbiz journalist. But the chances of that happening now seemed even slimmer after she'd embarrassed herself by spilling wine all over last night's host.

Willing away the humiliation, Storm turned her head face down into the pillow. She wouldn't be invited back after showing herself up in front of Nico like that.

Dermot chuckled as he pulled her closer. 'What did you do this time?'

'Can't talk about it. Too embarrassing.'

He trailed his fingertips across her shoulders. 'Sure, I bet I can get you to open up.'

She didn't know if it was his soft Irish lilt, or just the fact that she was too knackered to resist, but Storm found herself melting into his featherlight kisses.

'Knew I could get you to talk,' he whispered. Easing her cotton nightshirt over her head, he gazed lustfully at her.

Afterwards they sank back gratefully against the mattress, the duvet tangled around their legs. Dermot propped himself up on one elbow and said, 'So tell all, darling, how was the *craic* last night?'

'Brilliant.'

'And your man Nico?'

At the mention of his name, Storm shuddered.

'Let's just say, I let the host know exactly who I was.'

A smile played over Dermot's lips. He knew what that meant. In the two years he'd been going out with Storm, he'd seen many times at first hand just how clumsy she could be. She'd dropped countless cups of tea and coffee, and broken more than her fair share of mirrors. The first time she'd invited him round to her place for dinner had become legendary. Storm had proudly told him she had cooked a Spanish chicken stew from scratch, but as she carried the casserole dish from kitchen to table she somehow ended up dropping the entire thing on the floor.

She had been furious with herself as she and Dermot scraped bits of chicken and tomato off the carpet. But he thought it was sweet and after they'd cleaned up the mess had treated her to a pizza around the corner, promising never to mention the incident again. Privately, Dermot nicknamed his girlfriend Calamity, but valuing his knackers as he did this was something he kept to himself. He always reckoned there was a reason why Alan and Sally had had the foresight to call their elder daughter Storm.

'And how was Carly? Did she pull anyone?'

Storm sighed as she thought about her best friend's latest disaster. There was nobody who deserved a chance of happiness more than Carly did. No doubt she was feeling rough in more ways than one after last night. Storm looked at her boyfriend, wondering just how much to tell him.

They'd met when Dermot had joined the paper as chief reporter just over two years ago, and Storm had never forgot the first moment they saw each other. With his sandy blond hair, square shoulders, piercing blue eyes and cool exterior, she'd fancied him straight away – and it seemed the feeling was mutual. Making a beeline for her cluttered desk, Dermot Whelan skipped the small talk and asked her out for a drink that night.

'Are you always this forward?' Storm demanded.

Dermot grinned cheekily, his broad Irish brogue already

making her melt. 'No, but when I see something I want, I go for it.'

Since they'd been together, Dermot had seemed to have become as fond of Storm's friend Carly as she had of him. Besides, they were a partnership, they didn't keep secrets from each other.

'OK, I'll tell you about it. But promise not to tell another soul?'

'Scout's honour,' Dermot replied, raising his right hand to his forehead and giving her the traditional salute.

Storm grinned. 'Do you even have the Scouts in Ireland?'

'Sure we do. I might have been thrown out for smoking on my first day, but I still made the promise.'

'And broke it too!' she shot back.

'Just tell me! Or do I have to make you?'

As Storm squealed in delight, Dermot pinned her wrists to the bed. Trailing a row of kisses across her already erect nipples, he left her in no doubt of the pleasure that lay ahead . . .

Over breakfast in their sunny kitchen overlooking the sea, Storm popped a couple of Paracetamol. After pouring herself a second cup of coffee, she mopped up the pool of tomato ketchup on her plate with the remains of her bacon sandwich and flicked through her guilty pleasure – *Vida!* magazine. She'd been addicted to it since she was a kid. When she'd been taking care of Sally and the kids, it was her one luxury. Back then it had provided a release from the drudgery of her everyday life and Storm had adored poring over the pages of glamorous celebrities and reading about their lives. It was almost as if she could pretend that she was there too, transported to another world that wasn't filled with drunk mothers and dead fathers. She couldn't stop fantasising about what it would be like to live in an exciting world filled with celebrities and parties, where your biggest worry was what you'd wear or how you'd style your hair.

Even though she was grown up now, she still loved the mag as much as she ever did and dreamed of working for the title one day. Reaching the back page, Storm was delighted to realise her headache had nearly gone. But then two rounds of sex first thing in the morning always made things better.

Storm smirked to herself. Should be available on prescription.

Looking around, she sighed contentedly. This room never failed to put a smile on her face. It was bright, with tall ceilings and windows overlooking the sea. She and Dermot had spent an entire weekend painting it a cheery yellow when they'd first moved in. Or rather, she and Carly had painted it. Dermot had been too busy working, apparently, and hadn't done much. It was the first time Storm had realised he would always put his career before her.

Setting a plate of toast and Marmite on the table, Dermot interrupted Storm's daydreams by taking a noisy bite.

'Do you have to?' Storm groaned. 'My headache was just beginning to go.'

'Forget about your headache,' he replied, spitting toast

crumbs everywhere. 'No more keeping me in suspense. What's going on with Carly?'

Where to start? Storm pushed the coffee cup away from her and looked him squarely in the eye. 'She shagged a married footballer the other week.'

Dermot's eyes were out on stalks. 'No way!'

'I know, I couldn't believe it myself when she told me.' Storm sighed.

'Bloody hell! I didn't think Carly was like that.'

'She's not,' Storm said firmly.

'But Carly's gorgeous, she could have her pick of blokes,' Dermot continued, ignoring Storm. 'Why on earth would she drop her standards and shag a footballer? And who is the lucky bastard?'

'Aston Booth.'

Crumbs flew across the table. 'Shit. Aston Booth! His wife's well fit, and didn't he just win Celebrity Dad of the Year or some bollocks?'

'Apparently,' Storm said sarcastically. 'Obviously not a lot of research goes into these awards.'

'Is she sure it was him? Not being funny, Stormy, but it wouldn't be the first time a bloke had pretended to be someone they weren't to get a woman into bed,' Dermot pointed out.

Storm reached into her work bag and pulled out a mobile.

'Somehow I ended up with Carly's phone last night. Look, she took a selfie of them together.' As she showed Dermot the picture, Storm carried on talking.

'You know, I'm worried about her. This team mate of

Aston's was at the party, warning her off going to the press.'

'Like she'd ever do that.'

'I know, but the scumbag made her cry, I'm worried it'll send her right back to rock bottom again.'

'Carly will be fine, she's been through a lot worse than this, and that Aston fella will have moved on to some other yoke now,' Dermot reasoned as he finished his toast and stood up to dump his plate and Storm's in the kitchen sink.

'True,' she agreed. 'But . . .'

'But nothing,' Dermot said firmly. 'Lookit, in a way it sounds as though she's back to normal, if she's finally slept with someone else.'

Storm paused. She hadn't thought of it like that. Perhaps in a funny way this was progress. Maybe now Carly had got that awkward first shag out of the way she'd feel ready to meet a nice bloke.

'You off to work in a minute?' Dermot asked, interrupting her thoughts.

'Yeah, got last night's exciting meeting to write up and I'm already running late.' Storm yawned. 'I'm going to need coffee intravenously if I'm to get through today. Plus I want to drop Carly's phone off on my way there and check she's OK, so I'd better get my skates on.'

Leaving her phone on the table, Storm rushed out of the room, leaving Dermot staring thoughtfully at her phone, a sly smile on his face.

Fifteen minutes later, Storm was ready to go.

'I'm not in until eleven so I'll see you at the office.' Dermot said, giving her a swift kiss on the cheek.

'OK, babes. Love you.' Grabbing her phone and bag, she ran out of the door.

Stopping at Carly's flat on her way to work, Storm couldn't help noticing how down her friend seemed. Despite the fact they'd had a brilliant night out, the whole Aston Booth saga was obviously upsetting her. And who could blame her? As if she needed another man to make her feel like crap. Storm felt bad she couldn't stay, but Ron would kill her if she took a sickie.

As soon as she got into the office Storm called Carly, just to make sure she wasn't sobbing into her pillow, but there was no answer; she must have gone back to bed. Slumping down at her desk with a sigh, wishing she could be asleep as well, Storm turned on her computer and was surprised to see an email from Miles Elliot, editor of the *Herald*, a national Sunday tabloid where she'd been doing some freelance work recently.

Strange. He'd never contacted her directly before, always leaving one of his minions to do that. Curious, she clicked it open and, as she read, all thoughts of Carly and her problems left Storm's mind.

I've been impressed with the work you've done for us in the last few weeks. The interview with the young widow was brilliant, and you seem to have a talent for getting people to talk to you. So I'd like to offer you a position on the showbiz desk effective immediately.

Storm was stunned. She knew Miles had been pleased with the widow's story which she'd brought in, but the last thing she would ever have expected from him was a job offer. And not just any job! It was the one she'd always dreamed of. Staring at the screen, she checked the email. Was this some kind of joke? Quickly she punched Miles's number into her phone and was put straight through to his secretary, who happily confirmed that Miles wanted her to start as soon as possible but wasn't available to talk to her today. She just needed to email a response.

Putting the phone down, still Storm couldn't believe it. This was the opportunity of a lifetime – and covering showbiz too. Wow! Dreams really did come true. That left her just the small matter of Dermot to deal with. He'd been after a job at the *Herald* for as long as she'd known him, and she wasn't sure how he'd take this news. Perhaps it would be better to wait until she saw him in person. She had a horrible feeling he wouldn't be pleased. Storm bit her lip; she had no idea how to handle this situation.

She glanced around the office, desperate to talk to someone, but couldn't speak to anyone at work, not until she'd seen Dermot. Grabbing her phone again, she dialled Carly, waiting impatiently for her friend to pick up. But there was no reply. Throwing her phone on her desk in frustration, Storm read the email again, still not quite believing that her dreams were starting to come true.

After that the office was unusually busy for a Friday and Storm's phone wouldn't stop ringing, but though she tried to concentrate all she could think about was Miles's email, awaiting her response. Feeling sick from a mixture of excitement and her hangover, Storm couldn't take it any more. If she didn't talk to someone she'd go mad. Bolting down two flights of stairs to the ladies and locking the cubicle door, she called Carly, only to hear her voicemail again.

'Babe, call me! It's urgent!'

Aargh! She needed her best friend more than ever. Where was Carly?

Sitting on the toilet seat, Storm thought about how her life was about to change. Not only would she finally be doing what she'd dreamed about, but she'd have many more nights out like last night – champagne, dancing, celebrities, and fit chefs . . . what more could she want? But despite it all, she was scared. Would Dermot stick with her or would their relationship founder? And she hated leaving Carly when she seemed so down . . .

As if on cue her phone rang – Carly. Finally!

'What's up, babes? You sounded frantic.'

About to blurt out her news, Storm paused. Carly sounded croaky, as if she'd been crying. Maybe it could wait a bit. 'I was worried about you. You seemed sad this morning, are you OK?'

'Sorry. Monster hangover so I went back to bed after I saw you and slept it off.'

Storm felt a pang of envy. She'd have given her right arm for a lie in. Then again, she thought, blushing as she remembered the passionate sex she and Dermot had enjoyed that morning, waking early definitely had its advantages.

'So how are you feeling after last night?' Storm asked her.

Carly hesitated then said, 'I'm all right. I mean, I'm

still upset about what happened, but the way I look at it, we're all human, and we all make mistakes. I never have and never would go to the press, so I've nothing to worry about.'

'I'd just hate that wanker who threatened you last night to think his tactics worked,' Storm sighed.

'Yeah, well, he's a tosser, just like Aston. I've decided to forget about them both, chalk it up to experience and concentrate on single men only from now on.'

'Good for you, babe. He's definitely not worth it,' Storm replied, excited to hear her friend talk about future boyfriends. 'We'll soon find you a nice hot bloke, I promise. Anyway, listen, can I come round after work? I need to talk to you.'

'Why? What's up?'

Hearing someone come into the ladies, Storm dropped her voice to a whisper.

'Listen, I can't talk now, I've got to get back to work – I'll call you later, OK?'

Back at her desk after lunch, Storm flipped through her notepad. Scanning her notes, she wasn't surprised to find her scribbles were just as dull as the council meeting she'd been to the day before. God, how could she concentrate on this? She felt a bubble of excitement swell inside her. Soon she'd be writing up interviews with film stars. No more trying to make town parking issues interesting! Throwing the pad on to her desk, she looked up and spotted her editor walking briskly her way.

Shit! She was supposed to have finished this story an hour ago. He was going to have a right go at her. She may be about to leave, but she didn't want to leave anyone in the lurch. Sitting up straight, Storm stared ahead at her computer screen and pretended to be typing.

'Storm, where's Dermot?' asked Ron, getting straight to the point.

'Dunno . . . at his desk?'

Craning her neck over towards Dermot's cubicle, Storm expected to see his sandy curls peeping over the top of the divider. But there was nobody there. He must have popped out.

'Don't get clever with me,' Ron shot back at her.

'At lunch then?' she suggested brightly.

Ron Jones wasn't a patient man. An old school cockney with a reputation for taking no prisoners, he prided himself on slicing through bullshit like butter. Now it was Storm's turn to know he meant business.

'To take a lunch break he'd have to turn up for work in the first place, and nobody's seen him all day. Now, I'm asking you nicely. Where is he?'

'Um . . . maybe he's got wind of a scoop?' Storm suggested nervously. 'You know what he's like.'

'What sort of a story stops him answering his phone?' Ron snapped, bringing his fist down hard on Storm's desk, making her jump. 'I bloody well need him here. There's a crisis over at the town hall and I want my chief reporter to cover it. Find him!' he snapped before storming back to his office.

Storm looked down at her keyboard and tried to make sense of what Ron had just said. Dermot didn't have a day off. In fact, he'd said he'd catch up with her at the office.

She'd been expecting to see him any minute. Where the hell was he?

Reaching for her phone, she dialled Dermot's number but it just rang and rang. She tried again, but this time the call went straight to voicemail. What was happening?

Anxiously she called Carly, who answered on the first ring.

'Random question, but I don't suppose you've seen Dermot this morning?'

'No. Why the panic?'

Quickly, Storm explained.

'I wouldn't worry, babes. He's probably just gone to a meeting and forgotten to tell anyone.'

Ending the call, Storm realised Carly was right. But ten minutes later she was back in panic mode. What if Dermot wasn't in a meeting? What if he was lying in a ditch somewhere hurt? She couldn't stand it any more. Punching in the numbers of the fire and police press officers, Storm asked if there'd been any accidents that morning.

'Nothing serious, Storm, why do you want to know?' the police press officer asked.

'No reason, Mike. Just can't find Dermot.'

'He'll be fine, Storm, he's probably chasing some story – he'd wrestle an alligator if it meant he'd get a scoop.'

Storm hung up, knowing Mike was right. When she had first started dating Dermot she'd been impressed by his focus on reaching the big time. He fancied himself as the next Piers Morgan and often covered the weekend graveyard shift on the *Herald*.

Dermot's commitment to work was admirable, but it meant that Storm was often only at the back of his mind. He routinely forgot her birthday and their anniversary, and thought nothing of standing her up if he had a story to cover. Often Storm went for days without seeing him, which was why she'd started working freelance at the *Herald* herself.

If you can't beat them, join them, she'd thought when she'd emailed Miles Elliot, begging for a chance. It wasn't showbiz as yet, but she was gaining quite a reputation for herself as a reporter who could be trusted with a difficult interview.

One of the other *Herald* journalists had said that what set her apart was the fact that she cared about people, and made them feel as though they were chatting with a mate rather than an unfeeling journalist.

'I could do with picking up some tips from you,' Dermot commented after Storm had managed to persuade a young widow all the nationals had wanted to talk to, to give her an exclusive interview. She'd been proud of that piece, and the young woman had written her a note afterwards thanking her for being so sensitive. 'It's not a science, Dermot. I'm just interested in other people.' *Unlike you*, she'd thought to herself then. And now she couldn't help wondering whether this job offer would be the end of their relationship. God, where was he? She couldn't bear not knowing. But that was typical of Dermot. He always treated her as some sort of afterthought. Deep down she knew she deserved better. But damn it! She didn't know if it was the fact he was so focused on work, or just so irresistibly hot in bed, that meant she just didn't have the heart to dump him.

It was a murky, grey day and as Storm peered out of the window on to the street below, she realised this wasn't the first or last time Dermot would behave so irresponsibly. Watching a toddler having a massive tantrum with his mother, crying at the top of his lungs that he wanted to go home, Storm knew just how he felt. Because even though she'd just been offered the job of her dreams, until she knew Dermot was all right, she couldn't feel happy about it.

One thing was for sure: she couldn't sit here for the rest of the day worrying about her boyfriend. There was only one thing for it. Reaching for her bag and coat, she walked towards the exit, determined to find him. Just as she put her hand on the door she saw Ron surface from his office.

'Where the bloody hell's that planning story, Storm?' he bawled.

'Five minutes, Ron,' she promised.

Sighing, she slipped off her coat and returned to her computer.

Dermot sat on the tube with his head buried in a free newspaper. He'd just got to the middle of a story about a cat rescuing a dog when the doors jerked open at Wapping. Tossing the paper on to the seat next to his, he stepped off the train and headed towards daylight. Anxiously he checked his watch. Half-past one. Brilliant. Just enough time to grab some coffee and a sandwich.

Turning right out of the station, he walked for a couple

of minutes before pushing open the door to his favourite greasy spoon. 'Tuna melt and a flat white, please, darlin',' he said to the woman behind the counter.

'Coming right up.' The waitress beamed at him.

As he walked over to his usual window table, he took a deep breath and tried to relax before he saw Sabrina Anderson. With her hard as nails exterior, violet-blue eyes and long blonde hair, she was his ideal woman. He'd fancied her from the moment they'd bumped into each other in this very café twelve months ago. When he'd rung her this morning and told her he had something special for her, she'd played it typically cool.

'Trust me, this is going to be the biggest and best Christmas present you've ever had,' he cajoled her.

'Yeah, yeah,' she replied, playfully.

'Seriously. You'll be screaming my name in ecstasy by the time I've finished,' he teased.

'Just tell me what it is.'

'I can't say on the phone, but you won't be disappointed. Promise.'

'Meet me at two, usual place.'

Now, as he waited for his food, he pulled out his mobile and grimaced. Shit! Ten missed calls. Four from his editor and six from Storm.

'That's not a happy face,' said the waitress, bringing his coffee. 'Everything OK?'

'Fine,' Dermot replied. 'Just a bit of woman trouble, nothing I can't handle.'

He was setting his phone on the table when it rang again – Storm. For fuck's sake! Couldn't the girl take a hint? He was busy. She was the last person he wanted to talk to right now. And his editor wasn't far behind. If Dermot had to speak to either of them, he wasn't sure he'd have the balls to carry out his plan and play hookey with Sabrina.

Switching his phone to silent, he decided to deal with the consequences later. This was something he'd been looking forward to for a long time. He was going to enjoy every second of it. Sabrina walked in on the dot of two and sashayed over to his table, dressed in a slim-fitting black trouser suit. Dermot's eyes roamed appreciatively over her body. Her arse looked incredible.

'Good to see you,' he said as she sat down opposite him.

Touching his arm, Sabrina beamed, showing off a row of perfect white teeth. 'So what's this amazing Christmas present?'

Dermot took a deep breath. 'Aston Booth's cheated on his wife.'

Sabrina said nothing, leaving him on tenterhooks. Hadn't she heard him properly?

'Photos?' she asked finally, not mincing her words.

'Yeah, including one of him with the girl he shagged.'

Dermot reached for his bag, pulled out the snaps of Carly and pushed them across the Formica-topped table.

As Sabrina flicked through them he thought about his busy morning. While Storm was in the bathroom he'd sped into action. First he'd forwarded the photo on Carly's phone to his own. Then, when Storm had gone to work, he'd printed it out, along with some other pictures he'd found of Carly over the years, which were stored on Storm's laptop. After a quick shower he'd dressed in his work suit and walked to the station. He had to admit he'd felt slightly guilty about stitching up Storm's friend, but not enough to change his mind. Chances like this didn't come along twice.

'Pretty girl,' said Sabrina. 'Well done, Dermot. I knew you had it in you. I take it you've got time to talk this through with the chief?'

Dermot felt like punching the air with happiness. Instead he nodded and stood up. After he'd opened the door for Sabrina, they crossed the road. Dermot savoured the moment. Here he was, with Sabrina Anderson, the *Herald*'s news editor, about to walk into the national newspaper's headquarters and meet the editor. Finally, Dermot Whelan was making his name.

Chapter Three

Glancing around the now empty office, Storm reached for her desk phone and punched in Dermot's number for the last time. It was almost 10 p.m. and she'd long-since worn out the battery on her mobile. As the call went predictably straight to voicemail, Storm flung the receiver back into the cradle in frustration and let out a loud scream. Bloody Dermot!

Icy fear gripped her heart as she tried desperately not to let her imagination go into overdrive. About three months after she'd got together with Dermot, she'd caught him snogging a colleague in the stationery cupboard. It was laughable really, a cliché situation, and Dermot had sworn blind it hadn't meant anything. They hadn't been going out for long then so, after making him grovel for a good couple of weeks, she'd forgiven him on the understanding that it was never to happen again. But despite forgiving him, Storm had never quite forgotten his betrayal. Now, whenever he was out late or working overtime, she always felt a flash of insecurity and distrust. Was he really where he said he was?

Then there was the other option – that something truly awful had happened to him, just like it had to her dad. An image of Alan's smiling face flooded into her mind then and she felt her eyes start to water. There wasn't a day that went by when she didn't miss him.

Storm had been a real Daddy's girl, and the apple of her father's eye. On Alan's precious weekends off they used to stroll down to the pier first thing in the morning, where they'd eat fresh hot doughnuts from the stand at the front. They'd chat, laugh, and if the weather was good Alan would teach her how to skim stones over the sea. It had been their special time together, and Storm missed those mornings with her father as much now as she had just after his death.

Alan had been thirty-nine when he'd passed away. Sudden Adult Death Syndrome, the doctors had said, and after his funeral Sally had gone to pieces so it was Storm who had sorted through all her dad's belongings and decided what to keep and what to give to charity. The one thing she couldn't part with was his gold watch. He'd bought it with his first wage packet when he was eighteen, and had worn it every day. He said it brought him luck because if he hadn't gone into the jeweller's to buy it, he never would have met Sally, who'd been working behind the counter. Storm hadn't been able to part with it after his death, and carried it with her everywhere. Pulling the watch from her pocket now, she rested it on her desk and stroked the face. The action never failed to comfort her, as did a cup of tea with the one person she could always rely on. She needed to see Carly.

'Get that down you,' her friend said, handing Storm a mug of hot sweet tea.

'Thanks, babe.' Taking the mug, she curled up on Carly's huge grey sofa and glanced at the TV. *The Graham Norton Show* was on – she could do with a bit of light relief.

'Still no word then?' Carly asked.

Storm shook her head.

'The bastard!' Carly fumed. 'I could kill Dermot for this.'

Storm said nothing. She was well used to Carly's outbursts when it came to Dermot. Her friend had made no secret of the fact she thought he was a great bloke but a shit boyfriend, something she'd worked out when she'd temporarily moved in with Storm and Dermot following her break-up with Paul.

Over the years Storm and Carly had been through more than their fair share of ups and downs. When Storm's dad had died, Carly had been a huge support. A shoulder to cry on at school, not to mention a complete rock at the funeral. It was Carly's hand Storm had clung to as she sprinkled earth on to her dad's coffin while it was lowered into the ground.

Then, later, Carly made sure Storm ate lunch every day and frequently insisted she came over for a well-deserved night off. Not only that, Carly had thought nothing of spending weekends at Storm's house rather than out on the town, to help her friend babysit the kids and put her mum to bed when she was too drunk to make it up the stairs.

To Carly, Storm was a hero. It was amazing how she'd found the time to excel in her GCSEs, go to college *and* take care of her family. As for Storm, she was as devoted to Carly as she was to Bailey and Lexie. Although Carly had pretty much led a charmed life, she was the first to admit she'd struggled at school. She was by no means thick, but when it came to hitting the books, Carly preferred to spend a night in watching *Friends*, gossiping about boys, painting her nails and flicking through fashion magazines, rather than concentrate on her studies.

As a result she was always in trouble with teachers, who took great pleasure in dishing out detentions while telling Carly to remove her bright red nail polish and mascara.

Watching them pick her friend apart time and time again had left Storm fuming. She had always stood up to them in class, telling them to leave Carly alone and pick on someone else. Unsurprisingly the girls often both ended up in lunchtime detention, but the fact that Storm would put herself out like that had touched Carly and they had always remained close.

'Do you want me to call him?' Carly asked now, reaching for her phone.

Storm shook her head.

'It's pointless. When Dermot gets a story in his head, he forgets about everything else. Anyway, there's something else I've got to tell you. Miles Elliot offered me a job today.'

Carly's eyebrows rose. 'What! Why didn't you say? Doing what? Where? When do you start?'

Carly was so excited, Storm almost forgot her misery over Dermot. 'As soon as possible. Apparently there's a job going on the showbiz desk and he thinks I would be perfect for it.'

'Wow, babe! That's so brilliant! I couldn't be prouder,' Carly told her, leaping off the sofa to hug her friend.

'I know. I can't believe it,' Storm replied. 'It's everything I've ever wanted.'

'And everything you deserve,' Carly pointed out loyally. 'I take it you haven't told Dermot yet?'

Storm shook her head. 'And that's the thing . . . I've no idea how he's going to take it. Dermot's further up the career ladder than me and he's supposed to be the big rising star, not me.'

'Don't be daft, Storm,' Carly said. 'You're very talented, which is why Miles offered you this job. Dermot will be fine about it, and if he isn't, well, he'll have me to deal with. Now, you're welcome to stay here tonight if you want? That sofabed's pretty comfy.'

'Thanks, babe, but I'll go home.' Storm smiled gratefully at her. 'At least that way I'll be ready to kneecap the fecker when he finally puts in an appearance!'

Dermot lit the final candle and smiled as he surveyed the living room. The whole atmosphere screamed romance. As well as lining the flat with what looked like hundreds of tea lights, he'd arranged a huge bouquet of Storm's favourite flowers, red and white roses, on the kitchen table and put two bottles of champagne on ice. Then, to really sweeten the deal, he'd placed a small Tiffany box containing a silver bangle in the centre of the table.

Dermot wasn't a complete idiot, he knew he owed Storm one hell of an apology when she got home. But try as he might, he couldn't help grinning as he thought about how well that afternoon had gone. The moment he'd walked into Miles Elliot's office, he'd had the *Herald* editor eating out of the palm of his hand.

They'd bantered, joked and laughed, and Miles had been seriously impressed when Dermot revealed he'd got photographs to prove his story.

'You've done very well,' he said admiringly as he leafed through the stack of snaps Dermot had brought with him. 'Do I need to ask if you've done anything illegal?'

'Well, I didn't hack anyone's phone, if that's what you mean?' Dermot bantered.

'Good. And these photos are proof enough if we can't get either Aston or this girl to talk . . . unless you can help us out there too?'

Dermot shifted in his leather chair and sipped thoughtfully on his flat white. He knew if he even approached Carly about doing an interview he'd get a swift kick in the nuts, and Storm wouldn't be far behind her.

'She's my girlfriend's best mate,' he admitted. 'Might not be that easy.'

Miles scratched his chin thoughtfully. 'It's a good story, and I appreciate you bringing it straight to us rather than going to anyone else. Anything we can do to make the situation easier at home?'

Dermot couldn't believe his ears. Instinctively he knew he had to look out for Storm. He wasn't a complete bastard – she deserved something out of all this.

'Well, I don't suppose you've got any jobs going here, have you?' he asked.

'What did you have in mind?'

'A job for me, and something for Storm, my girlfriend. She's been working in features for the last few Saturdays.'

Miles chuckled. 'I know exactly who Storm is. She's a very good reporter and in fact I offered her a job first thing this morning.'

Dermot was surprised. It had taken him months to get the editor even to look at him; now suddenly Miles was telling him he was not only aware of Dermot's girlfriend but had also offered her a job. This wasn't supposed to be how it went. Dermot was the talented one, not Storm. Everyone at the *Post* was always telling him how brilliant he was. There had to be a mistake.

Miles gave him an amused look, and changed the subject. 'You remind me of a younger version of myself. When I was your age, there were no lengths I wouldn't go to for a story. We always need reporters like that here.'

Dermot smiled a lazy smile. Now that was more like it, and no more than he deserved after the hassle he'd gone through.

'So what do I get in return for the story?'

'How about I offer you a six-month contract as a news reporter? That way you and your girlfriend can move up here to London together, which will keep everything sweet at home. As a staffer Storm can use the company flat in Clapham till she can sort herself something else out, so you could move in there together. Last thing I want is to split up the Romeo and Juliet of journalism.'

'Has Storm got a six-month contract too?'

'No. I've offered her a permanent position. With her interviewing skills, I reckon she can get us some great stories.'

Dermot's heart beat faster. Was this guy serious? Storm was nothing without him. *He* was the one with the talent – Storm was just some chancer who'd managed to make a widow tell her sob story. Dermot should have been the one to have a crack at her . . . anyone could have done it. Still, he wasn't about to look a gift horse in the mouth. Getting to his feet, he pumped the editor's hand furiously. 'You don't have to worry about that, Miles. I can promise you, Storm and I will do you proud. When do we start?'

Feeling exhausted, Storm walked towards her front door with all the fight knocked out of her. As soon as she got in she planned on doing nothing more than collapsing in bed without even bothering to remove her make-up.

But nearing her home she was amazed to see the flat lit up like a Christmas tree. Thank God! Dermot was home.

'Where the hell have you been?' she yelled, bursting through the front door and straight into the living room. Stopping short, she couldn't believe what she was seeing. Dermot was standing nervously by the window, looking tired and dishevelled. On the kitchen table stood a champagne bucket with what looked like two bottles wedged firmly in ice, while next to it stood the biggest bouquet of red and white roses Storm had ever seen and nestling between them was a small robin egg blue box.

'What's all this?'

'For you, gorgeous,' replied Dermot, walking over to her and handing her a glass of fizz. 'We're celebrating.'

But her relief at seeing him quickly turned to anger, and Storm threw her glass of champers all over him. 'You might be celebrating, I've been worried out of my mind all day, you bastard!'

As liquid dripped off his forehead, Dermot hung his head and did his best to cover his anger with a semblance of shame. 'I'm sorry, babe, I was busy on a job in London and my phone ran out of juice.'

'You've been totally out of order,' Storm fumed. 'I was terrified you were lying dead in a ditch somewhere. And as if that wasn't bad enough, I've had to put up with Ron bollocking me all day because he couldn't get hold of you either.'

Dermot stepped closer to Storm. He needed her onside, and quickly. It was stupid not to have taken her calls, but if he'd spoken to her before his meeting there was a chance he might have pulled out. It was time for him to play his ace card. 'I'm really sorry, Storm, but the truth is, I've been spending the day sorting out our future.'

'What do you mean?' she snapped.

'What would you say if I told you that I'd landed a job as a news reporter at the *Herald*?'

'I'd say you were being a selfish dick,' Storm fired back. She was still fuming. The bloody cheek of him! And after she'd spent all day defending him to Ron. Enough was enough.

'That hurts, pet, especially since I know Miles has

offered you a position too. When were you going to tell me about that? Or did you want to make me suffer first?'

'Well, if you'd bothered to call me, I could have told you hours ago. You might have noticed I left a few messages on your phone?' she said sarcastically.

'So I assume you're taking it?' Dermot said, ignoring her accusation.

'I'd like to, yes,' she said quietly. 'This is my dream, Dermot. And now you've been offered a chance to work for Miles too, we can go to London together – it's perfect for us both.'

'I know, darlin'.' Dermot smiled at her. 'I'm just messing with you. I'm not mad, I would have done the same thing, and you're right . . . we can be together now, which is the only thing that matters.'

Storm breathed a sigh of relief. 'So tell me how it all happened?'

'Miles rang out of the blue this morning and asked me to come straight in,' Dermot explained. 'He said he'd been so impressed with my work recently, he wanted to offer me a full-time job.'

'So we both got offered jobs out of the blue this morning? Just like that?' Storm asked, incredulous.

'Just like that. So am I forgiven?' he said, nuzzling her neck once more.

'Just this once,' she teased, flinging her arms around him.

The following morning, Storm woke to the sounds of swearing in the kitchen. Blearily peering at the alarm clock, she was amazed to see she'd slept in until a record 11 a.m.

'You OK, babe?' she croaked.

'Fine. Just burned my hand on the coffee pot . . . don't move a muscle!' he called back.

Hoisting herself upright and sinking her head back against the pillows, Storm was delighted to see Dermot carrying in a tray loaded with toast and coffee.

'Am I still dreaming? Breakfast in bed. What have I done to deserve this?' she squealed.

'Thought it was more than justified after everything I put you through yesterday.' Dermot was outdoing himself with all this thoughtfulness. How had she got so lucky? She had her dream job and a boyfriend that gave her a Tiffany bangle and made her breakfast in bed. Reaching for a hot buttery slice of toast, Storm could hardly contain her excitement.

Taking a bite of toast, she pictured herself sashaying into a posh London hotel room, interviewing Jennifer Lawrence about her latest blockbuster. The interview would go so well, she fantasised, Jennifer would lean over and slip her personal mobile number into Storm's hand, insisting they paint the town red the next time she was in London.

Storm spilled hot coffee over the bed sheets and snapped back to reality.

'I couldn't speak to Miles yesterday, did he mention when he wanted us to start?' she asked.

'Next Monday.'

'That's ten days before Christmas!' she replied, horrified. 'We can't do that.'

Dermot said nothing. His raised eyebrow told Storm all she needed to know – they had to.

'Well, I suppose we only have to give a week's notice at work. And we can live in the *Herald*'s company flat in Clapham until we find somewhere of our own.'

'Exactly,' Dermot agreed. 'Aren't you excited?'

Storm grinned. 'What do you think?' The thought of no more council meetings or bollockings off Ron was like a dream come true.

'So have you told Carly your big news yet?' Dermot asked, nicking the last slice of toast.

Storm nodded as she shook the crumbs from her nightshirt on to the plate. Swinging her legs out of bed, she stood up and stretched. 'I told her about my job offer but she doesn't know you've got one too. Thought I might pop over to hers now and tell her the big news.'

'Brilliant idea. I've got a bit of work to do while you nip out. Then we could go for a celebration meal tonight at the Italian around the corner, if you fancy?'

Walking around to Dermot's side of the bed, Storm kissed him passionately on the mouth.

'Bloody hell, babe, you look like you ran a marathon to get here,' Carly laughed, spotting Storm's bright red cheeks as she opened the front door.

It was true. The moment Storm had jumped out of bed she'd wanted to get over to Carly's as quickly as possible. After pulling on her trademark grey skinny jeans and navy jumper, she'd gathered her hair into a high ponytail and raced over to her friend's flat just a few streets away.

'I've got some brilliant news,' Storm panted. 'Dermot's

been offered a job on the *Herald* as well. It means we can go together!'

'OMG! For real?'

'Totes for real,' Storm squealed as she clutched her friend excitedly by the elbows and together they jumped up and down, shrieking in delight. Bolting upstairs to Carly's kitchen, Storm reached into the fridge and pulled out the emergency bottle of champagne she always kept for special occasions.

'Sod tea,' Carly agreed. 'News like this deserves a real drink. Now . . . tell me all the details.'

Storm explained how a couple of positions had opened up at the paper that Miles thought they would be perfect for. 'Although I don't know why he insisted on interviewing Dermot when he just offered a job to me straight away,' she said. 'He emailed this morning with my contract and to congratulate me on my new position. Apparently he thinks I have unique skills, which the paper can benefit from. And all this without even giving me an interview!'

'Oh, yeah! I hope it's just your writing skills he's talking about.' Carly raised an eyebrow suggestively.

'Carly!' Storm giggled, throwing a cushion at her friend.

'Kidding! Seriously, Stormy, congratulations. If anyone deserves this chance, it's you.'

'Thanks, babe. It's just all so sudden, I can't quite believe it.'

It hit Storm then that she wouldn't just be leaving her job at the *Post* behind but also her hometown and Carly. Overcome with the emotion of it all, tears blurred Storm's eyes. Waving her hands in front of her face to stem the flow, it was only a matter of time before she set Carly off.

'What the hell am I going to do without you?' Storm exclaimed.

'I'm going to miss you so much,' Carly wailed. 'Even though we can still see each other in London, it won't be the same!'

After a full on tear-fest the girls stretched out on Carly's sofa with a family-sized bar of Dairy Milk each and watched their favourite movie, *The Notebook*. There was something about Ryan Gosling that always put a smile on their faces.

'I'm so full,' Storm moaned after devouring the entire bar.

'Me too,' added Carly. 'I hope you don't want any help packing today.'

'Nah, Dermot's given me the afternoon off. Besides, I want to know how you're doing.'

So far the girls had stayed off the topic of Carly's fling, but Storm was keen to know what her friend was thinking now.

'I'll live. I just can't believe how stupid I've been, sleeping with a married man.'

'It takes two to tango, you know.'

'I know. I just can't stop thinking about Aston's wife,' Carly said quietly. 'She didn't even enter my head before . . . what is wrong with me?'

Carly looked so fed up, Storm's heart ached for her.

'I just wanted to pretend I was in some bubble where me and Aston would live happily ever after.'

'Is that why you took that selfie?'

'Yeah. I've deleted it now. I feel sick at how badly I let everyone down. I wish I could say sorry to Tanya.'

'You've got to stop punishing yourself, babe. Anyway, sod being in a romantic bubble with Aston – thought you said he was shit in bed!'

Carly burst out laughing. 'Yeah, he asked me after we'd done it why I didn't blink. I told him it was because I didn't have time!'

As the two girls cracked up, they restarted *The Notebook* and prepared to ogle Ryan Gosling all over again. The only problem now was they'd run out of chocolate.

With the sun shining and the sea a crystal-clear blue, Brighton looked exactly how he felt, Dermot thought as he strolled along the seafront. The whole operation had gone better than he could have hoped. This was going to be one of the easiest interviews he'd ever done. *Probably because he'd got Storm, interview expert, to do it for him.*

Dermot smirked. It had been a stroke of genius, hiding a tiny recording device in her bag as she left the flat to see Carly. Dermot wasn't much of a follower of fashion but he loved a gadget and always kept ahead of the latest techno developments. He never liked to leave the house without his passport, iPhone and Apple laptop. When he'd spotted this tiny voice-activated recording device a couple of weeks ago he'd known it was another essential he had to have.

Slipping it into the bottom of Storm's bag earlier that morning as she showered, he'd taken a bet with himself that very soon the device would be filled with Carly's candid comments about Aston. After all, it would be the second topic they talked about after Storm's announcement. All he had to do was sit back and wait for her to come back. Then, when she was getting ready to go out, he'd retrieve the device, type up the girls' conversation, and . . . hey presto! Full interview to Miles.

Pausing to stop for a beer at one of the pubs on the seafront, he ordered a pint of Guinness, slipped off his leather bomber jacket and rang his new editor.

As he waited for Miles to pick up Dermot found it hard to believe how much things had changed in the past twenty-four hours. Yesterday, Miles Elliot barely knew who he was. Today, Dermot had access to his direct line.

'What have you got for me, Dermot?' Miles demanded, straight to the point.

'Just letting you know I'll have the interview with the girl for you later.'

'Nice work. Email me your copy as soon as you can. Looks like you've got your first front page, son.'

As Miles rang off, Dermot gulped his celebration pint and texted Storm. The sooner he could get her home, the sooner he could get his interview over to Miles, and then he was on easy street.

Babe when are you coming back? I miss you and can't wait to play!xxxxxx

While he slurped the froth off his Guinness, Storm texted straight back.

Back in ten. Love you. xxxxx

Finishing his pint, Dermot knew he was home and dry.

This time tomorrow he'd be celebrating his first national scoop. The only thing he had to worry about now was dealing with Storm. If he was honest, her reaction was something he'd been pushing to the back of his mind, but now Dermot knew he was going to have to come up with a plan. After all, this time tomorrow she would know that he'd eavesdropped on her conversation with her friend. Plus she'd more than likely want to kick the shit out of him for betraying her trust and selling Carly down the river.

He thought carefully while he ordered another drink. There was no denying it, things were going to get a bit rocky with Storm once his story broke. When he'd initially gone to Miles and asked for a job he had thought that if Storm kicked off too much he'd dump her then hightail it to London to make his name alone. It wasn't that he didn't love Storm – he did – but he loved his job more.

However, Miles had thrown him a curveball yesterday when he'd said that he had already offered her a job. Now it was in Dermot's best interests to try and win her over; he hated to admit it to himself but he needed her. Usually he knew exactly how to push her buttons to get what he wanted. As he downed his second pint, Dermot could only hope his tried and tested formula of begging for forgiveness would work for him tomorrow.

Chapter Four

The banging was so loud Storm's neighbours woke before she did. Peering out of their sash windows they couldn't believe a tiny woman, red-faced with fury, was responsible for making such a racket first thing on a Sunday morning.

'Keep it down, love,' one woman shouted. 'You'll wake my baby.'

But Carly didn't care if she woke the living dead. 'Storm, open the door this minute!' she yelled.

Storm, who'd been happily in the Land of Nod dreaming about a night out with Jay-Z and Beyoncé, woke with a start. Realising it was Carly at the door, she slotted her feet into fluffy slippers and padded downstairs, leaving Dermot still sound asleep.

Flinging the door wide, Storm did a double take. Her friend looked to be in a real state. Dressed in trackie bottoms and UGGs, with mascara streaming down her face, Carly was obviously upset. Shit! Had she bumped into Dillon again?

'What's going on, babe?'

'You know exactly what's going on. This!' Carly spat.

Seeing the copy of that morning's *Herald*, Storm ran her eyes over the headline.

Top Totty scores with Aston. Underneath was the selfie Carly had taken and next to it were three little words Storm had definitely not expected to see: *By Dermot Whelan.*

Her blood ran cold. Ignoring her friend, she snatched the paper from Carly's hands and flicked through the story, which ran across four pages. The details they'd got hold of were eye-watering. It was as though they'd sat down with Carly and interviewed her for hours. The piece revealed just what her night with Aston had been like, and even featured Carly's revelation that he was well hung but out of practice.

It didn't end there. Photos of Carly throughout her youth filled the pages, including one of her at school with a bucktoothed smile and hair in bunches. Then another of her at a fancy dress party where she'd donned a flesh-coloured bra and pants to look like Miley Cyrus, complete with foam finger. There was Storm too, in a striped suit, pretending to be Robin Thicke. Shaking, Storm turned back to the front page and looked in bewilderment at Dermot's name in big, bold letters.

Ignoring the stares from her neighbours, who by now had appeared in the hallway to see what all the fuss was about, she sank to the floor. What was Dermot's name doing on the front page of the *Herald*? Had he really betrayed her and Carly? How could he do this to them? She'd trusted him to keep it to himself when she'd told him about Carly and Aston, and he'd used her and her friend in the sickest way possible. Storm knew how desperate Dermot was to make a name for himself, but would he really go to these lengths? God, was this how he'd scored his new job? By selling out Carly? The revelations came thick and fast.

'Don't act like this is all some big surprise to you, Storm,' Carly spat. 'You tricked me into telling you and Dermot everything just so you could finally get your dream jobs. I hope you're proud of yourselves now.'

'That's not true, I knew nothing about this.'

But Carly wasn't buying it. 'Do you think I'm stupid?' she sneered. 'Don't forget, I know you. And I know how long you've dreamed of working as a showbiz reporter. You'd do anything to succeed.'

Storm was shocked by the look of hatred and disgust etched on Carly's face. Was this what her friend really thought of her? 'You know I'd never do anything to hurt you. You're like a sister to me, Carly.' Storm reached out, but her friend pushed her away.

'So if you didn't do it, how did your bastard of a boyfriend find out?'

Seeing Dermot walk down the stairs then, rubbing his eyes, Carly turned her attention to the man of the moment. Eyes blazing, she was on a roll and nothing would stop her.

'Get everything on some sort of secret tape yesterday, did you?'

'What's going on?' he murmured blearily.

Both girls looked at him, disbelief in their eyes. 'How could you do this?' Storm asked quietly.

'How could you both do it?' Carly screamed. 'This is a disaster, my life's over.'

'No, it isn't, babe,' Storm soothed her as the neighbours shuffled back inside, preferring another cuppa to a morning spent watching a row. 'It might seem like it now, but everyone will have forgotten about it by tomorrow.'

'Easy for you to say,' Carly fired back. 'Your life's not in tatters. So just how did you two plot this? Get me to forget my phone on purpose at Nico's party, did you, by getting me wasted?'

'No, Carly, you did a pretty good job of that all by yourself,' Storm snapped.

Dermot stood in the hallway in his tatty pyjamas unable to believe his eyes. He'd never seen the girls fight like this. Of course he'd witnessed the odd scrap over silly stuff like who got the last chocolate in a box of Thornton's but they'd never gone for each other before. Dermot knew he ought to feel guilty, but he was itching to take the paper from Storm's hands and read his story cover to cover. Seeing his name on the front page, he was bursting with pride – this was his big break, his very first national front page. He'd meant to get up first thing in the morning and savour the moment as he walked into the newsagent's, but he'd been so knackered last night after answering all Miles's queries he'd slept in.

One thing was for sure, Carly was in serious danger of ruining the moment. After all, she was the dumb slapper who'd slept with a married footballer. Girls like her deserved to be outed in the press. But he didn't want her falling out with Storm. They were off to London in a week to start their new life, and he knew he was going to have enough of a hard time winning her around, without Carly making it any more difficult for him. Time for him to fall on his sword.

'Girls, let me just say I'm sorry,' Dermot interrupted. 'Carly, it's true, Storm knew nothing at all about this. She told me about you and Aston after the party and I went to the *Herald* alone. But the press would have found out anyway in time. This way at least people get to know the girl behind the selfie.'

'Are you kidding me with this shit, Dermot?' Carly yelled. 'All my clients are going to think I'm scum for sleeping with someone else's bloke, and as if that isn't enough, Dillon told me he'd ruin me if I went to the press.'

'That's not going to happen,' Storm interrupted.

'Oh, you're going to sort it, are you, Storm?' Carly shot back. 'Just like you sorted this . . . by running to your boyfriend and telling him about my private life, even though I told you to keep it to yourself.'

'I did keep it to myself!' Storm protested.

'You didn't, you stupid cow, you told your lying scumbag of a boyfriend.'

'I didn't think he'd do this,' she said helplessly.

'No?' Carly looked at her in disgust. 'I did. You might not see him for what he really is, but I marked his card long ago. He'd sell his own grandmother if it meant he would get ahead.'

'That's a bit unfair,' Dermot grumbled. 'Both my grandparents died years ago.'

'You're not even taking this seriously. How did you get all those details anyway? I only told Storm about this.'

Dermot looked sheepish. 'I bugged her bag when she came over to yours yesterday. Then I listened to your conversation and emailed it to my editor.'

'Un-fucking-believable!' Carly spat. 'I spill my guts to my best friend, and you listen like some sort of perv. Funny how this story doesn't say how guilty I felt and how I couldn't believe I'd been so stupid. Why is that? Frightened it wouldn't make such a juicy read? I've a good mind to sue you, you bastard.'

'For what?' Dermot fired back. 'Correct me if I'm wrong but you did shag a footballer, and he was married?'

Storm had gone white. Looking at her boyfriend and best friend sparring in the hallway, she couldn't help wondering who Dermot really was. She'd thought she knew him, but the past ten minutes had been a wake-up call. To think she'd once thought he was the love of her life! No chance. Looking at him now, his face twisted and contorted with rage as he laid into her friend, Storm realised it was over between Dermot and her, and there was no way she was going to London if it meant being within spitting distance of his lying, cheating face.

'Look, Carly, I never wanted to hurt you . . .' Dermot said, trying to calm things down.

'Don't bother. All I can say is, revenge is a dish best served cold. And as for you, Storm, you and me are through – I never want to see you again.'

With that, Carly stepped out of the front door and

slammed it shut behind her. With a withering look at Dermot, Storm pulled open the door and raced after her.

'You can't mean that,' she said, as she caught up with her friend.

'Yes, I do,' Carly said as she coldly pushed Storm aside. 'What you've done is totally out of order and I'll never forgive you.'

'I'm so, so sorry,' Storm pleaded. 'I never thought Dermot would do this. I thought he loved you like I did. I would never do anything to hurt you, Carly, you're my world. Think of all we've been through – we've been friends for a lifetime. Please don't throw that away.'

Carly stared contemptuously at her friend, sweaty and out of breath, standing on the seafront dressed in her pyjamas.

'Up until this morning I would have said that nothing would ever come between you and me, Storm. I would have said we were best friends for life. But the moment I saw that headline I knew it was over. I never want to see you again, you're dead to me.'

For the rest of the week, Storm felt as if she was trapped in a nightmare. After eventually returning to the flat on Sunday, she'd had the mother of all rows with Dermot. Storm had never been so angry and they'd argued for hours over his betrayal.

'How could you do this to me . . . to us . . . to Carly?' demanded Storm.

'Don't be stupid, darling. You know as well as I do how brutal journalism can be.'

'But it doesn't have to be. There is such a thing as loyalty, you know.'

'When will you realise, I did it for us?'

'Please!' Storm snorted with disgust. 'You didn't do it for me or for us. You did it for yourself.'

Dermot stalked towards her, putting his face close to hers. 'That's not true. When I learned Miles had offered you a job, I couldn't stand the idea of being without you so I went to London with what I had.'

'Bullshit! The earliest you would have known about that was if Miles had told you when you were already *in* London, so if you think I'm falling for that you can think again.'

Realising he'd been caught out, Dermot went for her, all guns blazing. 'Well then, you'll know that in this business it's all about who you know, Storm, and you know Carly – who just happens to be a slapper who shagged a footballer. Now, enjoy the benefits of having your boyfriend working alongside you on a national tabloid and wake the fuck up!'

White-hot fury rose in Storm's chest. Before she knew what she was doing, she'd raised her hand and slapped Dermot hard across the face. First he had the nerve to deceive her, then he was having a go at her for being furious with his behaviour. He could fuck right off after the damage he'd caused.

'You bitch,' he said, clutching his right cheek.

'That's nothing compared to what you deserve. And in case you were wondering, I won't be taking that job in London . . . and you're dumped! If I never see you again it'll be too soon.'

Not waiting for a reaction Storm had flounced out of the flat, so angry she didn't even take a coat despite the fact it was snowing outside. Running all the way to Carly's, she hammered over and over on her door. She had to speak to her. Carly was her best friend, there was no way Storm could live in a world where they weren't pals. She was desperate to make things right. 'Open up, please, Carly,' Storm called through the letterbox. 'Let me in. I know you're in there. I just want to talk, I won't budge until we've talked.'

Five hours later, with teeth chattering and fingers so cold she could no longer feel them, Storm had to admit defeat. Shivering and with her eyes blurred with tears she walked slowly home, the bitter wind nipping at her ears. As she rounded the corner to her flat she walked straight past a group of carollers singing *'Tis the season to be jolly.*

Yeah, if you're anyone but me, thought Storm grimly.

The following morning she got into work early, intending to write an email to Miles saying thanks but no thanks for the job offer. She'd tossed and turned all night, agonising over what to do. On the one hand there was no denying that a full-time post working in showbiz journalism was a great opportunity. It was her dream, after all. But she couldn't stomach the thought of being so near to Dermot, and if working on a national tabloid could make you sink so low as betraying a friend, she just wasn't interested. It wasn't right for her. So instead Storm decided to stay put, and by getting in early hoped to prove to Ron just how committed she was to the *Post*, even if Dermot wasn't.

But Ron had other ideas. Storm had barely shrugged off

her coat and fired up her computer when her editor's dulcet tones were heard, bellowing across the office. 'Storm, my office, now.'

Gathering her notepad and pen, she hastened across the floor, aware of everyone's eyes boring into her.

'I've had your daft as arseholes boyfriend in here first thing and now it's your turn to be read the Riot Act,' Ron began as he slammed the door shut.

'But . . .' Storm began.

'I don't want to hear it,' he snapped. 'Now sit down and shut up.'

She perched on an uncomfortable wooden chair by the filing cabinet and braced herself.

'I thought you were better than this, Storm,' he sighed. 'I like to sell papers, but selling out your own best mate's a level even I wouldn't stoop to.'

'But I didn't . . .' Storm began, only for Ron to cut her off.

'You're a good reporter, but after witnessing everything you're capable of I'll be glad to see the back of you. You and Dermot make me sick.'

Wide-eyed with panic, Storm started babbling. 'What are you talking about? Ron, please believe me, I never had anything to do with that story. I want to stay here and keep working at the *Post*.'

'Correct me if I'm wrong, Storm, but Dermot insists you told him something your mate told you in confidence. Don't you remember the first rule of journalism school? Always protect your sources. No, I'm sorry, Storm, if you weren't resigning, I'd have to fire you, I don't want people like you working for me.'

She looked at her editor aghast. How had her life blown apart like this?

'Dermot tells me you're both off to pastures new, so I wish you luck with that,' Ron continued. 'Make sure you clean your desk before you leave.'

'But, Ron, seriously, I can explain all of this . . .'

He opened the door, signalling that the conversation was over. 'I'm sorry Storm. I like you, but I don't like what you've done. There's no job here for you any more.'

Walking back to her desk, head hanging down in shame, she thought quickly. Despite her best intentions she'd have to take the job in London after all. Journalism college hadn't come cheap and she was still paying off her student loans. She needed a job, and fast. She might not have wanted to take the job at the *Herald*, out of loyalty to Carly, but that was the only offer on the table right now. With the job market the way things were, who knew when she might find something else?

But the last thing she wanted was to spend any more time than she had to with Dermot. It was bad enough that they were still living together for the rest of the week. No way was she allowing the situation to continue in London.

'Look, there are two bedrooms in the Clapham flat. We can just be flatmates until we both find something more permanent,' Dermot pointed out when she confronted him about it later.

'Yeah, right. You've already proved you're a liar. For all I know this *Herald* flat could be a studio where we'd have to live in each other's pockets. I'm calling Miles and asking if there's anything else available.'

'Don't be ridiculous, Storm. The last thing you want to burden your new editor with is your personal life. It will make you look stupid and both of us unprofessional. The flat has two bedrooms, I promise, and I also promise that I'll leave you alone. I mean it, I'd do anything to get you to forgive me.'

'Yeah?' Storm fired back. 'Hell will freeze over first. We're not moving in together, and we're never getting back together. Got it?'

After that her week went from bad to worse. All her friends shunned her for her apparent betrayal of Carly. As for her colleagues, they continually made snide comments about her being a sell-out. The only one who offered any kind of support was her mother. Sally had been genuinely delighted when Storm told her she'd got a job on a national paper. Now Storm was touched that Sally had realised her daughter was in the middle of a crisis.

'I've read the papers,' she said, ringing Storm at work one morning. 'I sense there could be trouble for you.'

'That's an understatement, Sally.'

'Well, I'm here if you need me. You only have to ask. We all make mistakes, love.'

As for Dermot, he devoted much of the week to trying to win Storm back. Clearly he thought life would be easier if they could share the flat as planned, and Storm was sick of his campaign to make her give in. He showered her desk at work with flowers, cards and love tokens, all of which she dumped in the bin beside her desk.

One evening Storm got home late from work to find him on his knees, naked apart from a rose in his mouth.

'What do you think you're doing?' she shouted.

'I never should have done it. Honestly, Stormy, I just got carried away. I had this idea that selling the story would mean we could finally get the jobs of our dreams. I was thinking of us.'

'What do you mean, selling?' Storm asked.

Dermot shifted uncomfortably on his knees. 'Just an expression, babe. I promise you. I never would have done this if I'd thought Carly would be seriously damaged, or that you and her would fall out so badly. I mean, I figured she'd be a bit pissed off but that you would sort things out eventually – you two are solid.'

Storm had heard enough. 'Yeah? That's what people used to say about Brad Pitt and Jennifer Aniston, and look how that turned out the moment Angelina Jolie got in the way.'

'I'm no Angelina,' Dermot said hastily, getting off his knees.

'No! And you're no bloody Brad Pitt either.'

Walking over to the worn sofa, the only thing they hadn't packed for the move, Storm sank down heavily on to it. She was so tired she could hardly think straight. Cross with Dermot, devastated and sorry for Carly, not to mention keyed up at the prospect of a new job, Storm didn't think she could take any more. 'What do you want from me, Dermot?' she asked wearily.

'Well, I wondered, if you won't take me back, if we could at least keep up the pretence that we're still together when we start work?'

Storm lifted her head from her hands and eyed him

with suspicion. Was he taking the piss?

Sensing he was about to get slapped all over again, Dermot reached for his white towelling dressing gown and held out his hands as a shield. 'Now, Stormy, hear me out. The last thing we want is any more gossip about us. At the moment everyone at the *Herald* thinks we're a couple. If we tell them we've split, people are going to be too busy talking about how and why to pay any attention to the work we do. Surely it's better to break the news a few weeks after our arrival, when people have got to know us and it won't be the first thing they associate with us.'

Storm looked at him in disgust. He really was the most spineless man she'd ever had the misfortune to meet. She didn't care what people thought, and so much the better if they realised she'd dumped the loser. 'No, we bloody well can't pretend,' she hissed. 'And FYI you'll need to find somewhere else to live as I'll be in the Clapham flat alone.'

With that she turned on her heel, leaving him open-mouthed with shock.

Thankfully it at least looked as though Carly was weathering the media storm.

Earlier that week when Storm had turned on her TV before going to work, to find Carly making an appearance on the sofa of *Morning Cuppa*, looking innocent and demure in a high-necked blouse and knee-length skirt.

Sitting opposite the nation's sweetheart and *Morning Cuppa* host Poppy Mason, telling the world how lonely she'd been since she'd been dumped, and how much she wanted to make it up to Aston's wife, Carly had the audience eating out of her hand.

Suddenly the papers were full of Carly's pain as she went from tramp to victim in a matter of days. Storm was pleased Carly's life wasn't going to end in tatters as she'd feared but it seemed she was still no closer to regaining her friend's trust. Logging on to Facebook, she was horrified to see Carly's latest post in her newsfeed was a postcard with a quote about how it can often take years to find out who your friends really are. Scrolling down, she saw hundreds of people had 'liked' her comment and reposted it to their own feeds. For God's sake! Storm knew she was in the wrong, but since when did she and Carly communicate through the Internet? It was beyond childish.

By the time Friday morning rolled around Storm didn't want to stay in Brighton a minute longer. She was itching to put this whole mess behind her.

Arriving for work to see out her last day, she found herself largely ignored. 'It's because everyone expected better from you, Storm,' explained Wendy.

There was no arguing with that. As Storm cleared the last of her belongings from her desk and headed out of the newspaper building for the last time, her eyes brimmed with tears. She hated to admit it but Wendy's words had stung. Reaching the flat and packing the last of her stuff into the back of the van she had hired, she had to face facts – she no longer belonged in Brighton. There was a time she'd imagined a huge send off when she left for London, with all her friends gathering at her flat to say goodbye, complete with champagne and maybe even a few moving in gifts, but that was no longer on the cards.

Dermot had already left, saying he would sleep on a

mate's floor in London so only Sally was there to wave Storm off as she began her new life. Kissing her mother swiftly on the cheek, Storm fought back tears. Here she was, leaving her hometown after twenty-five years, and nobody other than the mother who had all but abandoned her as a teenager had bothered to say goodbye. Everything was such a mess. She was just about to get into the van when Sally grabbed her arm and pulled her close for a last hug.

'Storm, I know you won't believe me but Carly will come round and forgive you eventually. And it may not mean much to you but I'm proud of you for pursuing your dreams. You owe it to yourself to make the most of this opportunity.'

'I don't know, Sally,' Storm said quietly. 'I don't feel like I deserve this break.'

Sally released her daughter from her grip, and looked straight into Storm's eyes.

'Listen, my girl,' she said fiercely. 'You may have made a mistake, but you've more than paid your dues in this life already. This is a once-in-a-lifetime chance for you, don't be stupid and screw it up.'

Chapter Five

Checking her reflection in the huge mirror that dominated the ladies' loos, Storm brushed some imaginary dirt from her blouse, smoothed down her hair and took a deep breath to calm herself.

She hadn't felt so anxious for years, but that morning as she'd collected her new pass and made her way into the lift with all the other *Herald* employees it had hit her that this was her new life.

Suddenly the nerves had kicked in, and she'd felt so nauseous she'd been tempted to walk out and never come back. Thank God for her dad's watch. She'd had a feeling she'd need it more than ever this morning so had slipped it into her pocket for good luck. Now as she stroked the face the action grounded her. She remembered that she was a woman in control.

Since her arrival at the new flat Dermot had gone out of his way to help Storm settle in and prove that he wanted her back. He'd turned up offering to clean the place, to unpack her boxes, even go to the supermarket to stock up on food for her, but Storm had taken great pleasure in slamming the door in his face each time, telling him in no uncertain terms to get the hell out of her life and drop dead!

His behaviour had been nothing short of irritating if she was honest. Storm wasn't about to change her mind and take him back. He was a rat. A rat who had cost her the most precious relationship she'd ever known. No, as far as Storm was concerned, Dermot was ancient history.

Squaring her shoulders, she stopped at the sub-editor's desk and asked where she could find Sabrina Anderson. After she was pointed in the right direction, Storm said thank you and walked towards her new boss. Sabrina was on the phone and Storm hung back rather than interrupt. Something told her the call wasn't going well.

'I don't care if she's dead. Find someone else to talk or I'll get another freelancer who will!' Sabrina shrilled as she slammed the phone down. 'Amateurs,' she muttered, turning to an anxious-looking Storm.

'Who are you and what do you want?'

'I'm Storm, new writer on the showbiz desk.'

Sabrina said nothing but looked her up and down.

'Er, we haven't met before as I've done some Saturday shifts in features,' Storm continued, holding out her hand for Sabrina to shake. 'But I just wanted to thank you for this opportunity.'

Sabrina stared at Storm's outstretched hand as though it was something nasty stuck to the bottom of her shoe.

After leaving Storm hanging for what felt like an eternity, she shrugged and turned back to her desk.

'Your "opportunity" had nothing to do with me. But you can show me how grateful you are by getting me a coffee. Black, no sugar.'

Turning to Dermot who had already settled into his new desk opposite the news editor, Sabrina cocked her head to one side and plastered on her best smile. 'Dermot, how wonderful to see you. Our lovely new starter has offered to go on a coffee run, what would you like?'

'Flat white, please, babe,' he replied, not even looking at Storm. 'So, Sabrina, I've got some great leads I wanted to talk to you about . . .'

Storm flushed bright red with embarrassment before turning away and keeping her head down. She joined the queue in the canteen to get the drinks. The cheek of Dermot, calling her 'babe'! And that bitch Sabrina! What a bloody welcome this was turning out to be – she didn't even know where she was sitting yet.

'Don't worry about Sabrina,' said a voice behind her. 'She's rude to anyone who's not a bloke.'

Turning around, Storm saw a smiling blonde, dressed in a sharp black pencil skirt and grey biker jacket. 'I'm Chelsea, and I'll be working with you on the showbiz desk,' she said.

As Chelsea held out her hand, Storm took it and returned her grin. Thank God she'd met someone normal. 'I thought it was just me she'd taken an instant dislike to.'

'Oh, no, she hates all women so don't even think about trying to be friends with her.' Chelsea smiled. 'We

78

nicknamed her Supertramp 'cos she's shagged her way to the top.'

Storm couldn't help herself, she burst out laughing. That was just the sort of thing she'd have expected Carly to say. At the thought of her old friend, Storm felt a stab of pain. But today was meant to be a new start – it wasn't the time for letting old hurts get in the way.

Reaching the front of the queue, she gave her coffee order and, with Chelsea's help, successfully managed to deliver the drinks to Sabrina, Dermot and her new colleagues on the showbiz desk without spilling a drop.

'You must be a good influence on me. Normally I'm so clumsy these drinks would have gone everywhere.'

'Then consider me your guardian angel.' Chelsea smiled as she steered Storm to her new desk, and showed her where the tea bags and instant coffee were kept, along with the emergency stash of chocolate biscuits for when Sabrina was being particularly bitchy.

'There are only two left,' Storm noticed.

'Which should give you some idea of just how much of a cow she was last week. We had three packets of these in the drawer last Monday.' As Chelsea winked, Storm breathed out a sigh of relief. She didn't want to jinx things but she had a feeling she and Chelsea might become friends.

She wasn't wrong. All that week Chelsea showed Storm the ropes, telling her who and what to look out for. There was plenty to keep her busy. Although Sabrina was the news editor and officially oversaw the showbiz department, Chelsea was the one who'd been there longest and she ran the desk. She knew where to go, what to see and what to miss. Best of all, she knew all the celebrity goss on the circuit. Not a thing got past Chelsea and Storm had already been gobsmacked to learn one or two secrets about celebrities she would never have guessed.

'But they look to be so in love,' she protested after Chelsea had revealed the truth about one high-profile married couple.

'That's the point, Storm. They look committed, but they're living completely separate lives – she even lives in her own house next door to his.'

'But why all the pretence?' Storm asked innocently.

'You've still got a lot to learn, kid,' laughed Chelsea. 'They're celebrities, the public are supposed to want their lives. It's not going to look very good for them if the world discovers they're no different from everyone else, is it?'

'Which is where we come in,' Storm confirmed.

'Exactly, babe. That's why I want you at your first showbiz do tonight. It's a handbag launch and Mr and Mrs Golden Couple should be there – they haven't been seen together in months so if they show up tonight this is a big deal. I want you to look for any signs of a split, sit in the corner and just watch what goes on between them. Don't knock back the free champagne, tempting though it is. Getting pissed is not an option. Got it?'

Storm nodded her head. And later during the party at London's swanky Guildhall she did just as she'd been told. Although the promised Golden Couple failed to turn up, the place was wall-to-wall with other celebs and Storm hobnobbed with TV and reality stars, making sure she came up with loads of gossip for the paper's party pages.

As promised she'd sipped sparkling water rather than the free-flowing champagne on offer, but she'd been more than happy just to find herself on the fringes of this glamorous new world. She'd been unable to tear her eyes away from the latest *Big Brother* winner snogging the face off one of the *TOWIE* girls, and an *EastEnders* star emptying an entire gin bottle down her throat while pole dancing in a thong. As if that wasn't enough she'd bumped into another reality star, who announced she'd been offered a walk-on part in a Hollywood movie and was due to sign contracts next week.

'It's such a big opportunity,' she gushed. 'I wasn't supposed to say anything yet, but I feel like I could tell *you* anything! God, don't let me bump into you next time I end up snogging a man I shouldn't!'

The following day Storm wrote up her copy with pride, only to find it wasn't good enough for Sabrina.

'Your piece on that new handbag launch party was shit,' she said, slamming down Storm's copy on her desk.

'Sorry, Sabrina,' Storm mumbled. 'I did my best.'

'Well, your best was shit. It may have been good enough for the little backwater paper you came from, but not here.'

'Sorry again, Sabrina, I'll do better next time.'

'You'd better, otherwise it might be best for you to have a career rethink. I hear Sainsbury's are after shelf-stackers, perhaps that's more your thing.'

Storm just glared at her. Bitch! It was as if Sabrina had a hotline tapped directly into her junior's insecurities.

As Sabrina stalked over to her own desk, Chelsea gave her new friend a smile.

'Just ignore her, we all do.'

'Easier said than done,' Storm whispered back.

'She does this to every new girl who's any good. Sabrina thinks she can get away with it when someone's just arrived – trust me, she'll get bored in the end.'

'I hope you're right.' Storm sighed. 'There's only so much "yes, Sabrina, no, Sabrina, how many coffees would you like today, Sabrina" I can manage before I smack her around the face with a stapler!'

'Don't give her the satisfaction,' Chelsea chuckled. 'She's easily threatened by anyone with a hint of talent – don't let her get in the way of your big chance.'

Storm sighed. She knew Chelsea was right, and Sabrina wasn't the first awkward cow she'd ever encountered and wouldn't be the last. But it was Storm's first week. Couldn't the news editor at least cut her some slack?

'Does this qualify as a chocolate biscuit moment?' queried Storm.

Chelsea threw her head back and laughed. 'Not even close, babe.'

If nothing else at least the challenge of her new role helped to take Storm's mind off Carly. Although she had done her best not to think about her friend, Storm couldn't help it, she really missed her mate. Ever since they were small, they'd talked several times a week at the very least. Not being able to tell Carly all the details of her new life broke Storm's heart. It wasn't so much that she had lots of excitement and drama to fill her in on, but it was the chance to talk about the small things she'd taken for granted all these years – like whether she should be healthy and have grilled chicken for dinner or give into a craving for a greasy burger. Not only that, she would have killed to have confided in her friend about Dermot.

She kept checking her phone every five minutes to see if she had any missed calls, but nothing. Storm hadn't given up, though, and had rung Carly every day since she'd moved but her phone just rang and rang. Yesterday she'd rung and heard a disembodied voice tell her this number was out of service. Storm had stared at her mobile in horror. Had Carly really changed her number to avoid her? Storm couldn't believe it. But there was no getting away from the truth. Carly never wanted to hear from her again.

Storm was worried. Not just about the fact that she may never hear from Carly again, but also about how her former friend was coping. Desperate for information she texted the one person she hoped might still be speaking to her – Jez. Thankfully he texted her straight back, explaining he was working nearby and could meet her for lunch later that day.

Walking into the salad bar he'd suggested around the corner from her office, Storm was delighted and relieved to see a virtually orange man sitting in the corner, waving at her frantically. 'I've ordered us the carb-free lentil bake. It's disgusting but fabulous for the figure.' He smiled, pulling her in for a generous hug.

'Jez, it's wonderful to see you, thank you so much for meeting me.'

'Any time, sweetheart. I think it's madness you and Carly aren't speaking. I've told her there's no way she should be shutting you out like this but she won't listen. She knows as well as I do how the media blows things out of proportion.'

Storm fiddled with the corner of her napkin and fought back tears. What with splitting from Carly and Dermot in the space of a week, she'd needed to see a friendly face more than she'd realised.

'I honestly didn't betray her, Jez. I made the mistake of telling my boyfriend about her fling, a man I thought I could trust. Big mistake, which is why he's now my ex.'

Jez paused before he said, 'Storm, we've all made mistakes where men are concerned. Me more than most. One day I'll have to tell you all about a little indiscretion I enjoyed with a former boy-band member. He was such a swine in the end, I thought I was going to have to change my name and go into witness protection!'

Storm chuckled. 'That bad?'

'Worse. But what I'm trying to say is that, even though I made a huge mistake, things sorted themselves out in the end, and I know you and Carly will patch up your differences.'

'But she's changed her number, Jez. I don't think she's ever going to forgive me. Besides all that, I'm worried. We both know how badly she took it when Paul cheated on her. I'm concerned all this press attention will send her right back to square one.'

As their food arrived, they took a break from the conversation to tuck in.

'Look, Storm,' Jez said, reaching for the pepper grinder. 'This has done Carly no harm whatsoever. You might as well know she's never been busier at work and has even been offered a segment on *Morning Cuppa*, to dole out fashion and relationship advice to wronged women.'

Fork midway to her mouth, Storm paused. 'Are you joking? I thought Dillon said he'd ruin her?'

'Far from it. Carly may still be painted as a home-wrecker by some sections of the press but if anything she seems to be climbing the career ladder more quickly as a result, so I'd stop beating yourself up quite so badly if I were you.'

'I want her back in my life, Jez. She's my best friend, and being without her is unbearable.'

'And you'll get her back, you've just got to be patient. If nothing else you've got to get on with your own life, gorgeous. Carly's moved on, you have to as well. Why don't you try giving her some space for a while? Show her what she's missing.'

'You mean like when you've been dumped by a bloke?'

'Exactly like that.' Jez grinned. 'But don't hit the ice cream, my love. Now you're on the London party circuit, not to mention young, free and single, you need to stay in shape.'

After lunch Storm walked back to work feeling more light-hearted than she had in days. She was pleased Carly's career was soaring and that her friend was making the most of the situation she'd found herself in. If only she could find some way of forgiving Storm then life would be perfect for them both.

Flashing her pass at the security guard, she made her way to the bank of lifts. Waiting for one to hit the ground floor and whisk her back to her desk, she realised Jez was right. She couldn't keep chasing Carly like this. She'd go mad. There was only one thing for it, she realised. She'd just have to get on with her new life.

Thank God for Chelsea, who'd been an endless support since Storm had joined the paper. Not only had she been delighted with the way the new recruit had handled herself at the handbag launch, she now had a new assignment she knew Storm would be perfect for.

'You, Makayla and a hotel suite at five p.m. tonight,' Chelsea announced, handing her the details of an interview that had been set up.

Storm looked startled.

'What . . . THE Makayla ?'

'The one and only,' Chelsea agreed. 'Now she's plugging her new album and has agreed to give just two or three interviews to the press. Try and get something new out of her – I reckon you're good for it.'

At that Storm felt a little pulse of excitement. Makayla was one of the hottest pop stars on the planet. With a bigger following than Katy Perry and Lady Gaga put together, Makayla was seriously A-list. Was Storm really up to the challenge?

'I'm not sure I'm ready,' she said.

'Bollocks,' Chelsea replied cheerfully. 'Besides, I've got a hot date in Paris with a stockbroker tonight and can't be late.'

'Paris, France?'

'I only know one Paris. Come on, you'll be doing me a favour.'

Touched by her new friend's generosity, Storm vowed to do her best. Yet walking into London's swanky Dorchester Hotel later that day, she had to admit her palms and everything else felt more than a little sweaty as she was whizzed up to the penthouse in a private lift. Thankfully, Makayla couldn't have been more welcoming and immediately put Storm at ease.

'Come in, babe,' she said, pushing her PR people out of the way and greeting the reporter from the lift herself. 'Champagne?'

'Not for me, thanks,' Storm replied regretfully. 'On the job and all that.'

'Ooh, a bit like a policeman?'

Storm laughed. Whenever she'd seen Makayla on the telly, she'd always thought she was some super-professional icon who seemed untouchable. Now, she realised the star was a sweet, down-to-earth girl from Dagenham.

'Just like a copper, but without the uniform.'

Unleashing a Barbara Windsor-style belly laugh, Makayla reached for a fresh bottle.

'Well, don't mind me.' She smiled and poured herself a large glass. 'Bottoms up.'

After that Makayla answered everything Storm asked her, even when her publicity team butted in to tell her their client wasn't answering those sorts of questions.

'I can speak for myself, thank you,' the star said bolshily. 'Now then, babes, where were we . . . oh, yes, plastic surgery. Well, of course I've had me knockers done. Who hasn't?'

'I haven't.' Storm giggled. 'And I was sure I'd read you hadn't either.'

'I was embarrassed and ashamed to admit it at the time,' Makayla explained. 'I did it because I thought that was the way to sell more records. Now I realise that's bullshit, and I don't care who knows it.'

'Really?' Storm was puzzled. 'But why do you want to 'fess up now?'

'I don't know.' Makayla laughed. 'It's you! I never meant to tell you about that but you've got a way of getting the truth out of people. I like you!'

Once the interview was over, and Storm and Makayla had air kissed with genuine warmth, Storm walked through the hotel foyer and made her way out into the cool night air. With two days to go until Christmas, the West End pavements were jam-packed with last-minute shoppers, desperate to find gifts for their loved ones. As she negotiated her way around huge shopping bags and pointy elbows, she felt like running down the street cheering. Nothing could put a dampener on her good mood tonight. She'd secured a massive exclusive for the paper, and she'd only been in the job a week!

Nearing Marble Arch station, Storm felt like she was flying. Secretly, she'd been worried that after years of interviewing councillors about planning applications she would be out of her depth when faced with such a huge star. After all, Makayla filled stadiums. But she and the singer had bonded speedily. So much so that Storm had gone way over her allotted ten minutes. It was going to be quiet back at the office but she thought she'd go in to write up her notes.

Thinking of the scoop she'd just landed, she hoped this

was something that would not only give Chelsea a thrill, but finally put a smile on Sabrina's face.

'Nice one, babes,' Chelsea said, when they met in the lobby and Storm told her about the interview. 'I'd help you with your piece but Paris calls and all that.'

'My heart bleeds,' Storm bantered as the lift doors shut.

There was nobody else in the office apart from the night news guys and Storm was determined to make the most of the opportunity she had to get her piece word perfect.

By midnight she was knackered, having slaved over every sentence. She pressed send. With her copy safely delivered to Chelsea and Sabrina, Storm headed out to catch the drunk express. As usual at this time of year the night bus would be rammed with Christmas revellers determined to throw up in their handbags or pass out on her shoulder. What a shame she didn't have the energy to join them, thought Storm, already fantasising about crawling into bed. As she shivered at the bus stop, she thanked her lucky stars tomorrow was Christmas Eve, which meant it was her last day in the office before Christmas Day itself. Although there would still be a paper to produce, only a skeleton staff was on duty, meaning Storm could catch up on some much-needed sleep.

As for Christmas Day itself, she had thought hard about where to spend it. Sally would be in Canada this year with her relatives there, while Bailey and Lexie would both be away, they rarely came home these days – Lexie was fulfilling her dream, travelling the world working on cruise ships, and Bailey had joined the army and was currently stationed in Cyprus. Although they'd all speak on the day, Storm hadn't known what to do for Christmas.

Usually she and Carly saw one another on Christmas Day, but this year Storm had a horrible feeling her special day would mean a meal for one eaten slumped in front of the telly, with only her favourite box sets for company. Still, she'd had worse Christmases.

The following day in the office Storm was determined not to let Sabrina rattle her. She'd worked hard on the Makayla interview, and Chelsea had been thrilled with the story she'd produced, texting her late last night to thank her for a job well done.

It's brilliant babes! What an exclusive! Couldn't have done better myself. xxxx

Balancing a cappuccino and a bacon muffin in one hand and her mobile in the other, Storm was just about to sit down when Miles shouted that he wanted to see her in his office.

Predictably, she spilled coffee everywhere.

'Bollocks!' she hissed, mopping herself frantically with a wad of tissue.

'Stop mucking about, Storm,' Sabrina called. 'Miles is a professional even if you're not. We don't keep him waiting.'

With a heavy heart, Storm walked towards his office. She'd only been on the staff just over a week and had been working her fingers to the bone. What could she possibly have done wrong? Or was this down to Sabrina? It was obvious the woman hated her guts. Perhaps she'd successfully arranged for Storm to be fired. The perfect Christmas present, she thought.

Nearing her editor, she tried to read his expression. He

was smiling, which wasn't usually the look of a man who was about to give someone the sack. But perhaps he was like one of those killer assassins who grinned to put you at ease before shooting you straight in the chest.

'Don't look so worried.' He smiled more widely, ushering Storm inside. 'I want to congratulate you on a job well done.'

'Really?'

'Yes, I've just read your Makayla story – very nice work.' He gestured for her to take a seat. 'It's great you've landed such a big scoop so quickly – you're obviously settling in well.'

'Er, well, you know,' replied Storm, settling herself into the squashy armchair opposite Miles's desk, which was angled to overlook the Thames.

'Any new job takes time to settle into,' he replied reasonably. 'But it's clear you've got a knack for getting people to talk, which is why I've got a special undercover assignment for you. It means working on New Year's Eve but I don't think you'll find it too much of a hardship.'

He slid two first-class British Airways tickets across the desk towards her.

Storm gasped. 'What's this for?'

'Little job. We've got word that a celebrity couple host sex parties and are heading to a New Year's Eve party in Rome to enjoy themselves, with other like-minded individuals. Your job is to befriend them on the plane as they'll be on the same flight, so that they'll feel comfortable at the party revealing their saucy secrets to you.'

Storm wasn't sure she'd heard him correctly. 'You want me to go to a sex party?'

'That's right.' Miles chuckled. 'Don't worry, you don't have to have sex at the party and you don't have to stay for the whole thing, just long enough to get the details and some photos of our devoted celeb couple in action.'

This had to be a joke. Staring out of the window at all the other worker bees in offices across the Thames, Storm wondered how many of them were discussing sex with their boss.

'Look, it's just a bit of fun,' he continued. 'Besides, you'll have Dermot with you the whole time. I know you two aren't a couple any more but it won't kill you to spend some time together – and there's nobody else I can send. I can't imagine you'll need to be at the party for more than a couple of hours, meaning you two will have the rest of the night off. Think of it as a mini-break, no expense spared.'

Storm's mind raced. Her life was like some bad sitcom. Any minute now Ashton Kutcher was going to leap out of the filing cabinet and tell her she'd been punked.

Not only was she spending New Year's Eve at a sex party, but she'd be spending it with her ex. Life just got better and better. If only she could tell Carly, she thought. Her friend would die laughing. But no. She had to stop obsessing over her former friend. Jez was right. For now, she had to let Carly go.

Chapter Six

Sweeping into a Mayfair store on Boxing Day morning with the *Herald*'s company credit card burning a hole in her pocket, Storm felt like a million dollars.

'It's vital you look the part,' Miles had told her. 'All the other women at the party will be dressed in designer frocks so you need to be too – don't spare any expense. And don't forget the shoes either.'

But now, after traipsing up and down the shops for hours, Storm realised in despair that this was one of those days when nothing felt or looked right on her. She was staring at some hideous shiny dresses displayed in the window of a very expensive boutique when a man rounded the corner and collided with her.

'Jez! What on earth are you doing here?' she asked, delighted to see her new friend.

'I could say the same to you. I didn't think you were into granny frocks,' he teased, jerking his head towards the shop.

'Eurgh! I'm shopping,' Storm groaned. 'But everything I try on looks like it's come from a dressing-up box.'

'Well, of course it does if you've been looking in places like this. It isn't fit for anyone unless they're ninety-five or blind,' replied Jez, peering in the window and shuddering at the sight of a gold floor-length creation in the window. 'So what do you need a new dress for?'

Quickly Storm filled him in on her latest assignment. 'I thought it would be fun but I've been trudging up and down the shops for hours now and haven't found anything,' she wailed.

'Time for your favourite fairy godmother to step in.' He smiled, hailing a taxi and steering Storm inside. 'Harvey Nichols, please,' he told the taxi driver. 'Honestly, Storm, it's a one-stop designer paradise and you're going to love it.'

Entering the store, she quickly realised Jez was in his element as he flounced around each concession.

'Boring, boring, boring . . . perfect!' He grinned, reaching for a hot pink number and flinging it into her arms. 'I love shopping!'

'Me too,' Storm agreed weakly, by now barely able to see over all the outfits Jez had already piled into her arms for her to try on.

Finally, after Jez had exhausted the store, he herded her over to the changing rooms and insisted she show him every single outfit.

Storm, who was by now starving, was not in the best of moods.

'I'm not a model,' she whined. 'Can't I just show you the one I think will work best?'

Jez looked as if he could slap her. 'No, you can't. If it was down to you I know you'd turn up dressed in a bin bag. I want to see every single outfit – even if *you* think it's minging, *I'll* be the judge.'

Twenty minutes later Storm had found the dress of her dreams, a floor-length, cap-sleeved red gown, that clung to every curve, while still looking classy. 'Divine!' Jez declared as she stepped out of the changing room. 'You'll be the belle of the ball.'

'I hope not!' Storm protested as she gave him a twirl. 'The last thing I want is some dirty old perv picking my car keys out of the bowl.'

'Oh, sex parties aren't like that any more, Storm,' he assured her. 'That's so seventies. These days the venues are often very high-class.'

'How the bloody hell do you know?' she asked, gobsmacked, as they headed to the cash desk.

Jez shrugged. 'I've been around.'

Surrounded by shopping bags, Storm gratefully sipped a Dirty Martini in the bar of the plush W Hotel. She was exhausted after spending hours wandering around after Jez, who had insisted she bought accessories to match the dress. Storm had somehow ended up with a clashing hot pink clutch, diamond earrings, a beautiful ruby necklace, and a pair of red strappy Zanotti sandals that were so high, Storm was sure she'd topple over at any minute.

'They're more expensive than the dress!' Storm had gasped, gazing longingly at the shoes.

'It's on expenses, darling,' Jez wickedly suggested as he

guided her around the store. 'They expect you to spend all this money, so you might as well. Enjoy it while you can, I say. And anyway, with that dress and those shoes, you look like a goddess, darling. No one would dare touch you. Now enjoy it.'

Storm opened her mouth to protest, but realised there was no arguing with that, so she spent with abandon.

As for Jez, he'd refused to leave empty-handed and treated himself to an eye-wateringly expensive Omega watch. 'This is the life.' Jez smiled and clapped his hands together in delight as he rifled through Storm's bags. 'Nothing like a bit of shopping in the Christmas sales.'

'We didn't actually get anything in the sales,' she pointed out.

'No, but it is Christmas. Speaking of which, how was it for you?'

Storm sighed. She knew how much Jez loved this time of year, and it was no secret he liked to get all his nearest and dearest together for the perfect Christmas. This year he'd spent the day with Rufus and their best friends Gemma and Tony, as well as gorgeous glamour model Angel Summer and her über-hot husband Cal Bailey.

The last thing Storm wanted to do was rain on Jez's parade and reveal she couldn't give a toss about Christmas. Still, as Christmas Days went, this one hadn't been too bad. After speaking to Sally, Bailey and Lexie, she'd channel surfed, only to stumble across Nico Alvise presenting a festive cooking show. As she'd stuffed her face with a Christmas ready meal and chocolate Yule log, Storm couldn't tear her eyes away from the screen

– he was as gorgeous as she remembered. Watching him expertly slice a turkey crown, Storm felt butterflies in her tummy. She'd wondered if she'd imagined the strength of her feelings when she'd bumped into him at the party, but watching him on-screen it was clear she hadn't imagined anything.

After that she'd read a book and gone to bed early, but on the whole it hadn't been a bad day. Nobody had got drunk, passed out, vomited or hurled abuse. If it hadn't been for the fact she'd missed Carly every moment of the day and had drunkenly tried to see what she was up to on Facebook every half an hour, Storm would have said the day had been OK. If nothing else she'd at least had the chance to catch up on some sleep.

'It was all right.' She shrugged.

'How much time did you spend on Facebook trying to work out what Carly was up to?'

Storm looked at him in surprise. 'Sorry, did we spend Christmas together after all?'

'No, sweetness, it's just exactly the sort of thing I would do,' Jez said with twinkling eyes.

Storm laughed. Maybe she wasn't as insane as she'd thought she was. 'I've been doing my best to get on with my life, just like I know Carly's doing, yet I keep feeling guilty. I'm not sure I deserve to be happy after what I did to my best friend.'

Jez signalled to the waiter for another couple of Martinis, before turning to face Storm.

'You've got absolutely nothing to feel guilty about! I adore Carly, but she isn't hanging around feeling sorry for herself. Her work's going well and she's started seeing a new man.'

Storm gulped her drink in shock. Carly was dating again? Wow, that was brilliant news. She really was moving on. Storm knew it was none of her business but curiosity got the better of her.

'Who is he? Have you met him?'

Jez nodded. 'He's totes gorgeous with abs of steel like a Grecian god! His name's Roberto and he's an events manager in Brighton. He organised Nico's Christmas party, and after that awful story came out he called Carly to check she was OK.'

Storm's mind was in a spin. That party had changed both their lives, it seemed. She had a million questions, but there was just one she needed an answer to immediately.

'Is she happy?'

'Blissfully! And it's time you took a leaf out of her book. You can't put your life on hold like this for ever.'

Storm knew Jez was right. But knowing and doing were two entirely different things.

As the limo pulled up to the grand five-storey villa, Storm felt a thrill of excitement. She'd known the venue for the party wouldn't be a seedy dive, but even in her wildest dreams she'd never expected anything this posh.

The villa was gorgeous. It was painted a deep yellow, complete with little wrought-iron balconies and elegant shutters that framed the windows, while a huge stone archway decorated with ornate cherubs welcomed guests inside.

'Care to step this way, milady?' Dermot grinned as he stepped from the back seat of their limo and reached for Storm's hand.

'Don't mind if I do.' She smiled at him.

Dermot had been a perfect gentleman since they'd arrived at Heathrow. He'd treated Storm like a princess, carrying all her baggage, constantly ensuring her glass was topped up with champagne in the first-class lounge, and insisting she took the window seat on the plane.

By the time he had offered her his extra blanket, she'd had enough.

'What's going on?' she demanded. 'You're being too nice and it's weirding me out.'

Dermot looked hurt. 'Storm, I just want to make sure you're OK. We may not be together any more but I still care about you. Not only that but tonight's a big job for us, and I want to make sure you're properly relaxed.'

'Sorry,' she replied softly. 'I guess I just wish you could have been a bit more considerate when we were going out. It's a lot to take on board, that's all.'

'I know I messed up, Storm. You'd be mad ever to give me a second chance and I know I don't deserve one, but at the very least I want you to know I'm not all bad.'

Storm softened then and was about to reach for his hand when she saw Andy Markham, Olympic 1500-metre runner, and his wife Lisa – the reality star turned fashion designer, AKA their celeb swinging couple. They were last to board and sauntering down the aisle as if they had all the time in the world. Andy got Storm's back up straightaway by talking loudly on his mobile phone as he tried to cram half his lifetime's possessions into the overhead locker.

'Just think outside the box,' he bellowed before turning to the female flight attendant, who had asked him to get into his seat quickly as the plane was ready for take-off. 'I'll get off the phone when I'm good and ready! Don't you know who I am?'

Storm cringed. Cabin crew had enough of a hard time without dealing with wankers like him. Fury rose in her and she had half a mind to stand up and tell Andy to stop being such a dick when she caught Dermot's eye.

Leave it, he seemed to say.

Storm sat fuming in her seat, and when the stewardess came round with glasses of Prosecco for everyone, she took it gratefully. Hopefully it would help her relax and make Andy and Lisa a little more talkative. Dermot swung into reporter mode and leaned across the aisle, pretending to be nothing more than Andy's biggest fan, offering him sincere congratulations on his gold medal.

'Brilliant job, Andy. You made the country proud – you're an absolute legend.'

Storm wasn't sure such an obvious display of arse-kissing would go down well. But Lisa and Andy lapped up Dermot's praise.

'Thanks. 'Course winning the medal cost me. I had to get my legs insured for one hundred million each.'

'He really did,' chimed in Lisa. 'I insisted they were worth so much more, but the insurance company wouldn't go above one hundred mil.'

Storm squirmed in her seat in embarrassment, but she

knew she couldn't let her real feelings about the couple show.

Slapping on her biggest, fakest smile, she nodded encouragingly at Lisa.

'I know what you mean. My Dave's made a mint in stocks and shares so I wanted to get his brain insured.' She giggled inanely.

For this assignment, they'd both had to change their names. Dermot had imaginatively chosen Dave while Storm had gone for something a bit more mysterious with Destiny.

'This is my wife,' Dermot said, wrapping his arm around Storm and pulling her in for a squeeze. 'Destiny's got her own spray tan business.'

That was music to Lisa's ears. She wasted no time in asking Storm for a discount next time she needed her tan topping up. Storm assessed her as she sipped her Prosecco. If it weren't for the stringy hair extensions and badly applied slap, Lisa would have been jaw-droppingly pretty. With her long blonde hair, Barbie figure, piercing blue eyes and perfect skin, there was no denying she had model looks.

Sadly, she hadn't been to the less is more school of make-up. With her badly applied blue eye shadow, clumpy mascara and dodgy roots, she looked a lot older than her twenty-seven years.

By the time the four of them were on their second glass of Prosecco they were all getting on so well, Dermot casually mentioned they were off to a party near the Spanish Steps that night to celebrate the New Year.

'We like to do something special, don't we, love?' he said, turning to Storm, and kissing her lightly on the mouth.

'OMG!' Lisa whooped. 'We're hosting a party there tonight!'

'No way!' Storm exclaimed. 'What a coincidence.'

'Yeah, ours is strictly invite only,' Dermot explained. That much was true. The *Herald* had had to pull a number of strings to get invitations for him and Storm as the parties Andy and Lisa held were notoriously high end.

'Can I ask, is it the Four and Up Party you've been invited to?' Andy said in hushed tones.

'That's right,' Storm replied.

'Shit, babes! That's our party!' Lisa exclaimed. 'I thought there was something about you two that screamed good time! I can't wait to show you how to really party later.'

With that she shimmied the top half of her body in a side-to-side motion causing her boobs to jiggle at an alarming rate.

Andy didn't look impressed. 'Lisa, shut up!'

'Oh, don't be such a misery. If they're coming to our party then I'm not telling them anything they don't already know, or at the very least will find out about later.' She winked before beckoning to the flight attendant for another four glasses of Prosecco.

'To our new friends!'

By now Storm felt uncomfortable. Just how far would she and Dermot have to go to make their story convincing? Determined not to land herself in a sticky situation, she found her voice.

'It's our first time,' Storm babbled. 'But we've just celebrated our wedding anniversary and wanted to mark the occasion by doing something special.'

How easily the lies were flowing. Lisa squeezed Storm's hand, long manicured fingernails digging into her flesh.

'Don't worry, Destiny. It's all good clean fun,' she teased.

Andy nodded in agreement. 'I must say, it'll be nice to enjoy a bit more quality time with you both. Especially you, Destiny.' He leered at her suggestively.

Storm swallowed the bile rising in her throat. Cheeky bastard! Andy was bald, skinny, had pockmarked skin, and was also an arrogant prick. He hadn't stopped going on about how rich he was since winning gold. Apparently he'd been offered so many endorsement deals he was earning more money than he could count, and their house was now so big they needed two cleaners! And as if that wasn't enough, all his fans did his head in by asking for autographs.

'They should understand, I need my space,' he said uncharitably.

Storm wanted to smack him there and then. And had a feeling that if it hadn't been for Dermot she probably would have. As for Lisa, or Loser as Storm had secretly nicknamed her, she had her own set of issues.

'Sometimes the amount of clothes I own makes me feel physically sick, Destiny,' she confided. 'Honestly, since Andy won that medal, I've had designers throwing so many clothes at me we've had to build a new closet just to house all my shoes.'

'That is tough,' Storm sympathised, secretly thinking

how much she'd like to build a third walk-in wardrobe big enough to bury Lisa and her whining in.

By the time the stewardess told them to buckle up in preparation for landing, Storm felt that if they'd offered her the option to jump out now she would have taken it. She wasn't sure how much more she could take.

Later, Storm linked her arm through Dermot's and entered the Roman villa where the party was being held. The scene took her breath away. Everything was so elegant, a million miles away from the lurid sex den full of perverts she'd been expecting. As she took a glass of champagne from a passing waiter, her eyes darted everywhere. She drank in every little detail. Ornate mirrors that were twice the size of Storm herself hung on the stucco walls, while a white marble spiral staircase seemed to climb for miles overhead. In one corner stood a chic white velvet chaise-longue, so pristine Storm doubted anyone had ever sat on it. In the opposite corner she noticed a young man with thick dark hair and almond-shaped eyes, playing the harp as guests continued to flood into the room.

Moving into the grand ballroom, she scanned the crowd for famous faces. She spotted an MP who'd recently resigned over yet another expenses scandal, and over by the huge sash window, nibbling on canapés, stood a couple of minor royals, each married with children! Filthy buggers, she thought.

In the centre stood Marcus, master of ceremonies for the evening, who was in charge of welcoming everyone. Short, with blond hair and a northern accent, he'd been nice enough, and hadn't seemed to suspect anything when they were introduced. 'Always a pleasure to meet newcomers,' he'd said as he warmly shook Dermot's hand and planted a very slobbery kiss on Storm's cheek. 'Now, if you don't mind handing over your phones – we don't want any pictures getting out when we play later.'

Both Storm and Dermot had known they would have to give up their mobiles, so Dermot had found them both a couple of special camera key rings that doubled up as recording devices. As they slipped their phones into the plastic bag Marcus's assistant was holding out, the host was busily going through the rules for the event. Don't be pushy, don't disturb others, don't be rude, be explicit about your desires but don't exceed other people's limits.

'This sounds more like a boot camp than a sex party,' Storm grumbled under her breath.

At that moment Marcus caught her eye. Licking his lips, he wasted no time in showing her who was boss.

'If you have any specific questions, Destiny, ask me, Andy or Lisa, at any time.' Before turning his attention back to the crowd, Marcus ran his greedy eyes over her body. Despite the warmth of the red-hot fire burning in every room, Storm shivered. The bloke was worse than a drunk eyeing up a doner kebab. Gross!

When Marcus invited them to follow him for a tour of the house, Storm was entranced to see luxurious suites with flashy four-poster beds, chaise-longues and silk bedding. This was another world, and momentarily she forgot why she was in the house. There was nothing she loved more than poking around someone else's home and she had watched every episode of MTV's *Cribs*, desperate for a glimpse of the celeb lifestyle. Now she was living it – though she never would have imagined it would be quite like this.

Finally, as Marcus finished his tour and invited them all to enjoy a meal in the grand dining room, Storm began to relax.

Picking up her freshly filled wine glass, she took a long sip and tried to focus on the job in hand. She couldn't fail to notice that their hosts, Andy and Lisa, hadn't turned up yet. Storm nervously took another swallow of wine. Miles had specifically engineered it so that she and Dermot would be seated next to the couple, so Storm could work her magic on them and without their presence, the whole story would fall apart. And then, just as the starter arrived, Andy and Lisa – who was wearing a hot pink, skin-tight dress that left little to the imagination – burst through the double doors looking out of breath. Lateness seemed to be their speciality, Storm thought.

'Apologies!' Andy boomed as he marched into the dining room with Lisa tagging behind.

'Yes, Andy bought me a huge pearl necklace worth at least a million, which got us both in the mood for tonight,' cackled Lisa while everyone else tittered.

Andy had to have the last word. 'Certainly did! Looked marvellous against the new double-F boobs I paid for last summer. You blokes would all be lucky to get an eyeful of my wife, let me tell you.'

As the couple sat down, it was obvious that Lisa was blind drunk. Her eyes were unfocused and she virtually collapsed into her chair. Ever the professional, Storm smiled and got into character as she leaned towards them.

'So nice to see you again. It's a wonderful party.'

'And you, Destiny. We've been thinking a lot about you two this afternoon. We think you're our kind of people, if you know what I mean,' Andy replied, unable to resist ogling Storm in her figure-hugging red dress.

She gulped down more wine. Just the sight of Andy and Lisa was making her skin crawl. Thankfully, Dermot stepped in.

'Kind of you to say so, Andy. We were talking earlier and feel just the same way, don't we, sweetheart?' Dermot replied smoothly as he put his hand on Storm's thigh.

She didn't know which was worse. Being leered at by a creep or groped by her ex.

'Definitely,' she said, swiftly removing Dermot's hand from her knee.

'But enough about us. We want to know more about you – this place is incredible, how did you get started with these parties?'

But Storm's question was interrupted by the arrival of large plates of seared sea bass. Watching everyone around her tuck in, Storm felt increasingly nervous. How on earth were she and Dermot going to pull this off? Nibbling on a tiny piece of fish, she realised she'd lost her appetite, something that didn't go unnoticed by a drunken Lisa.

'You'll want to eat now.' She giggled. 'It's no good just drinking, Storm. We make sure we feed everyone so they've got plenty of energy for later!'

Storm simply smiled and shrugged. 'I'm fine, Lisa – watching my weight!'

Lisa rolled her eyes. 'You're gorgeous. Your weight's the last thing you need to worry about.' Looking down at her own busty figure, she sighed. 'Unlike me. All my weight goes to my bum, and sometimes I'd like to lose a bit. And now with my new boobs, men only ever want me for one thing. You know what I mean, don't you?'

Storm sipped her wine, and looked pityingly at Lisa. She was sure that any minute now the girl was going to burst into tears and start crying about how nobody loved her, a fact that hadn't gone unnoticed by Andy who shot Storm another suggestive glance before he glared at his wife. 'Lisa, leave the poor girl alone for a bit,' he said, then turned to Dermot. 'How would you like to come and enjoy a cigar with me in the library and have a look at my Olympic gold medal?'

Dermot took a sip of his wine and eyed Andy thoughtfully. 'Grand. I'd love to take a look.' Getting up, he bent down to kiss Storm on the cheek and whispered in her ear, 'Perfect timing. Don't worry, I'll get him to tell me all his sordid secrets now.'

As Dermot wandered off, Storm smiled brightly at Lisa and did her best not to panic at being left on her own. What on earth was she going to talk about? A list of dos and don'ts when it came to hair extensions?

But she needn't have worried as Lisa reached for the wine bottle and topped up both their glasses. She couldn't wait to get back to talking about her favourite subject – herself – and chatted with ease about her modelling career and recent attempts at fashion design.

'I've always enjoyed designing. Even when I was

modelling I was always drawing my own creations – you know, things I'd love to wear on the catwalk– but it's only lately it's really taken off,' she slurred. 'I'm hoping to show my first collection at London Fashion Week next year.'

Storm looked at her in surprise. Lisa might have been drunk, but it was the first time since they'd met that she had talked about something real.

'So why these parties?' asked Storm, genuinely curious. 'It seems a world away from Fashion Week!'

Lisa smiled at Storm and drained her glass before answering. 'Andy's always had a bit of an eye for the ladies, shall we say? I quickly worked out it was better to keep him interested with these parties than have a go at him about affair after affair. This way I don't have to worry about what he gets up to or who he's with because I'm there myself and know exactly what goes on.'

To her horror, Storm found herself pitying Lisa. She was doing all this just to keep her man. 'So when did it all start?' she asked, gesturing around the room.

'A few years ago. Then, after Andy won gold last year, we decided to start hosting exclusive parties for rich people just like us.'

'And do you always host parties in Rome?' Storm continued, ignoring Lisa's comment.

'Yes. Italians tend to be a bit more discreet.' Lisa smiled. 'Unlike Brits and the scumbag paps we have to put up with there. They're filth, Destiny. You've no idea what life's like for us. They follow us everywhere.'

Storm saw her chance and took it. 'Well, that's just it. How do you make sure the press don't find out?'

Refreshing their glasses once more, Lisa shrugged. 'We only invite our very best friends to our parties.'

'What do you mean?' Storm asked innocently.

Lisa, who by now had consumed nearly three bottles of wine, rolled her eyes. 'Well, we know the press go through everything . . . Christ, we even caught them going through our bins recently . . . so we only invite people we know we can trust or who have come recommended.'

Storm nodded understandingly and looked around her. 'This house is amazing, Lisa, and all this luxury and gorgeous food. These parties must cost a lot to put on.'

'Oh, they do. You wouldn't believe how expensive they are. But worth every penny.' Lisa winked suggestively, leaning closer to her.

Sensing she was on to something, Storm carried on with the questions. 'So Andy's endorsements pay for all this, do they?'

Lisa looked confused for a moment, and drank some more wine before answering. 'You know, I'm never quite sure where we get the money, to be honest, Destiny. I mean, don't get me wrong, we have loads of the stuff, and it just keeps coming, but Andy always says we should keep that just for us, you know? I think we pay for the parties by using any money that's left over from our charity. You know the one that helps amputee victims? Well, Andy's accountant says there's always so much money left over from the charity that we may as well use it to have fun.'

Gulping a mouthful of wine, Storm couldn't believe what she was hearing. Surely Lisa couldn't be stupid enough to believe that charities would have leftover money.

'So you don't help anyone through the charity?' she asked incredulously.

'Duh! 'Course we do, Destiny!' Lisa slurred. 'It's just, there's so much money, there's enough for us to have these parties too.'

Storm felt sick. The whole country thought Andy was a hero, and yet he and his wife were creaming off charitable donations. Any pity Storm had felt for Lisa quickly disappeared. Their life wasn't just dishonest, it was fraudulent too. They both deserved to be stitched up by the *Herald*. Quickly she glanced at the key ring attached to her bracelet. The light on it glowed a solid red, telling her she'd caught every last word.

As the lights went up, Dermot and Andy joined Storm and Lisa as everyone moved into the lounge area where more drinks were served. Storm was keen to go and finish the job. Dermot, however, pulled her down on to his lap and kissed her full on the lips.

'It's just for show,' he said softly, pulling away. 'We have to act like a couple to pull this off.'

Storm knew he was right. But all this pretence was doing her head in. Not only did she have a fake name but a fake boyfriend too. It wouldn't be so bad if she knew she could go back to her hotel room and chill in her trackie bottoms with a huge mug of builder's tea after all this was over, but she and Dermot were sharing a room – the only saving grace was the fact they'd been given twin beds.

Given the scoop she knew she'd landed, Storm realised it was vital they got out of here fast. Getting up, she pulled him off the chair and over to an alcove, where she quickly told him what she'd discovered. His eyes were as wide as saucers by the time she'd finished.

'Bloody hell, Storm! That's brilliant. I got nothing out of Andy, except an exhaustive account of his training schedule during the run up to the Olympics.'

Dermot looked at his ex-girlfriend with grudging respect. A year ago he wouldn't have been sure she'd have the courage to go through with something like this, but her new job was giving Storm a confidence he'd never seen in her before and, Dermot had to admit, he was finding it very sexy. She really did have the magic touch when it came to stories. However, he had a horrible feeling she was worth a lot more to the *Herald* than he was. Dermot wasn't stupid. He'd seen the look in Miles's eyes when Storm had pulled off that Makayla story. This was only going to send her stock soaring higher and Dermot realised it would make sense if he tethered himself to Storm, and fast. He hated to admit it, but he needed her.

'So do you think we can get out of here now? These people make me feel sick, and I'm not sure I can take any more,' she said.

Discreetly they found Marcus's assistant in the hallway, retrieved their phones and stepped outside into the cool night air.

An hour later Storm and Dermot had put their night of misery behind them and were enjoying champagne cocktails in a boutique hotel with a bar overlooking the Trevi Fountain. Rome was definitely in the mood to party, with everyone cheering excitedly, hugging and smiling as they took photos around the fountain and got ready for the countdown to the New Year.

Finally feeling relaxed, Storm checked her watch. Just half an hour to go before she could kiss goodbye to this miserable year and welcome in a new one. As she looked around she saw that the bar seemed to be full of happy couples having a good time. They all appeared to be so in love, with the world at their feet. Storm had never been one of those girls who needed a man to complete her. When she was at school she'd had no time for dating, and as she grew older she always put her mates first and blokes second. Feeling sorry for herself wasn't something Storm did, but at that moment she couldn't ignore the little voice inside her head that wondered: When am I ever going to find love like that?

With Dermot in the gents, she sat alone at the bar and flicked through the photos on her phone. There were so many of her and Dermot together, laughing, and having fun. Storm gazed at one Carly had taken when they'd enjoyed a barbecue on Brighton beach last summer. Dermot had treated them all to champagne and there was a picture of him shaking the bottle all over her as if he was a Formula One driver. Storm hadn't been able to stop laughing. She had to admit they'd had some happy times; it killed her they were over now. Taking a long drink of white wine, Storm felt a pang as her eyes came to rest on a photo of her and Carly, taken just after Dermot had soaked her with booze. With their arms wrapped around each other, it looked as though nothing could ever tear them apart – that all seemed like a million years ago. Since that photo was taken she'd lost her best friend and her boyfriend. And then there was Dermot. She was still furious with him, and though she hated to admit it, in her darkest hours she missed him.

'Thinking about Carly?' Dermot said as he returned to his seat.

His words surprised her. That was the second time tonight he'd seemed to know exactly what she was thinking. Dermot was many things, but intuitive wasn't usually one of them.

'Yes, something like that.'

'I know you won't believe me, Stormy, but I really never meant to hurt her and I certainly never meant for you two to fall out. Most of all, I never expected us to break up over it.'

'Don't be stupid, Dermot,' Storm snapped. 'You knew exactly what you were doing and you didn't give a shit. You were too busy thinking about your own precious career.'

Casting his eyes down, Dermot fiddled nervously with the stem of his wine glass. 'Thing is, I miss you so much it's killing me. I've been a complete twat, and I know that now. But I love you, Storm, and I want you to forgive me. The truth is I'd do anything to win you back.'

Storm was shocked. Never in all the time they had been together had he expressed his love for her so openly. Of course he'd frequently told her how gorgeous she was, and how wonderful it was to be with someone who completely understood his job, but this was the first time he'd ever spoken with such feeling. Seeing him close to tears moved her. For the first time since this whole mess had begun

Storm wondered if maybe Dermot genuinely was sorry for the upset he had caused.

She opened her mouth to speak, but just as she did the crowd in the bar started loudly counting down in Italian.

As they reached *uno*, Dermot locked eyes with Storm and leaned towards her. Realising he was about to kiss her she turned her head, leaving her ex with a mouthful of her hair.

'Stormy,' Dermot whispered, reaching for her hands.

Backing away from him, she shook her head. 'Dermot, I've told you before, you and me are over. I know you say you're sorry about what happened with Carly but you have to realise . . . we are never getting back together. Since we work together I'm happy for us to try and be friendly, but as a couple we're finished.'

Chapter Seven

'Good time in the land of pizza and pasta?' chuckled Chelsea, finding Storm sipping a latte at her desk.

'You could say that.' Storm smiled as she fired up her computer.

'Well, come on, I want all the details.'

Storm paused. Even though she'd told Chelsea about her history with Dermot over a bottle of wine during her first week at work, she was in no mood to dwell on the fact that he'd tried to kiss her on New Year's Eve. She shuddered at the memory – how funny that the idea of kissing him now was as tempting to her as snogging a fish. Instead she kept it simple and stuck to discussing work.

'The job went brilliantly.'

'So I hear. Miles has been full of your scoop all morning – Sabrina's mad with jealousy. I think she was expecting it to go spectacularly wrong.'

Storm smiled wryly. 'Yeah, I assumed that, seeing as she was so encouraging before I left.'

She reached for that Sunday's edition. After their Italian trip she'd had a few days off, but the thrill of seeing her name splashed across the front page still hadn't lost its novelty. *Swing When You're Scamming* had been the headline to the piece about Andy and Lisa. So far the response to Storm's scoop had been overwhelming. She'd worried that because Andy was considered a national hero and Lisa the nation's sweetheart, everyone would hate her for exposing them. But, in fact, the public were revolted by Andy and Lisa's behaviour and the police had launched an investigation. The comments on the paper's website had been incredible. Some had even thanked Storm for doing a public service in disclosing what a pair of scumbags they really were. Storm wouldn't usually have taken pleasure in seeing someone's career take a nosedive, but if anyone deserved it, Andy and Lisa did. As for Storm herself, Miles had rung her at home the moment she'd filed her story and given her a pay rise – effective immediately.

'Money well spent if you keep this up,' he'd told her.

At that moment Sabrina appeared before Storm's desk. As usual she was dressed to kill in a black power suit, sky-high heels and immaculate make-up. There was no denying Sabrina was gorgeous, but there was nothing warm about her beauty. Cuddling her must be a bit like hugging a cold radiator, Storm thought.

As Sabrina smiled sweetly, Storm waited for the ruthless attack about to come her way.

'Well done on the Italian job,' Sabrina announced while Storm inwardly waited for the sucker punch. 'You exceeded Miles's expectations.'

'Well, that's really good to know,' Storm replied cautiously.

'Yes. Of course, I did say attending a sex party in disguise was something I knew you'd be good at. In fact, I said to him, our Storm will have no trouble pulling off the part of a good-time girl.'

There it was, the inevitable put down, delivered with perfect timing. She might be the boss but Storm thought it was about time she let Sabrina know she wasn't putting up with her cheek for ever.

'Well, thank you for the vote of confidence, Sabrina. And I know you too understand how wonderful it can be when you get the chance to mix business with pleasure,' Storm replied with assumed innocence.

Out of the corner of her eye, she could see Chelsea smirking as she buried her head in her paperwork. Sabrina gritted her teeth and fixed Storm with an icy stare.

'I certainly don't know anything about that. Everything I've achieved has been down to good old-fashioned hard work.'

'Well, there's nothing like getting down on your hands and knees in the name of hard graft,' Storm agreed, still in apparent innocence of her double-entendre. 'Now is there something I can help you with, only I know how busy you are?'

Sabrina looked as if she was itching to give Storm the finger. Instead, she coolly turned her attention to the sheaf of paper in her hands.

'Yes, actually. Miles has asked you to go to a few celebrity parties this week, including the new Daniel Craig premiere tonight. Wear something nice, but this time don't put it on expenses. I hear Aldi occasionally carry women's wear, if you need to upgrade your wardrobe.'

Storm refused to take the bait. Instead she simply smiled at Sabrina and took the pile of invitations. With Sabrina safely out of earshot, Chelsea let out a snort of laughter, unable to contain her giggles any longer.

'You really told her!' she chuckled.

'Stuck-up cow deserves it. Anyway, aren't you meant to put rabid dogs down? I should call the RSPCA and put her out of her misery.'

Chelsea smirked. 'Forget her, babe, we all know she's a bitch. Anyway, I've got some good news for you. Tonight you won't be all on your own as you attempt to chat up Daniel Craig because I'll be joining you. And I have even got a gorgeous hot pink halterneck number you can borrow. What do you say?'

Storm smiled. What could she say? It sounded like she was in for yet another night of glamour.

Back at her flat Storm was determined to look her best just in case she came face to face with a certain Mr Craig. She slipped on Chelsea's pink halterneck dress and admired her reflection in the full-length mirror. It wasn't bad. She didn't usually do pink but this creation fitted like a glove, with a plunging neckline that made her fairly average-sized boobs look massive. To complete her look she blow dried her hair so that it fell in its usual soft waves around her shoulders. With smoky eyes and a slash of soft pink lipstick, she was done.

'Christ! You'll have someone's eye out with those,' Chelsea laughed as she spotted Storm rushing out of Leicester Square station.

'You don't have to tell me! I've already had my fair share of city boys perving over me on the tube. You could have told me this dress would give me Lisa Markham-style assets.'

Chelsea laughed as she linked arms with her new friend. 'Why else do you think I bought it? Us girls who don't have Lisa's legendary boobs need all the help we can get and I reckon you're going to have celebrities eating out of the palm of your hand tonight . . . or maybe your cleavage!'

'Chelsea,' Storm warned her, 'my name's not Sabrina, and I'm not that kind of reporter.'

'Don't worry, babes. I'm just teasing. To be honest, I think I'm a bit out of sorts because that stockbroker turned out to be more of a cockbroker, if you know what I mean?'

Storm realised with a sudden jolt of guilt that she hadn't asked Chelsea anything about her date in Paris just before Christmas. How self-involved was she? Usually there was nothing Storm loved more than a good gossip, particularly where sex was concerned.

'Was it that bad?'

Chelsea groaned. 'Bad doesn't cover it. Fair enough, he whisked me off to Paris in his private plane and we enjoyed a fabulous meal at the Plaza *Athénée*, but all he did was talk about himself all night long, then shag me before the plane had even left the tarmac on the way home.'

'Was he shit in bed?' Storm asked, getting to the heart of the matter.

'Yes! And the worst thing was his dick wasn't just the size of a party sausage, he had the nerve to tell me afterwards that I should get bum implants and he'd give me the number of a friend of his who was a cosmetic surgeon.'

Storm was astounded. 'He didn't! I hope you told him where to go?'

''Course I did. I said to him, you want to ask your surgeon friend if he's doing a two for one offer. That way you could get your dick and your personality surgically enhanced.'

Storm threw her head back and roared with laughter and was still chuckling as they arrived at the cinema. She'd wanted to watch all the stars walk up the red carpet, but Chelsea had told her not to be so lame.

'Only tourists do that, or mad fans,' she hissed as they marched straight past the crowds and into the foyer.

Storm desperately tried to be discreet and cool just like Chelsea but couldn't help scanning the achingly stylish room with its wall-to-ceiling glass front and hip white stools.

There were lots of wannabes, sipping cocktails and desperately trying to look as though they belonged, but so far no genuine celebs had arrived to watch the film.

'They don't watch the flick,' Chelsea explained. 'They walk the red carpet, get noticed, then head straight to the after party. Most of the stars have seen the film about a thousand times anyway so I'm afraid you're going to have to wait a little longer to meet Mr Craig.'

Storm sighed impatiently. She'd never been to a premiere before and had secretly hoped she'd end up sitting next to Mr Bond himself. She imagined him yawning as he casually put his arm around her shoulder – it was a move every fifteen-year-old could count as a winner. There was just the small fact that Daniel was married, but as Storm was strictly dealing in fantasy she didn't give herself too much of a hard time about it.

Slipping into her seat in the back row, she looked around her. This was one of the poshest cinemas she'd ever been in. Forget the tatty red velour of the multiplex; these seats were covered in leopard print and embossed with the names of the stars who'd sat in them at various premieres and award ceremonies. It was incredibly glam, and Storm would have loved to have taken some photos on her phone to show her sister Lexie, but they'd been made to hand in all mobiles before being seated. Now, as she scanned the audience, she realised that although there weren't many celebs in attendance, the place was packed with plenty of civilians, dressed up to the nines.

With Chelsea bagging the aisle seat, Storm slyly glanced to her left and found she was sitting next to a bloke in a charcoal grey suit. She couldn't help feeling sorry for him. At well over six foot, he was squeezed so tightly into his seat that his knees were practically around his ears. Storm took pity on him and patted him gingerly on the arm. 'Would you like me to ask my friend to switch seats with you?'

As the man turned, he treated her to a megawatt smile, sending Storm's heart racing. Bloody hell! It was only Nico Alvise. What were the chances? And what if he remembered their last meeting?

'I'm fine, I'm more than used to sitting like this.' He smiled, about to turn away from her, then he asked, 'Hey, don't I know you?'

Determined to style it out, Storm kept her face averted and pretended to find her arm rest fascinating. 'Er, no. Don't think so.'

But Nico was insistent. 'Yes, I do! You're that flight attendant who spilled red wine all over me at my Christmas party in Brighton.'

Storm groaned. That bloody party was going to haunt her for the rest of her life.

'Oh, yes! Sorry, didn't recognise you in here, you look so different with . . . er . . .'

'. . . with a white shirt that's not covered in red wine?' Nico bantered.

Storm scowled and wished for the thousandth time she'd never even gone to Nico's party when it seemed she was still dealing with the fallout.

'Look, I'm sorry, I feel terrible about that,' she began.

'I'm teasing, Storm.' As Nico smiled broadly at her, his gorgeous brown eyes twinkled with mischief.

Storm blushed. 'You remembered my name.'

'Hard to forget – like the rest of you.'

Oh, he was smooth, Storm had to give him that, and any awkwardness she felt disappeared as she laughed at the corniness of the line.

'So you're laughing at me now! Storm, I could take this personally. At our last meeting you threw wine at me and now you sit here cruelly snickering at my attempts to make you feel better.'

'If you want to make me feel better, I'd appreciate an invitation to dinner in one of your restaurants a whole lot more.'

Oops – she hadn't meant it to sound as if she was inviting him on a date. That had always been her trouble, Storm thought, she never knew when to quit while she was ahead. As for Nico, if he was taken aback he didn't let on. Instead he treated her to another smile. He was about to open his mouth and reply when the cinema lights dimmed and the opening credits of the film began.

Storm found herself unable to concentrate with Nico sitting next to her. His every move caused her pulse to quicken and the hairs on the back of her neck to stand on end. There was something about him that sent her pulse-rate soaring. When his leg accidentally brushed against hers, she felt the same charge of electricity she'd felt when he'd gripped her wrists at his party. Momentarily shocked, she sneaked a glance at Nico only to lock eyes with him. Had he felt it too? By the time the film had ended Storm felt giddy with lust and couldn't wait to get out of the cinema. Grabbing Chelsea, she murmured a hurried goodbye to Nico and raced from the auditorium. What was it about that man? She wasn't usually shy around blokes, but she felt like a schoolgirl around Nico.

'What's got into you?' Chelsea grumbled as Storm hustled her outside. 'I need the loo and to rid my cleavage of all the popcorn I dropped down it.'

'You can pee when we get to the after party,' Storm said, signalling to a passing taxi and practically shoving Chelsea into the back seat. 'And, babe, newsflash. Your cleavage isn't big enough to hold a lot of popcorn!'

By the time they pulled up to The Chiltern Firehouse, Storm had put Nico out of her mind and instead was buzzing with excitement about the after party.

'Bloody hell! Is that really a giant inflatable Daniel Craig?' she exclaimed to her friend.

Chelsea laughed. 'You ain't seen nothing yet, girl. Trust me, when we get inside there'll be more A-listers guzzling Cristal and pressing more flesh than you saw at your sordid sex party the other night!'

Storm considered Chelsea. 'Just how do you know all this, babe? Exactly how long have you been doing this job?'

'Long enough to know that any celeb worth their salt doesn't really want to be here, they just want to get in, get out, and get into bed before they have to do it all over again tomorrow. What was it Cameron Diaz once said: "The movies I do for free, the publicity I get paid for".'

'You old cynic, anyone would think you hated your job,' laughed Storm.

'Don't get me wrong, I love it. But I can see through the bollocks of the celeb lifestyle. Trust me, I'd rather be me than some A-lister.'

'Even when you date dickhead stockbrokers?' Storm put in.

'Even then,' Chelsea agreed as she flashed her press pass at the bouncer on the door.

Once inside, Storm struggled to get used to the low lighting. As usual Chelsea was right: the place was wall-to-wall with celebrities. This time there were genuine A-listers too, like Bradley Cooper and Kate Upton. Up close they were just as gorgeous as they were on screen.

'Wow!' sighed Storm, momentarily star-struck.

'For fuck's sake, babe,' chimed Chelsea. 'You look like every other civilian in here, gawping at Bradley like that. You're a professional, so act like it. Plus you've got no chance of pulling if you keep your gob open like that. Keep your fingers crossed for me – I'm off to work the room.'

With Chelsea out of the way Storm headed to a table in the corner to observe the action. Just as she sat down a waiter approached her table with a glass of Cristal. 'From the gentleman at the bar with his compliments,' he said, setting the glass on the table. Storm swivelled around and saw Nico at the bar. Shit! She should have known he'd be at the after party. Catching her eye, he raised his glass as if to toast her and then walked slowly towards her table. She felt a thrill of anticipation as he gestured towards the seat next to hers and sat down, making Storm feel unusually tongue-tied.

'Thought I'd give you the chance to spill another drink over me,' he joked.

'Generous. But I wouldn't waste good champagne on you,' she bantered, not wanting to let Nico know how much his presence was unsettling her.

'So why do I keep finding you at showbiz celebrations? Shouldn't you be up in the skies somewhere, jetting off to glamorous destinations?' he asked.

'Oh, you know, us flight attendants get the occasional day off.' She shrugged, not keen to elaborate on the lie.

She knew she ought to tell Nico the truth, that she was a journalist, but somehow didn't want to break the spell she was caught up in and swiftly changed the subject. 'My friend Chelsea invited me. But what about you? Shouldn't you be cooking up some gastronomic feast in a kitchen somewhere?'

'Us chefs do get the occasional night off, you know,' he mocked. 'No, my manager tells me I have to come to these events to keep my profile high. To be honest, I'd feel more comfortable in the kitchen.'

'Celebrity lifestyle not agreeing with you then?' Storm asked as she sipped her drink.

'I wouldn't say that. I'm grateful for everything that's happened, it's just the TV thing has taken off so quickly, I'm still finding my feet.'

Storm arched her eyebrows as she noted Nico's designer suit and a watch that would have cost thousands of pounds.

'But I'm guessing the pros outweigh the cons.'

He followed the direction of her gaze and shrugged. 'Fair point. Yes, the money helps. But still, all the press attention can be intrusive and I'm sick and tired of women sending me their underwear.'

But Storm couldn't resist teasing him some more. 'Well, that's what happens when you top those sexiest man lists. It's your girlfriend I feel sorry for. How does she cope with women throwing their knickers at you, left, right and centre?'

Nico looked awkward as he replied, 'Francesca and I have known each other many years. She trusts me and thinks it's funny.'

'Well, she's more understanding than I would be!' Storm continued, now in full flow as she finished her champagne. 'If I were your girlfriend, I'd be furious.'

Now it was Nico's turn to look surprised by Storm's outburst. 'Well, if I were your boyfriend, I'd feel like the luckiest man on earth to have such a loyal, beautiful woman by my side.'

His words hung in the air and Storm wanted to brush them aside with a joke, or shoot him down with a feisty reply about keeping his corny comments to himself. But something stopped her. From nowhere an image of Nico kissing her, overwhelming her with his strong, tall body, flooded her mind. For a second she lost herself, wondering what it would be like to lie on top of him and feel his fingers glide over every inch of her skin. Something told Storm she was in dangerous territory. He was attached – flirting was the last thing they ought to be doing. Getting to her feet, she pushed her chair back and smiled at him. 'I think I should go.'

Needing a few minutes to calm down, Storm rushed up the stairs to the ladies and went to open the door. She froze in shock as she realised who was standing directly in front of her – Carly. She looked incredible, dressed in a black chiffon strapless dress and Jimmy Choo pumps. Carly's hair gleamed and her eyes sparkled. In fact, she seemed a world away from the last time Storm had seen her just before Christmas. Now she appeared happy and in control, unlike Storm. Looking down at her borrowed pink dress, she realised she'd spilled champagne down it.

Carly noticed, of course. Wrinkling her nose in disgust,

she gave Storm the once over. 'So it is true what they say.' She looked directly into Storm's eyes. 'Shit really does rise to the surface.'

But Storm barely registered Carly's hurtful words, so great was her astonishment at seeing her. 'Carly! It's amazing to see you. You look so well . . . Jez told me you'd got a new boyfriend too, and of course I've seen you on TV. Looks like everything is going brilliantly for you.'

Storm knew she was babbling but didn't care. There was so much she wanted to say to her old friend, she didn't know where to start. Maybe this was an opportunity for them to talk and repair their relationship. But Carly shut her down in an instant.

'No thanks to you! My whole life could have been in tatters after what you did, and you've got the cheek to stand there telling me how well everything's going for me!'

Even though they were just inches apart on the marble floor, Carly pressed her face close to Storm's and jabbed one perfectly manicured finger into her chest.

Storm tried to remain calm. 'I'm not going to row with you, Carly. How about I let you go? There must be people you need to see.'

But Carly was gunning for her. 'I'm in no rush, but perhaps you are. Desperate to get back to your dick of a boyfriend, are you?'

Bollocks! Storm knew how badly she'd hurt her friend, but those words stung. 'Like I said, Carly, I'll let you get on if we can't at least be civil.'

'You'd like that, wouldn't you?' Carly spat. 'For me to roll over and pretend everything's fine. Well, forget it, you skank. I couldn't give a shit if everyone here found out what you did. 'Cos let's face it, if you hadn't stitched me up you wouldn't be here. In fact, the only way you'd know anything about this premiere would be by reading about it in your precious *Vida!* magazine! So, no, Storm, I won't play nice with you because, unlike me, you don't deserve any of this.'

Carly's words stung, but it seemed she still wasn't satisfied. 'You know what? You remind me of someone in that dress,' she continued as she peered down at Storm's outfit. 'Yes, with all that booze down your front, you resemble your mother.'

Storm felt as if she'd been punched. She knew she'd hurt Carly, but this was a step too far in retaliation.

All she wanted to do now was go home, but as she shook herself free from Carly's hand and turned her back on her former friend Storm was greeted by a fresh horror as she saw Nico standing at the top of the stairs.

Carly paused, brushed some imaginary fluff from her dress as she composed herself and pushed past him to return to the party, leaving Storm flushed with shame.

Nico walked straight over to her. Despite her anguish, Storm felt a flash of desire as his fingers wrapped themselves around hers.

'Silly question, but are you OK?' he asked, brown eyes brimming with concern.

'Fine, fine,' Storm lied, trying unsuccessfully to stop hot tears from spilling down her cheeks.

She could have kicked herself. Storm hated to show weakness at the best of times, let alone in front of a stranger. Shyly she glanced up at Nico, but he didn't seem to mind. Instead he carefully brushed her tears away with his thumb. The kindness of the gesture only set Storm off again. She couldn't put her finger on it, but there was something about Nico that made her feel as though he'd known her all her life and understood who she was.

'That was my former best friend.' She sniffed. 'We had a disagreement before Christmas because she felt I'd betrayed her, and I'm ashamed to say I did. Tonight was the first time we've seen each other since then and I deserved everything she threw at me.'

'You've tried making up with her?' Nico asked gently.

'Almost every day. But Carly's not interested and I don't know how to reach her.'

At the thought of all she'd lost, Storm felt exhausted and dropped to the floor. Nico joined her and sat beside her, cross-legged.

'I know what that's like,' he confided. 'I used to have several very good friends in Italy but many years ago we had a disagreement and we never spoke again.'

Storm rested her head on Nico's shoulder as though it were something she'd been doing for years. 'What was your row about?' she asked.

Nico buried his face in her hair and paused for a moment. 'To cut a long story short, they didn't stand by me during a very difficult time.'

Storm nodded. It sounded tough. 'Do you miss them?'

'Every day,' he replied simply. 'But there's still a chance you and Carly will make up.'

'I don't think so,' Storm replied. A gaggle of girls

rounded the stairs towards the loos. At the sound of their cackles of laughter the spell was broken and she got to her feet.

'Time for me to leave . . . again.' She smiled at him. 'But thank you for everything.'

Nico squeezed her hand once more, reluctant to let her go. 'Any time, Storm,' he whispered.

Too tired to negotiate the tube home, Storm treated herself to a cab. After the night's events all she wanted was to crawl into bed. The sound of Ed Sheeran's 'Drunk Again' coming from her handbag interrupted her thoughts – Sally. Storm stared at her smartphone. Could she really deal with her mother right now? Whatever she had to say, it wasn't likely to be something that would add to Storm's evening. She checked the time. Just after eleven, a bit late for a routine call, perhaps something was wrong.

'Hi, Sally, what can I do for you?' Storm answered cautiously.

'Nothing, love, just ringing to see how your posh premiere went.'

She sounded remarkably upbeat. Was it possible she'd been boozing?

'Yeah, fine. Sal, are you OK? You sound strange.'

'Fine, love. The real reason I rang is because I've got something to tell you.' There was a brief pause as Sally cleared her throat and took a deep breath. 'Thing is, I've met someone at bingo. I've known him for years, and he's a good, kind bloke. You'd like him, Storm.'

She began to feel sick. Sally hadn't dated anyone since

her husband had died and had always insisted she wasn't interested in finding love again, arguing that Alan had been the only man for her.

'Who is he?' Storm finally asked.

'His name's Jeff. He's a gardener, and like me he lost his partner.'

Is he a drunk like you too? Storm thought uncharitably as pictures of her mother falling down the stairs time and again after drinking too much vodka flooded her mind. Sally sensed what her daughter was thinking.

'I've told him everything, Storm. He knows all about my drinking and how I relied on you to take care of the family, plus he knows how proud I am of you and all you've achieved. He's curious about you and wants to meet you. Why don't you pop down for Sunday lunch sometime? There's no rush.'

Storm stared out of the cab window and watched the lights of the city pass her by.

As they neared Chelsea Bridge her mind wandered. Of course she wanted her mum to be happy, it was just a shock to hear there was someone else in her life after so many years. From nowhere she remembered the Saturday morning ballet lessons her dad always insisted on taking her to, and the strawberry milkshake they'd enjoy together afterwards. Then there were the school holidays when Alan would teach her vital life skills, as he called them. As his trusty assistant Storm had learned what went on under a car's bonnet, how to bleed a radiator, fix a plug, put up a shelf and paint a wall. It was almost as if Alan had a sixth sense his daughter would need those skills around the house when she became mother, father and handyman after he died.

'Trust me, Storm. You don't want to rely on a fella for everything. You keep your independence for as long as you can, earn your own money, pay your own way, and only be with a man because you love him,' he'd advised.

But Storm at just eleven then had been too embarrassed to heed her father's words. Instead she'd clamped her hands over her ears, willing her dad to go back to talking about anything but boys.

'Dad!' she'd protested. 'Boys are disgusting! I don't ever want a boyfriend.'

At that Alan had smiled knowingly. 'It won't always be that way, Stormy. Believe me, when you're older you'll find a man out there who'll give you everything you need.'

Storm hadn't thought about those conversations with her dad for years. Somehow her mum's shock news had sent her mind spiralling back to the past.

'I'm not replacing your father, Storm,' Sally insisted, bringing Storm back to the present. 'I'm just grabbing a little bit of happiness before it's too late. You know better than anyone what that's like.'

Storm knew she wasn't being fair to her mum. 'I'm really happy for you, Sal, and I'd love to come down some time and meet Jeff. I'm a bit busy at work at the minute, but I'll call soon, I promise.'

Chapter Eight

For the next few weeks Storm buried herself in her work. Sally's bombshell had left her feeling unsettled and she knew she needed a distraction. The paper's annual awards ceremony, celebrating the nation's favourite stars and their charities, was coming up so Storm volunteered her services on top of her regular reporting duties and threw herself into organising interviews with people that each charity had helped. That task, combined with ringing each star's agent and asking about their dietary requirements for the awards do, kept her busy and more often than not she wasn't home before midnight.

Apart from the occasional coffee with Jez and glass of wine with Chelsea, Storm spent a lot of time alone. She didn't mind on the whole, but there were times when she felt lonely. Since she and Dermot had returned from Rome, she'd kept her word and been friendly. She'd asked how things were going sleeping on his mate's floor, enquired after his Christmas back in Dublin and even had lunch with him. Friends they were not, but she was doing her best to keep things cordial for the sake of their jobs.

Now, after another day spent running around chasing stories, Storm poured herself a huge glass of wine and ran a long hot bath. She had always done some of her best thinking in the bath. Immersed in a tub full of soapy bubbles she considered her mother. Sally had emailed her earlier in the week to say she'd told Lexie and Bailey about Jeff, and they'd both taken it well. A lot better than Storm, by the sound of things. They'd agreed to meet him for lunch when they were next in Brighton, something Storm knew she wasn't yet ready for. Instead she'd fobbed her mum off with excuse after excuse, hoping that if she closed her eyes and wished hard enough all her troubles would go away.

Her mind wandered to Nico. Despite trying to lose herself in her work, Storm hadn't been able to stop thinking about him. His eyes, his touch, the way he made her feel.

Being with him was like being with a lifelong friend, except with all the best stories yet to be revealed. Storm felt he had a hotline straight to her heart, and knew just what to say and do to connect with her. She dreamed of seeing him again, but knew it was a lost cause. She felt like a stupid teenager – it wasn't as if they'd even kissed and of course he lived with his girlfriend Francesca who adored him, if what she'd read in the press was anything to go by.

But no matter how hard she tried to tell herself Nico was out of bounds, Storm had felt a real connection to him on the night of the premiere, and she wished she could see him again. As she began sloshing water over her face, an image of Alan with his head firmly under a car bonnet as he explained how to check the oil popped into her mind. She could almost hear him now, reminding her that she should never need to be with a man. She should be with him because she wanted to, and because she loved him. It really was that simple.

Just then a knock at the front door interrupted her thoughts. Stepping out of the tub and roughly towelling herself dry, she hurried to open it, only to find a beaming Dermot on the doorstep.

'I was just passing,' he said as he gestured towards the bottle of red wine he was carrying. 'Thought we could split this.'

Storm looked at him in amazement. 'Why would I want to do that, Dermot?'

He shuffled his feet, looking sheepish. 'Well, you know, I just thought . . .' He stopped talking, and looked at her uncertainly.

Storm bit her lip. She wanted to tell him to bugger off, but she'd meant what she'd said about them being friends for the sake of working together so where was the harm? 'Come in then,' she said, 'but I warn you, I'm exhausted and was planning on going to bed quite soon. I just need to put something on.'

'No problem,' he replied, pushing past her and into the kitchen to root around for a couple of glasses.

Coming out of her room a few minutes later, she saw that Dermot had made himself at home and was slumped on the black leather sofa, eating peanuts and watching *Question Time.*

Storm glanced at him. 'Make yourself at home, why don't you?' she said sarcastically.

'Hope you don't mind,' he said. 'Thought I'd get myself settled while I was waiting for you.'

Storm fought the urge to thump him. Instead she sat down and reached for the glass of wine he had poured for her.

'So what were you doing in this area?'

'Sorry, what was that?' murmured Dermot, unable to tear his eyes away from the TV screen.

'I said, what were you . . . oh, never mind,' Storm snapped.

'Sorry, Stormy,' Dermot said, giving her his full attention. 'To be honest, I wasn't passing, I wanted to talk to you about something.'

She was immediately on red alert. 'Oh, yes?'

Swinging his legs off the sofa and turning to face her, Dermot cleared his throat nervously. 'Well, the thing is, Storm, my mate's asked me to move out – he's got a girlfriend and she doesn't like me being there. Truth is I don't have anywhere else to go, and after our lunch the other day, I thought, now you've forgiven me and we're friends again, well . . .'

'. . . you thought you could move in here with me?'

'Not with you,' he said quickly. 'Just as flatmates. You've plenty of room. And you know I can knock you up a mean fried breakfast in the mornings.'

Storm looked at him. Not for the first time he'd left her speechless, and not in a good way. She felt like a prize idiot. Here was she, doing her best to keep things friendly and professional for the sake of their careers, and here was Dermot, wondering how he could best use that situation to his own advantage. Sod being professional. Enough was enough.

'Sure. Why not?' she said.

'Really?' replied Dermot, unable to wipe the smug grin off his face.

'Yeah. I'll tell you what . . . the place is all yours, in fact.'

Dermot looked confused. 'What do you mean?'

'I mean, you move in here and I'll move out. You seem to think I'll just forget what you did, but I won't. I don't want you in my life, Dermot. You're always looking for a way to get something over on someone, searching for an opportunity to haul yourself up, and I'm sick of it. Other than to say hello, goodbye or anything work related, I want nothing to do with you. I was going to move out soon anyway. You've only got a couple of weeks left here, they want the flat back.'

'Look, Storm, you're tired, you're upset, you don't know what you're saying . . .'

'Jesus, Dermot, what do you take me for? You and me are finished. You're the worst thing that ever happened to me. If you're coming here, I'll move out.'

''Course you can move in with me, babe,' Chelsea exclaimed when Storm told her how Dermot had tried to worm his way back into her good books. 'Spare room's all yours for as long as you need it.'

'Thanks so much, Chelsea. I wouldn't ask if I wasn't desperate,' Storm sighed.

'Are you trying to tell me you're too good to stay at my place?' Chelsea teased. 'I know Stratford's a bit of a come down after Clapham but we're very trendy in East London these days.

'Look,' she continued kindly, 'I think you're great, Storm. Sadly, I've never felt the same way about Dermot. He's always given off an air of what I like to call eau de weasel.'

Storm looked surprised. Usually everyone loved Dermot. 'What do you mean?'

Chelsea sighed. 'Sorry, I didn't mean to speak out of turn, but to be honest with you, Storm, you were way too good for him. I've seen Dermot's type come and go before. He's been hanging on to your coat tails for long enough. You've got more talent in your little finger than he'll ever have. It'll be interesting to see what happens now he no longer has you to fall back on.'

Storm was speechless. She'd half expected Chelsea to tell her she was making a big mistake. If his true character was that obvious, Storm wished she herself had wised up a bit sooner.

'Anyway,' Chelsea continued, swiftly changing the subject, 'I've got something to take your mind off your troubles – I've been invited out to Barcelona for a couple of days to stay with Angel Summer at her mansion and cover her new wedding dress launch. I need you to come with me as it's going to be a really big deal, with lots of celebs.'

Storm looked like a rabbit trapped in headlights. 'Are you serious?'

'Deadly. Why?'

How could she explain? Angel was something of a hero to Storm. The fact that Angel was just a few years older, had gone to the same school, grown up just a few streets away and had enjoyed a meteoric rise to fame, wasn't lost on Storm as a kid. When she'd flicked through her beloved *Vida!* magazine and seen pictures of Angel living her glamorous celeb life, her spirits always lifted. If Angel, a girl from just around the corner, could live out her dreams, who was to say Storm couldn't as well? After all, Angel was living proof that you could change your life; not only had she enjoyed a stratospheric modelling career as one of the world's most stunning women, but she'd bagged the ultimate prince in Cal Bailey, the ex-England footballer who had recently been tipped for the England manager's job.

'When do we go?' Storm breathed.

Chelsea grinned. 'Valentine's Day.'

Angel's wedding dress launch was being held in a luxury mansion just a short drive from Barcelona city centre. In true celeb style she'd arranged for a limo to collect Storm and Chelsea from the airport, and even though she couldn't be there to greet them herself, had ensured there was a bottle of vintage champagne on ice waiting for them in the back to celebrate their arrival.

'I could get used to this.' Storm smiled, taking a delicate sip and enjoying the feeling of the bubbles fizzing all over her tongue.

'Say what you like about Angel,' Chelsea replied, 'but the girl is class all the way.'

'How do you know her?' Storm asked.

'Oh, we go way back,' Chelsea said as she explained she had been fortunate enough to interview Angel several times over the years and they'd always got on well. When Angel had revealed she'd suffered from post-natal depression, Chelsea was the only showbiz reporter who had insisted their paper shouldn't cover the story. 'Women suffering like this should be encouraged to speak out and get help, they're not going to do that if we reduce Angel's condition to nothing but gossip,' she'd told Miles, much to Sabrina's disgust. When Angel had heard of the lengths Chelsea had gone to on her behalf, she'd been more than impressed and had taken the unusual step of inviting her over for dinner – something she had never done with a journalist before, as she usually hated them all on sight. Since then the unlikely pair had become firm friends, with Angel realising Chelsea would always have her back.

When they arrived at the mansion they found a whirlwind of activity in progress. Technicians were setting up lights, carpenters were building the stage, while a team of engineers were rigging up a complicated sound system ready for the models to strut their stuff to. Storm couldn't help noticing Angel's signature colour, pink was splashed everywhere, from the fairy lights and chandeliers to the colour of the stage. Storm thought it all looked incredible and, if she was honest, felt more than a little overawed. Everything was so glamorous and perfect, including the glossy pristine paintwork and giant marble staircase that was so grand it could be considered a work of art in its own right.

But there was no time to dwell on her own feelings as together with Chelsea she moved through the venue. They found Angel giving instructions to a team of florists.

'I thought you were too posh to get your hands dirty these days and had people to do this sort of shit for you?' Chelsea joked as she leaned in for the obligatory air kiss.

'Oi! Don't bite the hand that feeds you.' Angel grinned, kissing her in reply.

'And you must be Storm,' the model exclaimed. 'I've been dying to meet you. Chelsea's told me so much about you, including how you've been telling your cow of a news editor where to go.'

Storm shot Chelsea a WTF face.

Angel sensed Storm's discomfort. 'Don't worry. I've told Sabrina Anderson to fuck off a few times myself.'

Angel had never forgotten how Sabrina had hounded her night and day after she'd briefly split from Cal following his short-lived affair with an Italian WAG. When other reporters had gone home Sabrina had stayed put, determined to land a scoop, and had thought nothing of trying to interview her daughter Honey right in front of Angel.

While Angel finished giving instructions to her team Jez and Rufus sidled into view. Smiling in delight, she waved at them and the two hurried over. The couple kissed Chelsea and Storm hello and Jez wasted no time in getting to the point. 'You've seen the pink palace then?'

'Mmmm, I think you mentioned something about it looking a bit Gypsy Wedding this morning. Cheeky bastard!' Angel smiled as she spoke.

'I was merely pointing out that there are other colours in the world besides pink.'

'It's Valentine's Day and a wedding dress launch, Jez! I think for once pink is entirely appropriate.'

He shrugged. 'I suppose I'll let you off just this once. But more importantly have you shown them your new rock yet?'

'They've only just got here,' said Angel, playfully batting her best friend on the shoulder.

Rufus winked at her. 'You know my husband . . . large pretty things excite him.'

'Yes! Enough with the bullshit, show me the bling,' Chelsea exclaimed as she reached for Angel's right hand.

'Crikey, that's bigger than Ayers Rock,' Storm gasped, unable to tear her eyes away from the huge pink diamond nestled on Angel's ring finger.

'It's a Valentine's Day present from Cal.' She sighed contentedly. 'An eternity ring and good luck gift for today. He had it 'specially made.'

Storm was stunned. She'd never seen such a large diamond.

'So what's the plan . . . or are we going to admire your diamond all day long?' Chelsea asked cheekily.

'I've booked you in for some treatments at the spa around the corner, and then we're off to Lasarte for dinner later.'

'Fabulous!' said Jez, clapping his hands in delight. 'I'll need to be relaxed before I get my hands on some of your brides tomorrow. I will not be held responsible for my actions if I see one bride-to-be wearing a scrunchie or a Croydon facelift.'

As part of the launch, Jez and Rufus had teamed up to offer a wedding bootcamp campaign. Jez was going to be giving hair demonstrations while Rufus would demonstrate wedding day workouts guaranteed to get results.

'As you can see, Jez went to the "customer is always right" school of hairdressing,' Rufus teased.

'Let me stop you right there!' he replied theatrically. 'The customer is never right. Got that? Never! Some of them deserve to be hung, drawn and quartered for crimes against hair.'

'And you see it as your role to tell them that?' Storm couldn't help joining in.

Jez sniffed. 'What can I say, Storm? It is a tough job, but someone really does have to do it.'

There was no other way to describe it, the day had been truly perfect, reflected Storm as she got ready for dinner. After Angel had shown them all to their rooms, which turned out to be luxurious suites, complete with mini-bars stocked with nothing but champagne, Storm had considered the contents of her suitcase. She hadn't known what to pack for a weekend with her heroine so had decided to keep it simple and settled on a short black shirt dress. As she sat down to do her make-up she realised the full body massage, hydrotherapy treatment, facial and mani/pedi she'd just enjoyed, courtesy of Angel, were exactly what she'd needed after everything she'd been through recently.

The therapists had magic hands, and Storm had left the

spa feeling like a new woman. After Carly's outburst at The Chiltern Firehouse, Storm had felt hurt for several weeks, but eventually she realised it had given her the closure she badly needed. It was as though she could shuck off her guilt once and for all as, despite her best attempts, she hadn't been able to mend bridges with Carly. Now Dermot was finally out of her life, she felt as though a giant weight had been lifted from her shoulders and she could move forward. It was just a shame he hadn't got the message yet. Since Storm had moved out of the Clapham flat he'd sent her flowers and texted her every day.

She found this all a bit creepy, especially as she strongly suspected he was now sleeping with Sabrina. God only knows what *she* thought about the situation – or if she even knew.

'Cocktails or champagne?' Jez asked as they were shown to their table in the restaurant.

'Let's start with cocktails. Slippery Nipples all round?' Angel grinned.

'Oh, you can take the girl out of Brighton but you can't take Brighton out of the girl!' Jez mocked, rolling his eyes at his old friend.

Angel protested, 'And what's wrong with a Slippery Nipple? Or Sex on the Beach . . .'

'. . . or a Screaming Orgasm?' joked Storm.

'Ooh, I enjoyed one of those last night.' Jez smirked as he turned to his husband. 'Or should I say, we did?'

Rufus playfully squeezed his hand and calmed him down. 'Nobody likes a show off. Now let's order.'

Two rounds of cocktails later the conversation was flowing. Storm was giving them a blow by blow account of the swingers party, Chelsea was moaning about her love life, and Angel proudly showed the group pictures of Honey along with her new baby boy Ryder, as well as giving them the lowdown on Cal's new football academies.

'He's got four now. As well as the Lewisham and Brighton ones, he's set up one in Chatham and another in Clacton-on-Sea,' she revealed proudly.

'I don't know how he does it,' Jez marvelled. 'Though I like to think I do my fair share for the disadvantaged youth of today.'

'Making interns run around picking up your dry-cleaning, fetching your coffee and searching the Internet for vaguely pornographic pictures of Ryan Gosling, is not the same thing, sweetie,' Angel shot back as the table hooted with laughter.

Storm had to admit, the whole evening was going brilliantly. Although she had got to know Jez and Chelsea quite well by now, she'd been worried she wasn't quite in Angel's league. But she realised she had nothing to worry about. Angel was such a brilliant host, and so wonderfully grounded despite her superstar status.

The following morning Storm woke up starving. After slipping on a pair of grey skinny jeans and a t-shirt, she hurried down to breakfast in the vast, sunny kitchen that overlooked the city. There she found everyone apart from Angel, who had been up for hours, busy devouring a feast.

'Those waffles look amazing, Chelsea.' Storm beamed, pulling up a stool next to her friend.

'That's because they are,' she said, mouth full of waffle, chocolate and banana.

'Yes, they're so good that in fact they're Chelsea's third helping,' Jez pointed out.

'Who are you? The food police? Mind your own business,' Chelsea shot back as she reached for more chocolate sauce.

'Just saying, a moment on the lips is worth a lifetime on the hips,' he said, smugly tucking into half a grapefruit.

'Say that again and you'll be wearing that grapefruit instead of eating it!'

'Children, children!' Rufus interrupted, desperate to avoid war until at least lunchtime. 'Storm, can I get you a coffee?'

'God, yes, please!' she said gratefully. Storm didn't feel remotely human until she'd had at least three cups of the black stuff before even attempting food.

'How did you all sleep?' she asked, taking the espresso gratefully.

'Badly,' Jez replied playfully. 'There's nothing like a little European getaway to inject romance into a relationship.'

Rufus looked at his husband warningly. 'Nobody wants to hear about our love life. Again.'

'Definitely not. At least not when we haven't had a bit for ages,' Chelsea moaned.

'No! Are you in the middle of a sex drought?' Jez asked. 'That's terrible. Happened to me once, so I went to visit a white witch who gave me a spell . . .'

148

Storm couldn't resist interrupting. 'Sorry. You went to a white witch and got a *spell*? There's so much wrong with that sentence, I don't even know where to start,'

Jez glared at her. 'FYI it worked. I hadn't had sex for months, but the witch told me to race around Glastonbury Tor after dark, naked, with a white feather in one hand and a white candle in the other, while chanting "My body is yours to worship" three times. Then I had to wait.'

'Oh, yeah! And how long did you have to wait?' Chelsea scoffed.

'Not long actually,' he said conspiratorially. 'On my way back down the hill, I bumped into this gorgeous hippie with huge rippling biceps and dreadlocks down to his navel. I don't normally go for hippies, but on this occasion I made an exception and . . . *voilà* – drought broken.'

Storm gazed at him in surprise. 'Are you serious?'

Jez tipped his head to one side and paused before he burst out laughing. 'Nah! But you should see the look on your face!'

She shook her head. 'You bastard! I believed you then. Still, let me just say this. I may be single, but I don't care how bad it gets . . . no hairy hippy will ever get anywhere near my muff!'

Chapter Nine

After breakfast Storm was determined to make herself useful and threw herself into the launch, admiring all of Angel's hard work. Their host really had thought of everything. Towering plates of chocolate truffles stood proudly at the entrance, along with romantic displays of vibrant red roses and glossy pink peonies, ready to get the guests in the mood for love. Elsewhere, huge photos of Angel and Cal's weddings, the first and second time around, lined the immaculately painted walls, while a string quartet played classic love songs in the garden and caterers set up plates piled high with to-die-for canapés. Outside, the thick grassy lawns had been mown into immaculate stripes, the kidney-shaped swimming pool was a vivid blue, and the marquee (pink, of course) had just been erected. As for the driveway, the beautiful white gravel had been replaced with pink stones. Best of all, there wasn't a cloud in the sky as the sun gently beat down.

The whole place looked as though it had come straight

from the pages of a style magazine and Storm felt a little out of place. She was just some chancer from Brighton – she had no business being here.

'Come on, stop dreaming, there's work to be done.' Angel smiled, cutting into Storm's thoughts. 'Could you be my meet and greet person for a couple of hours, to give me a break from the press? You and Chelsea are one thing, but the rest of them I can't stand and I know they'll be trying to trip me up.'

'Absolutely,' Storm exclaimed. 'What do you want me to do?'

'Stand at the entrance, look pretty and hand them a press pack and goody bag,' Angel said briskly as she guided her to the front of the house.

'Ooh, what's in the goody bag?' Storm asked, curiosity getting the better of her as she peered into one of the pretty pink carriers that stood on a long table by the solid oak front door.

'Just a selection of my perfumes, a slice of pink wedding cake, a voucher for a set of bridal lingerie and some jewellery.'

'Very generous,' said Storm approvingly.

'Well, the one thing I've learned with these bastards, Storm, is that the press can be bought very easily!'

As Storm went upstairs to change out of her jeans, she thanked her lucky stars she'd had the foresight to bring the dusky pink bandage dress she'd bought from ASOS in the sale last summer. She'd almost left it at home, thinking it was far too summery for Barcelona in February, but thank God she'd given in to temptation. The dress was unbelievably flattering, making her look slim without being skinny, and somehow it made her feel a little less tall. Teaming it with the trusty pair of nude slingbacks, she was good to go.

Two hours later, Storm had seen at first hand exactly the kind of shit Angel had to deal with from the press on a daily basis. Not only had the handful of journalists Storm had met been rude, surly and downright ungrateful, she'd even caught a couple of paps taking pictures of her when she'd bent down to adjust her shoe strap, inadvertently flashing a bit of cleavage! They really do give us a bad name, she thought, giving them another eyeful by flipping them the finger.

'Don't do that, they'll never get over the shock.' Chelsea smirked as she came to relieve Storm from her post. 'Some of those paps see you as the new girl who can't put a foot wrong at the moment. Watching you flip the birdie at them like that will give them palpitations.'

'Well, they shouldn't try and take pictures of my boobs, should they? Pervs,' Storm muttered darkly.

'Looks like I've arrived just in time. Go and get a glass of fizz and enjoy yourself. I'll deal with this shower of shit . . . sorry, colleagues!' Chelsea said, shooing her away.

As Storm joined the throng in the garden she helped herself to a glass of pink champagne from a passing waiter dressed in a fuchsia-coloured tuxedo and watched Angel do her thing. The whole place was teeming with beauty and gossip journalists, actors, actresses, pop stars and sporting heroes. As for the star of the show herself, Angel was in her element, smiling and welcoming all her guests, ensuring that nobody felt excluded.

'Darling! That dress looks sensational. So lovely to see you in something a little less funereal.' Jez had appeared by her side. Dressed in a pink linen suit that was on the verge of clashing with his slightly orange skin, he looked surprisingly macho.

Storm considered his outfit carefully. 'I think you are the only person I know who could pull that off,' she said finally.

'What can I say? You've either got it or you haven't.' He smiled, doing a little twirl. 'What are we doing anyway? Eyeing up the journalist competition. Rest assured, Storm, Angel will make sure you leave with a little exclusive that should keep Sabrina Anderson off your back for a while.'

At the sound of Sabrina's name, Storm groaned and helped herself to another glass of champagne. That woman had a very sobering effect on her. 'Can we please discuss anyone but her?'

'Anyone but who?' asked Angel as she joined them mid-conversation.

'Sabrina,' she and Jez chorused in unison.

At the mention of the news editor's name, Angel grimaced. 'Yeah, you're right. Can we please discuss anyone but that woman today?'

Storm was about to open her mouth and say something else, when she saw Angel wave at a man in the distance.

'There's someone I'm desperate for you both to meet,' she said.

'I'd brace yourself for a chat about football if I were you,' Jez whispered in Storm's ear. 'I might have a thing for the players, but if you're anything like me you'll find discussing the sport about as interesting as watching paint dry.'

Storm giggled as she gratefully sipped her glass of champagne.

'Happy Valentine's Day, Storm. Don't tell me, another day off?' a voice bantered behind her.

Storm turned round – Nico. 'What are you doing here?' She was amazed to see the man she couldn't stop thinking about before her once again.

'Oh, you two already know each other? I was just about to introduce you. Nico's doing the catering for me today,' explained Angel.

He turned to Angel and Jez, his eyes full of mischief. 'We've met a couple of times, but usually I've found Storm likes to spill her booze rather than drink it.' Nico chuckled softly.

Cheeky bastard! Two could play at that game.

'What can I say, Nico? If you serve quality refreshments like Angel does, then there's less temptation to get them everywhere but down your throat.'

Just being next to him was doing something to her. Even now, dressed in sparkling chef's whites and with his hair slightly dishevelled, he looked gorgeous.

'Actually I was going to invite you into the kitchen to test some of my new dishes. I believe last time we met you mentioned something about dinner . . .'

As Nico's voice trailed off, Storm found herself blushing. Jez and Angel looked at them, surprised expressions on their faces.

'That wasn't how it sounds . . .'

'I'll just bet it wasn't,' sniggered Jez. 'Well, I suggest you hop to it. When a man's offering you a private viewing of his canapés, Storm, it's rude to say no.'

After giving Jez the evil eye, she smiled at Nico. 'If you'll excuse my friends, I'd love the opportunity to see you at work.'

'And I'd love to show you,' he replied softly. 'So will you join me?'

Storm nodded and followed him across the garden towards the house. As they walked inside the mansion she realised that the sound of her high heels was the only thing punctuating the silence.

'Where is everyone?' she asked, spooked by the quiet.

'Most of the team have gone home now the party's underway.'

As the kitchen door loomed ever closer, Storm found herself feeling strangely guilty. She hated telling lies, and knew it was time to tell Nico the truth about what she did for a job. As he opened the door and led her inside she vowed to tell him the truth immediately, but then the sight of the kitchen distracted her momentarily.

'Not bad, Mr Alvise.' She smiled, looking around. The kitchen was small and industrial-looking, with steel worktops and cupboards, but extremely well organised, with pots and pans hanging from the ceiling and knives stuck on a magnetic board on the wall.

'This is where the magic happens.' Nico took her hand and led her towards the fridge. Pulling out a tray of miniature beef tartlets, he held one up to Storm's mouth.

'Taste this.'

Storm didn't need asking twice, and bit into the tart with enthusiasm. 'God, that's so good,' she groaned in appreciation, taking another bite. As the hairs on the back of Nico's hand tickled her top lip, Storm felt consumed with lust. It took every ounce of self-control she possessed for her not to devour that hand as well as the canapé. Instead she focused on the food.

'If nobody's ever said it to you before, let me tell you you're a miracle worker when it comes to food.'

'It's been said before!' Nico laughed, running his eyes over Storm's face. 'Wait a minute, you've got something on your lip.'

As he gazed into her eyes and rubbed his thumb across her mouth, Storm felt it was one of the most erotic and intimate gestures she'd ever experienced. Closing her eyes with longing, she suddenly heard the unmistakable sound of the click of a camera from the kitchen window.

Swinging round at the same time as Nico, she saw a paparazzo flee, camera swinging from his shoulder.

'You scum! Get back here now!' Nico shouted, his face red with anger. 'Who do these people think they are . . . interfering in my life?' He reached for one of the pans hanging from the ceiling and threw it across the room.

Storm jumped back in shock. How had the paps even known they would be in the kitchen, or had they just got lucky? It wasn't as if they'd been doing anything newsworthy. Still, Storm could just imagine the look on her face as she'd eaten from Nico's hand. Innocent it was not.

'I can't believe that just happened,' she said, voice shaking.

At the sound of it, Nico calmed down. 'Forget them. Those paps are nothing, but this is the price of fame. Everything in my life is up for grabs. Even you,' he said sadly.

Storm hesitated. She wanted more than ever to tell Nico what she did for a living but instinct told her that now wasn't the right time. The last thing she wanted to do was make him even angrier. Instead she reached for his hand and squeezed it reassuringly. 'Maybe we should return to the party?' she suggested.

But Nico shook his head. 'No, *bella*, I must go back to my hotel and speak to my manager and Francesca about what's just happened. Maybe I can track down the scum that did this too. I'll see you soon.'

As Storm watched him walk out of the kitchen, she was gripped by a feeling of sadness.

After a night spent worrying about what she was going to find in the next morning's papers, Storm woke after a couple of hours' sleep at about 11 a.m. Desperate for a cup of coffee, she reached for her dressing gown and went downstairs to the kitchen, only to find Angel, Chelsea, Jez and Rufus in full flow.

'Have you lot been to bed?' Storm asked. 'You were all in exactly the same seats when I said goodnight.'

When Nico had left, she had agonised over their encounter for hours with her friends, who'd all done their best to cheer her up, but it was pointless. She couldn't stop

157

thinking about how if that snap got into the wrong hands it could damage both her career and Nico's. The rumour mill would go into overdrive, accusing her of having an affair with him behind his girlfriend's back – something she would never do, no matter how tempted she was – and Storm wasn't sure she could take any more scandal.

'Grab yourself a mug and stop looking so worried.' Chelsea smiled as she pulled out the chair next to hers so Storm could sit down. 'I've sorted out your little problem with the paparazzi so you can stop fretting about that photo making it into the press any time soon.'

'What have you done?' Storm gasped.

Chelsea shrugged as if it was no big deal. 'Let's just say I made a certain pap see reason, and he realised it was in his best interests not to let that image get out.'

Storm was touched Chelsea had gone out of her way like this to help.

'Honestly I don't know what to say,' she replied, helping herself to coffee and buttering a piece of lukewarm toast.

'All in a day's work.' Chelsea smiled. 'So can you stop worrying now, please?'

'Yes. And I ought to tell Nico, he'll be so relieved.'

Angel held up her hand. 'Already done. I phoned this morning to let him know Chelsea had sorted it.'

'What did he say?' Storm asked, her heart pounding.

'He was obviously delighted, but realises that this won't be the last pap intruding on his personal life. It's the price of fame,' Angel replied, shaking her head sadly, understanding only too well.

Storm chewed her bottom lip absent-mindedly. It

sounded silly, but she'd been hoping to break the news to him herself.

'Did he ask about me?' she said finally, only for Angel to shake her head.

'There was no time. It was only a short call.'

'Just what is going on between you and Nico?' Chelsea said, getting straight to the point. 'It's obviously none of my business, but I think I speak for everyone when I say the sexual chemistry between you two yesterday was as obvious as Jez's fake tan.'

'Do you mind?' he fired back. 'It costs money to maintain this level of bronzing.'

'Really? I thought you just went out and got yourself Tangoed!' Chelsea giggled.

But Storm was hardly taking in a word of the chatter around the table – she was too busy breathing a sigh of relief that a crisis had been averted.

'We're just friends,' she said quietly, finding the idea unsettling. How could she say what they were when she really had no idea herself?

Jez raised an eyebrow. 'Friends with benefits more like.'

'You haven't shagged him?' Chelsea exclaimed.

'No! 'Course not,' Storm protested.

Chelsea wasn't convinced. 'Well, be careful. Mr Alvise might be shacked up with the lovely Francesca, but he's no stranger to the ladies.'

'What do you mean?' Storm demanded.

'I mean that Nico has a girlfriend on the side. Or did up until very recently.'

'Really!' exclaimed Angel. 'I never knew that.

Chelsea shook her head and took another sip of tea. 'No, he's very discreet, doesn't want to upset Francesca.'

'So why hasn't it been in the press?' asked Jez.

'Because Nico's just too nice. He treated his last girlfriend like a goddess, with spa days, first-class hotel stays and so on.'

Chelsea glanced at Storm, who had gone as white as a sheet.

'But he seems so devoted to Francesca,' she protested. 'He as good as told me he was the last time I saw him.'

'Yes, he is devoted to her – but I dunno, they've grown apart or whatever.' Chelsea shrugged. 'Let's face it, the only people who really know what's going on in a relationship are the ones directly involved, so don't judge him too harshly. Nico's a good guy. Just be careful. You could get your heart broken by someone like him.'

'Perhaps the reason he's so into you, Storm, is because he's hoping for a free upgrade next time he goes back to Italy!' Jez chipped in.

'What's he on about?' Angel asked, puzzled.

Storm shot Jez a look of reproof and quickly outlined the facts to her new friends.

'So he's got no idea you're a reporter?' Chelsea asked.

Storm nodded. 'It's so stupid, I had no reason to lie to him, and the story's spiralled out of control. I've a feeling if I tell him now it won't go down very well.'

Angel agreed. 'I think you have to tell him eventually, Storm, but given what happened with the pap yesterday, now may not be the best time.'

*

As Storm and Chelsea weren't flying back to London until later that night they had plenty of time to relax. After breakfast Angel, the boys and Chelsea decided to head into Barcelona for a bit of retail therapy, but worried she wouldn't be good company, Storm offered to stay behind and cook lunch for when they got back as a thank you to Angel.

'You cook? Wow, Storm! I'm impressed, I can't even boil water,' Angel laughed. 'What time do you want us?'

'How about two-ish? That should give you plenty of time to shop 'til you drop.'

After air kissing everyone goodbye Storm changed into her blue and white striped bikini and dived into the outdoor pool. Even though it was February, the pool was heated and the water was so refreshing. The more she swam, though, the more she thought about Nico, the same questions going round and round in her mind.

Was he really a cheat? Did he view her as just another potential notch on his bedpost? Was that why he hadn't asked about her when Angel called him? Was he angry with Storm? Had he already worked out she wasn't a flight attendant? Or had she been imagining things all along and any feelings in this situation were purely one-sided. After thirty laps she admitted exhaustion, having never been a strong swimmer. Hauling herself out of the pool, Storm had just started to dry off when she heard the doorbell.

Knowing she was alone in the house, she hastily wrapped a towel around herself, went inside to open the door and came face to face with Nico.

'What are you doing here?' she gasped.

'I just wanted to check you were OK after what happened yesterday.' He shuffled anxiously from foot to foot.

'I'm fine. Chelsea managed to convince the pap not to sell the photo.'

'Yes, I heard,' he replied. 'Are you going to invite me in or should I just stay on the doorstep and watch you drip water everywhere, half-naked?'

At the mention of the word 'naked' Storm flushed bright crimson. In her surprise at seeing Nico again she'd completely forgotten she was wearing just a towel. Worst of all it was freezing – her nipples were doing all the talking. Shit! Of all the times to be caught out. Quickly she hoisted up the towel and opened the door wider to let him in.

'Can you give me five minutes to change?' Without waiting for an answer she sprinted up the stairs, dried off and slipped on a cute navy mini-dress. Running a slick of balm across her lips, she raked her fingers through her hair and hoped Nico was a fan of the just got out of bed look.

'Can you pass me the chicken stock please, Chef?' Storm smiled, pointing to the steaming hot jug just behind Nico. Today she was cooking her famous chicken risotto and, now that she had invited Britain's sexiest chef to join her friends, she knew she had to pull out all the stops. He had of course offered to help, but instead Storm had told him to sit in the corner and look pretty. This was her turn to cook, and Nico was not going to ruin it.

'I'm impressed you're attempting a risotto, Storm,' he mused, handing her the jug. 'Many people would be far too frightened to cook this classic Italian dish, especially for a classic Italian chef.'

Storm laughed as she ladled the stock into the heavy-bottomed pan. 'You don't frighten me. Trust me, my risotto is the business, and when you've tasted it you'll be begging me for the recipe.'

'Is that right? I think you'll find my risotto has won awards. And of course I'm Italian so, let me assure you, it'll be impossible for you to cook one better than I do! Still, it doesn't look to me as though you're doing a bad job,' Nico bantered, as he watched her dicing the onions. 'Where did you learn to cook?'

'I taught myself mainly. My mother wasn't much for cooking so I did most of it.' She shrugged.

'Why was that?'

Storm snuck a glance at Nico. He wasted no time in getting to the point, she'd noticed. Usually she avoided questions about her childhood but something about Nico's questions made her want to open up. It was just a shame she hated talking about her past. It wasn't that she was ashamed, far from it. Storm had grown up tough and independent, but her memories of her younger years were still painful. Unexpectedly, she felt a pang as she recalled one Christmas where she'd spent hours decorating the house and wrapping the presents, then preparing the dinner, only for Sally to destroy it all while she was drunk. The kids had got up early and found Christmas lights ripped from their sockets, the tree upended and their presents, that Storm had worked so hard to buy, smashed in a drunken rage.

Reaching for a clean wooden spoon, she focused her attention on stirring the creamy rice as she explained how she'd had to cope with Sally's alcoholism and raise her brother and sister for years. The fact that they'd had no immediate family to help didn't make life any easier. Alan's parents had died before Storm was born and Sally's mum and dad had emigrated to Canada years earlier. Once Alan's life insurance ran out Storm became mum, dad, sister and breadwinner, juggling two cleaning jobs around school as Sally was incapable of working. Together with the benefits Sally received they had just about enough to cover the bills and rent on their three-bedroomed council home, but Storm's wages put food on the table, clothes on the kids' backs and bought a few treats at Christmas.

'It wasn't what I would have wished for, but it's made me strong and the person I am today,' she finished.

For what felt like ages Nico said nothing and Storm worried her story had shocked him. After all, some people judged alcoholics very harshly, unable to understand that alcoholism was a disease. But if Storm thought she'd successfully hidden her tears from Nico, she was mistaken. He'd seen the quaking of her shoulders and the tears sliding down the sides of her nose. As a salty tear dripped into her risotto pan he felt a pang of concern. Getting up from his stool, he strode towards her and pulled her into his arms.

'It's getting to be a habit, this,' Storm blurted. 'You mopping up my tears.'

Nico hugged her tighter. 'I don't mind. I get the feeling

your past isn't something you talk about very often.'

'How did you guess?' she replied, burying her head in his shirt.

The smell of fabric conditioner mixed with the tangy scent that was unmistakeably Nico's immediately soothed her. Taking a deep breath, she looked up into warm, chocolate brown eyes that were filled with nothing but kindness.

'It's not good to keep things to yourself. You should talk, get your feelings off your chest,' he said gently.

'I can't,' she said. 'I feel too guilty about it all.'

Dipping her head back against his shirt, Storm tried to suppress her feelings about her childhood. The memories were too painful, and for years now she'd successfully managed to distract herself from thinking about old hurts. But Nico refused to let it go.

'What could you possibly have to feel guilty about, Storm? I'm sure you did the very best you could.'

Nico's perception left her rattled. He was right, she had done the best she could, but it wasn't enough. 'I'm ashamed to admit it, but for all those years, I cared more about raising Bailey and Lexie than I did about being there for Sally. Of course I tried to encourage her to get the help she needed, but she put us through hell. I know I should be able to forgive her now. I feel terrible I'm still so cross with her when it wasn't her fault. She was ill. She was grieving for her husband.'

Burying her face back in his shirt, Storm tried to hide her face from him.

Damn him. She'd never talked over her real feelings for

her mother with anyone, not even Dermot or Carly. What was it about Nico that had her baring her soul?

'We all live with secrets and demons, Storm,' he said, breaking the silence. 'Even me. You probably think I have a perfect life filled with fame and fortune. On the outside it must seem that all I have to do is click my fingers and I get whatever I want, whenever I want, but the truth is I want a simple life. I'd give anything to come home from work, cook a simple meal for my girlfriend, and for us to spend the evening curled up in front of the telly together. But that will never happen.'

'Why? You and Francesca always look so happy together in the press.'

'We are happy. I've known her since I was ten years old and we've been through so many things together. She's supported me from the very beginning of my career, but now the only meals we share together are ones I prepare for her fancy lawyer friends when she's entertaining.'

Storm frowned. So Francesca worked a lot – that didn't give him a licence to cheat on her. Storm was just about to open her mouth and point out as much when Nico started to speak.

'The press isn't always right,' he continued. 'Nobody but me and Francesca knows what really goes on between us. What I will say is that since meeting you, I've been thinking a lot about my mother.'

Storm rolled her eyes. 'Please don't tell me I remind you of your mum?'

Nico nudged her and smiled. 'No, you're nothing like her. But something she said to me before I left for London was that I shouldn't close myself off from marriage.'

'Is it something you're against?' Storm asked.

'It's not something I ever saw in my future, and it's not something that's right for me and Francesca,' he replied carefully.

Storm was confused. Was he saying their relationship wasn't special? That he didn't want to be with Francesca? That he'd met someone else? She paused before asking her next question, aware that directness might offend him.

'Have you met someone you think might be a better fit for you than Francesca?'

Nico looked at the floor, eyes downcast as he nodded. 'But it's hopeless. I can't leave Francesca . . . not now. And this girl, this woman, deserves so much more than a cheap affair.'

'Unlike some of the other one-night stands you've had?'

A look of anger then disappointment flashed in Nico's eyes. 'Who told you that?'

Storm shrugged. 'I hear things, but wasn't sure they were true.'

Letting out a long sigh, Nico sank down on a stool and put his head in his hands.

'It's not true. But this is all such a mess,' he groaned.

'What's a mess?' she asked, sitting down next to him. 'You can talk to me.'

'All this,' he said, raising his face to look at her. 'I always thought *Mamma* was talking rubbish, all those years ago, about "the one".'

'You don't believe in "the one" then?'

'You do?'

Storm thought for a moment. For years she'd thought Dermot was the one for her, but if she was honest their relationship had always been riddled with problems. That and the fact there was something about the two of them together that had always felt a little off key. He hadn't been her one, but that didn't stop her from believing that somewhere out there he existed.

'I do believe there's someone out there who is meant for me. I just hope one day I'll find him.'

'What if you already have?' Nico asked quietly.

'Then I'll grab him with both hands.'

'But what if you can't? What if he lives on the other side of the world or is already involved, for example?'

Storm looked at Nico in shock. The realisation of what he was saying hit home. Nico was involved, but her feelings for him were reciprocated. She felt breathless.

'Then it would be a no go,' she forced herself to say. 'Because if he really was my one it would be easy for me to be with him. There would be no complications to keep us apart,' she whispered.

'Even if you thought you were meant to be together?'

'Even then.' She fell silent.

Nico was the first to speak. 'Then I can't keep doing this, Storm.'

'Doing what?'

'This.' He shrugged helplessly. 'Bumping into you when I know I can't have you. It's killing me. I think about you all the time, but if I know there's no chance of any kind of future for us, I think it's better if we stay away from each other.'

Storm felt as if she'd been punched in the stomach. How could they go from talk of the one to never seeing each other again? Pain seared her heart as she contemplated a life without Nico. It was unbearable, unthinkable, but deep down she knew it was the best solution all round. He was spoken for, end of.

'I think you're right,' she replied, raising her eyes to meet his.

They were so close she could feel the warmth of his breath. Suddenly she felt Nico's lips on hers. It was every bit as good as Storm had imagined it would be. Soft at first, then as their passion for each other built, their kiss gained intensity. It felt so good, so warm, so natural, Storm thought she could lose herself in kissing Nico for the rest of her life. Waves of desire rippled through her as she felt his fingers in her hair. Then all too soon reality kicked in and she pulled away.

'We shouldn't have done that.'

Nico's forehead rested against hers. 'I know,' he breathed. 'But I couldn't help myself. I wanted to say goodbye properly.'

As he got to his feet and walked away Storm's heart sank. It was the sweetest, saddest first kiss she had ever known.

Chapter Ten

Six Months Later – August Bank Holiday

'*Et voilà*! Just scramble the egg into the pan.' Nico beamed out from the TV screen. Watching the programme as she flung clothes from the hotel wardrobe into her suitcase, Storm felt a pang of desire. She hadn't seen him in person since Angel's launch, but that didn't stop her missing him, thinking of him, wanting him. Their kiss had been sensational, everything a first kiss should be, but it had also made it a lot harder to stay away from him. It was as though she'd had a bite of the very best chocolate cake in the world only to have it taken away from her – she knew what she was missing. Of course their pact hadn't stopped her from looking out for him on TV and in the press. She ransacked the gossip magazines for news of what Nico was up to and made a point of watching him on TV. Every word he uttered, every dish he made, every interview he gave, brought him closer to her heart.

Looking at him now, smiling so easily into the camera, no doubt causing hearts to flutter up and down the country, Storm smiled back. She had to hand it to him, he made great telly. He made great everything, she mused longingly. When she'd turned the television on an hour ago she hadn't expected to see Nico – she was in Venice after all.

But it seemed fitting that she should find him here in his home country just as she was returning to the UK. For the last few days Storm had been lucky enough to cover the Venice Film Festival, and had been excited to hobnob with the likes of George Clooney, Matt Damon and Cameron Diaz. A year ago she'd have been too star-struck to do much apart from stutter in the presence of A-listers, but she'd come a long way since her days on Brighton's *Daily Post*. And thanks to Chelsea's guidance, Storm had mastered the art of appearing cool towards a celeb.

Now she was headed back to the UK for a meeting with her editor. Miles had rung late last night and demanded Storm return to the office immediately.

'It's urgent – I want you to come straight from the airport when you land.'

'But, Miles, I'm meant to be here all week,' Storm had protested. She was having a lovely time in Venice. The weather was warm, the parties were stylish, the champagne flowed (not that she could drink much of it), the people were beautiful and the hotel room overlooking St Mark's Square was Storm's idea of paradise, but Miles had been less than understanding.

'I don't give a shit,' he'd blasted her. 'Get your arse on the first plane back.'

As she expertly zipped her suitcase shut, Storm shivered when her eyes caught sight of a huge bouquet standing on the dressing table. It had arrived yesterday, and was so large the poor bellboy who'd been forced to deliver it had struggled under its weight. Taking the blooms from his arms, Storm had set the arrangement down and found the card. As she tore the envelope open her heart was pounding. She found herself hoping the bouquet had come from Nico. If only.

Hope you're having a wonderful time in Venice. Thinking of you today and always. Yours for ever, Dermot xxxx

She'd dropped the card as quickly as if she'd been burned. What was he doing sending her flowers in Venice? The barrage of texts and late-night calls over the past few months had been bad enough. It was always the same message. He was sorry, he wanted to make amends, he wanted her back. But Storm was adamant and repeatedly told him no. When that hadn't worked he'd called and called at any hour, trying to get her to pick up. A few weeks ago she'd been horrified to discover she had endless missed calls from him and immediately changed her number, giving the office strict instructions not to hand it out to anyone without her permission. She'd hoped that finally Dermot had got the message as she hadn't heard a peep out of him since, but the bouquet was further proof that he hadn't.

As the plane hurtled along the runway and soared into the air, Storm looked out of the window. She knew she shouldn't be too upset about going home early. The last six months had been hard work but a lot of fun as she had landed scoop after scoop after scoop. Still, a lot of the stories she'd been assigned to had troubled her, if she was honest. Reporting on people's failed relationships or drinking habits didn't really feel like proper journalism to her. Back when she'd been dreaming of becoming a showbiz reporter she hadn't thought the job would entail so much muck-raking. But Storm was determined to do her best and although she was still living in Chelsea's spare room, had thrown herself into her job following the split from Dermot, working all the hours under the sun. Her diligence hadn't gone unrecognised. Just a month ago Miles had made Chelsea showbiz editor, and she had insisted Storm was promoted to be her deputy, meaning neither of them need have anything to do with Sabrina any more.

Both girls had been delighted with their promotion, especially when Miles treated them to champagne to celebrate. Everyone around the office made a point of congratulating them – everyone that is apart from Sabrina and Dermot.

Inevitably, Sabrina told Storm she'd been sleeping with him for months behind her back. Collaring her in the ladies' loos one day, as Storm was peering into the mirror reapplying her lipstick, Sabrina couldn't wait to share all the gory details.

'Just thought you should know – Dermot and I are together,' she drawled, leaning against a cubicle door. Storm said nothing, merely glanced at her in the mirror.

For a woman who made a big show of having everything, Sabrina looked strangely unhappy. She had huge bags under her eyes, her skin was grey and her mascara smudged. Turning her gaze back to her own reflection, Storm checked on how she felt to hear this news and realised she wasn't remotely bothered. Dermot was a loser and Sabrina was welcome to him.

'I hope you'll be very happy together.'

This calm response was clearly not what Sabrina wanted to hear. Eyes flashing, she walked towards Storm and stood menacingly behind her. 'Oh, we will be. I know how to make sure he's satisfied in every way. In fact, I've been keeping him satisfied for months.'

Storm snorted and shook her head in disgust. Dermot was a lying, cheating wanker, she'd lost nothing and certainly wasn't going to give Sabrina the satisfaction of getting into a catfight with her about him.

Putting her lipstick back in her bag, Storm turned away from the mirror and walked towards the door. She paused there to eye Sabrina coldly. 'You know, I'm curious – if you're not a slut, what are you?'

With that she'd walked out of the bathroom, Aretha Franklin's '*R-E-S-P-E-C-T*' her own personal soundtrack as she returned to her desk.

Arriving back at London's City Airport at a little after four, Storm jumped in a cab and twenty minutes later strode into a deserted office. She wasn't surprised, it was a bank holiday after all. Dumping her luggage under her desk, she raked her fingers through her hair and walked towards

Miles's office. Her heart sank when she saw Dermot and Sabrina waiting on the sofa outside.

'Storm. So glad you could join us, and so sorry to tear you away from Venice.' Sabrina smiled cattily.

'What can I say, Sabrina? Life's a bitch. Oh, no, wait . . . that's just you.' Storm knocked firmly on Miles's door before entering. She perched on the nearest chair as Dermot and Sabrina filed in behind her.

'So what's all this about?' she asked pleasantly.

Miles leaned back in his office chair, hands clasped behind his head. 'Got a special little job for my star reporter,' he explained. 'It's a delicate one, and needs careful handling.'

'What, more careful than catching out the Markhams?' she teased.

'Dermot here's been working on a story for several months now and we need a bit of help bringing it to life,' Miles continued, ignoring Storm's last comment. 'Are you up for the challenge?'

'Of course Storm's up for it,' Sabrina put in. 'Our rising star is always up for it, if the graffiti in the ladies is anything to go by.'

Storm couldn't even be bothered to reply. The stupid cow was only showing herself up with comments like that, something that didn't go unnoticed by Miles.

'That'll do, Sabrina. Why don't you pop out and get us a round of coffees?' he said to her before turning back to Storm. 'So what do you think?'

She shifted uncomfortably in her chair as Sabrina flounced out of the office. Normally Storm wouldn't dream of turning down a job but she had a horrible feeling

175

that if Dermot was involved then there was every chance someone was going to get stitched up and she didn't want anything to do with that.

'Well, er, I'd need to know more about it.'

Miles turned to Dermot and gestured for him to take the floor. 'Perhaps you can fill Storm in.'

She watched nervously as he got to his feet holding an A4 file.

'I'll get to the point – a few sources have told me that a very high-profile celebrity has been cheating on his girlfriend. This certain someone routinely has had a long-term relationship with a woman and is no doubt in the market for another, despite having lived with the same woman for years. We've tried to get his previous girlfriend to talk, but she's not having it. We want to expose him for who he really is.'

Storm raised her eyebrows. How ironic that Dermot wanted to expose someone else's duplicity when he was a cheating bastard himself. 'Where do I fit into this?'

'We want you to be the honey trap. Go on a few dates with the guy, see if you can get him to invite you back to his place, that sort of thing.'

Storm was speechless. Her instincts had been right. This job was as dodgy as hell. 'Let me get this right. You want to turn me into a hooker?'

'No! It's not like that, Storm,' said Miles, leaping to Dermot's defence. 'It's just an undercover job, like the Markhams' party. It's all legit, we certainly don't expect you to have sex with the bloke. We just need enough pics and info to prove he's up for it.'

Storm sat in her chair stubbornly looking down at the floor. 'Well, you can get someone else. I'm not doing that.'

Cheeky bunch of bastards. She wasn't the resident sex reporter. But Dermot wasn't put off. Turning his attention to his file, he leafed through a sheaf of papers until he found what he was looking for.

'I think you will do this, Stormy,' he said softly. 'Otherwise I've got something here that could cause you to be in the press for all the wrong reasons.'

As she took the sheet of paper from her ex, her heart almost stopped beating. It was a printout of the pap shot of her taken with Nico at Angel's launch.

'How did you get this?' she gasped.

'Like I said, Stormy – contacts. Now, if you won't do it Miles has suggested we print this instead and then you'll be the focus of the story. I've a few lurid tales of my own I could share, and I'm sure Carly would be good for a comment or two to really spice things up.'

Storm looked at her editor. 'Really?'

He shrugged. 'Papers don't sell themselves. I obviously don't want to print a story about my best reporter, but it's a bloody good picture. I'm disappointed you didn't come to me yourself with this, Storm, but instead tried to cover it up. It shows a certain lack of trust. You should realise nothing gets past me. Although, I'll admit, I didn't realise you and Mr Alvise were quite so intimate, but that's one of the reasons we've picked you for this job.'

'What do you mean?' she asked quietly.

'You've already got a relationship with the man himself

– that's why it'll be easy for you to lure him further. Unless you're already at it?' he added.

Storm's head was spinning as the penny dropped. 'You want me to honey trap Nico Alvise?'

'The one and only,' Dermot said cheerfully. 'You can start tomorrow. He's launching a new charity at Tower Bridge – perfect opportunity to start chatting to him there.'

'But I haven't seen him for months,' she protested. 'He probably doesn't even remember me.'

'Well, tomorrow will be the perfect time for you to find out,' Dermot put in. 'When you see him at his press launch.'

Taking a deep breath, Storm knew she had to think quickly. Deep down she wanted to tell them all to shove their job but she knew that wouldn't help Nico. Even if he was playing away he didn't deserve to get stitched up like this – but there was a chance that if she went along with their plan, agreed to play her part in the honey trap, she could protect him, make sure there was nothing to report. After all Miles, Dermot and Sabrina clearly thought that the fact she knew Nico would be an advantage. Instead she intended to make sure nothing got back to any of them about Nico's private life.

'Fine,' she said.

'Excellent,' replied Dermot as he walked towards her with the file.

Handing her the paperwork, he whispered in her ear, 'How did you like the flowers by the way?'

Storm shot him a look of pure hatred. This, the job, the flowers, the phone calls, had to be his version of payback.

And all because she'd had the nerve to dump him. Refusing to give him the satisfaction of an answer, she stalked out of the office.

Watching his ex march back to her desk, Dermot smiled. The meeting had gone so much better than he'd expected. When a pissed off pap had shown him the photo of Storm and Nico taken in Angel's kitchen months earlier, Dermot had been shocked to see what could only be described as a look of pure desire in Storm's eyes. He couldn't take his eyes off the image, stricken with jealousy. She looked beautiful, and she'd certainly never gazed at him that way. For years now he'd run rings around Storm, and exercised complete control over her. It killed him to admit it, but she'd been good for his career, was a far better reporter than he would ever be. He couldn't help noticing that while her reputation soared at the paper, his was foundering, something that hadn't gone unnoticed by Miles either. Just last week he'd called Dermot into the office and laid down the law.

'I'm wondering what happened to that go-getting reporter I hired at Christmas,' Miles snapped at him. 'The biggest stories you've brought me so far have all been ones you've worked on with Storm. What's the problem, Dermot, got no ideas of your own?'

He had been furious. 'It's not like that, Miles. My stories require investigation and guts, unlike Storm's. She just has to bat her eyelashes and show a hint of cleavage.'

'I think we both know she does a lot more than that,' Miles blasted him. 'There'd better be an improvement in your success rate. I'll be honest, I'm starting to think I made a mistake in hiring you, Storm's clearly the only one with the talent – what that makes you, I'm not too sure.'

The meeting had left Dermot rattled. He knew he needed to up his game, which was why he desperately needed this story about the chef to come off. If he hadn't started dating Sabrina, who he'd been shagging on and off since they'd met, he doubted he'd even have a job at all by now – it was only because she'd put a good word in for him that his six-month contract had been extended on a month-by-month basis. The truth was his life was no good without Storm in it. He needed her back – and fast.

Over the past few months Dermot had tried everything to win her over but Storm had resisted his charms and he was secretly furious with her. Nobody ever said no to Dermot. When he'd discovered Nico had had a girlfriend on the side, he felt like he'd won the Lottery – if he couldn't have Storm, he'd make darned sure her heart's desire couldn't either.

As Storm forced her way on to the Central Line and jostled for a space with her nose pressed into another commuter's armpit, she tried to shake off her feelings of anger and prepare for the day ahead. Since her meeting with Dermot and Miles she'd felt sick to the stomach. Honey trapping wasn't news and Nico sure as hell didn't deserve what Dermot wanted to dish out to him. All she could do was hope against hope that her plan would work and she could save Nico from having his private life splashed across the front page. Last night she'd barely slept and this morning had agonised over what to wear.

In the end she chose an outfit she felt comfortable in, teaming her favourite black boyfriend blazer, white slub t-shirt and navy skinny jeans with a pair of metallic gladiator sandals.

Emerging into the daylight at Tower Hill station and marching towards the venue, Storm shivered despite the early-morning sun and tried to ignore the knot of fear in her stomach. She'd been desperate to speak to Chelsea for advice, but her boss and friend had been sent out to Venice to cover the Film Festival after Storm had been ordered home and she hadn't been able to reach her. More than anything she needed Chelsea to help her keep a level head about all this. Her heart and her mind felt as if they'd been put through a washing machine. Nerves and guilt were eating away at her, but more than anything else, the prospect of seeing Nico again was overwhelming. She dreamed of him most nights. Happy dreams where somehow they would find each other and live happily ever after. When Storm woke, she often felt an overwhelming sense of grief that her dream wasn't the truth. That she and Nico weren't together, and never could be.

All too soon she reached Tower Bridge and saw a huge crowd had already gathered for a glimpse of the man himself. His newest project was incredibly worthwhile, it was no wonder it had drawn such public interest. This time he wasn't opening a fancy restaurant or announcing a new TV show. Instead he was launching a new cookery training scheme for disadvantaged kids – a brilliant cause that had caught the attention of a couple of royals who had offered their support. Today was the launch event, where Nico had invited members of the press and public to find out about the course.

As she reached the venue and showed her press pass to security, she noticed a large part of the bridge had been sectioned off ready for Nico's arrival. There was a small stage at the front that had been set up with a kitchen, and a bar area with drinks and refreshments for later on. The plan was obviously for Nico to show off some of his cooking skills to the crowd. Behind the makeshift kitchen hung huge posters of the chef dressed in a sharp charcoal suit. Looking at them was like looking at the man himself and she felt a pang of nerves – could she really do this? Storm wasn't sure and half considered running back to the office until she remembered that if it wasn't her it would be someone else sent to ensnare him and then Nico really would be stitched up. She might hate what she was doing, but she'd hate someone else doing it more, and at least this way she could keep him safe from harm.

Ignoring her instinct to run, she pushed her way towards one of the nearby restaurants that was helping to host the event. There she milled about, picked up some press information and even managed to talk to a couple of the students who had already enrolled on the course. One was a former burglar who'd been released from Feltham Young Offenders just last week and the other an ex-drug addict desperate to turn her life around. Hearing their stories was heart-warming, and reminded her of just how worthwhile and necessary this cause was. Once again she felt a flash of fury with Dermot for turning her into the muck-raking reporter she'd never wanted to be. They were meant to

182

expose scumbags like the Markhams, not decent people like Nico. Still, his launch would make a good enough story in itself. She decided to pass it on to the features team and encourage them to use it this Sunday as one of the paper's more in-depth pieces.

As she walked back out of the restaurant towards the crowd, she arrived at the fringes just in time to hear everyone erupt into a deafening round of applause. Flushed with embarrassment, Nico walked on to the stage flanked by two women. One looked like his press officer, while the other Storm recognised from the press photos she'd studied – Francesca.

Storm did a double take. There was no denying it, Nico's girlfriend was stunningly beautiful. With long glossy black hair, olive skin and deep brown eyes, she radiated success and warmth, and seemed very proud of Nico. With her arm linked through his, she accompanied him on stage then stepped behind to applaud and give him his moment. They really did make the perfect couple.

Wearing a fitted navy suit and pale blue shirt unbuttoned to reveal just a flash of chest hair, Nico glanced at his notes before addressing the crowd.

'*Signori e signore*, thank you so much for coming here today to the launch of my new cookery school. It means a great deal to me that so many of you have come to show your support, or maybe you are more interested in the free food I'll be offering later?'

As the crowd laughed, Storm saw Nico scan them with his eyes. He paused and locked his gaze on her. She froze. For what felt like hours it seemed as though she and Nico were isolated in their own private world where the crowd didn't exist. Storm watched Nico recover himself, look down briefly at his notes and then address the crowd once more. The rest of the launch passed her by in a blur. So much so she didn't even notice when it was over and Nico was walking through the crowds, appearing suddenly by her side.

'Storm, how lovely to see you.'

She jumped at the sound of his voice and spun around in shock, only to find the chef wasn't alone.

'I'd like you to meet Francesca,' he said, kissing Storm twice with genuine warmth.

Storm returned the kisses to his cheeks, catching the musky scent of his aftershave as she leaned in against his stubble.

'A pleasure.' She beamed, holding out one hand to Francesca, who immediately batted it away and also leaned in to kiss her.

'Nonsense, we greet the Italian way with kisses not handshakes,' she said.

As Francesca kissed Storm warmly on each cheek she locked eyes with Nico once more. Despite their pact, his delight at seeing her again was obvious in his eyes.

'So what are you doing here?' Nico enquired. 'No flights to tend to today?'

'Er, no, I've actually left the airline.'

'Really? What are you doing instead?'

Bugger! Storm quickly looked around for inspiration until her eyes caught sight of the posters about his cooking school.

'I've decided to change careers and go into the hospitality trade,' she lied. 'I've just enrolled at the same college where your cookery classes are held and I heard about your launch there so thought I'd pop down.'

Nico regarded her closely before his face broke into a huge smile.

'But that's wonderful news, *bella*. I worried about you up in the air with so many crashes and planes going missing . . .' His voice trailed off.

A smiling Francesca told her, 'As you can see, Nico is a worrier. But a change of career is always a good thing. Life is too short. You must grab your opportunities with both hands . . . something else I am always saying to Nico.'

Storm found herself warming to this woman who was so natural and welcoming. In any other circumstances she was sure they could have been friends. 'Well, it's early days,' she found herself saying. 'Who knows how many drinks I'll spill before I'm thrown out?'

'You're too hard on yourself, Storm,' Nico replied. 'I bet you'll be brilliant.'

'Me too,' Francesca assured her. 'Now if you'll excuse me I really need to find the bathroom.'

With that she turned and half walked, half ran to the nearest bathroom. Funny, thought Storm, she would never have expected a top barrister to be so down to earth and she could see why Nico adored her – Francesca seemed perfect.

'I hope you're not angry I'm here,' Storm began to say to him. 'I just saw the posters at college, and well, it seemed like fate.'

Nico shook his head, his face lit up with his megawatt smile. 'Not at all, *bella*. It's the best thing to have happened to me in a long time. I've missed you.'

Storm couldn't stop smiling back at him. Any feelings of anxiety were long gone as she basked in Nico's obvious delight at seeing her again. With butterflies in her stomach and her heart pounding, she felt like a teenager all over again.

'Come for coffee with me?' he suddenly suggested.

'What?'

'A coffee. You, me, some *biscotti*, a table. We'll talk, get to know each other properly,' he babbled.

Storm felt rattled. Nico was making her job much easier than she'd anticipated. 'But I thought we'd agreed it was best not to see each other again.'

'You're the one who turned up to my launch,' he pointed out.

Storm lowered her eyes and toed the ground with her shoe. She had a feeling she was going to regret this. 'You got me. OK, coffee sometime.'

Nico lit up, his already handsome face suddenly becoming more attractive. 'Perfect. How about after I finish up here?'

Storm laughed at his eagerness. 'No. I have things to do later. But how about next week sometime?'

'Next week would be good. I'll call you.'

'You'd need my phone number for that,' Storm teased.

He fished inside his jacket pocket. 'Here's a card with my personal mobile number. Feel free to call any time and we'll fix a meeting.'

As Storm took the card from him, she trembled with anticipation.

Putting the card carefully into her satchel bag, she pushed her hair out of her eyes and squared her shoulders. 'Well, I'd better be going. Do say goodbye to Francesca for me, it was a pleasure to meet her.'

Nico leaned forward and softly kissed her cheek. 'Until next week, Storm,' he said, his eyes never leaving hers.

As Storm got off the tube at Stratford and walked slowly home, she couldn't stop smiling. Even though pretending to be a college student wasn't the way she would have chosen to see Nico again, it had been worth it. She replayed the scene in her mind. As their eyes had met across the crowd it had felt so romantic, like something out of a film. And now she had his number and a plan to meet for coffee next week. Storm knew this was probably going to end badly, that somehow she was going to get her fingers burned, but at this precise moment she didn't care. Nico had appeared in her life once more and suddenly everything was sunny.

Rounding the corner, she stopped in her tracks. Sitting on a bench near Chelsea's flat was a man who looked suspiciously like Dermot.

It couldn't be. He was at work. And she'd only popped home herself to change into something more business-like before returning to the office. She was going mad, she thought, as she neared the front door.

But edging closer to the bench, she realised there was no mistake. There he was, her ex, larger than life and twice as ugly, sitting there smiling at her.

'What are you doing here?' she growled.

'How was it?' he said, ignoring her question as he got up and walked towards her.

'Yeah, fine,' she replied, barely glancing at him as she took her front door keys out of her bag.

But Dermot wasn't put off. 'Come on – you can give me more than that. I saw the photo, Stormy, I know you've got the Italian Stallion eating out of your hand. Share the wealth.'

'I repeat, nothing went on. I don't think he's even interested in me – perhaps he prefers blondes. And who uses phrases like Italian Stallion any more!'

'Ah, don't give me that, Stormy, I've seen you work your charms when you want to. I'm sure you can get him to do anything you want him to.'

Storm looked her ex squarely in the eyes as she unlocked the door. 'Dermot, you can't make a guy fancy you if he doesn't fancy you.'

'But that picture showed you looking pretty cosy.'

'Not really. He was probably just helping me wipe sauce off my face. Anyway, you haven't answered my question. What are you doing here?'

'Just thought I'd check you were OK.' He grinned. 'Can I come in?'

Storm grimaced and blocked the doorway. 'No, you bloody can't. Now was there anything else? Only I have to get ready for work.'

Sensing he wasn't getting any further, Dermot backed away from the door.

'Well, keep me or Sabrina updated, we'd like to know how our story's progressing.'

Storm looked at him in horror. Keeping Dermot up to date was one thing but there was no way she was talking to that skank. 'What's Sabrina got to do with any of this?'

'In case you hadn't noticed she's still news editor, and she and I have worked very hard to put this together.'

Storm finally lost her temper with him. 'Dermot, there's a café on the corner. Why don't you do us all a favour and pop over there for a nice hot cup of fuck off and die?'

'You told me she was gorgeous but you didn't say just how gorgeous,' Francesca commented once they were safely in the back of their chauffeur-driven Bentley.

'Storm?' Nico asked.

Francesca rolled her eyes. 'No! The waitress doling out the Prosecco. Of course Storm.'

Nico smiled at Francesca. 'You really liked her?'

'I thought she was wonderful. Pretty, genuine, bright . . . I can definitely see why you would like her so much. She's perfect for you, *moroso*.'

Nico trailed his fingers across the back of Francesca's perfectly manicured hand and let his mind wander. He had done his best to forget about Storm over the past six months, but she was always on his mind. He'd stopped going to showbiz events so he could avoid seeing her, but that didn't stop him from hoping he would run into her again. Every time he boarded a flight he looked out for her, and he had even toyed with the idea of getting in touch with Angel and asking her to help him by passing on a message. But he'd stopped himself. He knew it wasn't fair to Storm – he couldn't give her what she deserved.

That didn't stop him from thinking about her all the time, hoping fate would intervene. And then suddenly, as he'd looked out into the crowd, there she was – like some sort of miracle. Inviting her out for coffee had been an impulse. Finding her in front of him like that, he couldn't stand the idea of never seeing her again. Of searching strangers' faces in the restaurant, the street and on the tube, hoping one of them would be her. He hadn't really expected her to say yes, but was delighted they would see each other again at least once.

He was suddenly aware of Francesca clicking her fingers in front of his face.

'Earth to Nico.' She smiled. 'Hello. Anyone home?'

'Sorry. I was a million miles away.'

Francesca snorted. 'Yes. With Storm, I imagine.'

Nico shrugged. Was it that obvious?' Francesca wasn't stupid. Even though he hadn't seen Storm for months, he occasionally dropped her name into conversation. Just saying it was a way of keeping the connection alive. It hadn't gone unnoticed by Francesca.

'I've known you for twenty-five years, Nico Alvise, and I've never seen you like this over a woman before.' She sounded astonished.

'It's nothing. I just . . .'

'You just?' Francesca encouraged.

'I just really like her.'

'So why aren't you pursuing her?'

Nico shook his head and smiled. Nothing got past Francesca. 'I don't want to just sleep with Storm,' he said, brushing a piece of imaginary fluff from his trousers. 'And

I can't offer her any more than that so I don't know where that leaves us.'

As he stared out of the car window at the London skyline, he felt stumped. He wanted Storm, but she was worth more than some cheap affair. He loved Francesca, she was his best friend and he'd never wanted to end their relationship . . . until now. What he felt for Storm left him both elated and miserable. Never in his life had he been so confused. He was not a dishonest man, yet he'd been living a lie for years.

'Why don't you tell Storm the truth about us?'

Wide-eyed with shock, Nico spun his head to stare at Francesca. Her mouth was set and she had her head cocked slightly to one side. He knew she was serious. But no, it wouldn't be fair on her, on either of them, and could do irreparable damage to their careers.

'I couldn't . . .' he began, shaking his head.

'I want you to be happy, Nico – you have a real chance of that with Storm. Meeting her today has proved to me what I've suspected for months. She likes you as much as you like her. When you see her for coffee, tell her about us then let her make up her mind.

'After all, doesn't everyone deserve a chance at true love? It turns up when you least expect it, and you shouldn't waste this gift. I haven't.'

Nico glanced at Francesca as she admired the delicate platinum eternity ring that sparkled on her hand. He knew she had found the one, and more than anything wanted him to do the same. His best friend had always had the power to amaze him. They had known each other since they were children, becoming friends initially through the church they both attended. They were so close, both families had assumed it was only a matter of time until the couple married, but Nico and Francesca had other ideas. They'd moved to the UK when they were both eighteen. Francesca qualified as a barrister and then helped Nico establish his first restaurant in the city.

He soon made a name for himself with customers loving the theatricality of his cooking. Then there were the customers he was unafraid of standing up to, even going so far as to throw out objectionable diners on occasion. It was no surprise he quickly caught the attention of TV execs, who wasted no time in signing him to front his own show.

Since then his success had grown and grown, along with his popularity with women. Nico had never known anything like it, but he'd not taken advantage of it, sticking to his long-term girlfriend. But despite her, he had never once fallen in love, and suddenly he realised he was terrified of the prospect.

Chapter Eleven

'Those filthy bastards!' Chelsea exclaimed as she downed her second shot of limoncello. 'I can't believe they're making you do this. I'll talk to Miles, this is completely out of order.'

'I don't think it'll do any good, Chelsea,' Storm said, shaking her head. 'He pulled me back from Venice himself to set this up – he thinks it's a brilliant story, and the fact that I already know Nico makes me the perfect bait.'

'Fuckers!' Chelsea growled, pouring them both another generous measure of limoncello. 'I've never heard of anything like this.'

Storm raised her eyebrows. 'But you've heard, seen and done everything.'

'I thought so, babe. But using one of our own in a honey trap's a new one even on me. And the deviousness of Dermot, getting hold of that pap pic, is shocking. I'm going to have a word with my sources.'

'Would that be a word or a slap?' Storm enquired.

'Same difference.' Chelsea shrugged. 'So what's your plan?'

'To protect Nico and give them nothing,' she replied, taking a sip of limoncello and wincing. 'Shit, Chelsea! Why did you buy this? It's gross.'

'It was on offer at the airport.'

'So is meths at the corner shop but we don't buy it,' Storm pointed out.

'Any port in a storm,' Chelsea replied, finishing her drink and topping herself up. She had only arrived back from Venice a couple of hours earlier and had insisted on catching up with Storm immediately.

Dumping her luggage in the middle of the living room, Chelsea had barely even taken off her jacket before she'd pulled two bottles of sticky lemon liqueur from her duty-free carrier bag and insisted Storm tell her everything.

'So you're meeting him for coffee?'

'That's the plan. I've got to ring Nico next week to set something up.'

'And have you told Dermot?'

Storm choked on her drink. 'No way! I'm not telling that weasel anything.'

Chelsea smiled. 'Good! With a bit of luck this story will be his downfall. I'll help you all I can.'

Storm looked at her gratefully. 'Really?'

''Course! You're my mate, and whatever the hell is going on between Francesca and Nico, neither one of them deserves to have Dermot Whelan upending their lives just so he can get his by-line in the paper. Something I've noticed has been a bit lacking lately.'

Storm paused. She had noticed that too. Despite Dermot's hunger for stories, he didn't seem to be reporting on an awful lot these days.

'Between you and me,' Chelsea said conspiratorially, 'Miles is really pissed off with Dermot. All his stories keep falling down, and he hasn't had a good idea in months.'

'Great!' replied Storm uncharitably as she flopped back in her chair. 'About time the bastard got his comeuppance. Anyway, enough about him. Tell me about Venice.'

An enormous grin spread across Chelsea's face. 'All right, I met someone when I was out there. A gorgeous unknown actor called Adam Stark who's played a few minor roles in a couple of action blockbusters. He's just getting his big break after fourteen years of trying and was out there raising his profile.'

'Oh, yeah! Sounds like it wasn't just his profile he was interested in raising.' Storm smirked.

'Come on, a lady doesn't kiss and tell. But as you know I'm no lady, and quite honestly he was hung like a donkey! I told him he was wasted in Hollywood, and he should give soft porn a go.'

'You didn't?' Storm chuckled.

Chelsea slid further down the sofa and let her legs dangle over the edge. 'Nah, I didn't, but he's definitely got what it takes.'

'So I take it you spent most of the festival shagging rather than scribbling?'

'Afraid so, Stormy. It's a hard life, but someone has to do it.' Chelsea grinned.

'And are you going to see him again?'

'I hope so. We've exchanged numbers and he's already Skyped me.'

'Bloody hell, he's keen! You only got back a few hours ago.'

Chelsea looked smug. 'What can I tell you? I've got the X-factor.'

'You certainly do, babe. And of course this means the drought's finally over.'

'Yep! The drought is well and truly over. In fact, it's more like the floodgates have been opened.'

'Oh, gross.' Storm shuddered as the unwelcome image entered her mind.

'How about I fix us a real drink? I can't face any more of this lemon shite,' she said, getting to her feet.

'Thought you'd never ask,' Chelsea replied, handing over her empty glass.

Storm walked to the huge American-style fridge that dwarfed Chelsea's tiny galley kitchen. She pulled out a bottle of ice cold Chablis and poured them both large glasses. Just then there was a knock at the door.

'I'll go,' Chelsea called, as she raced down the stairs to the front door.

Carrying the glasses back into the living room, Storm had just set them on the coffee table when Chelsea shouted up the stairs. 'Storm, get down here.'

Sighing, she made her way down. What was it this time? More Jehovah's Witnesses? She was quite sure Chelsea didn't need help telling anyone to get lost.

'Delivery for you,' explained her friend, jerking her head towards the florist's driver who was busy pulling bouquet after bouquet after bouquet of white roses from the back of his van.

'What's going on?' Storm hissed.

'Storm Saunders?' asked the delivery driver. He handed her an electronic notepad and pen. 'Sign here.'

'Wait, what is all this?'

'Twenty-five bouquets for you.'

Storm's ears rang with shock. 'What?' she gasped. 'Who from?'

The driver shook his head as he hauled yet more bouquets from the van.

'No idea, love. There'll be a card on one of them, that ought to tell you. Quite the gesture though. Usually people say it with one bouquet, not a van full.'

Chelsea giggled as the flowers piled up on their little patch of front lawn. 'Maybe they're from Nico,' she suggested.

Storm didn't think so. So many blooms suggested something sinister rather than sweet. Snatching up the bouquet that contained the card, she ripped the envelope open.

It eats away at my heart that you won't return my calls. Maybe the flowers in Venice weren't enough. But I hope these bouquets, one for every year of your life, will convince you to take me back. Dermot xxx

Staring at the card in disbelief, Storm felt sick.

'What is it?' Chelsea asked, taking it from her. As she read Dermot's words she put her arm around Storm, who seemed to have gone into shock.

'Jesus, this sounds weird. One for every year of your life? What's he planning? To make sure you don't reach twenty-six? And what does he mean about flowers in Venice?'

'He sent flowers to my hotel room while I was away.'

'What! Why? And what does he mean about the phone calls?'

Storm looked at her friend. She'd been trying to shrug off Dermot's weird behaviour for a while but she had to admit this latest stunt was getting to her. Quickly she outlined what he'd been doing.

'This is seriously creepy.' Chelsea frowned. 'Are you OK, babe?'

Storm nodded. 'Fine. I just wish he'd get the message once and for all that we're over.'

Chelsea called over to the delivery driver, 'Mate. Any chance you can take these back to your shop?'

But the driver shook his head as he piled the last of the bouquets into Storm's arms. 'Not a chance. I'm paid to deliver, not return.'

'But she doesn't want them,' Chelsea pointed out. 'They're from her weird ex-boyfriend who's making her life a misery. Seriously, what normal person sends this many bouquets?'

The delivery driver looked sheepish. 'I'm sorry, love. Wish I could help.'

With that he turned on his heel and clambered back into the van. Looking at the mound of flowers on their tiny patch of lawn, Storm couldn't help noticing that the huge number of white blooms resembled funeral flowers more than any declaration of love.

'Look, we'll both keep an eye on Dermot. As for these flowers, let's stick them in the back of my car and deliver them to the local hospital. They'll be grateful for Dermot's insanity even if nobody else is,' said Chelsea.

Storm let out a sigh of relief. Typical Chelsea, she had an answer for everything. 'Brilliant idea. Thanks, babe.'

Chelsea pulled her in for a hug. 'Any time. What are mates for if not for sipping disgusting lemon drinks and sorting out deranged exes?'

'What do you think, the blue or the red?' Storm asked nervously.

In the middle of reading some juicy gossip about Blake Lively over a bowl of granola, Chelsea didn't appreciate the interruption. 'What are you on?' she exclaimed. 'These are more like red-carpet dresses. Storm, seriously, this is getting well out of hand. It's coffee, go for jeans – keep it simple!'

'But what if it turns into something besides coffee?' Storm protested.

Chelsea smirked. 'Thought you said you didn't shag men with girlfriends?'

'I'm not worried about that!' she gasped. 'I mean, what if we go on somewhere?'

'Storm, you're meeting at eleven on a Friday morning – it's not exactly cocktail hour.'

'I s'pose not,' she muttered. 'Fine, I'll go with the jeans.'

Frustrated, Storm wandered back to her bedroom, only for Chelsea to knock on her door a few minutes later.

'Can I come in?'

Storm nodded, clearing away clothes, make-up and magazines to create space on her double bed for Chelsea to perch on.

'You're getting this meeting way out of proportion,' she said gently. 'Remember, you're going to make sure nothing ever gets out about Nico so you're doing him a favour. Now just enjoy this for what it is – coffee with a bloke you really fancy.'

In spite of her fears, Storm laughed. If nothing else this was a chance to spend more time with Nico, something she definitely wanted though she didn't like to admit it.

'Jeans it is then,' she said, slipping on her favourite pair.

Nico had suggested Storm meet him in an old Italian café in Soho. Feeling the warmth of the late-summer sun on her back as she turned into the narrow street, Storm was pleased she'd gone for an outfit she felt comfortable in rather than dressing to impress. She had teamed a striped blazer with her favourite pair of wedges and kept her make-up simple, choosing a hint of brown shadow and a slick of her favourite Clinique Chubby Stick on her lips.

Reaching the coffee shop, Storm took a deep breath and opened the glass door, pausing at the entrance as she scanned the room for Nico.

It didn't take her long to find him, fiddling with his smartphone at a table along with what looked like ten cups of coffee. Amused, Storm walked straight over.

'Either you've been here a long time or you really like coffee.' She smiled gesturing to the different varieties on the tiny table. Along with an espresso, there was a cappuccino, Americano, flat white, and God knows what else.

'Storm!' Nico smiled, immediately getting to his feet and kissing her on both cheeks. 'Please sit down. I realised

I didn't know what sort of coffee you like so I got you a choice.'

'Thank God for that.' She grinned as she sat down on a banquette opposite him. 'I thought you had some awful caffeine addiction. But FYI, I usually order a double shot cappuccino without sugar.'

Reaching for a cup and taking a careful sip, she took in Nico's appearance. As always he looked gorgeous. His olive skin gleamed with health. He was wearing a pair of loosely fitted jeans with a classic navy polo shirt. Storm found her heart thumping as he treated her to a broad grin.

'It seems funny to see you somewhere so normal, somewhere that's not an event or launch party,' he said shyly. 'Just you, me . . .'

'. . . and a table full of coffee! People will definitely talk,' Storm laughed as she interrupted him. 'So how come you can squeeze me in for a drink today, Mr Alvise? I thought you celebs never got a minute to yourselves.'

'Shhh!' Nico teased, putting his finger to his lips in mock seriousness. 'I don't want to dispel the rumour. No, actually I have taken a few days off. The restaurants run themselves thanks to my team of brilliant managers and head chefs, and the TV stuff doesn't start again for a few weeks. So I have all the time in the world for you, Storm.'

She sipped her coffee while she thought about how to reply to him. There was so much she wanted to know about this intriguing man. 'So come on then,' she said finally. 'Tell me about yourself. And not the stuff I've read in the press, tell me things I wouldn't know.'

As Nico spoke Storm became intensely aware of his voice, each word sounding as warm and velvety as chocolate. God! She could listen to him talk all day.

He told her all about his childhood, growing up in a small village on the east coast of Italy, with three elder sisters who thought nothing of dressing him up as a fourth sister in their mother's old clothes, and how he and his friends had always played football in the garden until they put the ball through his parents' living-room window and afterwards he hadn't sat down for a week.

Nico was a good storyteller with a passion for detail. Storm realised she hadn't enjoyed herself so much in ages. As he moved on to telling her about how he'd developed a passion for cooking when his mum taught him to make everything from *antipasti* to *dolce*, all thoughts of her job and the honey trap were forgotten.

'I knew then there was nothing else I wanted to do with my life,' Nico finished.

'And now?' Storm pressed him. 'What's next for you? Is cooking still something you love?'

Nico gazed at her thoughtfully and then smiled. 'I'm not sure. Maybe another restaurant, maybe more cookery courses . . . But enough about me. I want to know more about you.'

Storm told him stories about her own childhood. For once, instead of focusing on the unhappy memories, she told him about growing up in Brighton: days spent at the beach with Alan, helping Lexie learn to ride a bike, taking her brother for a McDonald's milkshake when their parents had expressly forbidden it. Then there were the books and films she liked to read, plus the soft spot she had for Ryan Gosling.

'Honestly, I think Carly and I have watched *The Notebook* at least a hundred times,' Storm laughed. She hadn't felt so light-hearted and unburdened in a long time. Aside from Carly, she couldn't remember anyone before who had been so interested in her life and it felt good.

'I loved living by the sea. That's the one thing about London I can't stand. There's nowhere to go fishing,' Nico commented.

'Leigh-on-Sea?' Storm suggested.

Nico arched an eyebrow. 'I'm very fond of Leigh-on-Sea, Storm, but fishing in an Essex estuary doesn't compare with the blue waters of the Adriatic.'

Storm giggled. 'Point made.'

'Anyway, how are things going for you at college?' he asked.

'Oh, fine. I haven't started properly yet so I've just been doing a bit of pre-course reading. So far, so good.'

Her latest lie was the last thing she wanted to talk about. An image of Pinocchio came into her mind, and as she shifted uncomfortably in her chair Storm found herself rubbing her nose. She wouldn't have been surprised if it had suddenly grown in the last thirty seconds, the lies tumbled from her mouth so quickly.

Sensing she wanted to change the subject, Nico signalled to the waiter for two more cappuccinos and decided to go all out. 'And what else is going on for you, Storm? I cannot believe a girl as beautiful as you is single. Do you have a boyfriend?'

'You don't waste time getting to the point, do you?' she chuckled.

'Sorry. Always a habit of mine. I didn't mean to offend you.'

Storm shrugged and dipped her finger into the froth of her cappuccino. As usual Nico had got her to open up and be who she really was. 'You didn't. For a long time I thought my last boyfriend Dermot was the one,' she admitted. 'I thought we would be together for ever. But the truth is he was a lying, cheating bastard who did his best to destroy my life and I'm better off without him.'

If Nico was surprised by this outburst he didn't show it. Instead he reached across the table for her hand and traced his fingers across its palm. As he touched her Storm felt a pang of desire. She wanted to spend every moment of every day with this man. Locking eyes with Nico, she saw his expression suddenly become grave.

'There's something I want to discuss with you.'

'Sounds serious?'

'It is. And you can tell nobody, especially not your reporter friend Chelsea.'

Storm's heart started to thump wildly. What if he knew about the honey trap plan? What if he'd lured her here to have a go at her, accuse her of fraud, deception, or, worse, tell her he never wanted to see her again? In that moment Storm didn't think she could stand it. Not for the first time she wished she had never gone along with Dermot's stupid plan. Being unemployed was better than duping someone like this.

Nervously, she withdrew her hand from Nico's and

braced herself. 'OK, I'm listening.'

'There's no easy way to say this,' he began. 'I've developed feelings for you, and I don't mean to sound arrogant but I think you care for me too. You're the first person I think about when I wake up and the last person I think about when I go to bed. When I create a new dish it's your opinion I want, and when I'm in bed it's your arms I want to feel around me.'

Storm didn't know what to say. These were the words she'd longed to hear, but it was pointless. Nico was with Francesca and if he couldn't remember that then she had to help him. Suddenly she felt very tired. It would be so easy to let herself be swayed by his words but there was just the little matter of his girlfriend getting in the way. She knew she was falling for Nico but it was time he realised it wasn't ever going to happen.

'Francesca joining us in this little scenario, is she?' Storm leaned forward so that her face was close to his. 'I liked Francesca. I thought she was warm, fun, classy. She deserves better than this.'

Nico winced, and reached for her wrist. 'Francesca very much likes you too. She's part of the reason I'm here. It's with her blessing that I want you to learn the truth about us. I've hardly told anyone what I'm about to tell you, Storm, but the truth is, I'm single. Francesca isn't my girlfriend, we're not getting married – she's gay.'

'What?' Storm gasped. Leaning back in shock, she considered all the photos she had ever seen of Francesca and Nico together. They'd seemed so happy and in love – everyone said so. 'What are you talking about?' she asked finally.

Nico looked at her anxiously.

'It's true,' he said quietly. 'Francesca's gay. Always has been, always will be. She has a girlfriend, Paula, and they have been together for a couple of years and are very much in love.'

'But why lie?' Storm spluttered.

'Even in this day and age people are prejudiced, Storm.'

'But not that badly,' she protested.

'You'd be surprised,' he replied. Taking a deep breath he told her how Francesca had been brought up by her very strict grandparents after her parents were killed in a car crash when she was only a baby. 'From the moment I met Francesca when we were just ten, I sensed she was vulnerable – her grandparents were very strict with her and both devout Catholics. It was a cold existence so I made it my own personal mission to look out for her, make sure she was OK. I sat next to her at school, invited her around to my home to play with me and my sisters, and made sure her grandparents thought I was a good influence on her, so that Francesca would have a little more freedom.'

'Wow, what an amazing friend you were!'

'It wasn't all one-sided,' Nico put in. 'One day she punched a much older boy who had tried to bully me at church. Her bravery and strength impressed me. And you know what, Storm? After twenty-five years she is still doing that today.'

'How do you mean?'

'Well, after that day, Francesca and I became inseparable, sharing each other's secrets as we grew up in and out of each other's houses in our tiny village. But then when we were eighteen both our lives were turned upside down after a group of kids caught Francesca behind the village church, kissing a girl she went to school with.'

'What's wrong with that?'

'This was in the early nineties,' he explained. 'It doesn't seem so long ago but things have changed dramatically since then, especially in small-town Italy. Francesca became the subject of nasty gossip. In a small village like ours, it was hard to get away from the whispers and name calling . . .'

'That's awful,' Storm breathed. 'Poor Francesca.'

'That wasn't the worst part,' Nico replied grimly. 'Her grandparents considered Francesca's behaviour so disgusting they threw her out. It was a terrifying time for her, and she came straight to me. I was furious, couldn't believe her grandparents could behave in that way. I went to see them to try and get them to change their minds.'

'And did you succeed?'

Nico shook his head. 'I didn't come close. They threw me out too. Said I'd encouraged her by not asking her to marry me! It was a joke. They refused to believe Francesca was the kind, loving person she has always been and instead viewed her as some sort of terrible sinner. I hated seeing her treated that way. Because her grandparents were so well-respected in the community, many people – even former friends – shunned us both.'

Storm winced. 'That's horrible.'

'It was, but I didn't need friends like that, and neither did Francesca. But that's why she has never come out. She still worries now about what people will say should she choose publicly to reveal her sexuality. When all this happened I had a place at a top London cookery school and invited her to join me in the UK, to make a fresh start. She'd been due to study law, and once we got here, she studied hard and managed to win a place at a London university . . .'

'Then what?' Storm asked.

'Francesca began her law degree and I vowed to love and protect her no matter what. She's my best friend and there is nothing I wouldn't do for her, she's been through far too much already.'

'So that's why you let everyone assume you're a couple?'

Nico nodded his head. 'It hasn't done either of us any harm. Francesca has never been back to Italy, and pretending we're a couple makes her feel safer. It's suited us both to keep up the pretence.'

'And your parents have supported you?'

Nico nodded. 'They're the only ones in our village who have. I have always stood by Francesca and always will.'

'And what about the affairs you've had?'

Nico shrugged. 'I'm single, Storm. I haven't had lots of affairs. I had a long-term girlfriend for many years, who understood my situation with Francesca. But then she wanted more, wanted me to encourage Francesca to come out so we could be together once and for all, but if I'm honest I didn't love her anywhere near enough to do that. So I ended it. Now Francesca's away a lot at Paula's, or rather at the house they both own in Dorset, and when she is I do my own thing here.'

'So you're not really cheating then?'

He shook his head. 'I would never cheat, Storm. It's not who I am. Before my restaurant career took off we talked about Francesca finally coming out and living the life she wants with Paula. But she became nervous and insecure, and I couldn't see the point of putting her through it. As I said before, I hadn't met anyone else I wanted to get serious with . . . until I met you.'

'And when you did . . .' Storm's voice trailed off.

'I couldn't stop talking about you, and she . . . how do you say? . . . cottoned on that my feelings for you were strong. When she met you, she saw how I felt and said I owed it to her, you and me to tell you the truth. And maybe, just maybe, there was a way we could be together.'

Nico finished his speech and looked at Storm, waiting for her to say something.

She let out a deep sigh and leaned back against the banquette. She couldn't get her head around any of this. But the one thing she realised was that she had to protect Francesca now as well as Nico. If this ever got out they'd be splashed across the front pages for weeks as skanky reporters and paps delved into their private lives and dug up all kinds of horror stories. She shook her head sadly. Neither of them deserved that. It was up to Francesca when and how she came out. Storm knew she had to carry on with the honey trap plan. She felt unbearably trapped in a situation she just did not know how to handle. She needed to get away from Nico so she could think clearly.

But that wouldn't be fair after he'd just bared his soul to her. She tried to say something, anything, that would relieve the tension that his words had caused, but nothing came. Instead, she picked up her bag and rushed out the door, leaving Nico staring after her with a dejected expression on his face.

Chapter Twelve

'You ran out of the coffee shop? Have you lost your freaking mind?' Chelsea blasted.

It was gone six and the two girls had gone for post-work drinks at a pub in Covent Garden well away from the prying eyes and ears in the office.

Storm shrugged and sipped her glass of Sauvignon Blanc.

'I didn't mean to. I was just so overwhelmed by Nico's confession.'

'It must have been quite something to rattle you like that, babe,' Chelsea said thoughtfully. 'It's not like you to go off on one.'

Storm took another sip of wine. She hadn't told Chelsea the details of Nico's news. It wasn't her secret to share. It wasn't that Storm didn't trust Chelsea; she hadn't known the other girl for very long but already felt she would trust her with her life. But after everything that had happened with Carly, Storm had learned her lesson. Some things were meant to stay private – and Nico's relationship with Francesca was definitely one of them.

'It was the last thing I was expecting,' was all Storm said.

'I can see that, babe,' Chelsea said quietly. 'What did he do when you legged it?'

'I didn't look back to find out. I just grabbed my stuff and raced out of the café.' Storm sighed and took another sip of her wine. They'd done well to grab a table outside, usually the place was packed with tourists and day-trippers.

'I feel terrible about it. There was Nico, baring his soul, and I just left him there. It was a horrible thing to do. I haven't heard from him since.'

Chelsea folded her empty crisp packet into a triangle and wedged it into the hole in the middle of the table before regarding Storm carefully. 'Do you think that whatever he told you was the truth?'

Storm nodded her head sadly. 'I Googled where Francesca works straight after I saw Nico and called her. She confirmed what he'd told me.'

'I see,' replied Chelsea, nodding. 'Did you tell her you'd deserted him?'

Storm nodded. 'She laughed and said it was the first time a woman had ever ditched Nico.'

She paused then and thought about the conversation she'd had with Francesca. Much as she'd wanted to stay with Nico, the pressure of everything had suddenly become too much for her and she had fled from the coffee shop to a nearby churchyard. Perching on a bench, she had thought long and hard about what to do before deciding to find Francesca. Punching in the number for the chambers general office, she'd asked to be put through to Francesca. Storm had half expected her to tear strips off her when she heard what had happened, but the other woman had been nothing but warm and sympathetic.

'He's falling for you,' she said. 'We have kept my sexuality a secret for many years, but now I have found love. It would make me very happy if Nico could do the same.'

'But I just left him there,' Storm wailed.

Francesca sounded unconcerned. 'He'll get over it,' she said soothingly. 'Leave Nico to me.'

Swallowing a pang of guilt about the lies she had told him, about working as a flight attendant and then about studying catering, Storm had hung up and returned to the office where she'd done little more than daydream over her computer screen and leave unanswered messages for Nico every half hour. The only glimmer of sunshine in her whole day had been the fact that nobody at work had asked her how she'd got on with him. Sabrina and Dermot had been out on a job all afternoon and Miles had been tied up with meetings so hadn't called her into his office for the lowdown.

Now, almost two glasses of wine down, Storm could see the error of her ways. 'I shouldn't have run off like that. It was a shit thing to do.'

'So tell him, apologise.'

'Not that simple. He won't answer his phone and I don't like to bother Francesca again.'

'Go over there.' Chelsea was surprisingly single-minded sometimes.

'Duh! I don't have his address. And even if I did, I couldn't just turn up.'

'Why not?'

Storm looked at her friend as if she was an alien from another planet. 'Paps, babe! They see me, they'll think I'm there for a booty call.'

'No, they won't. They're all across town at some huge premiere with Jennifer Aniston – they're not hanging about to catch Nico out.'

Storm drained her glass and got to her feet. 'Another?' she asked.

As she waited to be served, Storm considered Chelsea's advice. Maybe she should go over there, explain and tell Nico how sorry she was. She knew she wouldn't sleep a wink if she didn't speak to him this evening.

By the time she'd ordered two more drinks and a couple of bags of salted peanuts, Storm had made up her mind.

'OK, it's a good idea,' she said, placing the drinks carefully on the table and for once not spilling a drop. 'But I don't know where Nico lives.'

'Well, luckily for you, I do,' Chelsea replied, fishing in her bag for a notepad and pen and scribbling down an address in thick black print. Tearing the page from her pad, she handed it to Storm. 'There you go. Now get yourself in a cab and get over there.'

Storm took the piece of paper and stared at the address in front of her. Was there nothing Chelsea couldn't do?

'Thanks, but I can't leave you here in the pub alone.' She pointed to their two full glasses. Chelsea reached across the table and helped herself to Storm's glass of wine and bag of nuts.

'Problem solved,' she said firmly, noticing a gorgeous dark-haired stranger at a nearby table giving her the eye. 'Besides, I don't think I'll be alone for very long.'

It was one of those beautifully warm nights that made the summer feel like it would last for ever. The sound of laughter and good times provided the soundtrack to Storm's evening as she left the pub and walked towards the nearest taxi rank. It felt to her as though her senses were on fire as she noticed how alive the city seemed, with people spilling out of bars and cafés on to the street, enjoying drinks as they soaked up the late-summer sunshine. She was about to fish out her mobile and check for messages when a movement across the street caught her eye. Glancing up, she was horrified to see Dermot standing across the road, smiling and waving at her.

Shock pulsed through her. What was he doing here? She and Chelsea had only just decided to go for a drink in Covent Garden after they left work. How did he know where to find her?

Determined not to show she was rattled, she ignored him and instead focused on catching the attention of a passing taxi. Right now all she wanted was Nico, not Dermot. Clambering into the back of the next cab, Storm gave the driver Nico's address in Hampstead then turned to look out of the back window.

Dermot was still there, mouthing 'I'll call you'.

Shuddering, Storm did her best to forget him. Tonight

was about Nico, not Dermot. She pulled her compact from her bag to check her appearance. Not too bad, she thought, grateful she didn't have mascara rings around her eyes. Reaching into her bag for the packet of mints she always carried, Storm put two into her mouth to freshen her breath.

Nico's home was every bit as gorgeous as Storm had expected: a large, detached red-brick house, set back from the road behind trees and with a tall hedge at the front to keep out prying eyes. After she'd paid the cabbie, she made her way towards the red front door. As her feet crunched on the gravel drive she did her best to calm down; at least the place was free from paps just as Chelsea had promised.

Raising her hand to rap the brass knocker loudly, Storm couldn't help hoping nobody was home. Apart from a couple of lamps on in what looked like the living room, the place seemed deserted. Just as she was convincing herself it would be for the best if Nico weren't in, the front door swung open and there stood the man himself, dressed in cut-off grey sweatpants and a baggy white t-shirt that showed off just a hint of his tanned, taut stomach muscles, Storm was mesmerised. God, he was sexy! Nico could wear a bin liner and still be the most gorgeous man in the room.

'What are you doing here?' he asked, shocked to see her.

'Er . . .' Storm suddenly felt so nervous, she couldn't get the words out. 'I just wanted to say I'm sorry. I shouldn't have run out on you like that this morning. It was an awful thing to do after you'd told me something so personal.'

The words didn't seem to be enough when she looked at Nico's impassive face. He was giving nothing away and

Storm realised that turning up out of the blue had been a very bad idea. 'I'm sorry, I should never have come.'

As she began to walk away, Nico grabbed her wrist and spun her back round to face him.

'Don't go.'

As his eyes met hers, Storm weakened and her pulse raced. 'I'm sorry, I was overwhelmed . . .' she began. Nico silenced her by gently placing a finger over her lips.

'Shhh,' he whispered, bending down to kiss her. As his beautiful mouth met hers she was sure she heard fireworks going off around her, the passion of it all leaving her breathless. Nico's tongue darted into her mouth and Storm reacted instinctively, moving her lips to the rhythm of his. Butterflies fluttered wildly inside her as ripples of desire pulsed through every part of her body. By the time Nico had gently pulled away she had the strangest feeling it was as if she'd finally come home.

'Do you want to come inside, Storm?' he murmured. 'I'm not ready to let you go when I've only just found you.'

'I think I never want to leave,' she replied softly, taking his hand as he guided her inside.

As Nico led her into the huge open-plan kitchen-diner, Storm couldn't believe the luxury of it all. The room was decked out with glass and steel and by rights should have looked overpowering and masculine, but instead it looked and felt warm and inviting.

But there was no time for a guided tour as he pushed her gently on to the red leather sofa at the end of the kitchen and kissed her again. This time his lips were greedier. 'My God, Storm,' he breathed, breaking away and looking at her in wonder. 'I've fantasised about this moment for so long, but wasn't sure it would ever happen.'

By way of reply she kissed him back, hungry for more, feeling like a different version of herself, more confident, daring, and alive with a craving she had never experienced before. Her hands moved to his torso. She slid her fingers underneath his t-shirt and savoured the feel of his smooth, warm skin. As she caressed his rock-hard abs, Nico tugged off her dress and knickers. He unclasped her bra, leaving her totally naked, and she realised she would usually have felt self-conscious, a new lover seeing her without any clothes on, but not today.

This time Storm felt powerful in her own skin, excitement coursing through every nerve in her body. At the thought of what lay ahead her nipples stiffened in anticipation – all she could think was how much she wanted this man. Drunk on love and lust, Storm couldn't get enough, wanting to consume every inch of him. Melting into his touch, she slipped her hand into his boxers and moaned with pleasure at the feel of his hard, waiting cock. Storm's touch sent Nico into overdrive. Lustfully, he scooped her into his arms.

'Are you always this masterful?' she giggled as he carried her up to his bedroom.

'Only when I'm really turned on,' he said gruffly, kicking the door closed behind him. Suddenly Storm's laughter gave way to pure passion as they fell on to the bed. Their hands were everywhere, each desperate to touch and please the other. Storm shucked off Nico's sweatpants and gazed at him. He was as perfect as she'd imagined.

Reaching for her, Nico trailed his fingers across her shoulders, then sucked and kissed at her hard nipples, sending waves of desire through her core. As he travelled further down her body, slipping a hand between her legs, Storm bucked and writhed with sheer pleasure. There was no denying it, Nico was an expert lover, his touch sensuous, slow, and at the same time thrilling. He made her feel as though he had all the time in the world just for her. But Storm wanted to prove to Nico just how much she wanted him. Pushing him onto his back, Nico gasped as she slid her mouth lower and lower, eager to taste all of him.

'Let me just put something on . . .' he murmured, pulling her up and reaching into his bedside drawer for a condom.

'Now, Nico, now!' Storm begged, lying back on the bed, unable to wait any longer.

Pausing just for a moment to look at her face, Nico found his way inside her, the sensation so pure and perfect each of them shuddered in delight.

As Nico plunged deeper, all too soon Storm felt her orgasm build, until finally she couldn't hold back any longer. Burying her face in his chest she screamed in ecstasy as wave after wave of pleasure rippled through her body, and then Nico was reaching his own climax. As she felt him thrust into her he called out her name, and Storm thought it was the most beautiful thing she had ever heard.

Storm woke up the next morning to find herself alone in Nico's king-size bed. Sitting bolt upright, she took in the scene – there were clothes everywhere, including her best lacy briefs. Just as she was trying artfully to reach for them and shove them under her pillow, Nico appeared wearing nothing but a pair of boxers and holding a huge tray laden with coffee, croissants, fresh fruit, and what looked suspiciously like huge bacon sandwiches.

'Wow! Is all that for me?' Storm asked, unsure which was more impressive, the contents of Nico's tray or the contents of his closely fitting boxers.

'I was thinking we might share, but having discovered last night just how greedy you can be, you can eat the whole lot if you want,' he teased, putting down the tray on a bedside table and leaning over to kiss her good morning.

Feeling Nico's lips on hers, Storm too was reminded of last night. It had been amazing, incredible, she didn't think she'd ever had such good sex before in her life. After they'd made love the first time, they'd lain together, limbs entwined, laughing and talking before making love again, and again, and again. Nico had serious prowess, and Storm had lost count of the amount of orgasms he'd brought her to.

Smiling at the memory, Nico brushed a stray tendril of hair from her face. 'What are you smirking about?'

'Nothing.' She laughed, sneaking a bite of buttery fresh croissant. 'Just remembering last night.'

Nico playfully batted her arm before leaning over to gently suck her nipples. 'Last night was just the warm up.' He smiled, inching his boxers down. 'Let me show you just what us Italians can really do.'

'Mmm. I like the sound of that, Mr Alvise. It sounds like it's going to be a long day.'

*

220

Exhausted, that was the only word for it, Storm thought later as her head hit the pillow. Exhausted, but definitely ecstatic. If she'd thought last night was good, then Nico deserved a medal for the performance he'd just put in. Actually, they both did. Turning her head towards him, she gazed at his closed eyes.

'Stop watching me, Storm,' he whispered, making her jump out of her skin.

'You nearly gave me a heart attack,' she cried, wrapping the duvet tightly around herself.

'Hmmm, don't cover up your beautiful body,' he protested, wriggling closer. 'You're too gorgeous to be covered up. In fact, I think you should be naked all the time.'

'Yeah? I think people in the street might have a problem with that.'

'Well, if they do, they can take it up with me. I know a top barrister who will make their lives a misery!'

Storm felt guilty then. How could she have been so thoughtless as not even to consider Francesca? She'd been so swept up in the heat of the moment she'd totally forgotten about her. OK, so Francesca was a lesbian, and involved with someone else, but Storm reckoned she still might not like to find Nico in flagrante in the house they shared.

'Relax.' He smiled as if reading her thoughts. 'Francesca and Paula are in Dorset for the week. We've got the whole place to ourselves.'

Storm felt a rush of relief. 'Really? So what do you feel like doing?'

Nico pulled her towards him and started caressing her neck. 'I think you know exactly what I'd like to be doing.'

By early evening Storm begged for mercy. She'd never had so much sex in all her life.

'Seriously, I'm knackered!'

Nico pretended to look put out. 'Oh, Storm! Come on, let me make love to you once more.'

As he leaned over to kiss her, she playfully pushed him away.

'No! I need to get up, I'm starving. I can't believe I've spent all day with a chef, and only had a croissant.'

'And there was me, thinking I'd filled you up in other ways.'

Already recognising the lustful glint in Nico's eye, Storm put her hands up. 'Stop! I'm getting in the shower and then we are going out to eat.'

Leaving Nico wanting more, she hopped into his huge en suite and turned the rain shower on to full blast.

Over dinner in a gorgeous neighbourhood Thai restaurant Nico counted as one of his favourites, the two of them swapped more stories about their lives. Being a journalist for so long, Storm naturally found it easier to listen to others rather than to reveal details about her own life. With Dermot it had taken her months to open up and share, but with Nico it was different. She felt instantly connected to him. Storm was able to be herself, so when Nico asked how she was coping following her row with Carly, she was honest.

'I haven't seen or heard from her in months,' she

admitted sadly. 'I still miss her every day and wish we could make up – she's been such a huge part of my life for so long – but I know I have to face facts, I doubt it will ever happen.'

'Never say never, Storm.' Nico smiled at her. 'A couple of my old friends from Italy emailed me the other day, apologising for their behaviour. We ended up having a very long conversation. They said they were sorry for not standing by us when we fell foul of Francesca's grandparents. They were just kids who didn't know what to do. It made me realise you never know what's around the corner.'

'Wow, Nico, that's incredible.'

In spite of her own friendship problems, she was delighted for him. He had seemed so sad, almost haunted by the loss of so many friends. It must be a huge weight off his shoulders to know they would be in each other's lives once more.

'Does Francesca know?' she asked shyly.

Nico nodded. 'She's my best friend, Storm. There's nothing I keep from her. And yes, before you ask, she knows you stayed over last night and is incredibly happy for us.'

Storm flushed with delight. The rest of the evening passed in a blur of happy laughter and chat. As she reached into her bag to pay for her half of the meal, Nico waved her gesture away.

'Don't be silly,' he insisted. 'This is on me.'

She was flattered but not easily put off. 'I'm not one of those girls who thinks a man should pay for everything, you know. I insist on paying my share.'

Nico grinned. 'How about a compromise? You pay for breakfast in the morning?' Storm roared with laughter at his forwardness. The cheeky bastard! Just because she'd put out once, he expected her to stay over again.

'You know what they say about assumptions, don't you, Mr Alvise?' She stared at him stern-faced. 'To assume makes an ass out of you and me.'

'Don't talk about your ass, Storm – just the sight of it drives me wild,' he groaned.

She laughed again. The man was shameless!

'Well, I hate to see someone in pain, so as a favour to you, yes, I'll stay.'

Nico smiled broadly. 'Excellent. Now grab your stuff and let's get out of here. You're wearing far too many clothes for my liking.'

Hand in hand, they left the restaurant and walked back to his house. They were just metres from his front door when Storm's mobile rang.

Letting go of Nico's hand, she reached for her phone and peered at the screen – Chelsea.

'I should get this. I haven't managed to speak to her so she's probably wondering where I am.'

'I'll give you some privacy,' Nico offered considerately, unlocking his front door as Storm pressed answer.

'Thank fuck for that! You haven't answered your phone all day, I thought you were dead in a ditch somewhere,' Chelsea said dramatically.

'Don't be daft, I'm with Nico,' she replied, before lowering her voice. 'Actually I'm staying over again tonight.'

Chelsea cackled. 'You dirty bitch! Good on you. So how was he?'

'None of your business.' Storm laughed. 'But I'll be back in the office on Monday.'

'Well, that's what I rang to tell you. I've told the office that you've got a nasty case of tonsillitis and the doctor's signed you off for a week, so nobody's expecting you in for a few days, meaning you and lover boy can spend some time getting to know each other. Don't worry, I've cleared it with HR.'

Not for the first time Storm felt beyond grateful that Chelsea was her friend.

'I don't know what to say. Thanks, babe.'

'I'm not that selfless. I want you out of the way because I've persuaded Adam to come over for a few days and I'd quite like a bout of hot, dirty sex myself without you interrupting, thanks very much.'

Storm giggled. Typical Chelsea. Still, she appreciated the gesture. Heading inside the house to find Nico, she couldn't wait to tell him they had each other all to themselves for the next few days.

Chapter Thirteen

Thanks to Chelsea, Storm and Nico were in a complete and utter state of loved-up bliss. With time to spend together without any pressure from paps, friends, family or work, the couple were able to enjoy the simple luxury of falling in love.

They went everywhere together and couldn't stand being apart, though Storm did insist on returning to Chelsea's flat briefly to pick up some fresh clothes.

It might have taken them a while to get their relationship off the ground but the two of them were more than making up for lost time now. Storm had assured Nico that her college course didn't start for another week, meaning they were free to enjoy days out, including a romantic trip to Bath where Nico arranged for them to have the gorgeous Roman Baths all to themselves. When they weren't out, they would lie in the garden talking and laughing for hours, or Nico would whip up a delicious meal while she perched on a stool at the countertop, chatting and sipping wine.

They never seemed to run out of things to say to each other and Storm felt totally absorbed in his world. When she was with him nothing else seemed to matter. And at night they enjoyed mind-blowing sex.

Over the next few days they felt untouchable, locked in their own private world, and Storm felt happier and more free than she had in years. Her connection with Nico was so intense, it was like nothing she had ever experienced before. She had never really believed in the idea of soulmates, but now she felt sure that's what Nico was. He already seemed to understand her better than she did herself, and they had been eager to learn as much as they could about each other, no detail too small for them to share.

Storm had loved finding out just how he liked his coffee (cappuccino first thing in the morning, followed by espresso throughout the day), that he hated butternut squash, and was secretly fond of *Grey's Anatomy*.

'It's Patrick Dempsey's hair,' he admitted as Storm caught him engrossed in an episode. 'It's so thick and beautiful, it should have its own show.'

As for Nico, he found everything Storm did enchanting. The way she liked to eat satsumas in bed, carried dental floss in her bag, using it after every meal, and had a crush on all the boys in One Direction.

Nico wanted a life with this woman, and already knew he had fallen head over heels in love with her. From the few details he'd learned about Dermot though, and how badly he appeared to have treated Storm, Nico knew he had to tread carefully. He wanted to prove his feelings for her. Whizzing up a homemade pesto sauce for dinner one night, he looked at Storm who sat in her usual place opposite him.

'So I was thinking, why don't I drive you to Brighton some time and join you for lunch with Sally and Jeff? We could eat in my restaurant, that way it's neutral ground for you both,' he suggested casually.

'Really?' Storm stared at him in amazement, surprised that he was volunteering to get involved in her family life. With Dermot she'd got used to doing things on her own, and on the rare occasions he could tear himself away from work he'd frequently moaned about having a million and one other things to be doing – it had to be said, she appreciated the difference. But old habits were hard to break and she was just about to open her mouth and tell Nico that she was fine and could manage by herself when he leaned across the breakfast bar and silenced her with a kiss.

'I know you were about to tell me thanks but no thanks, but for once stop trying to be so independent and let someone help you. I want to meet your mum, and I want to be there for you.'

'OK then.' She smiled, won over by his thoughtfulness. It had been a long time since she'd felt cared for, and she realised just how close she and Nico had become in a short space of time. Which was why it pained her that she had kept some huge secrets from him, such as the fact she wasn't a hospitality student and had never been an air hostess.

More than anything she wanted to tell him she was really a showbiz reporter who had been asked to entrap him, but she knew if she did then the spell would be broken. Storm felt terrible about deceiving him. The only thing that stopped her from telling him was knowing that what she was doing was the best way to protect him, since she had no intention of selling him out.

But all too soon Monday morning arrived and their magical week was over. Not only was Storm due back at work, or college as Nico assumed, but he himself had to return to his flagship restaurant. He was recruiting a new sous-chef and always made sure he did the hiring and firing personally.

'Don't look so sad.' He smiled, catching sight of Storm's expression as she layered on her mascara in the bathroom mirror.

'I'm not sad,' she said, doing her best to sound as if she wasn't bothered.

Nico snorted. 'Yeah, right! Never play poker, Storm, your face would give you away every time.'

Doing her best to hide a smile, she eyeballed him in the mirror. 'So you're not bothered our week together is over?'

'Is that all I am to you?' He laughed, slipping his arms around her waist and kissing her neck. 'Some irresistible boy toy you can put down after a week.'

'I hate to break it to you but you're in your mid-thirties so you're less of a boy toy and more of a man plaything.'

'Hah! Well, if that's all I am to you then I'd better make sure I leave you satisfied for the day.'

Pushing her up against the bathroom door, Nico unbuttoned her blouse and started kissing and sucking her breasts.

'I'm going to be late,' she protested weakly.

'Who cares? Storm, you drive me wild,' he said, expertly tweaking her nipple in a way he knew she loved. After this she would be smiling for the rest of the day.

'You're a sight for sore eyes.' Chelsea smiled as she saw Storm sashay across the room holding two giant cups of coffee. 'Glad to be back?' she asked, gratefully taking the paper cup Storm offered her.

'What do you think?' she sighed, throwing her bag on the desk and taking a long swig of coffee.

'Yeah, I bet it sucks to get back to reality.'

Storm glanced at her friend, unsure if she was taking the piss. 'Hey, I mean it.' Chelsea insisted. 'Adam's gone back to LA now, meaning it's just me, and my Rampant Rabbit for company on a nightly basis.'

'Oh, babe! TMI!' Storm shuddered. 'How was lover boy then?'

'Brilliant.' Chelsea smiled. 'We got on amazingly well all week and he's even asked me to move in with him.'

Shocked, Storm choked on her coffee.

'What did you say? You've only known him five minutes.'

'Talk about judgey,' Chelsea grumbled. 'Anyway, for your information, I may be loved up but I'm not totally stupid. I told him it's far too early for anything like that.'

'Thank God. What did he expect you to do about your career anyway?'

'Well, exactly,' Chelsea replied. 'I told him it would be a nightmare trying to get a job in the States, but he reckons he knows people and could wangle something.'

'Or he could come over here in a few months' time and you could try living together on a trial basis before you commit to something more serious,' Storm put in sensibly.

'Who died and made you the relationships guru?'

'Nobody. I'm just saying, you've got a life here and he shouldn't expect you to drop everything.'

'It's not like that,' Chelsea protested. 'Look, I know it's early days but everything feels so right with him. I can't put my finger on it, it just feels easy.'

Catching the flicker of emotion that crossed her friend's face, Storm softened.

'I'm sorry. I just worry about you, that's all.'

'Right back at you. How's it all going with Nico anyway? Still shagging for Italy?'

Storm chuckled. 'Something like that. God, Chelsea, I think I've really fallen for him. I hate us being apart. I want to be with him all the time, and I'm pretty sure he feels the same way. He's even offered to come with me to meet Sally and Jeff.'

Chelsea raised an eyebrow as she took another sip of coffee. 'Wow! That is serious. And I take it he's still got no idea who you are or what your job really is?'

Storm frowned. 'None at all. And I hate all this deception. I've already come close to blurting out the truth about my job and what I've been asked to do. The only thing that's stopping me is the worry about what will happen if I don't pretend I'm doing the job. I have to protect him.'

'I know, babe. I haven't said a word, though that slimebag Dermot's been round here sniffing for dirt like a

231

fly around shit. That bastard would sell his own granny if he thought it would help him get ahead.'

Storm considered what Chelsea had said. She hadn't told her friend that he was still bombarding her with text messages urging her to give their relationship another go. Last week he'd sent her a load more, asking how she was, begging forgiveness and telling her Sabrina meant nothing to him. Obviously Storm hadn't answered, but she was worried he'd guessed Chelsea had been lying about her being ill. Knowing him, he'd have turned up at the flat while Chelsea was at work and realised she wasn't there. He was starting to really get to her, his behaviour was seriously unhinged, so she had started to keep a log of all his weird behaviour in case things got out of hand.

Spotting Storm across the office, Dermot wasted no time in coming over to her. 'Ah, you look gorgeous as ever, pet. No one would ever guess you'd been ill for the last week. Hope you don't mind my asking, but now you're better when are you planning on seeing Nico? It would be great to get something on him soon.'

Storm eyeballed him. 'I've just got in, Dermot. I'll keep you posted.'

'And I've got a couple of jobs I need covering this week that'll keep Storm pretty busy, but I'm sure she'll fit you in when she can,' Chelsea added sweetly.

Dermot walked around to the back of Storm's chair and whispered in her ear menacingly.

'How was Bath, Storm?'

Storm dropped her pen and turned her head in shock to

face him. How would he know she'd been there? Had he followed her to Bath? 'What do you mean?'

'Nothing,' he replied smoothly. 'Now, to business. I know you're already screwing the chef, but I meant what I said. If you don't give us a story soon then I'll print what I've got, and believe me, I think it will be enough. *Capisce*?'

Anger pulsed through her veins. She stood up so she could look him in the eye. 'If anyone should be issuing threats, dickhead, it's me . . . or have you forgotten all those text messages you sent me last week, telling me it was over with Sabrina and you'd never stopped loving me? If you don't leave me alone and let me deal with this in my own way, I'll tell her everything. And while I'm about it, I'll go straight to Human Resources and have you for sexual harassment.'

'You wouldn't dare,' Dermot hissed.

'Try me. And FYI, even Italians don't say *capisce*, you loser. Now fuck off back under your rock.'

'What a dick! I'm glad you told him where to go,' Chelsea said as Dermot stalked moodily back to his desk.

Groaning, Storm sat down. She didn't know how much more of him she could take. How many other people had to put up with seeing their exes on a daily basis? Not many, she bet. Glancing at her phone, ready to text Nico, she saw she already had a missed call from him along with a voicemail.

Dialling her mailbox, she couldn't help smiling as she heard his chocolatey tones flooding into her ear.

'I just called to see how your day's going and to tell you I miss you,' he said. 'Also, I wanted to check you

233

were still coming over later. Your man plaything is eager to please.'

Laughing, Storm put the phone down.

'I take it all is well in paradise then?' Chelsea asked.

'Never been better,' Storm replied dreamily.

The rest of the week passed in a blur. Storm spent her days interviewing and writing, then at night would rush home to Nico and make love until the small hours. All too soon Friday arrived and Storm was over the moon – for two days it would be just her and Nico. OK, so she'd promised her mum she'd meet her for lunch on Saturday but that wouldn't take long, then Storm would have Nico all to herself again.

But on Saturday morning she woke up in his luxurious bed with a heavy ache in her heart. Not only were they driving down to Brighton for lunch today with Sally and Jeff, but Nico had announced when she got in from work last night that he was heading to Italy for a fortnight on Monday, to do some research on street food for his next TV show. The idea of fourteen days without him in her life seemed like torture to Storm. Determined to shut the world out for a little while longer, she buried her face in her pillow.

'Hey! Cheer up,' Nico whispered, snaking his arm around her waist and pulling her close. 'I won't be away long.'

'I know.' Storm sighed. 'I just don't know what I'll do without you.'

Nico lightly ran his palm over her face, then kissed her gently on the mouth.

'Who said anything about you having to do without me? It's only a fortnight. Besides, there's such a thing as phone sex, you know.'

With that he inched himself under the covers, trailing kisses softly down Storm's back.

'Giving me an idea of what I'll be missing, are you?' she gasped.

'Something like that,' he whispered as he slipped his hand between her legs, bringing her quickly to a shuddering orgasm.

By the time they finally got up, they were running dangerously late to meet Sally and Jeff so skipped breakfast.

'I warn you, I'm moody when I'm hungry,' Storm growled as she settled herself into the passenger seat of Nico's Range Rover.

Sliding his key into the ignition, Nico snorted. 'I thought I left you more than satisfied this morning, Ms Saunders!'

Storm raised an eyebrow. Cheeky bastard. But before she could come out with any quip in return, Nico reached into the back seat and pulled out a picnic hamper.

'Gorgeous Storm, I know you better than you realise, and the one thing I've picked up on is the fact you're no good when you're hungry, so I threw together a simple breakfast picnic for you this morning.'

Staring at the wicker basket Nico had placed on her lap, Storm was lost for words. 'I don't know what to say. Nobody has ever been this thoughtful before.'

'Take a look inside,' he urged, unfastening the leather straps to reveal a fresh fruit salad, hunk of ham, bread, a flask of coffee and even *Panettone*.

'You made all this for me?' Storm was amazed.

'Of course,' Nico whispered, as he stroked her face. 'When will you realise, Storm, I would do anything for you.'

Looking into his eyes, she felt a lump come into her throat. This had to be the most romantic thing anyone had ever done for her. How had she got so lucky, finding the most perfect man in the world?

When they finally arrived in Brighton, and Nico had smoothly parked the Range Rover near Churchill Square, Storm's palms felt sweaty. She hadn't been back since moving to London and she felt strangely nervous.

Sensing Storm's anguish, Nico reached for her hand and together they strolled towards his restaurant. Sally and someone Storm assumed was Jeff were waiting outside.

'Sally,' she said, plastering on a fake smile and kissing her mother lightly on the cheek. 'You should have waited inside.'

Her mum, dressed in a long floral skirt and plain white t-shirt, looked uncomfortable loitering on the pavement, as did Jeff, who was standing just behind her looking incredibly smart in dark trousers, white shirt and navy blazer.

'Oh, you know me, love. It didn't seem right when we hadn't booked a table,' she said, shuffling from foot to foot.

Storm tried to refrain from rolling her eyes. When she'd rung Sally earlier that week to suggest meeting for lunch her mother hadn't been keen on eating at Nico's restaurant, arguing it was a bit fancy for her and Jeff.

But Storm had insisted it was Nico's treat, and Sally had reluctantly agreed.

Now Storm wondered if it had been a good idea to force the issue. Thank God for Nico, who swung into action. He kissed Sally warmly on each cheek, then pumped Jeff's hand furiously. 'Such a pleasure to meet you both. Storm and I have both been looking forward to this very much. Now, please, let's go inside, eat and enjoy ourselves.'

As Nico opened the door for her mother and boyfriend, Storm shook her head in amazement. If he ever fancied a career change, he could enter the diplomatic service, she thought.

Surprisingly, it turned out to be a good lunch. After her initial nerves had settled, Storm took the time to get to know Jeff and was delighted to discover he was a lovely bloke, kind, gentle and warm, with lots of funny stories about his job as a gardener, and the bingo hall where he and Sally had met.

'We'd been friends for years,' he told her. 'And one day, when the girl behind the bar told me they'd run out of chicken and chips, your mother overheard and generously offered to let me have her plate.'

''Course he didn't take them,' Sally chuckled.

'What sort of bloke would I be if I took a woman's chicken and chips, eh?'

'So you two fell in love over . . . what is the dish you say? A bird in a basket?' Nico asked.

The whole table fell about laughing at his mistake. 'It's chicken in a basket,' Sally corrected him.

'A bird in a basket is a very different thing,' Jeff put in. 'But, yes, I think that is how we fell in love.'

'Certainly is.' Sally beamed, giving him a peck on the cheek.

Storm was very surprised by the change in her mother. She seemed so different, relaxed and happy. Storm hadn't seen this side of Sally since before Alan died. Perhaps Jeff was just the tonic her mother needed.

'Am I right in thinking you used to work there, Storm?' Jeff asked, interrupting her thoughts.

'Did you?' Nico looked amused. 'Were you the one who shouted "two fat ladies" and "Kelly's eye"?'

'Not quite, I was just an assistant. I used to stand there with a microphone and when someone called House, I'd run over and read the numbers.' She laughed. 'When I was bored I used to try making up stupid rhymes for the numbers. Don't think many people found it very funny, though.'

Sally tutted. 'Stop putting yourself down. You worked very hard, just as you do now. What you've achieved at work has been incredible . . .'

Before her mother could say anything else, Storm kicked her furiously under the table, reminding her to keep her mouth shut. When Storm had spoken to Sally earlier in the week, she'd explained she had a new boyfriend, and after Sally had got over the shock of her daughter dating a TV chef, Storm had revealed the fact that Nico didn't know what she did for a living.

Listening to herself explain, Storm felt it made their whole relationship sound like a sham, but her mother had agreed not to say anything. Keen to cover her mistake, Sally quickly changed the subject.

'So tell me about your family, Nico. What do they do?' she enquired.

'My parents live in a village on the east coast of Italy. My father is a train driver, my mother runs a small café.'

'And is that where you get your love of cookery from?'

'I think so. My mother and I are very close. She passed her skills on to me from a young age, and it helped that my sisters had no interest in cooking at all. For years it was just me and my *mamma* together, and later I helped her when I could in the café. She helped to fire my passion for cooking. I thank God I was blessed with a loving and happy family.'

As Sally choked on her mineral water, Storm turned bright red while Nico looked horrified as he realised he'd been tactless, considering Sally and Storm's troubled past. He was about to open his mouth and try to smooth things over, when Jeff reached across the table and patted his hand.

'Don't worry, lad. We know you didn't mean anything by that.'

Storm caught Jeff's eye and gratefully mouthed 'thank you'.

Thankfully the rest of the meal passed without incident. After rounding off lunch with a calorific helping of delicious *tiramisù*, they went for a walk along the seafront.

Nico had Sally eating out of the palm of his hand, showing an interest in her and her life that Dermot had never done, giving Storm the opportunity to chat to Jeff. She had been unsure what to expect, but he was easy to talk to and chatted about his work and his two sons, who had grown up and left home.

They were nearing the Pier when Jeff stopped walking and turned to her. 'Can I be frank with you, Storm?'

'Sure,' she said, hesitantly, worried about what was coming next.

'I just want to say I know that after your dad's death, along with everything you and Sally have been through over the years, it can't have been easy for you to come here today, but both Sally and I appreciate it.'

'Well, thanks . . .' she began, before Jeff cut her off.

'I just want to say I know this is difficult, but I love your mother and we're serious about each other. I realise you and she have had your issues, and I understand why. Heaven only knows how I would have felt if I had been the one who had to cope with bringing up two kids and dealing with a drunk for a mother, but I can see why Sally is so proud of you. It's important to me you realise that while I will never, ever try to replace your father, if ever you need someone to talk to . . . you know, a bloke's opinion sort of thing . . . then I'm here for you.'

Tears sprang into Storm's eyes. Jeff's words had unexpectedly moved her. She hadn't wanted to like him, if she was being honest, and had been looking forward to a good old-fashioned moan in the car with Nico on the way back about what a dick her mother seemed to have found, but incredibly she had taken to Jeff from the moment they'd met. He seemed to get her relationship with Sally, and didn't want to push her or try and get her to accept him as a daddy figure either.

Wiping tears from her eyes, she cocked her head to one side and looked at him. 'You're not what I expected. But you know what? I think I'm going to like you.'

Out of the corner of her eye, she could see Nico and Sally waiting for them to catch up. Struck by an unexpected pang of emotion, Storm linked her arm through Jeff's. 'We'd better hurry up before those two get sick of waiting for us.'

'Well, that went well!' Nico exclaimed as they drove along the A23 towards London.

'It did,' she replied. 'I really liked Jeff.'

'And I thought your mother seemed nice,' Nico put in carefully.

Storm thought for a moment. 'Yeah, she's OK. I'm glad she's met Jeff. It's like the old mother I knew and loved as a kid has come back.'

'How do you mean?'

'Well, normally, Sally's so keen to please and make up for lost time that she totally overdoes the perfect mother act. It was nice to see her relaxed and having a laugh for a change.'

'Maybe Jeff isn't the big bad wolf you thought he was going to be.'

Storm laughed. 'No, I definitely don't think he's the big bad wolf. If anything I think he's bloody Prince Charming, putting up with Sally.'

'He does really seem to love her,' Nico mused. 'And your mum really seems to love you.'

Storm groaned. 'What did she say to you once I was out of earshot?'

'That's between me and her,' Nico said, tapping his nose. 'But she loves you, Storm.' His voice softened. 'And all she wants is to make up for the past. She's so proud of you. As am I. I told her she must have done something right because you are perfect. Perfect for me.'

Storm looked over at him, feeling completely dumbstruck. She knew she had fallen for Nico, and she'd hoped he felt the same, but hadn't expected this now. She wanted to fling her arms around him and never let him go.

Nico cleared his throat and looked back at her, his expression serious. 'So, I was thinking, now might be a good time to talk to Francesca about publicly revealing the truth about our relationship.'

Storm gasped in shock. 'What? Why?'

'Because I've fallen in love with you, Storm. I've never felt like this before, and I know I never want to lose you.'

Chapter Fourteen

Watching Nico sling his black leather wash bag into his expertly packed Louis Vuitton suitcase, Storm felt a twinge of sadness. Since the moment they'd got back from Brighton she'd been dreading this parting. She could have kicked herself for it as well. Christ, this wasn't who she was. She didn't need some bloke to complete her. But Storm had a horrible feeling that life without Nico was going to feel very empty indeed.

But if she was honest, his departure wasn't the only thing on her mind. Over the weekend she had been unable to switch off from work. The previous week she'd gone to Claridge's to interview a soap star who had just been killed off and the chat had gone better than anticipated. The star had been a hugely popular character, and now had her sights set firmly on Hollywood. But halfway through the interview Storm got her to admit life wasn't quite as peachy as it seemed.

The actress wasn't sure she was going to like LA. Worse

than that, she was worried about what was going to happen with her boyfriend, a fellow soap star. She didn't trust him as it turned out he'd cheated on her with a lap dancer the year before last. Storm had been nothing but sympathetic, but came away from the interview with a heavy heart. Other people's dirty washing wasn't news, and it wasn't anyone else's business either. She'd written up the interview as sympathetically as possible, but when Miles had praised her for a job well done, and told her it would make the front page on Sunday, she hadn't felt any sense of achievement. In fact she felt as if she'd betrayed a confidence. It wasn't the first time she'd felt it, but this time it was stronger than before, and finally she knew what she needed to do.

The past couple of weeks, spent largely away from the office with a man she knew she loved, had given Storm time to think. She realised that although she loved journalism, the dream of becoming a showbiz reporter was in fact turning into a nightmare. The events the paper asked her to cover weren't glamorous or newsworthy. In fact, she was discovering the job of showbiz reporter was actually quite grubby, pretending to be a swinger one minute and embroiled in a honey trap the next. It wasn't what she'd thought the job would entail.

OK, she was delighted to have been given a promotion, but all this deception and spilling other people's secrets wasn't her. Not only that but it occurred to her that she should never have taken the job after what happened with Carly. If anything should have put her off, that should. Especially as she had to work with Dermot. She felt as if she'd profited from a friend's downfall, and that was out of order. Now she knew she had to make things right between her and Nico, so they could enjoy a trusting and happy future.

She couldn't believe she was thinking it but she wished more than anything she could go back to covering council meetings and planning hearings, reporting on things that really mattered to people. She just couldn't carry on in showbiz any more and she vowed to talk to Chelsea and Miles about it and ask to be transferred to features. Once she had a new position, she would be able to tell Nico the truth and warn him the press were after him. Perhaps she could encourage him to talk to his lawyer and take out one of those super injunctions.

'I promise I'll call you as soon as I land,' said Nico, interrupting her thoughts.

'OK, but don't stress if you can't,' she said, doing her best to sound casual even though her heart was breaking into a million pieces at the thought of even one night away from him. Looking up into his face, she memorised every detail of it: the slope of his Roman nose, the thickness of his brows, the mole on his left cheek. All ready to store in her own personal memory library, to call up at a moment's notice when her desperation at not seeing him got too much for her.

Pulling Storm close to him, he cupped her face in his hands. 'It's no stress, I want to. When are you going to realise you're never getting rid of me?

'Can I have that in writing?'

'You can have it any way you want it.' He smiled, kissing her with such force, Storm was left in no doubt of how he felt.

'How about I have you now?' she replied, running her hand down his chest and slipping it into his boxers.

'You're a wicked woman, Storm Saunders,' he murmured, already pushing up her pencil skirt.

Storm had toyed with the idea of not going into work and playing hookey all day. The thought of trudging into the office and pretending to feel excited about some pointless celebrity interview before a talk about Nico with Dermot and Miles made her feel sick. She thought she could go shopping instead, have a bath, read a book . . . but finally realised that skiving wasn't the solution. She'd made up her mind about her job and wouldn't rest until she'd spoken to Chelsea and Miles about it.

Walking into the office with two extra-large coffees for her and Chelsea, Storm got straight to the point.

'I need to talk to you,' she said, tracking down her boss by the photocopier.

'Sure. Is here OK?'

Storm shook her head. 'Can we go somewhere more private, please?'

Chelsea nodded and they both walked through the double doors towards the lifts. Once they were outside in the fresh air, Storm couldn't hold back.

'I can't do this any more, Chelsea. This job isn't me.'

'What do you mean, babe?' she asked gently.

Storm hung her head, tears springing to her eyes. 'I don't want to let you down, Chelsea, you're my friend and you've been so good to me, but I don't want to be a showbiz reporter any more. I can't hack it. Swingers, honey traps, lies. I'm turning into someone I don't recognise, and I don't like what I see.'

Chelsea bit her lip as she pulled her friend in for a hug. 'Don't be daft, babe, I'm the one who should feel guilty. You've been looking downbeat and sad for week. I thought it was because Nico was off for a couple of weeks but I should have realised it was more than that. I may only have known you a few months, but I know you're not the kind of girl who puts her life on hold the minute you get a new bloke.'

Storm pulled away and smiled sheepishly at Chelsea. 'Not my style, hon.'

'I know. And you know what? No job's worth feeling like this for. You've been put through more than your fair share of shit here and that's out of order. I should have done more to help, so let me help you now. What do you need from me?'

'I want to be transferred to features. It's nothing personal, I love working for you, Chelsea, but this isn't what I want . . . which is terrifying because for the last twenty years being a showbiz journo has been my dream.'

Chelsea gave her friend a rueful smile. 'I understand, Storm. Please, babe, don't worry about this any more. Let me see what I can do.'

Storm shook her head. 'You've done more than enough for me, Chelsea, I'll talk to Miles myself. I need him to understand that I'm not cut throat enough for this life. The press has cost me one best friend, I can't afford to let it wreak any more havoc in my personal life.'

But Chelsea was insistent. 'As your boss, I'm asking you

to let me talk to Miles and see what I can sort out. You can speak to him yourself later, but trust me, this will be a lot easier for him to deal with coming from me. I know Miles of old, and I understand exactly how to handle him.'

As Storm let out a sigh of relief, Chelsea brightened. 'Now, do you reckon I can get you to edit some freelance copy for me while you're still here? A five-year-old could have done better, which is surprising because I think this woman actually got her five-year-old daughter to write it.'

Storm laughed in spite of herself. ''Course I can. Thanks, Chelsea.'

Hailing a black cab, Nico pulled open the door, told the driver to take him to Heathrow as fast as he could and hauled his luggage on to the seat beside him. He was running seriously late! If he missed this flight he'd be in trouble. He was meeting some of the TV crew in Rome and had a feeling his producer wouldn't be too forgiving if he was made to wait for hours until Nico got on the next plane, even if he did have a good excuse.

At the thought of Storm a smile played around Nico's lips. Their morning together had been amazing, and he knew that if he did miss his flight it would all have been worth it. Storm was incredible, and there was nothing he wouldn't do for her. He couldn't put his finger on what it was about her but he just couldn't get enough of her. She hadn't been the only one with sad eyes that morning. In fact, half the reason he'd initiated sex was because he'd felt himself on the verge of tears and had wanted to lose himself in her.

Still, they would be apart for only two weeks, it would pass in a flash, he told himself. And there was always phone sex, as he'd mentioned to Storm on more than one occasion. He had a feeling she'd thought he was joking, but when he checked into his hotel that evening it might be time to let her know he was deadly serious. He smiled at the thought. Everything about Storm took his breath away, in bed and out, it all felt so right and he was overwhelmingly grateful to Francesca for encouraging him to follow his heart.

Smiling, Nico allowed himself a moment to catch his breath. He looked out of the window as the cab sped through west London before the city gave way to the urban sprawl that led to one of the world's busiest airports. Nico liked flying, and enjoyed the feeling of constantly moving, it kept his overactive mind engaged. Taxi journeys, however, he wasn't too keen on, and found it hard to settle in traffic.

Spotting a discarded paper on the seat next to him, Nico idly reached for it and flicked through the sports section. He made a point of never reading the paper itself but on the brief occasions he did glance at the tabloids, he usually only looked at the sports section to find out how his beloved Lazio were faring.

Ten minutes later he was bored. Bad enough the paper was a day old, but football season had only just begun and there wasn't much to report yet. The rest of the news about cricket, horse racing and darts didn't appeal either. Darts, he mused. Yet another crazy English custom he didn't think he'd ever understand. He threw the paper back on to the seat, but glancing down, something on the front page gave him a start. Picking up the copy of the *Herald*, Nico's hands started to shake as he stared at it in disbelief.

The front page carried a story about an ex-soap star's betrayal, but that wasn't what bothered him. It was the by-line next to the headline: *By Storm Saunders*. Could this really be by his beloved girlfriend? After all, the name Storm wasn't common. But surely there had to be a mistake? Storm was an airline stewardess. A student. But according to this she was also a reporter. What was going on?

Storm was doing her best, trying to inject some life into a particularly bad piece of freelance copy, when she heard her mobile ring.

Peering at the screen, she couldn't help smiling as she saw Nico's name flash up.

'Hello, gorgeous. Missing me already?'

'How could you?' Rather than the warm, soothing voice she'd expected to hear, Nico's tone was ice cold.

Storm was gripped by fear. 'How could I what?'

'Don't play me for a fool. How could you lie to me like that? I've just seen yesterday's paper with your fucking story on the front. Did you really think I wouldn't find out, Storm?'

Dread coursed through her body as she felt her entire world come crashing down around her. The last thing she'd wanted was for Nico to find out like this. She'd pictured breaking the news to him when they were in bed, maybe after a leisurely breakfast once she'd got her transfer to features. She'd expected him to be a bit hurt that she hadn't told him the truth straightaway, but once she'd made him understand her reasons for keeping her job from him, he would understand. Stupid as it sounded she hadn't factored in the possibility of Nico seeing one of her stories. He'd told her he didn't read English newspapers, and most people never registered journalists' by-lines, so what were the chances?

'Please, Nico, let me explain . . .'

'Explain? That's the best joke I've heard all year!' snarled Nico, cutting her off. 'Let me guess. You and your journalist friends thought it was funny to dupe me into believing you were an air hostess so you could dig up all the dirt you could on me. Well, you got lucky, didn't you, sweetheart? Bet you never thought you'd get wind of a juicy story like mine.'

'No, Nico, please! It wasn't like that . . .' she began.

'I bet all that stuff with Carly was part of it as well,' he continued. 'I trusted you. I thought we were going to build a life together, to think I was actually stupid enough to fall in love with you. Shit! Scum like you make me sick.'

Hearing Nico use the past tense, tears flooded Storm's eyes. This couldn't be over, she had to make him understand.

'Nico, I know you're upset, but you've got to listen to me.'

But he wasn't interested in hearing anything Storm had to say.

'I thought you understood . . . I hate journalists and paps. They're like parasites, feeding off my life.' By now Nico's voice had taken on a cruel edge that Storm had never heard in it before. Gone were the chocolatey tones that made her feel loved and protected. 'I thought I'd seen it all until I met you, but you've stooped to a new low. I may have misled people about my relationship, but I've never tricked someone into loving me and fucked them under false pretences. You are worse than a whore, Storm Saunders. I never want to speak to you again.'

He hung up the phone and Storm raced from her desk and bolted to the ladies where she threw up the contents of her breakfast. It felt as though her heart was shattering into a million pieces, she had never been in so much pain. Nico had said some terrible things, labelling her worse than a whore. If it had been anyone else she would have hoped for a chance to explain, but she had always known how Nico felt about the press. The fact he had been lied to didn't help, and the worst thing of all was that she had nobody to blame but herself. It was time to face facts. Once again she'd destroyed her chance of happiness with someone she loved.

In the end Nico did miss his flight to Rome, and the one after that too. He'd been so angry after speaking to Storm he couldn't face being cooped up on a plane and had paced up and down the airport, not knowing what to do with himself.

Eventually he'd realised there was only one other person who would understand and called Francesca. She'd been as stunned as Nico to learn the truth, but was upset to learn he hadn't given Storm the chance to defend herself.

'I agree, Nico, that what she has done is terrible, but there must be some mistake here. You should have let her give you her side of the story.'

'What? So she could spin me more lies,' he spat. 'Christ, Francesca, she's already got more than she bargained for from us, and to think I trusted her! I can't believe I was so stupid.'

'You weren't stupid and I don't think you were wrong to trust Storm either. She loves you, Nico, that much I am sure of,' Francesca said carefully.

He laughed angrily. 'You're a bigger fool than I am if you believe Storm ever loved me. The only things that girl loves are herself and her career. We're just two more victims along the way.'

Sinking on to a nearby bench, he sat there for a moment allowing the enormity of his discovery to sink in. It seemed hard to believe that just a couple of hours ago he had been ridiculously happy and in love. For a moment he wished he hadn't ever seen that newspaper and had gone to Rome as planned. But he would only have been living a lie, something he was sick and tired of doing.

'I have to go. I just wanted to warn you there's every chance the press will be sniffing around you and Paula. I want you to know I'm sorry, Francesca. I was wrong to believe there could be any passion in my life other than in the kitchen. From now on that's where I'll focus my energies.'

As Nico hung up, he realised there was nothing Francesca could say or do to change his mind. He'd been betrayed in the worst way possible. As he headed to the flight gate, all he wanted now was the chance to heal.

Once Storm had thrown up she rinsed her mouth out with cold water and splashed her face. Then she returned to the office where she found Chelsea and told her exactly what had happened. Chelsea was too shocked to come up with any of her usual quips. Instead she listened in disbelief as the words tumbled from Storm's mouth.

'I'm sure he's just upset. Once he's calmed down, he'll give you the chance to explain,' Chelsea told her.

'No, he won't,' replied Storm, shaking her head. 'You didn't hear him, Chelsea, he was so bitter and angry. Nico never wants to see me again, let alone give me the chance to explain.'

Storm looked around her. Pap shots of various celebrities lined the walls, along with a planner and tear-sheets of scoops they were particularly proud of. It all seemed so meaningless now. To think this stupid office was once her idea of a dream come true was crazy. It had brought her nothing but trouble. She felt winded, as if all the stuffing had been knocked out of her. How could she ever have believed in a happy ending?

'I really don't think that's true,' Chelsea continued. 'I think you should just give him time. Why don't you let me try and talk to him in a couple of days? I can put your side of the story across and get him to talk to you.'

Storm shook her head. 'Please don't. I've caused Nico enough trouble for one lifetime, I don't want to upset him any more. I've just got to accept it's over. Just as I have to accept I don't belong at the *Herald* any more.'

Reaching for her bag, Storm stuffed her notepad and pen inside then cleared out her drawer. Aside from a spare pack of tights and some mints, she didn't have many belongings at work, preferring to keep things minimal.

'Where are you going?' Chelsea asked as Storm stood up and pulled on her coat.

'To do something I should have done long ago. I'm quitting.'

'Don't be daft!' Chelsea gasped. 'Let me talk to Miles about that transfer to features, he won't want to lose you.'

Storm walked over to Chelsea and hugged her tight. 'You've been brilliant, a better friend than I could ever have hoped for, and I'm going to miss you. But my mind's made up. I don't belong at this paper or in London.'

'Where are you going to go?' Chelsea wailed.

Storm pulled away and looked her friend in the eye. 'I'll be fine. I just need some space to figure out what I'm going to do next.'

As expected her resignation hadn't gone well. Miles had begged her to reconsider, mentioned a pay rise, and when that didn't work he brought out the big guns.

'This is deeply unprofessional, Storm, I expected better.'

But she was in no mood for Miles's bullying. 'Just as well I don't want to work in journalism any more then, isn't it?'

Life at the *Herald* had left a bitter taste in her mouth. She worried what she'd turn into if she didn't get out while she could.

'I'm sorry, Miles, but my mind's made up. I want to leave immediately.'

He looked defeated. He could see Storm was serious but wouldn't give her the satisfaction of knowing how much her departure would hurt him personally. 'Just as well I want you out now then, isn't it? We don't need people like you cluttering up the place. But let me be quite clear with you, Storm. You will regret this decision and you will come to me begging for your job back.'

'I don't think so,' she said quietly, before racing out of the office and returning to Chelsea's apartment for the final time. There she stuffed a few things into a suitcase and scribbled a note to her flatmate.

Will be back for the rest soon. Thanks for everything! Sxxxxxx

By the front door she looked around the place she'd called home for the last few months, then banged the door shut behind her. She flagged down a passing cab and threw herself inside, desperate to get out of London as soon as possible.

'Where to, love?' the cabbie asked.

'Victoria station, please,' she replied, letting out a sigh of relief as the London streets whizzed past her.

When she'd woken up the day had been sunny and warm. Now the weather had turned and, despite the fact it was only mid September, the afternoon had taken a decidedly wintry turn. Like so many others before her, Storm realised she'd come to London full of hopes of a brighter future, only to have her dreams crushed.

As the rain lashed down on the cab windows, Storm pulled her parka tightly around her and fished out her mobile. She scrolled through her contacts, paused when she saw Nico's number and deleted it. There was no point in keeping that now, they'd never speak again, it didn't seem right to store his number any more. Instead she found the number of the one person she was sure wouldn't turn her away.

Clicking on the message icon she tapped out a text.

I need a bit of time out. Would it be OK if I stayed with you for a couple of days? x

She received a reply almost instantly.

Course you can. I've got the day off today, let me know what time you're getting here and I'll come and pick you up. x

Twenty minutes later the cab pulled up to Victoria station and Storm rushed inside. Anxiously she scanned the departures screen for the train to Brighton and was delighted to see the next service left in ten minutes. Storm walked determinedly towards the train she hoped would take her away from her pain and misery. Maybe she'd had it wrong all these years and had been looking for love in the wrong places. Perhaps unconditional love began with her mother after all.

Chapter Fifteen

'Another drink, love?' Sally asked brightly. Curled up on her mum's sofa, hands wrapped around a stone cold mug of tea, Storm stared blankly at the TV screen as *Morning Cuppa* blasted through the living room.

'Storm! Did you hear me?' Sally asked, standing in front of the telly, waving her hands in front of her daughter's face. 'Do you want another cup of tea?'

She reluctantly lifted her gaze from the TV and looked at her mother. 'No, thanks. I'm fine.'

'Really? Because you've been hanging on to that mug for over an hour now, and haven't moved a muscle,' Sally exclaimed. Walking over to the sofa, she sat down next to her daughter and took the mug from her hands. 'You've been like this for the past week now and I'm worried about you,' she said carefully. 'You barely eat and have hardly left the house.'

Storm tucked her legs underneath herself and returned her gaze to the telly. These last few days had been a major role reversal for mother and daughter. From the moment Sally had picked Storm up from the station she'd been brilliant: listening for hours as she sobbed over Nico, not to mention cooking, cleaning and trying to coax Storm out of the house with trips to the cinema or local café. She'd even taken time off work to look after her daughter. Storm had been grateful, and a little surprised. Rushing back to Brighton had seemed like the right thing to do, but Sally's determination to look after her had knocked Storm for six. For the first time in years she was able to see the woman her mother was now, rather than the drunk she used to be. But despite Sally's best efforts to help Storm heal, the idea of getting on with her life was too much for her. Right now all she wanted to do was slob out in her pyjamas, watch telly and drink tea.

'I'm OK, I promise. I'm sorry I'm being a pain but it won't be for long. I'll sort myself out soon.'

But Sally wasn't giving up. 'You're not being a pain, love, but this isn't you. I liked Nico very much, he seemed the perfect match for you, and I know you're hurting, but Storm, if you two are meant to get back together then you will find a way. What I do know is you can't sit here on the sofa day after day. You're a bright and determined girl, you need to start getting your life back on track.'

Storm felt her hackles rise. It was all too much. She couldn't cope with anything at the moment and had been silently sobbing herself to sleep every night, grieving for everything she had lost. 'I just told you, I will soon,' she said, struggling to keep her voice even. 'I need a bit more time first. In case you hadn't noticed my whole life's fallen apart, so it's not surprising if all I want to do is sit around the flat, is it?'

'But it's not like you, Storm,' Sally said gently. 'I'm not saying you haven't had a rough ride, but trust me, wallowing in self-pity will not make you feel better. Today I want you showered and dressed, and as I've got to go back to work, I'd appreciate it if you'd nip to the post office and pay a couple of bills for me.'

Storm looked at her, about to protest, but spotting the heady mix of frustration and concern in her mother's eyes, changed her mind. Storm knew if it hadn't been for Sally she'd have gone under – she owed her.

'OK,' she said, giving Sally a kiss on the cheek as she walked towards the bathroom.

Storm hated to admit it but strolling down Western Road in clean clothes, with her hair washed and brushed, she realised Sally was right – she did feel a lot better. After paying her mum's bills it struck Storm she now had a whole day to fill. As she had finally worked up the courage to leave the flat all by herself she didn't feel much like going back so decided to wander down to the seafront.

Zipping her parka tightly around her to keep out the coastal breeze, Storm strolled past the pubs, art galleries and merry-go-round. She tried to make sense of her life. She had always loved it by the sea, and the sound of the waves crashing against the shore helped focus her mind as she started thinking about the very thing she'd been avoiding over the past seven days – where she went from here. Sally had been more than generous, saying she could stay with her for as long as she wanted, but

Storm knew it wasn't exactly ideal. The flat was tiny, and Jeff, lovely as he was, would understandably want Sally to himself as he'd only just moved in. Storm knew she needed to get her own place, and fast. Thankfully she'd managed to save some money while staying with Chelsea, and had enough for a small deposit and a couple of months' rent, but she would need a job – doing what she wasn't sure.

Anything so long as it wasn't journalism.

Then there was Chelsea. She'd rung and rung Storm every day for the past week to find out how she was doing, and Storm knew she owed her a phone call. Truth was she couldn't face speaking to anyone at the moment. She knew it was cowardly, especially after everything Chelsea had done for her, but she'd sent a quick text earlier that morning letting her know she was OK, in Brighton, and that she'd be in touch soon.

Storm realised as she strode across the beach that she needed to take baby steps if she wanted to move forward. It was time to stop crying and pick herself up. OK, she hadn't expected to have to start life all over again but if that was what it took, then that's what she was going to have to do. Shit happened! If anyone knew that she did. It was time to deal with it, and throwing herself a pity party wasn't going to help.

Passing a beachside coffee shop, Storm ducked inside for a break from the chilly air and ordered herself a latte. Perching on a stool, she looked around her as she waited for the barista to make her drink. This place was only small, with a handful of rustic wooden tables and chairs and a small fridge by the door filled with freshly made sandwiches and healthy smoothies, but it was surprisingly welcoming. On the counter stood an eye-catching display of chocolate cakes that made Storm's mouth water.

Peering across the counter for a better look at the calorie-busting treats, she caught sight of an open copy of *Hot* magazine and saw two pap shots of Nico in Bari shooting his latest TV show. At the sight of him, laughing along with a group of local schoolchildren who were taking part in the show, Storm felt like she'd been kicked in the stomach, the pain and grief of the way they'd split still so fresh and raw. Pulling the magazine closer to her she scanned the picture, drinking in every last detail. Nico looked just the same as he had when she'd last seen him: happy, vibrant and full of energy. She realised the picture must have been taken recently as he still had a nick on his cheek from where he'd cut himself shaving the morning he was flying out to Italy.

As the memory of their last moments together flashed into her mind, Storm lost control and let out an anguished howl, making the barista spill hot milk all over the wooden countertop, soaking the magazine.

'You all right?' he asked as he frantically mopped up.

Miserably, Storm nodded her head. 'Yes. Sorry, I didn't mean to startle you. Here, let me help you clean up.'

As she dived into her bag for the tissues she always carried, the barista waved away her offers of help. 'Forget it. My fault, not concentrating as usual.' He grinned at her and, pouring some fresh milk into her latte, pushed the steaming mug towards her. 'On the house.'

Storm looked at him in surprise as she wiped away her tears. 'You don't have to do that.'

'I don't, but I want to. Besides, anyone who cries in my café deserves a free coffee.'

'Thank you.' As Storm took a sip she considered him gratefully. He looked to be a couple of years older than her, with curly blond hair, big blue eyes and a sloppy grin. She found she felt strangely relaxed in his company.

'What's making you so unhappy?' he asked.

'I wouldn't know where to start.'

'I know the feeling. Come on, try me.'

Storm shrugged. 'OK. In the past week I've lost my job, my house and my boyfriend.'

The barista raised his eyebrows. 'Ouch!'

'Yep. And now I'm living with my mum, which is great . . .'

'. . . but you don't want to stay there for ever.'

Sheepishly Storm nodded.

'What did you do?'

'I was a journalist. Used to work on the *Post* up until last Christmas when I moved to London and worked on the *Herald* as an entertainment journalist.'

'Wow! You hit the big time.' The barista let out a whistle of appreciation. 'So what happened?'

'To cut a long story short, I decided the job was a bit scummy and I'd sooner be homeless, jobless and penniless than spend another minute of another day turning over celebrities.'

'Ah.' The barista paused before asking his next question. 'And the boyfriend?'

'He was a celebrity I'd been asked to screw over. He found out.'

'Bloody hell. You don't do things by halves. I suppose it's pointless me asking who the celeb boyfriend was?'

Storm shot him a murderous stare. He held up his hands and backed away.

'Fair enough. Well, I reckon today is your lucky day. How do you fancy a job here?'

Storm threw back her head and laughed. 'Do you usually go around offering strangers jobs? Besides, if you knew me, you definitely wouldn't hire me. I'm the clumsiest person I know.'

'Well, I'm hardly God's gift myself, am I?' he said, gesturing to the milk-sodden worktop. 'Come on, you'll be doing me a favour, my last waitress ran off to join the circus. Seriously, it's true.' He grinned, clocking her stare. 'And I'm stuck here on my own all day. It's not rocket science. It's coffee, slicing up cake and working the till.'

Storm paused. It wasn't exactly a natural leap from journalism but maybe that was just what she needed. What did she have to lose?

'You're on! But before I start, I think I should know your name.'

'Ed.' He grinned, sticking out his hand.

'Storm,' she replied, returning his grin.

'Well, you've cheered up since I saw you this morning,' said Sally as she bustled through the front door and saw Storm cooking dinner.

'I got a job.' She grinned while she sliced tomatoes.

'That's great, love!' Sally exclaimed as she kicked off her shoes and threw her coat on the back of a kitchen chair. 'And that smells great too. What is it?'

'Just Bolognese sauce. Thought we'd have pasta tonight.'

'Perfect. Now what about this job?'

'It's in a coffee shop on the seafront. The little one tucked under the arches. I just walked in, and after I'd made the owner spill my coffee, he offered me a job.'

Sally laughed. 'You made him spill a drink! That's a new one. Seriously, though, I'm delighted. This is brilliant news, Storm. When do you start?'

'Thanks.' Storm grinned. 'I start tomorrow. Didn't think there was much point in delaying it. I need to get on with my life so might as well start sooner rather than later.'

'That's my girl.' Sally beamed. 'How about we celebrate with a nice cup of tea?'

Flicking the kettle on, she pulled out two mugs and put a teabag in each. 'I'm so proud of you, Storm. I just want you to know that,' she said, handing her daughter a steaming mug.

'Thanks, Sal. But it's just a job in a coffee shop.' Storm shrugged.

'No, it's more than that,' said Sally seriously. 'You never fail to surprise me. You pick yourself up, refuse to let life defeat you, and who knows where this will lead?'

'Thanks,' replied Storm, getting a bit teary-eyed. She knew she was too old to want her mother to heap praise on her but, she had to admit, it felt nice hearing it.

'Anyway,' said Sally, sensing they were both getting a

bit emotional, 'more importantly, what's this guy you're working with like? Is he fit?'

Storm laughed as she thought about Ed. 'He's really sweet. But he's not my type. Think Justin Bieber before he came over all foul-mouthed and got done for drink driving.'

'Oh, that's a shame. I was hoping you were going to tell me he was just like Harry Styles.'

Storm looked at her mother in surprise. 'What do you know about Harry Styles?'

'I know he likes an older lady.' Sally winked.

As the two women erupted into laughter, Storm thought how nice this was. Cooking in the kitchen with her mother, laughing and drinking tea. She never would have thought it was possible a year ago. It was funny how life changed.

Dermot had barely slept following Storm's resignation, he'd been so angry about losing his story and, if he was honest, worried about his future at the *Herald* too. This scoop had been his lifeline, his chance to show Miles he was talented, but now his stupid cow of an ex had ruined it for him. Concerned, he'd tried to talk to Sabrina about other ways of setting up Nico, but she wasn't interested.

'Just move on,' she had said. 'You used to be full of good ideas, don't get hung up on just the one scoop.'

But moving on was the one thing Dermot couldn't do. He knew there was a story on Nico Alvise somewhere, one that could make his career, he just had to prove it.

'I don't understand how the stupid bitch could allow herself to get caught out like that?' Dermot had raged to Sabrina.

'Because she's talentless and was out of her depth,' replied Sabrina, who in truth had no idea what she herself would have done in that situation.

'And in the meantime where does that leave us?' Dermot moaned.

'Look, Dermot, you've got to let this go,' Sabrina insisted. 'This isn't doing you any good at all. Why is this story so important to you? There are plenty of others out there.'

Dermot fell silent. He couldn't explain why exposing Nico was so important. He just knew he wouldn't be satisfied until he'd revealed the truth about the chef one way or another.

About a week after Storm's departure Dermot still couldn't sleep. Sick of spending his nights tossing and turning until the alarm went off, he decided to kill time by pacing up and down Sabrina's kitchen instead.

Flicking the kettle on, he reached for a mug and teabag and waited for the water to boil. Leaning against the worktop, he realised he was as tightly wound as a coiled spring. He knew going over and over Nico's story in his head wasn't doing him any good, that he was on the verge of becoming obsessed. But throughout his entire career he'd never let a story go, and he wasn't about to start now. There had to be some way of proving Nico was a cheat without using Storm.

As the kettle boiled he made his tea then walked over to the chrome breakfast bar, his eyes resting on Sabrina's mobile. Funny, she had exactly the same fluffy pink case as Storm had. Then it hit him: he'd hack Storm's phone and email. Sure, it was technically frowned upon these days after all those celebrities had wept crocodile tears about invasion of privacy and all that bollocks, but this was different. Storm was his ex, and he was pretty sure that she wouldn't have changed the password to her voicemail. She was always so terrible at remembering security information she wrote all of it down in the back of her diary. This wouldn't be phone hacking, this would be more like liberation of information, he told himself.

Besides he'd already placed a GPS tracker on her phone so he knew where she was at every minute of the day. He'd done it when they split, sure it would help him to wreak revenge on her in some way. When she'd changed numbers, all he'd had to do was sweet talk Becki on reception and he'd had Storm's new digits in a flash. He'd hoped his plan to freak her out with flowers, messages and surprise appearances would send her round the bend, but she'd been surprisingly unfazed by it. He'd show her Dermot Whelan was a man you didn't forget, and what better way to do that than by hacking her phone?

Sitting at the chrome breakfast bar, Dermot reached for his phone and punched in Storm's number. Crossing his fingers, he entered her voicemail password and let out a silent whoop of delight when a disembodied voice told him he had no new messages and several saved messages.

Pulling a pad and pen towards him with his free hand, he started listening to all of Storm's voicemails. The first was a boring message from Sally, thanking Storm for lunch, but the next three were from Nico. Each more or less the same as the other: he missed her, he loved her, the sex between them was incredible and he couldn't wait until he saw her again.

Dermot's cheeks flamed with excitement. This was the proof he needed that Italian sweetheart Nico Alvise was no more than a cheating bastard. Still, he thought as he listened to the messages again, he was surprised Storm had actually gone to the trouble of sleeping with Nico. He didn't think she would do that for a story. Then, like a bolt from the blue, the reality of the situation hit. Storm hadn't slept with Nico for the scoop, she'd done it because she'd fallen in love with the guy. He'd known it since he saw that pap shot of them together but had told himself it couldn't be true. Hearing Nico's voice, warm with love, he knew there was no way Storm would come back to him. He'd give anything to listen to Nico's messages. In fact, he thought, why didn't he listen to Storm's messages to Nico? All he had to do was press whatever key gave him the message details and the number would be there for him to hack.

Minutes later Dermot had successfully managed to get hold of Nico's number. He checked his watch. It was shortly after 5 a.m. Chances were Nico would still be in bed and his phone on silent – worth trying to hack in now. Trembling, Dermot dialled Nico's number and tried accessing his voicemail, already thinking of various number combinations that might form his password. But, incredibly, Nico didn't have any security set up on his phone! Dermot could hardly believe it. Were these celebrities stupid? They deserved to get hacked if they didn't even try to protect their information.

As a second disembodied voice told him he had one new message and one saved message he waited with bated breath. The saved message was from Storm. She was crying into the phone, begging and pleading with Nico to call her. The message rambled on for ages as she wept about how sorry she was, how much she loved him, how he was her one, and how she would do anything if he would only talk to her. Dermot made a note of every word, ready to use in the future. It was all the proof he needed that Nico was a cheat but curiosity got the better of him as he pressed the right key to listen to the new message. This was from the girlfriend, Francesca.

Nico, please listen to me. You have to talk to Storm. I have never seen you so in love, you two are made for each other just as Paula and I are made for each other. Nico, don't be stubborn. You owe her the chance to explain herself. Please, I just want you to be happy.

Putting the phone down, Dermot was both excited and confused. Why was Nico's partner encouraging him to be with Storm and who the hell was Paula? Dermot knew he had some digging to do, but something told him this story was going to be one hell of a lot bigger than he'd originally thought.

Chapter Sixteen

It was a busy few days for Storm as she got used to life working in a coffee shop. Although she was no stranger to hard work, she'd forgotten how physically demanding being on your feet, rushing around after customers and constantly clearing and tidying, could be. She found she was too busy to think much about Nico or her old life in London. After a day at work in the café, Storm would rush home and fall straight to sleep, too exhausted to cry, then wake up, ready to do it all over again the next day.

The job was exactly what she needed. She got to stare at the sea, drink coffee and eat cakes. She had access to as many free newspapers as she liked, though she did her best to avoid them. Not only was she terrified of seeing more pictures of Nico doing God knows what, but she didn't really feel like seeing Dermot's name in the *Herald* either. Thankfully he'd left her alone since she'd resigned. Now she was no longer in the journalism game, she had stopped being of any use to him whatsoever.

Brighton was turning out to be a great fresh start for her. She had hoped that some of her old friends would have been ready to welcome her back, but it seemed they were still siding with Carly, and just like her former best friend nobody else here was ready to forgive and forget. Not for the first time Storm found herself thanking her lucky stars she'd found Ed. Sweet, lovely, funny Ed. He was like the big brother she had never had. Although they didn't have a lot in common, they spent their days chatting, laughing and joking. Ed was a typical surfer dude, who was relaxed, unambitious and had recently left his beloved St Ives for Brighton after falling in love with the place during a stag do with his mates.

'So why coffee?' Storm asked.

'I own a coffee bar in St Ives. Opening one here as well seemed like the next step, until I realised there was no surf but by then it was too late.' He grinned as he cleaned the expensive cappuccino machine before they opened.

Storm whistled in appreciation. 'I never knew there was so much money to be made in coffee?'

'Pah! Have you never heard of Starbucks?' he teased. 'No, it's not a huge money-spinner, but it's chilled and gives me enough money to fund my dream.'

'Which is?' Storm probed.

'To surf my way around Australia for a year. Catch some of those really big waves.'

'Wow! That sounds amazing.'

'Yeah! But I need to sell a lot more coffee to do that.'

'So what do you do when you need a surf fix?' she asked. 'I mean, Brighton's great, but like you say it's not known for its surfing.'

'I go back to Cornwall whenever I know the surf's going to be good, which is probably why my last assistant ran away to the circus!'

'But Cornwall's hours away!'

Ed laughed. 'It is. But I like the chance to get in my Beetle with my surfboard strapped to the top, just me, the open road and the dream of catching the perfect wave. Anyway what about you? What are your dreams?'

Storm continued sweeping the floor as she reflected on Ed's question. For years the answer would have been obvious: editor of a major newspaper or magazine. Now she had no desire to do either and was at a bit of a loss. 'You know what, Ed? I've got no idea any more.'

'Well, sometimes that's good. Means you're more open to whatever new opportunities come your way. Speaking of which, I can give you a hand to move your stuff tonight, if you like?'

Storm looked at him gratefully. She was moving into a studio flat above a newsagent's in town later that day and although she didn't have many belongings she didn't fancy shifting them all by herself. Jeff had offered to give her a hand, but Storm wouldn't hear of it. He'd done more than enough finding her the flat in the first place, never mind getting him to shift heavy luggage when she knew he had a bad back.

Jeff had looked so embarrassed when he'd got in from work a couple of days earlier and asked Storm if she was interested in living in a studio. 'I don't want you thinking you're not welcome here,' he said nervously. 'But a mate of mine has got a little flat, and knew you were staying with us, so he asked if you might be interested. I've been to see it and it's small but very nice. It needed a bit of redecoration, so I've painted it all bright white to make the most of the space. Other than that it's got all mod cons, and it's right in the heart of town with views of the sea . . . if you crane your neck and stand on one leg!'

Storm had been both surprised and touched that Jeff had gone to so much trouble on her behalf, but couldn't resist teasing him. 'Finally got tired of me cramping your style then?'

'Don't be like that,' Sally said, swatting her daughter's arm as her boyfriend went puce. 'You know Jeff's just trying to help.'

'And you know I'm kidding.' Storm grinned at them both. 'Seriously, you two have been great letting me stay here, but I need my own place and this flat sounds perfect. Thank you!'

After that Sally had gone into maternal overdrive, sorting out bed linen and food ready for Storm to take with her.

'I have moved out before, you know, Sal,' she said as she watched her mother fly around piling things together.

'I know, I know, I just want to help,' she insisted.

Now, as Storm opened the café door, ready to welcome in the first customers, she was surprised to see her mother striding purposefully towards her.

Dressed in jeans, trainers and biker jacket, Sally looked like she meant business.

'You're up early. What are you doing here?' Storm asked. 'Can I get you a coffee?'

'No, thanks love, I can't stop,' Sally replied breathlessly. 'I just wanted to ask you if you'd prefer white or navy towels? There's a sale on in town, and I thought I'd treat you to a few new things – fresh start and all that.'

'You don't have to!' Storm exclaimed, touched that Sally was going to so much trouble. 'I'll sort something out later this week.'

'I don't want you too, Stormy,' her mother protested. 'Let me do this for you.'

Storm said nothing. She knew she had to let Sally get on with it. This was her way of making up for those lost years and she was clearly relishing her second chance to play mum again. Storm found she didn't want to spoil it for her.

'Well, classic white would be lovely – thank you. But I insist you come in and have a coffee on me before hitting the shops. Besides you haven't met Ed yet.'

Not taking no for an answer, Storm hauled Sally inside and sat her at a cosy corner table.

'Ed,' she called to her colleague, who was emptying the bins out the back. 'Come and meet Sally.'

Hands full of sacks of rubbish, Ed appeared with a huge smile on his face. 'Mrs Saunders. Lovely to meet you at last. I'd offer to shake your hand, but as you can see . . .' he said, waving the bags around to make his point.

Right on cue rubbish spilled everywhere, leaving Ed red-faced as he bent down to start picking it all up.

'Please, call me Sally,' she said, leaping up from her chair to help him. 'Mrs Saunders makes me feel very old.'

'Oh, Sal, sit down,' Storm chided, shooing her mum away from the rubbish. 'You'll get your nice coat all grubby.

275

Besides, me and Ed have got a system going. This happens on an almost daily basis.'

'Please don't tell me you're clumsier than Storm?' Sally chuckled, returning to her seat. 'I don't think the world could stand another one of you chucking tea, coffee and heaven knows whatever else everywhere.'

'I'm afraid so, Sally.' Ed grinned as he shovelled the last of the rubbish back into the bag. 'I make Storm look graceful.'

'Wonders will never cease,' she said in mock amazement as he walked past her to the commercial bins outside, leaving Storm to make her mum's drink.

'Cappuccino, Sally?' she called over her shoulder to her mum, who was now engrossed in the latest copy of *Me Time*.

'Yes, please, love.'

As Storm filled the cappuccino maker with water, she heard the sound of the door opening and a pair of heels click-clacking their way across the flagstone floor.

'Can I get a latte to go and one of those skinny blueberry muffins too, please?'

At the sound of the pure Brighton accent Storm froze. It couldn't be? Not again. With a heavy heart she peeked over the coffee machine and saw it was just who she was terrified of bumping into again – Carly. Even though her head was bent over her smartphone and her blonde curls covered her face, Storm would have known her anywhere.

Taking a deep breath, she emerged from behind the machine and wiped her palms on her black apron.

'Carly, hello,' she said cautiously.

At the sound of her old friend's voice, Carly's head jerked up. She looked shocked.

'Storm! What are you doing here?'

'I work here.'

'You work here?' Carly exclaimed. 'Since when?'

'Since a couple of weeks ago. Things didn't work out for me in London,' she said quietly as she reached for a muffin and placed it in a brown paper bag. 'Did you want the latte and muffin to go?'

'You've got to be kidding me!' Carly spat as she stepped closer to the counter. 'I don't want *anything* from you. In fact, if you're working here, I'm never coming in again. I don't know who you think you are but this is my local coffee shop. You know I only live up the road. You've done this deliberately, just to annoy me. You're well out of order. I'm talking to Ed and getting you fired!'

Sally, who had previously been sitting in the corner minding her own business, leaped straight to her feet.

'Now just you wait a minute, my girl,' she butted in.

'Sally!' said Carly, visibly shocked. 'I didn't see you there.'

'Obviously,' Sally fired back at her. 'Now I know you think you've got the right to lay into Storm but you need to hear a few home truths, Carly. It's time you faced up to the fact that Storm has never been anything but a bloody good friend to you. Her stupid ex-boyfriend might have hurt you, but the only thing Storm has ever been guilty of is having terrible taste in men. Something you know all about if the papers are anything to go by. I mean, correct me if I'm wrong, but it was you who slept with a married man, and you who was stupid enough to take a bloody picture on your phone of the two of you.'

Carly flushed bright red, lost for words. 'Er, well, I . . .' she began, but Sally was just beginning to warm to her theme and in no mood for interruptions.

'It's time you took responsibility for your part in all this, lady. Nobody held a gun to your head and made you sleep with that bloke, you did that all by yourself. And Storm here has apologised until she's blue in the face for something she had no control over. It's time you got a bloody grip and stopped being so childish. Life's too short for stupid grudges, if anyone knows that it's me. My daughter's been like a sister to you, Carly, and I know you think I was so drunk when you two were kids I didn't know what was going on, but I did. I know Storm helped you with your homework, stood up for you in class when you were always getting into trouble, and I know that she was there for you when that scumbag you were engaged to cheated on you.

'Can you say that, Carly? Have you always been there for Storm? If you would but see it, she's been through hell and high water this year and could have done with a friend. But you've been too badly wronged, haven't you, to see any of that? Not only that, but correct me if I'm wrong . . . since you were in the papers you seem to have bagged yourself a nice little telly job. I suggest you start looking in a mirror, love – you might not like what you see.'

As Sally finished her verbal attack Carly raced out of the coffee shop in tears, almost knocking Ed over in her haste to get away.

'What happened?' he asked, standing in the doorway, covered in muck and scratching his head.

'Something and nothing,' Sally replied, before turning her attention back to her daughter.

'Now, love, do you mind if I get that coffee to go? I want to make sure I find you those towels before the shops sell out.'

Storm was dumbfounded. She'd had no idea her mum knew what had gone on at school, and couldn't believe she'd stood up for her like that. Looking at Sally, she felt a sudden rush of love. 'Coming right up, Mum,' she said softly.

Arms laden with boxes and bags, Storm and Ed pounded up two flights of stairs. Reaching the front door of her new home, Storm dumped her stuff on the floor, pulled the key from her jeans pocket and fiddled with the lock.

'Ta-dah!' she said, opening the front door.

Ed whistled as he walked in behind her. 'Not bad.'

'It's OK, isn't it?' exclaimed Storm as she walked around her new surroundings, taking them in.

There was no denying the place was tiny but all the furniture had been carefully chosen to make the best use of the space. A double bed had been raised to create a mezzanine, while underneath stood a small sofa, desk and large wardrobe. To the right stood a door to the en suite bathroom complete with shower and loo, while on the opposite side of the room stood the kitchen that looked as if it had been completely refurbished with glossy white cabinets and granite-effect worktop. Freshly painted white walls and birch-effect laminate flooring finished the flat off to perfection.

'I reckon this place is perfect for you,' said Ed.

'Me too.' Storm beamed. 'And the rent's super cheap.'

'Just as well, given that your boss is tighter than tight.'

'Agreed,' bantered Storm.

Walking over to the large bay window that overlooked Brighton's hustle and bustle, she realised Jeff had been right. If you stood on one leg it was just about possible to make out the sea.

It wasn't where she would have expected to find herself, or if she was honest the flat she would have chosen if she had gone house hunting herself. But as fresh starts went, this one wasn't bad. She had a home, a flat, a family . . . what more did she need to start the healing process?

'How about a takeaway?' Ed asked, interrupting Storm's thoughts. 'I'll nip out and get a curry, if you fancy one?'

Storm clapped her hands in delight. 'Perfect. You have given up your Friday night to help me, so it's only right we salvage some of it! Jeff also gave me a bottle of wine somewhere, I'll dig it out and we can start celebrating.'

'Sounds good to me. I'll be back in five.'

In fact Ed was gone the best part of an hour, but Storm didn't mind. It gave her the chance to sort out her new bed, dig out her pyjamas and give her fresh towels pride of place in the bathroom. By the time he returned with a huge bag of chicken tikka, lamb bhuna, rice and onion bhajis, Storm had only just found the wine and all-important glasses.

'You timed that well,' she said as he set the takeaway down on the breakfast bar. 'Red OK?'

'Lovely,' he replied, already digging into the poppadoms.

As Storm handed him a glass, she got to work dishing out the curry on to two mismatched plates.

'So, I'm curious,' Ed began. 'What was all that business with that woman earlier?'

'What woman?' replied Storm, buying time by playing dumb.

'The one your mum was screaming at earlier.'

Storm sighed. So much for the fresh start.

'She's an old friend. Very old actually as she now hates my guts. Mum was giving her hell for it. Anyway, I thought she was a friend of yours. She told me she'd get you to fire me.'

Ed snorted on his poppadom. 'I hardly *know* her. She's been in for a coffee twice. Though she does look familiar.'

'She's on the telly,' Storm explained. 'She has a style section on *Morning Cuppa.*'

'That's not where I know her from,' he said, shaking his head. 'No . . . wait! Got it. Wasn't she the one that was in the papers a while back for shagging that footballer?'

Storm groaned. Despite her promises to Carly that the story would be forgotten, it seemed sleeping with a footballer was still the one thing she was known for.

'Yeah, that's her.'

'So why does she hate you? You didn't go to the press with her story, did you?

Storm avoided Ed's gaze; he obviously didn't know how close to the mark he'd got. Storm had hoped that when she returned to Brighton she could finally stop talking about all of this, but it seemed her past was always going to haunt her. Taking a deep breath, she told him about Carly, Dermot, her move to London, job at the *Herald*, and why she'd left.

'Blimey!' Ed exclaimed when she'd finished. 'You've crammed more drama into the past year than most people get in one lifetime.'

'Tell me about it,' Storm sighed.

'And you're still not going to tell me who your celebrity boyfriend is?'

Storm laughed, and threw an onion bhaji at him. 'No way! All I want now is to leave this all behind and move on with my life, I'm saying no to any more drama!'

'I'll drink to that.' Ed smiled and raised his glass.

'Cheers!'

Dermot had to admit it. The last few days had been wildly stressful as he stalked, chased, researched, and sat in his car for hours, following both Nico and Francesca to get to the bottom of what was really going on in their relationship. It had been relentless and he had hardly had a chance to get home, but now as he saw Miles reading over his story with a huge smile on his face he knew it had all been worth it.

After listening to Storm and Nico's voicemails, Dermot had leaped into action and hacked into Storm's email. He hadn't uncovered much, but he did find a brief message from Francesca expressing her sorrow that Storm and Nico had split up. The message itself hadn't been a lot to go on but as Francesca had sent the email from her work account it told Dermot exactly where she worked and he vowed to go straight there. He'd sat outside all day until she left and then followed her home. He'd expected her to go to the Hampstead house he knew she shared with Nico, but instead she'd taken the tube to Waterloo station where she boarded a train to Bournemouth. Dermot hadn't had time to buy a ticket so had to buy one on the train at a heavily inflated price.

When Francesca got out at Bournemouth he followed her out on to the concourse and watched a petite young woman with auburn hair and blue eyes wave frantically at her. Francesca caught sight of the woman and her face broke into a huge smile. She rushed towards her and kissed her passionately. Together the two walked hand in hand out of the station and got into a nearby Volkswagen. Dermot, thinking on his feet, summoned a cab and told the driver to follow them. Twenty minutes later, they'd arrived at their destination – a little cottage near the sea. Watching the petite woman unlock the front door, Dermot realised the house belonged to her and wondered if this could be the mysterious Paula. After asking the cabbie to take him back to the station, he got the train to London and immediately started researching the house and its owner.

It didn't take long to get results. He soon discovered the house was jointly owned by Francesca and Paula. More digging into Paula's background revealed she was an architect and a proud lesbian, frequently campaigning for gay rights. Dermot's head was spinning as he tried to make sense of it all but more trips to Bournemouth, taking secret shots of Francesca and Paula together, told him what he wanted to know – they were lovers, meaning Francesca's relationship with Nico was a sham.

Realising his scoop had the potential to be one of the biggest of the year, Dermot had confided in Sabrina, sheepishly admitting he'd learned the truth through phone hacking.

'Well, don't tell Miles that, for fuck's sake,' she'd said. 'All you do is say you did an interview with Storm. There's enough in there on the voicemails she left Nico for it to sound as though you've spoken to her directly. Then we can put in the truth about Nico, Francesca and Paula afterwards.'

Dermot kissed Sabrina passionately on the mouth. 'You're a genius!'

Now, as he finished the final line of his article, Dermot felt like punching the air with delight. Finally he'd got his scoop, and it was a much better story than the stupid honey trap he'd tried to make Storm go along with. Popping his head around Miles's door, he checked that his editor was happy.

'Good work, Dermot,' he said thoughtfully, as he finished reading the story. 'This will make a brilliant front page on Sunday, and well done for getting Storm to give you an interview. I don't know how you managed it but you've obviously got better people skills than I gave you credit for.'

Dermot flushed with pride. 'Thanks, boss.'

He walked back to his desk, gathered his coat and headed to the pub to celebrate. Life had never tasted sweeter.

Chapter Seventeen

Storm woke to the sound of seagulls outside her flat. Climbing down from the mezzanine, she walked over to the window and looked out across the city beneath her. It was her first Sunday morning in her new home and although it pained her to admit it she had been dreading it. She had never lived alone before, and over the years had got so used to spending the day with family, Dermot, and later Chelsea, she wasn't sure how to fill so many lonely hours. Before she met Nico, she and Chelsea often headed to Spitalfields on Sunday mornings where they'd grab coffee, bagels and a vintage bargain. Then, they'd gossip over a couple of glasses of champagne at Bedales.

Then there were the few precious Sundays she had spent with Nico. Lying in bed, talking, laughing, watching movies and making love, she had felt such hope for their future. Naively she'd thought they had years and years of Sundays to spend together. At the memory of it all she felt a stab of fresh pain. Nico was gone for ever, there was no point in thinking of him any more.

Now it was just Storm. With nobody else to please or consider she watched the street beneath her preparing for the day ahead. Tourists had arrived early to soak up the atmosphere, while directly below locals were popping into the newsagent's for papers and pints of milk. She frowned as she saw them walk out of the shop armed with copies of the *Herald*. If there was one thing she didn't miss about her old life, it was working for that newspaper. She knew it had been the right decision for her to leave. She still felt bad about the way things had been left with Miles, though. Checking her watch, she realised it was only 8 a.m., far too early for her to be up on a Sunday morning. Taking her tea, she went back to bed and pulled the duvet high over her head. Time to shut out the world for a couple more hours.

The sound of the phone ringing woke Storm from a bizarre dream where she was making coffee in a racing stables. The job was relentless as she handed steaming hot cups out to everyone, from the jockeys to the grooms. Scrambling for the mobile that was right by her bed, Storm saw that she had three missed calls from Sally and now her mother was calling again. Shit! There had to be something wrong.

'Mum, is everything OK? Are Bailey and Lexie all right?' she asked frantically.

'They're fine, love,' Sally replied urgently. 'They're not why I'm calling. Have you seen the paper?'

'No. What paper?' Storm was confused.

'The *Herald*,' Sally replied.

Storm's blood ran cold. What had happened? Had Dermot somehow managed to turn Nico over after all?

'What is it, Mum?' she begged.

Sally took a deep breath before she answered. 'There's a story about you, Nico and Francesca.'

Storm didn't need to hear any more. Shocked, she dropped the phone and raced downstairs to the newsagent's, still dressed in her pyjamas. Quickly, she scanned the shelves for the paper and soon found a pile of them on one of the bottom shelves.

Snatching a copy, she was horrified to see her own face staring back at her, underneath the headline *Sex, Lies and Lesbians.*

The picture was a pap shot Dermot must have taken of her and Nico holding hands as they walked along Royal Crescent in Bath. Seeing it, Storm felt a wave of fresh hurt. The glance the two of them were sharing was so intimate – it was the look of two people falling in love. Shaking with rage, she glanced at the story below and immediately saw the piece had been written as though she had talked directly to the paper about her feelings for Nico.

She checked the paper again to see who had written it. As if there could be any doubt – *Exclusive by Dermot Whelan.*

The rat! The rat! The fucking, double-crossing, slimy, cheating rat.

Slamming a handful of change down on to the newsagent's counter, she ran back into her flat and read the piece. It spanned seven pages in total and the amount of information Dermot had managed to get hold of was extraordinary. Every gory detail of her affair with Nico had been laid bare for the world to know about. How they'd met, how they'd fallen in love, and how they'd split up along with Storm's pleas for them to be reunited, how sorry she was that she hadn't revealed she was really a journalist.

The reporter, who was worried her career would impact on her new relationship, told Mr Alvise she was really an airline hostess.

'You mean the world to me, Nico, how can I ever make this up to you? I have never loved anyone in the way I've loved you. I would do anything to make this right,' she was quoted as saying.

She had never told anyone that. How had they got this? She read the rest of her so-called interview, feeling sicker by the second. It was peppered with quotes, things she and Nico had said to one another during and after their relationship, personal things she would never have told anyone. The rest of the piece was all about Francesca being a lesbian and how she had been in a relationship with Paula Manning for some time. Dermot had managed to find out that they had bought a home together near Bournemouth and even got hold of a pap shot of the two of them sharing a kiss.

Further down, he had pointed out that Nico was as guilty as Storm of telling lies. That his pretence of being in a committed relationship was nothing more than a sham, and he'd been making money off the back of his wholesome image when in fact he was nothing more than a playboy who slept his way around town. Which was a blatant lie.

By now Storm had read enough. Throwing the paper in

the bin, she felt fury growing within her. That fucker! How dare he do this to her, Nico, and poor, poor Francesca? Storm's heart went out to them both – this would devastate their lives, and the lives of their families. They didn't deserve this. And neither did she.

Instinctively she reached for her phone to try and call them, before common sense kicked in and she put it down. Storm realised she was the last person they would want to hear from. The whole piece had been written as if she had spoken to the paper first hand – there was no way either of them would forgive her or believe that she'd had no idea this was going to be in the press. She wondered how on earth Dermot had got hold of all those details, never mind the quotes. The things he had unearthed were so personal, things Nico had only ever said to her, and she had only said to Nico . . . well, more specifically, Nico's voicemail as he had never actually taken her calls.

Suddenly the truth dawned on Storm – Dermot had hacked her voicemail. She'd rip that lying little bastard limb from limb! She would have said this was a new low, even for him, but she already knew there was nothing he wouldn't do to further his career. Looking back, she should have reported him to the Press Complaints Commission when he'd confessed to bugging her conversation with Carly all those months ago. And she should have been suspicious that he'd suddenly stopped sending flowers, texts, and calling her after she'd left the paper. She could have kicked herself – she'd been so stupid, making mistake after mistake. Storm assumed he had left her alone after she'd quit the *Herald* because she was no longer of any use to him; she should have known better. It was clear as day to her now – he'd been plotting the ultimate revenge.

Rage tore through her as she reached for her phone and punched in his number. But it went straight to voicemail and she was in no mood to leave a message. Instead she rang Miles.

'Storm, admiring your front page?' he said, picking up on the first ring.

'Don't be stupid, Miles. I want to know what Dermot told you about this story. It looks as though I spoke to you exclusively about this.'

'Well, you did, didn't you? He told me that he'd spent days talking you into it. I actually thought he had no chance, but he surprised me. Perhaps he picked up some interview tips from you.'

'No, Miles,' Storm sighed. 'He picked up nothing from me. What Dermot has actually done is spent days hacking into my voicemail, and then pretending I spoke to him directly.'

'What?' Miles was incredulous. 'You mean, you didn't give him an interview?'

'Do you honestly think that's something I would do?' she fumed. 'I mean, I know you hate me for the way I left, but I never thought you would stoop as low as him and dress up phone hacking as an interview.'

The editor sounded flustered for once. 'Storm, I'll get to the bottom of this, you have my word, but if what you're telling me is true, I'll fire Dermot.'

'I don't care what you do to him, but I'm suing you for this. You've ruined my life, and the lives of others, and for what? You should be ashamed of yourself,' Storm blasted him. 'If I ever had any lingering doubts about leaving a career in journalism, you've just convinced me I made the right decision.'

She slammed the phone down and stared glumly at the handset. Shock and disgust were pulsing through her veins. She couldn't believe this was happening. All she wanted to do was curl up in her bed and shut out the world. She glanced at her phone. There were three missed calls from Chelsea and one voicemail. Flinging herself back on to her bed, Storm propped herself up on her pillows and dialled her mailbox. As she heard Chelsea's voice she felt a pang of loneliness. If ever there was a time she needed a friend it was now.

'Babes! I've just seen the paper and want you to know I'm sickened. I've told Miles there was no way you'd ever have given an interview about Nico, certainly not to Dermot, and I've handed in my notice, babe. Since you've left the place has gone from bad to worse, and I told him there was no way I'd work for a paper that would behave like that. The bastard's making me work my three months' notice, but I don't care . . . I'm on my way to LA now to see Adam, but I'll give you a call in a few days. Maybe you could come out here for a break? I know Adam would love to meet you and have you stay. Anyway, babe, chin up and forget those fuckers.'

Storm couldn't believe her friend had quit her job over this. Not for the first time she realised she owed Chelsea big time. And if she was capable of making a grand gesture then so was Storm. Reaching for her diary, she looked through her contact information for Nico's mobile number. Storm might have deleted his number from her mobile, but she'd still kept a physical note, just in case she ever needed to contact him.

Slowly she punched in the digits and waited for the call to connect. As the phone rang Storm found she was holding her breath, trying to think of the perfect thing to say when Nico answered. But after two rings her call was diverted straight to voicemail. Worried there was a fault on the line she hung up and redialled, but this time there was no mistake. Nico's phone had been permanently switched off, and after realising Dermot had hacked her voicemail she didn't wait to leave a message.

She pressed the end call key, tears welling in her eyes. All she wanted to do was explain to Nico what had happened. But this was no time for a pity party. She wouldn't give Dermot the satisfaction. Instead she rooted around her wardrobe for her trainers and trackie bottoms and decided to deal with her frustrations by going for a run.

She wasn't a good runner, but it was the only thing she could think of that would help blow off some steam. The day was as overcast as Storm felt, wet, cold and windy, and as the rain beat down around her, Storm pounded the pavements harder and faster, each strike making her feel stronger. She would get through this latest nightmare, she told herself. She still had her family, her job and a new flat, this would not ruin her fresh start.

As if to prove the point, as she ran along the promenade and passed the coffee shop she decided to head into work and talk to Ed.

'Fancy seeing you here.' He smiled as she appeared in

the doorway, a hot sweaty mess. 'What's the matter . . . can't keep away?'

'Something like that.' She grinned. 'Any chance of a smoothie?'

He grinned back. 'Take a seat and I'll bring it over.'

As Storm took a seat by the window, she ignored the prying stares of other customers and instead turned on her smartphone. She saw there were over fifty missed calls, all from numbers she didn't recognise, as well as a text from her mum.

The house is overrun with paps, love. But they've no idea where you are and I've no intention of telling them. Jeff says he's going to throw a bucket of cold water over them soon if they don't bugger off. In the meantime, stay strong, love. Mum xxx

Reading the message, Storm felt her heart melt. Thank God for her mother. At least she was taking on the paps for Storm. That really would be the last thing she could cope with. Interrupting her thoughts, Ed placed a glass of green gunk in front of her.

'Power smoothie,' he told her proudly. 'It's got kale, spinach and wheatgrass in there – just the thing for the recovering athlete.'

Storm looked suspiciously at the glass. It looked gross, but she wasn't about to say so.

'Thanks.' She smiled, taking a tentative first sip.

'How is it?' Ed asked eagerly, pulling out the chair opposite and sitting down.

Trying desperately to choke it down, Storm smiled at him. 'Very, er, nice. A bit lumpy, but then kale can be hard to break down.'

Ed burst out laughing. 'You should see your face! Sorry, I made you a berry one, I just thought this might take your mind off what's been going on today.'

Storm arched an eyebrow. The cheeky bastard! Still, he was right. Drinking that disgusting concoction had been the first time all day she'd thought about something other than being on the front page of the country's leading weekend tabloid.

'So,' said Ed, as he returned with Storm's favourite berry blast smoothie, 'I wasn't expecting to see you on the front page this morning. Are you all right?

'Fine.' She shrugged, taking a big gulp of her drink.

'Did you know the paper was running the story?' he asked, getting straight to the point.

Storm shook her head as she drained her glass. 'Not a clue. I'm used to being the one writing about other people, not the one being written about.' She smiled ruefully.

'Well, that must suck.'

Storm eyeballed him, unsure if he was taking the piss. 'Yeah, it does. Still, I'm sure some people would say I deserved it.'

'Bullshit. Everyone should be allowed a private life. I take it that story was written by your ex?'

Storm nodded.

'What a bastard!' Ed exclaimed. 'He would only have done that out of revenge.'

Despite her pain, Storm couldn't help smiling. Ed certainly had the measure of Dermot. What a shame she hadn't seen straight through him herself three years ago.

'Well, on the bright side, at least I don't have to keep

asking you who your celeb boyfriend was.'

'Every cloud . . .'

'So, can I ask, how much of that story was true?' Ed spoke more gently this time.

Storm sighed, pushed her empty glass to the edge of the table and wondered just how much to tell him. She'd wanted to keep her life with Nico a secret; it sounded silly, but she'd felt that the fewer people who knew about him, the more easily she might be able to move on. Little chance of that now.

'Most of it was true,' she admitted.

Quickly she outlined the facts to him. How she'd met Nico, and how she had been asked to honey trap him.

'Nico and I did fall in love, and, yes, Francesca is a lesbian, but they didn't let people assume they were a couple to try and fool the public, as Dermot tried to make out. It's because her grandparents disowned her when they discovered her sexuality when she was a teenager, and in the end the gossip drove her out of her village. The whole experience has left her paranoid it could happen again. And after reading this pack of lies, I can't honestly say I blame her. The worst thing is, I think they were on the verge of coming clean when Nico found out I was a reporter and assumed I was screwing him over.'

'Which you weren't,' Ed put in.

'I wasn't,' Storm agreed. 'I only went along with the honey trap plan to try and protect him from something like this. I was about to ask my editor for a transfer to another department so I could tell Nico the truth, but then he found out and the rest is history.'

'So what are you going to do now?' Ed continued.

'Nothing.' She shrugged. 'What can I do apart from carry on with my life and hope it all blows over?'

'Not tempted to ring Nico and explain?'

Storm shook her head. 'I tried, he wouldn't take my call. I'll keep trying, but I'm not holding my breath. He made it pretty clear when we last spoke that he never wanted to hear from me again. I can't imagine now he and Francesca are front-page news that he's changed his mind.'

Ed's expression softened as he leaned over the coffee table to give Storm's arm a reassuring squeeze. 'Well, I suppose you could always take a leaf out of your friend Carly's book, and get your own style segment on a morning TV show on the back of all this.'

Storm laughed bitterly. 'Yeah, because I'm a real style icon, aren't I? I think battered trainers and faded trackies, combined with eau de stinky sweat, are very this season. Nah, think I'll stick to making coffee if it's all right with you?'

Ed smiled. 'That's more than all right with me.'

Nico walked over to the window and gingerly peered through the Venetian blinds.

'Don't do that,' Francesca warned. 'You'll only encourage them.'

As if by magic, a flurry of flash bulbs went off and what seemed like hundreds of journalists screamed his name. *'Nico, Nico, just give us five minutes.' 'Aren't you going to say anything, Nico?' 'How do you feel about deceiving the British public, Nico?'*

Scowling, he snapped the blind shut and sat down at the

kitchen table next to Francesca, who was trying to get on with some paperwork.

'Fucking scum,' he hissed. 'Haven't they got anything better to do than harass innocent people? I feel like going out there and tearing them apart.'

'You've been saying that all morning,' Francesca pointed out, head bent over some files. 'Can't you just ignore them? They'll get bored and move on to someone else soon enough.'

'They shouldn't be bothering us at all,' he shouted, leaping to his feet and pacing up and down the room. Usually, if Nico had a problem or stress to work out, he'd go for a run, but with paps on his doorstep there was no chance of that. Instead he'd had to resort to pacing up and down inside the house and felt like a prisoner in his own home.

Ever since his agent had rung late last night to tell him about the story that was due to break, he had been livid. Seeing the front page in the morning had done nothing to lighten his mood. He'd read it and re-read it over and over, unable to believe that Storm would betray him like that. And with Dermot, her ex, of all people. That is, of course, if she really was his ex. Maybe they'd never split up in the first place. Sighing, Nico ran his hands through his dark hair. He didn't know what to think any more. What he did know was that he should have realised Storm was just stringing him along. And to think he'd actually fallen in love with her!

Being in Italy for a couple of weeks had given him chance to think. Perhaps he had been too hasty. Perhaps there had been a perfectly good explanation. He hated to admit it but he missed her . . . where was the harm in talking to her? Francesca had been right, he'd mused. He owed her that much at least.

But waking up to this mayhem had shown him how much of a sucker the girl obviously thought he was. And he'd thought he'd found the one! What a joke. No, as far as Nico was concerned, Storm had taught him a very valuable lesson. All women were trouble and he was steering clear from now on.

As for Francesca, his heart went out to her. To her credit she had taken it remarkably well, Nico thought. When he got the call last night, he'd rung her immediately at Paula's and warned her about the breaking story. He'd expected her to stay put in Dorset or even to go away somewhere with Paula, but she'd driven straight back to London to support him. She'd also called her friends and bosses at work and told them the truth about who she really was.

'Are you sure you're OK about all of this?' he asked, flopping on to the huge leather sofa.

Francesca looked up from her work, and pulled her glasses off her face. 'You know what? I'm surprisingly calm about it. I've been dreading this day for a long time, but now it's happened I realise that I can't keep hiding my true self from the world. It's time to be me.'

Nico looked at Francesca with admiration. She really was incredible. It was just a shame her grandparents never came round to seeing that. They had died years ago without ever forgiving her. But it was their loss, Nico had always felt.

'Are you sure?' he asked.

Francesca smiled and nodded at him. 'Very sure. And, Nico, I feel like I need to apologise to you. If anything, I've held you back all these years. Your *mamma* was right, you should never have given up on love and marriage just to protect me. I can cope on my own. It's time for you to go out and live your real life now.'

Smiling, he pulled her into his arms and held her tight, He would always be grateful that this incredible woman had entered his life, he was proud to call her his best friend.

'How did it go with your boss?' he asked, releasing her from his arms.

Francesca sighed. 'They've really surprised me. When I told him he said he was proud of me and that I should have come to him sooner. He laughed and said I had some very old-fashioned ideas if I thought that being gay might impact my career. It's all going to be fine.'

'How has Paula taken it?'

'Well, she's delighted I'm ready to face the world as myself but worried about the effect this horrible story will have on all of us.'

'She's not the only one,' he growled. 'I've made an appointment with my lawyer in the morning, to see if we have any kind of case against the *Herald*. I still don't know how Storm could do this to us.'

'I'm not so sure she did,' replied Francesca thoughtfully. Pushing her paperwork aside, she got to her feet and joined him on the couch. 'It all seems very out of character.'

'Pah! Don't make the same mistake I did, Francesca.

She played you and me for fools, and I never want to hear that woman's name mentioned again.'

'I take it I can't persuade you to hear her out then?' Francesca said, swinging her legs up and resting them on top of Nico's.

'Hell will freeze over first.'

'But she's called you several times today. She wouldn't do that if she was as guilty as you suspect.'

Nico frowned. There was nothing Storm could say to make any of this better, and she was the last person he wanted to hear from. As if by magic, his phone rang again – Storm.

'Just talk to the girl,' Francesca insisted, spotting his caller ID. 'It's not fair to blame her for all of this without at least finding out her side of things.'

Nico thought for a minute and picked up his phone. 'Storm, if you ring me again I'll have you prosecuted for harassment. Now leave me and my friend alone.'

'I thought you were going to talk to her!' Francesca wailed.

'I listened to everything she had to say.'

'But you didn't let her say a word.'

'Exactly. That girl tells nothing but lies, I wasn't going to give her the opportunity to tell a few more.'

Nico turned his phone off and threw it on the coffee table. Storm might have played him once, but he was damned if he was giving her the chance to do it again.

Storm stared at her phone in despair. When Nico had finally answered her heart had leaped. Finally she was

300

going to get the chance to talk to him. But he had sounded so menacing, she'd felt almost frightened. She didn't think it was possible for him to have been any angrier with her than when he'd last spoken to her, but somehow he'd outdone himself. She felt like screaming. They'd both been stitched up and yet she was going through this alone.

Wandering over to the fridge, she pulled open the door and examined the contents. Aside from some leftover curry and half a pint of milk, it was bare. She sank to the floor and buried her face in her hands. She wasn't sure how much more of this she could take. Seeing Ed at the coffee shop earlier had left her feeling positive and she'd jogged back to her flat in the rain in a surprisingly upbeat mood.

But turning on her phone again and seeing over one hundred missed calls, all from journalists begging her to reveal more of her story, she felt trapped. How much longer was she going to have to keep paying for one stupid mistake? Ever since she'd told Dermot about Carly she'd been plagued by bad luck. Usually she prided herself on her ability to bounce back after any setback, but now Storm's resilience was wearing thin.

Too exhausted to stand, she crawled over to her bed and pulled the covers over her head. She didn't care that she was still dressed in her sweaty running gear, and even had her trainers on. What did any of it matter any more? Her eyes wandered towards her bedside table where her dad's gold watch was lying next to her alarm clock. She reached for it and gently rubbed the face as she so often did when she needed reassurance. But it was no good, even her usual comforts were failing her now. As the rain lashed down against the window, she drifted off into a dream-filled sleep where queues of people snaked outside her front door, all screaming and shouting at her that she was a terrible person.

As the rain turned to thunder, Storm found the shouting only got louder and louder.

'Open up. I want to talk to you!' one insistent voice was yelling over and over again.

Coming to, Storm sat bolt upright in shock only to discover the claps of thunder that she thought she had dreamed were actually the sound of someone banging at her door.

'Storm, will you open this door?'

Scrambling out of bed, Storm unlocked her front door only to come face to face with the last person she'd expected to see – Carly.

Chapter Eighteen

'What are you doing here?'

'Thought it was time you and me had a talk,' Carly replied.

Storm ran a hand through her hair, sweaty and tangled from her run, as she drank in Carly's appearance. Although she was wet from the rain, she looked as gorgeous as ever. Her long blonde hair looked as if it had been recently highlighted and her natural make-up made her eyes sparkle. Dressed in a fitted black wool jacket, jeans and knee-high boots, her appearance screamed style and Storm could fully understand why she had become such a hit on *Morning Cuppa*. It was wonderful to see her doing so well, but Storm was too tired to deal with any more today.

'Carly, I know you want to tear strips off me, but not now, all right?' she said, about to shut the door in her former friend's face.

'Actually that's not why I'm here. Can I come in?' she said quietly.

Surprised, Storm opened the door and ushered Carly inside.

'This is sweet,' she said, standing in the middle of Storm's flat and looking around her.

Looking at her flat through Carly's eyes, Storm almost felt like laughing at her ex-friend's politeness. With cardboard boxes and dirty washing all over the floor sweet was the very last thing the place could be described as.

'No, it's not. But thanks for saying it. Can I get you a drink?'

'Tea would be nice,' Carly said, perching on a large cardboard box and setting her bag on the floor. 'So how are you?'

'Fine, you know,' Storm replied as she flicked on the kettle and quickly rinsed two mugs under the kitchen tap.

'Good, good. And the job at the coffee shop?'

'Well, I haven't been fired yet, if that's what you mean? Look, I don't mean to be rude, but what do you want? I've had a hell of a day and if it's all right with you I'd love to postpone our next fight.'

Carly took a deep breath. 'I've seen the papers this morning. Storm, you must feel awful.'

'I do,' she replied, pouring boiling water into the mugs and adding milk to the tea. 'Is that why you're here then? To gloat over my downfall?'

'Actually, I've come to say I'm sorry for the way I've treated you.'

Shocked, Storm dropped the mugs she was holding,

causing scalding hot tea to spill everywhere.

'Bollocks!' she shouted, brown milky liquid running down her legs. Grabbing a roll of kitchen towel, she frantically started mopping up. Carly joined her.

'I see you haven't changed,' she said wryly. 'Still as clumsy as ever.'

'Yeah, well, why change the habit of a lifetime?' said Storm, standing up. 'So . . . tea?'

Carly shook her head. 'I've a better idea. How about we go to the pub? I reckon you could do with it after the day you've had.'

Storm stared at her in surprise. Of all the endings to this day she could have imagined, she would never have predicted this.

'Sure. Give me ten minutes to get showered and changed.'

The pub at the end of Storm's road was a quiet traditional place. With large fireplaces, wooden beams and red velour banquettes, it was a world away from any bright, trendy London watering hole, but Storm had always found the place homely. Sitting in a quiet corner, she poured two large glasses from the bottle of red Carly had bought and eyed her cautiously.

'So . . . you mentioned something about an apology?'

'Christ!' Carly groaned. 'You're not going to make this easy for me, are you?'

'I'm just curious,' Storm explained. 'You've got to admit that our last few meetings haven't exactly gone well. I'm wondering what's changed.'

305

Carly paused and took a sip of wine before she spoke. 'I've been so cross with you for such a long time now, Storm. I hated you for telling Dermot about what had happened between me and Aston.'

Storm hung her head in shame. If she could turn the clock back she would. 'I know, I wish I could change it. In fact, I wish I could change a lot of things, including ever getting involved with Dermot Whelan.'

'Well, that's the thing. All this time I've been cross with the wrong person. It wasn't your fault, Storm, it was mine,' Carly said. 'Sally gave me a wake-up call the other day when she yelled at me. I was so upset after she said all that stuff, but you know what? She was right. I was the one who slept with a married man and I was the one who took a stupid picture on my phone. I blamed everyone but myself.'

Storm shook her head. 'No, Carly, you made a mistake, that's all. You didn't deserve to have your face splashed all over the papers. Dermot's the one who's to blame. He lied to us both, but I was stupid for not seeing any other way out other than to move to London.'

'We've both made mistakes,' Carly agreed. 'But the biggest one has to have been letting this affect our friendship. Sally was right again about that. You have always been there for me, and I was stupid ever to forget that.'

Storm smiled. 'Mum's been right about a lot of things lately.'

'Wow, you've started calling Sally Mum! When did that happen?'

'When she started behaving like one.' Storm shrugged. 'A lot's happened, and I felt we should forgive, forget and move on.'

'Any chance we can do the same?' Carly asked quietly. 'I can't tell you how much I've missed you, Storm.'

She nodded. 'I know how you feel. It seems so weird that I don't know what's going on in your life. Although I know you've got a job on the telly now.'

Carly rolled her eyes. 'It seems sleeping with Aston Booth wasn't such a bad career move, but I'm still not proud of what I did. However, yes, the telly job is going well, but the public haven't let me forget my mistake. I still get hate mail sent to the TV studios calling me a home-wrecker, or journalists raking up my past when I'm mentioned in the press.'

'I'm still very proud of you, Carly. You've done so well after everything that happened,' Storm assured her.

Pouring them both another glass of wine, Carly shrugged. 'If there's one thing I've learned it's that you've got to make the most of any opportunity that comes your way.'

'And what about this boyfriend of yours? Jez told me you were seeing some events organiser?'

'Oh, him. Nah, that was over months ago,' she replied, shaking her head. 'But I have started dating this hot TV producer at work.'

Storm smiled at her. 'What's he like?'

'Young and fit.' Carly smirked. 'It's not serious. But what about you? I read the paper but I'm so confused. When did you start dating Nico Alvise? And why the hell did you give Dermot an interview? Finally why are you back in Brighton, working in a seafront coffee shop? What's going on with you, Storm?'

Shaking her head, she topped up their glasses. 'This story definitely requires more booze.'

Slowly, she filled Carly in on everything that had been happening in her life since she'd moved to London. Careful not to leave out any detail, she told her everything in a way that only two women who have been friends for a lifetime can communicate.

When she'd finished Carly was speechless. 'I don't know what to say, babe. Shit. I'm so, so sorry.'

Storm shrugged. Nothing anyone could do would change anything. She would just have to get through it all as best she could.

'So what are you going to do now? I mean, you're not giving up journalism, are you?'

'I think so, yes. It doesn't feel right to me any more.'

'But it was all you ever wanted to do,' Carly pointed out.

Storm fiddled with one of the paper coasters on the table, shredding it into tiny bits.

'Dreams change,' she replied. 'I'll find something else that excites me the way journalism used to. Who knows? Maybe I'll become the UK's go to barista.'

'Not the way you spill drinks!' Carly teased. 'But what about Nico? You still love him, I guess?'

At the mention of his name, Storm felt a rush of emotion. She'd been so strong all day but now the combination of shock, exhaustion and alcohol sent her over the edge.

'Yes, I love him.' She sighed hopelessly. 'But I have to start getting over him. He never wants to see me again, Carly, and I have to accept that.'

Dragging her chair over to Storm's side, Carly wrapped one arm around her old friend.

'Storm, let me tell you something you told me all those years ago, when that cheating bastard devastated my life. You will get through this, and you won't always hurt this much. I promise.'

As Storm rested her head on Carly's shoulder, she wiped her tears away with the back of her hands.

'When did you get so wise?'

'When I started hanging out with the smartest girl in the class,' Carly whispered. 'My biggest mistake was letting her go. What do you say, Storm? Do you think we can be friends again?'

Storm drew back from Carly's embrace and looked her up and down. For so long now she'd thought they were over; that she would never make things up with Carly no matter how hard she tried. She'd grieved for their broken friendship, the loss hitting her as hard as if someone had died. But now the unthinkable had happened. Carly was here, begging for forgiveness and offering Storm the chance to make things up. Was it really possible they could wipe away everything that had happened and go back to being friends once more? Or had too much happened and this was all too little too late?

Storm sighed as she opened her mouth to speak. 'Carly, I've always been your friend and always will be,' she replied, pulling her in for a hug. 'I love you like a sister, and you'll never, ever get rid of me.'

As Dermot sat down outside Miles's office, waiting to be called in, he tapped his feet up and down nervously. This morning, wearing his best navy suit and arriving at work with Sabrina by his side, he'd expected to be greeted like a conquering hero. Usually when a reporter landed a scoop this big there'd be high fives, pats on the back and talks of long pub lunches with plenty of booze. But since sitting down at his desk he'd felt like he was being given the cold shoulder by everyone. When Karen, Miles's secretary, told him the editor wanted to see him immediately, Dermot felt a rush of fear. Usually Miles came straight out to the huge open-plan office and announced hearty congratulations on a job well done. Being called in for a private meeting didn't signal anything good.

Finally Miles was ready for him, and as Dermot walked into the glass-walled office, he knew he was in trouble when he saw not just the editor but Polly from Human Resources.

'Take a seat, Dermot,' Miles said, gesturing to the hard office chair opposite his desk. 'Before we begin I want to ask you a question. How was Storm when you interviewed her?'

Miles's bluntness left Dermot on the back foot. 'Sorry. What do you mean?'

'Storm. You remember, your ex-girlfriend, a highly gifted journalist and former colleague. How was she when you interviewed her?'

'Fine. You know, getting on with her life,' he replied quickly.

Miles regarded him thoughtfully. 'I notice the article didn't say anything about where Storm's living now, or what she's doing. We've referred to her in the article as an ex-*Herald* journalist, but usually we mention people's current jobs and the town they're living in. Why are those details missing from your piece?'

Dermot flushed. Shit! Why hadn't he thought about that? He knew she was back in Brighton, the GPS tracker told him that much, but he had no idea what she was doing there. He should have asked Chelsea. She and Storm had been as thick as thieves. But then Chelsea also hated his guts, Dermot reasoned. The chances of her telling him anything would have been zero. Quickly he thought on his feet.

'Just an oversight, Miles,' he replied smoothly. 'But it doesn't affect the story. We've had so many hits on our website along with emails from people saying how much they enjoyed the piece.'

What Dermot didn't add was that most of the emails he'd received congratulating him on a job well done had been from his mum and his aunt. And actually the public had been surprisingly hostile to the story, saying things like they felt sorry for all three people involved and why couldn't they be left to live their lives in peace? If that was the sort of story the *Herald* wanted to cover the readers would be buying another paper in future.

But Miles had heard enough. Getting to his feet, he walked menacingly towards Dermot. 'It wasn't an

311

oversight, you didn't know. And the reason for that is because you didn't bloody interview her! Now tell me the truth about how you got that story.'

'That is how I got the story. I called Storm, and asked for her side of things and she agreed, out of loyalty to me, to give me an interview,' he said, panicking.

'Bullshit!' Miles roared. 'I know the truth. You hacked her phone and then you hacked Nico Alvise's. I've had them both threatening legal action, thanks to you. When will you learn that nothing gets past me? Now, for once in your life, tell me the truth. Did you get Storm's story by hacking her phone?'

For a minute Dermot said nothing. Then, realising the game was up, he nodded. He knew there was no getting out of this one.

Miles returned to his seat beside Polly, and pursed his lips. 'You don't need me to tell you how serious this is, Dermot. Phone hacking is illegal, and we don't use stories like that here. You've left me with no choice. You're fired. Clear your desk and get out immediately.'

'What! You can't be serious,' he protested. 'I made one tiny mistake but the story was all true. Storm did have a relationship with Nico and his alleged girlfriend is a lesbian.'

Miles said nothing. Instead he turned to Polly.

'Dermot, phone hacking is grounds for instant dismissal,' she said. 'Security will be here shortly to escort you from the premises.' She opened the office door, gesturing for him to leave.

'Miles, please don't do this to me,' Dermot pleaded,

turning to his editor. 'Look, I'll do anything . . . please give me another chance. I'll find you even greater stories, the right way, I promise.'

Miles laughed. 'I don't think so, Dermot. You're so bent, you can't even lie straight at night.'

But Dermot wasn't going anywhere without a fight. Leaving his dignity at the door, he got down on his knees and clasped his hands together. 'Miles, I'm begging you, please don't fire me. I'm nothing without this job.'

'You're nothing anyway, Dermot,' Miles sighed. 'The biggest mistake I ever made was hiring you in the first place. Now get out of my office and don't come back.'

Realising his career was over, Dermot let out a massive howl as two security guards walked into the office. They hauled him to his feet and pushed him towards the door, but he had one last thing to say.

'You'll be sorry you did this to me!' he screamed. 'I'll make you pay for this. You haven't heard the last of Dermot Whelan!'

After being front-page news Storm had worried her world would be turned upside down, but in fact life settled down fairly quickly for her. Of course, she still had several requests from journalists asking her to tell her story, and Carly also offered her the chance to go on *Morning Cuppa* and explain how she'd been a victim of phone hacking, but Storm refused. As for the paps, once they realised Sally and Jeff weren't going to give them Storm's location they too gave up, meaning Storm could get back to living her life in peace.

Over the next few weeks she hired a no win, no fee lawyer to help her sue the *Herald* for hacking her phone. Her lawyers had been more than happy to help and told her she had a watertight case. Worryingly, Chelsea had called a few days earlier, telling her that Dermot had rung asking where Storm lived. He'd worked out thanks to some old friends of theirs who had seen her in Brighton that she was working in the beachfront coffee shop. Chelsea wanted to warn Storm that he might come looking for her. 'Give him a kick in the nuts from me if you see him,' she fumed.

Meanwhile Storm threw herself into her job at the coffee shop, constantly thinking of ways Ed could improve the business. It was the only thing she could do to take her mind off Nico. Since he'd told her he never wanted to speak to her again, Storm had thought long and hard about trying to reach him. She toyed with the idea of going to his house, calling Francesca or even writing to him, but something always stopped her. He had made his feelings perfectly clear and she ought to respect that after all the damage she had caused him. And she couldn't really blame him for wanting her out of his life. They might have had a connection, but she'd lied to him, and caused his private life to be splashed across the front pages. No, Nico would see her as nothing but trouble now, and as the old saying went, if you loved someone you had to let them go.

That didn't mean she stopped missing him or thinking about him though. Every morning when she woke he was the first thing she thought about, and if she happened to catch his TV show, she'd look at the screen and pretend he was talking just to her.

Bustling into work one cold and drizzly November morning, Storm couldn't wait to show Ed her latest Christmas ideas. She'd been up half the night devising festive plans and, with Christmas around the corner, had come up with a file full of recipes and new ideas to tap into the hungry shopper market.

'Why don't we do a late-night opening on Thursdays to coincide with late-night shopping?' she suggested before they opened. 'We could encourage all those shoppers to unwind with a glass of mulled wine, or a Christmas coffee with a mince pie.'

'That's not a bad idea,' Ed replied. 'Though it would mean overtime for us both.'

Storm shrugged. 'So what? It would be great for business and we could add other events over the month.'

'Have you been watching Dragon's Den?' he teased her. 'It's brilliant. Have I told you, hiring you was the best decision I ever made?'

'Not since yesterday,' Storm bantered. 'But I've no problem with you telling me again.'

It was funny, she thought as she started clearing coffee cups and wiping tables. She had never seen herself working in a coffee shop, but she had to admit she was really enjoying it. Ed was a dream to work for, and it was brilliant not having to worry about deadlines or sit at a desk for hours on end. She might have been earning a pittance and was back to doing her clothes shopping in Tesco, but Storm realised she was a lot happier these days than she ever had been working at the *Herald* doing her supposed dream job. But then a lot of that might have something to do with Carly.

Since the two girls had made up, they'd quickly fallen into old habits and saw each other most days. Carly always stopped off for a coffee on the way to the station in the morning, and after work the two of them would either enjoy a gossip and a bottle of wine at each other's flats or go to catch a movie. It had been like old times.

'That reminds me, Carly had a good idea as well,' Storm said to Ed as she finished wiping the tables ready for the day.

'Oh, yeah?' he said cautiously. 'It's nothing to do with reinventing my style, is it?'

Storm frowned. 'No, why?'

'Ever since you two made up she keeps telling me I need to change my image. She says I'm never going to attract a woman if I wear camo shorts all year round and flip-flops. Plus she keeps fiddling with my hair.'

Storm tipped her head to one side and took in Ed's appearance. 'She does have a point. Don't you get cold dressed like that? I mean, it's almost the end of November – don't you think you ought to at least put long trousers on?'

Ed shook his head. 'I don't feel the cold. Besides, too many clothes make me feel trapped.'

'You're a funny boy.' Storm smiled fondly, shaking her head at him. 'Anyway, Carly suggested holding a Christmas party outfit session at the coffee shop. You know how everyone always struggles with what to wear at the

Christmas party? Well, she thought it might encourage more customers.'

'I like it,' Ed replied. 'As long as she doesn't start trying to style me. I'm happy as I am.'

'Even with the beard?'

'What's wrong with it?' he exclaimed, touching his chin self-consciously.

'Nothing, nothing.' She smiled. 'You just look a bit like Tom Hanks in that movie where he's stranded on a desert island for a year with only a football for company.'

'You cheeky cow. I'll have you know women love a beard.'

'If you say so.' Storm chucked her wet cloth into the sink and walked over to the door to open up for the day.

'I say so! And, Storm, you missed one of those tables.' He waited for her to turn round then threw the wet dishcloth straight at her, hitting her full in the face.

Storm had spent the day rushed off her feet. They'd been overrun with shoppers and day trippers, and by the time Carly came to collect her for a drink and a gossip in the nearby pizzeria, Storm was done in.

'Don't even think about cancelling on me,' Carly warned her. 'The thought of you, me, a glass of wine and a lot of carbs has been the only thing that's kept me going all day.'

'All right, all right,' replied Storm, taking off her apron and checking her appearance in the café window. Not bad after a day spent wiping, clearing and serving, she thought. Storm ran her hands through her hair and reached into her jeans pocket for her lip butter. That would have to do, she mused. Turning to Carly, she reached for her bag and coat.

'Come on then. Tell me all about your hectic day as the face of British television, and I'll reward you with tales of how I had to unblock the sink.'

'You do lead a very glamorous life,' Carly teased.

'Tell me about it. One minute washing dishes, the next slopping coffee over my favourite customers.'

'Still not tempted to go back to journalism then?' Carly asked.

Storm shook her head. 'I don't think so. Don't get me wrong, I miss writing. You know, actually talking to people, finding out about their lives and who they really are, but I don't miss all the bullshit that goes with it.'

'How do you mean?'

'Well, all the pressure, the deadlines, the boring council stories.'

'Come on, it wasn't that bad at the *Post*,' Carly reasoned.

Storm paused. No, it hadn't been all bad. There were times when she'd got a genuine thrill out of covering stories. Especially the crime ones. She loved the high drama of a criminal trial. And she'd liked her work when she'd reached out sympathetically to any family who had been a victim of crime or loss, and offered them the chance to talk freely.

'No. It wasn't all bad,' she said finally. 'I think my trouble was I got so fixated on the idea of being a showbiz journalist, I didn't think about any other area of journalism.'

'So what about going back into another field then? You're very talented, it would be a shame to waste that.'

Storm smiled. 'Yeah, my old editor Ron came in this morning and said much the same thing.'

Carly dropped a fork full of pizza. 'Why didn't you say? Bloody hell! How was it seeing him again?'

'Fine. He was really nice actually. Told me he was proud of me for resigning from the *Herald*.'

'Really? What did you tell him?'

'I said that I'd finally realised what was important in life.'

In truth, the meeting with Ron had rattled her. He'd had no idea she worked there and had popped in for a coffee on his way back from a meeting with one of the local councillors. Seeing Storm making lattes had given him a start.

'Storm! How lovely to see you, but what are you doing here?' he'd asked.

'Working,' she replied. 'But it's good to see you too. How's everything at the *Post*?'

'Fine.' Ron grinned. 'But we miss you. Things haven't been the same since you left. Me and Miles Elliot were at journalism college together. He rang to tell me you'd quit your job in London and, I have to say, I'm proud of you, Storm.'

She blushed as she made Ron his flat white. 'Thanks. But you shouldn't be. My life has lurched from bad to worse since I left the *Post*. And didn't you always tell me that a good journalist should write the news, not be the news? I messed up that golden rule, didn't I?'

319

Ron took his drink and slapped a fiver on the counter. 'You're too hard on yourself. You've handled a difficult situation very well and I'm proud of you. If you ever want your job back, just say the word. I was too harsh on you once, Storm, but there will always be a place for you at the *Post*.'

Giving Ron his change, she'd looked at him in surprise. Given the way they had left things, she'd been sure he would never want to see her again. Still, her mind was made up. No good could come from a career in journalism and she was better off doing anything else. 'Thanks, Ron, I appreciate that, but I don't think journalism is for me.'

'So now you've ruled out journalism, what's next?' Carly asked her.

'You sound like my mum!' Storm groaned. 'I don't know. I guess I'll find the right thing eventually. I'm really enjoying working for Ed at the moment.'

At the mention of her boss's name, Carly flushed, something Storm noticed straight away.

'Oh my God!' She grinned. 'Have you got a crush on Ed?'

'No way!' Carly exclaimed. 'He's nice, but he's really not my type. He's got no sense of style, lives in shorts, and his big ambition is to go surfing around Australia. No, thanks.'

'He's also got a heart of gold, a sweet, kind nature, and runs his own business,' Storm pointed out loyally. 'Also, he's given your style night idea the go ahead.'

'Really?' Carly beamed. 'Wow, that's great! When does he want to do it?'

'He suggested next week. First week of December, when Christmas really gets into full swing.'

'Great. I've got a stack of ideas.'

'Does one of them include snogging Ed under the mistletoe?' Storm teased.

'No, it does not!' Carly flushed, before cheekily adding, 'Maybe. You have to admit, he's cute.'

'He's very cute.' Storm smiled. 'I think he'd make someone a lovely husband one day.'

Chapter Nineteen

As Storm draped tinsel around the pictures in the coffee shop she did her best to ignore the sounds of Mariah Carey belting out her classic hit 'All I Want for Christmas' on the radio.

'Stupid song,' she snarled. 'Should be banned at this time of year, when people are feeling lonely.'

'What's got into you?' asked Ed in surprise. Storm had been grumpy all day – scowling at customers, moaning when she had to take out the bins – and despite his constantly asking her what was wrong, she'd refused to confide in him.

'For the final time, nothing,' Storm growled, just as Carly walked through the door with her arms full of clothes for that night's style event.

'Hi, guys.' She beamed as she looked around her at the twinkling Christmas tree lights and decorations. 'How's everything going?'

'Wonderful, thanks, Carly.' Ed beamed at her. 'You're

a breath of fresh air. Storm's been in a mood all day and refuses to tell me what's wrong. I can only think it's because she's secretly Scrooge.'

Carly glanced at her friend, currently wrestling with a piece of mistletoe. 'Yeah, it's not her favourite time of year. But I think she's probably more upset about the fact that Nico was in the papers this morning, looking loved up with a mystery blonde.'

'Carly!' Storm snapped as she slammed the mistletoe down in frustration. 'It has nothing to do with Nico. I'm just a bit tired, that's all.'

'Yeah, right,' Carly said. 'Storm, it's OK to be upset that Nico's seeing someone else. God, I'd be devastated.'

'Me too,' put in Ed, only for both girls to give him a glare, warning him to shut up. 'How about I pour us a glass of wine before the punters arrive?'

'Best idea you've had all day,' Storm replied, sinking into a nearby chair and throwing the remaining mistletoe across the room.

'So,' Carly began gently, 'how are you feeling?'

'Really pissed off!'

'Nico's a good-looking guy. He wasn't going to stay single for ever. Not only that but he's been badly hurt. I'm sure this is just a rebound thing, it doesn't mean anything.'

'Well, they look pretty close to me,' said Storm, snatching a tabloid from a nearby table and opening it to the page where Nico and his mystery woman had been papped.

Carly stared at the image. 'You're right. They do look close. But you know better than anyone how wrong the press can get things.'

'I know.' Storm sighed. 'It just hurts so much to see him with someone else like that. They look as though they're in love.'

Peering at the picture of Nico with his arm wrapped around the blonde sent a stab of pain through Storm and she burst into tears.

Putting an arm around her, Carly did her best to calm her friend down. 'I know this sucks, babe, and I know how much it must hurt to see him with someone else, whether it's real or not. But to be honest even if Nico is seeing someone, although it hurts it doesn't matter any more. You and he are done now; it's time for you to move on. New Year's around the corner, what better chance for a fresh start?'

'Yeah, except I just have to get through Christmas first.'

'It won't be that bad surely. Are you going to Sally's?'

Storm shook her head. 'No. Mum's going back to Canada and taking Jeff to meet her family there. Lexie and Bailey will be away with work again. They like Christmas as much as I do.'

Carly bit her lip. 'I'm sorry I won't be here either, Storm. Mum and Dad booked this ski-ing trip months ago to Val d'Isère. I can see if there's room for you, though, everyone would love to have you along.'

Storm was touched Carly would try to include her in her family's plans. 'No, don't worry. It's really sweet of you but I can't afford it. That's why I'm not going to LA to see Chelsea or to Canada with Sally either. I just haven't got the money.'

'Which is why I don't understand why you won't let

me loan you some?' put in Ed, appearing with three large glasses of red wine.

'Because I'm not a charity case!' she protested. Seeing Ed's hurt expression, she felt a pang of guilt. He had been nothing but nice to her, and certainly didn't deserve to be shouted at.

'Sorry. I just feel bad. You've done so much for me already. It wouldn't feel right to take your money as well.'

'What are you doing, Ed?' Carly said, changing the subject.

'Going back to St Ives for Christmas. It's the same every year. The whole family get together, sing carols, eat turkey and go to midnight mass at Truro Cathedral.'

'Wow, you sound very close.' Carly smiled at him.

'We are. Well, apart from my brother and sister, who refuse to go to mass and instead drink Dad's whisky and watch Clint Eastwood films.'

'Ah. Thought it sounded too perfect.' Carly nodded knowingly.

'See, Carly, there's no such thing as a perfect family,' put in Storm. 'Which is why I will be fine on my own, eating a ready meal and watching telly. Let's face it, it won't be any worse than last Christmas.'

Carly smiled sympathetically at her. 'Well, let's look forward to New Year then. You and me can go out on the pull together and look for Mr Right.'

'What happened to that hot TV producer you were seeing?'

'I binned him. He was more interested in how I could rework his wardrobe than a relationship with me.'

'So does that mean you're single then?' Ed asked bluntly.

'Single and very ready to mingle.' Carly smiled straight at him.

Storm looked at the two of them beaming into each other's eyes and smiled to herself. They weren't a likely couple but she reckoned there was a chance they could really suit each other. Perhaps she could give them a shove in the right direction.

Letting out a huge yawn, she stretched and got to her feet. 'I'm really sorry, you two, but would you mind if I went home instead of giving you a hand tonight? All this Nico stuff has really knocked me sideways and I don't think I'll be that much use to you.'

Concerned, Carly pulled Storm in for another hug. ''Course not, babe. You go home, have a nice hot shower and chill.'

'Thanks so much,' Storm said gratefully. 'Why don't you tell me all about it when you stop by for coffee in the morning?'

Carly stepped back and turned her attention to the huge bundle of clothes she was organising. 'I'm not going in tomorrow. I've got a day off.'

Storm was confused. 'Really? Since when?'

'Since I asked for one because I knew I'd be knackered the day after organising this event.'

'But it's the run up to Christmas. Surely the TV show needs you now more than ever?' Storm quizzed.

'No,' Carly said. 'They were fine with it. Now get off home before I change my mind and make you stay.'

Frowning, Storm was about to ask her friend for more

details but something told her that pushing Carly wouldn't do any good. She would come clean when she was good and ready, and Storm would be waiting. In the meantime she was off home, well aware of the expression two's company, three's a crowd.

Nico drummed his fingers on the Formica-topped table and wondered again why on earth he'd agreed to this meeting. When his agent had suggested it, his instinct had been to say no immediately but Natasha, who had worked with him for years, was very insistent, making it clear no wasn't really an option.

Realising there was no getting out of it, Nico tried to look on the bright side and thought that at least this would be a chance to lay some demons to rest. What he hadn't counted on was this particular demon being over twenty minutes late. Getting to his feet, he left a handful of pound coins on the table and reached for his coat just as the door swung open.

Spotting a short blonde woman standing at the doorway, frantically scanning the crowded café, he raised his hand to attract her attention.

'Carly,' he said quietly. 'Over here.'

Seeing Nico had waited, Carly rushed over to him, looking apologetic. 'I'm so sorry I'm so late. The train from Brighton was delayed. I tried to reach Natasha to get a message to you but she was stuck in meetings.'

'It seems our agent has been very busy lately,' Nico mused, sitting back down and gesturing to the waiter for another round of coffees.

Carly pulled a face. 'Yes. I know it was a bit naughty to get her to insist you meet me, but when I realised you and I shared an agent I saw it was the only string I could pull.'

Nico smiled. There was something very charming about Carly. She seemed so calm and poised on television, but in person she was unashamedly honest and warm. He could see why Storm had been so devastated to have lost her friendship. At the thought of his ex, his face darkened.

'So why did you want to see me so desperately?' he said. 'I have a funny feeling it has something to do with our mutual enemy.'

Carly flinched at his use of the word. 'Actually Storm and I have made up.'

'Pah! What lies did she tell to get you to come round? I thought you'd seen the light, Carly. I admired you for seeing straight through that girl's bullshit and getting out before she did any more damage.'

Carly shook her head. 'Storm's not like that. She's been hurt as badly as you have. You've got to understand.'

Nico shrugged. 'I don't have to do anything. So, it's Storm you've come to talk to me about, is it? I take it she sent you?'

'No. She has no idea I'm here. But, Nico, she's so unhappy without you. I know I never saw you two together, but what I do know is I've never seen Storm this besotted with a man. You clearly got under her skin.'

Nico frowned at Carly. Why had she come all this way to plead Storm's case? She was wasting her time; he should put her out of her misery right now.

'You should know that I'm suing both Storm and the

Herald for damages. My phone was hacked and my lawyer tells me I have an excellent case.'

Carly looked at him coldly. 'Well then, your lawyer should have informed you that Storm's phone was also hacked and she's also suing, which is how that dickhead of an ex of hers got hold of the story about you two in the first place.'

'You mean, she never gave an interview?' Nico asked, incredulous.

'No! That's the last thing she would ever do. She doesn't even work at the *Herald* any longer. She quit the day you dumped her, saying she'd realised how much of a shit job being a showbiz reporter was. She was going to tell you the truth about her job once she'd asked for a transfer to another department, but you beat her to it by dumping her.'

'And what about this honey trap business?' he scoffed. 'Oh, yes, I know Storm was asked to take part by her ex, Dermot, that's if he even was her ex. My lawyers have found out Storm was only going out with me in the first place to try and uncover the truth about my life, so she could run an *exposé*. I'm sorry, Carly, but that doesn't sound very innocent to me.'

'She was just doing that to protect you,' Carly replied, sounding exasperated. 'I know it's a lot to take in, but it's absolutely true. She never wanted anything to appear about your private life, and felt that if she pretended to go along with Dermot's plans then she could keep you out of the limelight. The last thing she ever wanted to do was hurt you.'

'I don't believe you,' Nico jeered.

'It's true. She's back in Brighton, with a broken heart, living in a tiny studio, earning a pittance making coffee in a seafront café. She says she never wants to work as a reporter again, which to be honest is stupid because she's a brilliant journalist.'

Nico sank back in his chair and swept his hands through his hair as he tried to take in everything she was saying. Storm was as much of a victim as he was. Storm was going to tell him the truth. Storm didn't want to honey trap him. Storm loved him. He shook his head. It was all too little, too late. Storm was gone, and no matter what he may or may not still feel for her, she'd done nothing but wreak havoc in his life.

'I'm sorry, Carly. My mind's made up. I never want anything to do with her again. And even if she had organised a transfer for herself to a different department it still wouldn't have made a difference. I hate journalists, they're the scum of the earth – she knew that.'

'What? You'd let someone's job stop you from loving them?' Carly exclaimed. ''Scuse my French but how fucking stupid!'

'It's not stupid at all. In fact, I'm surprised you've sorted things out with her after what she did to you.'

'How do you know what Storm did to me?' Carly asked, surprised.

'She told me a version of the truth, and my lawyers did some digging and found out the rest.'

'Well then, you should realise that my life without Storm was pretty miserable. On the outside I pretended to hate her because I was so hurt. But I realised her only crime really was telling someone she thought she could trust a secret.'

'Well, that's the other thing, isn't it?' hissed Nico, jabbing his finger on the table. 'Even if I did talk to Storm again, I would never, ever trust her. There's no getting away from the fact she lied to me. I'm sorry, you can't have a relationship without trust.'

Convinced he'd made his point, Nico looked at Carly triumphantly.

'It's true, trust can be hard to regain. But if the love is there then it doesn't have to be gone for ever,' she said thoughtfully. 'Sally told me some home truths a little while ago, which made me realise it was wrong to blame Storm for everything that happened. Ultimately I was the one who slept with a married man and you were the one who lived a lie. I mean, if we're getting down to it, wasn't that the real reason you hated reporters? Because you were worried they'd uncover the truth?'

Nico's face flushed with anger as Carly hit a nerve with her question. 'That is the biggest load of bollocks I've ever heard. My relationship was my business, and even if I let people believe we were together, I was doing it for the best of reasons.'

'So was Storm.'

Neither of them spoke for what seemed like an eternity, each staring at the other in frustration, until finally Nico got to his feet.

'Carly, I'm sorry but you've had a wasted trip. I hate Storm and never want to see her again.'

'Well then, it's nice to see you've moved on so quickly . . . if those pap shots of you in the papers with that blonde are anything to go by.'

'That's none of your business,' replied Nico smoothly as he pulled on his coat. 'Please leave me alone now. Storm and I are over.'

Carly grabbed his wrist as he made to leave. 'Wait just a minute,' she begged, pulling a pen from her bag. Reaching for a napkin from the chrome canister on the table, she scribbled something on it and pressed it into his hand. 'This is Storm's address. Just in case you change your mind.'

Nico released his hand from Carly's. 'I won't!' he called as he reached the door.

The Christmas atmosphere all around town and at work was beginning to do Storm's head in. Everywhere she went people seemed to be whistling carols, wishing each other a Merry Christmas and discussing their holiday plans. Usually this time of year didn't bother her; after all, she'd long ago got used to Christmases that were less than happy and instead looked forward to the new beginnings January always brought. This year was different, though, and Storm couldn't put her finger on why. She had a lot of reasons to be cheerful, including the new relationship she'd forged with her mother.

For the first time since she could remember Sally felt like a proper mum, and now Storm looked forward to their time together. They met every week for a gossip and a cup of tea, and Storm had even accompanied her and Jeff to their beloved bingo!

No, Storm knew she had more reasons than most to feel thankful, but this year she was finding it impossible to get into the Christmas spirit. Deep down she knew the reason – Nico. During their time together they'd actually made Christmas plans. Nico had offered to take her away to his holiday home in the Italian Lakes where he said they'd light fires, relax by the water and eat a huge Christmas dinner before spending the day making love. Storm had been doing her best to remain strong since returning to Brighton, but this endless Christmas cheer was bringing back memories of him and all she had lost. She knew there was no point getting upset, that what was done was done, but being without him still hurt and there were times she struggled to get through the day without crying.

Storm felt as though she was walking around under a great big cloud of unhappiness. More than anything she wished it would lift. As she opened her front door ready to leave for work, she ran through her mental checklist, phone, purse, keys . . . then realised they were the one thing she didn't have. Scrambling around her flat, desperately searching for her keys, she let out a torrent of swear words. She wasn't usually this disorganised and could only put it down to the curse of Christmas. Frantically she checked her watch and groaned. She should have left ten minutes ago if she had any hope of being on time and she'd promised Ed she'd open up this morning.

He and Carly had gone on their first date last night after they'd shared a kiss at Carly's style event. Knowing it was such a special occasion, Storm had offered him the chance of a lie in, just in case he got lucky! Not that Carly was that kind of girl, she'd assured him as he flushed bright red with embarrassment. She hoped it worked out for them; they both deserved someone special, although Storm had noticed Carly had been really weird for the past week. Always dropping in on her at home and at work to check she was OK, bringing her clothes from the set of *Morning Cuppa* which apparently she didn't have to return, and being generally over-attentive and positive about a brand new start in January. Storm didn't know what had got into her and had tried asking her what was wrong, but Carly had said everything was fine with such a bright sunny smile on her face that Storm had given up asking.

She could only put it down to the fact her friend was worried about how Storm would feel about Ed and her best mate going on a date, but she had nothing to worry about there. Storm was delighted for them both. It was nice to see Cupid fire his bow at this time of the year and she couldn't wait to find out how their date had gone.

Finally spotting her keys on top of the fridge, Storm heaved a sigh of relief as she grabbed them and raced out of her front door. Half jogging and half walking towards the café, she didn't notice the man on the opposite side of the road, who had been watching her flat waiting for her to leave.

'Storm!' a voice called. At the sound of her name, she whipped around and got the shock of her life when she saw Dermot.

Astonished, she stood rooted to the spot as he crossed the road and hurried towards her.

'Storm,' he said again, more warmly this time. 'It's so good to see you.'

As he leaned in to give her a kiss on the cheek she backed away, speechless. What the hell was he doing here? And how did he know where she lived?

'Why are you here?' she croaked, finally finding her voice.

'I had to see you,' he said, putting his hands in his pockets to ward off the chill of the December air. 'One of our old colleagues at the *Post* told me you were living here.'

As Dermot spoke, Storm took in his appearance. With greasy matted hair, an unshaven face and dark shadows under his eyes, he didn't look a well man. Still, Storm had no inclination to feel sorry for him as shock gave way to anger.

'Well, I don't want to see you, Dermot. Now fuck off and leave me alone.'

'Please, Storm,' he begged. 'Just listen to me . . . there's something I need to tell you.'

'What?'

'I need to tell you how sorry I am. I should never have hacked your phone and I should never have got you to honey trap Nico. I was jealous, and wanted revenge. You were doing so much better than me at work, and you'd fallen in love with another man. I didn't know what else to do, but I'm so, so sorry.'

'Wow, Dermot, thanks, I feel so much better about it all now,' she said sarcastically.

'Really?' He smiled, a flicker of relief passing across his face.

'No, not really!' she snarled, as she angrily jabbed her finger into his chest. 'You ruined my life, you piece of shit. Now, for once in your life, think of someone else and leave me alone.'

Pushing past, she picked up her pace and walked quickly away from him, but Dermot wasn't giving up. He chased her down the road.

'Just give me a chance to talk to you, Storm.'

'You've talked. I listened. Now go,' she said, continuing to walk faster down the street.

'Don't be like that. Please! I came here to ask you for another chance. I know I've asked before, but I got it wrong sending you all those flowers and text messages. I see that now. But what *you* need to understand is that ever since you and I split up our lives have fallen to bits. Look at us. You're here in Brighton again, doing a shit job and living in a shit apartment, and I'm kipping on a mate's sofa without any hope of getting a job in journalism again. We belong together, Storm. I need you and you need a grand gesture.'

To her horror, Dermot ran in front of her then blocked her path by getting down on bended knee. Reaching into his coat pocket and pulling out a tiny black box, he opened it to reveal a ring. 'Storm, you're my world. Please will you marry me?'

Looking at Dermot, down on one knee, holding a ring in the air, his expression brimming over with seriousness, Storm couldn't help herself. She broke into peals of laughter. 'Have you lost your mind?' she said, when she'd finally calmed down.

'No,' he said earnestly. 'This feels so right. We should be together, we belong together.'

'Really?' said Storm, arms folded against her chest. 'And what does Sabrina make of all this?'

'That's over,' he said, waving one hand. 'Has been for a while now. She blamed me after she was fired.'

Storm frowned. Sabrina was Miles's rising star – what on earth did she do to get fired? Still, it proved there was some justice in the world. The woman was the biggest bitch on the planet.

Seeing Storm's confusion, Dermot put her in the picture. 'She knew I'd hacked your phone. Miles fired us both.'

Instantly, Storm backed away from him. This was all too much, him being here in her life, with all his lies and deceit, after she'd worked so hard at a fresh start.

'Just go away, Dermot,' she said, losing her patience. 'How many times do I have to tell you before you get the hint?'

But he wasn't listening. 'Storm, I'm serious. All this has made me realise what's important in life, and I know for me that's you. I can't live without you. Since you left me everything's gone wrong, I need you back.'

Storm had not been expecting any of this and suddenly felt exhausted. 'You just don't get it, do you, Dermot? I know what love is now; I know what it feels like. Even if I never love anyone else again, I've experienced how good it can be when you're with the right person, and what you and I had was not love. At best it was good sex, but it wasn't love. Why on earth would I ever go back to life with a selfish twat of a man like you, who has tried to ruin me over and over again?'

'Don't be stupid, Storm,' snapped Dermot, getting to his feet. 'Nico will never have you back. You're wasting your time if you're waiting around for him.'

'Thanks, but I'm not waiting for Nico,' Storm replied. 'I know it's over, but I'd rather have nothing and be alone for the rest of my life than be with someone like you.'

'But it's Christmas,' he protested. 'Surely you don't want to be alone at Christmas?'

'It never bothered you when we were dating, and quite honestly I'd rather spend a lifetime of Christmas Days eating meals for one than spend another minute in your company!'

'And what am I supposed to do with this ring?'

'I couldn't care less what you do with it. Give it to Sabrina, give it to charity, throw it in the sea, but just leave me alone, Dermot,' she said. 'And if I ever see you near my flat again, I'll take out a restraining order.'

'Don't worry, I'm going,' he hissed. 'You know your trouble, Storm? You always look a gift horse in the mouth.'

She couldn't resist one final putdown.

'And you know your trouble, Dermot?' she called, walking away from him. 'You're like school in August – no class.'

Nico strolled purposefully along the seafront, feeling more hopeful than he had in months. When he'd woken early that morning this was the last place he'd expected to find himself, but he'd had the strangest dream. He and Storm had been lying in bed, eating croissants. Storm had been flicking crumbs at him, and he had pinned her to the bed and made delicious love to her. When he woke, sleepy and blurry-eyed, he reached across the bed expecting to find her by his side and felt a stab of shock when he realised she wasn't there. Propping himself upright against his pillows, he realised how much he missed her. How everything in his life had seemed brighter, shinier and simply better with her in it. He missed the way she smiled at him in the mornings, the way she scrubbed her teeth rather than gently brushed them, he even missed the way she sang really bad show tunes in the shower each morning. Had he made a mistake? Were Carly and Francesca right? Should he at least give Storm the opportunity to tell him her side of things?

His gaze fell on his bedside table where he saw the napkin on which Carly had scribbled Storm's address. It had been lying there in a crumpled heap along with a pocketful of change, receipts and a spare button. He'd wanted to throw it out the minute Carly had given it to him, but for some reason had kept hold of it. Now he knew why.

For a tantalising moment Nico considered the possibility that he could end this misery just by talking to Storm. That they could spend Christmas together after all. He fantasised about the two of them waking up on Christmas morning together. They'd open presents, eat dinner and spend all day locked in each other's arms. Life could be perfect, Nico realised, if he'd just swallow his pride. Too keen to get going to bother with a shower, he slipped on jeans and a jumper and grabbed his car keys. With a bit of luck he should catch Storm before she left for work.

On the drive down, Nico practised what he was going

to say. How he had been wrong not to listen; how although he was still angry with her for lying, he was now ready to work things out. He would blame his crazy Italian temperament, and ask her if she thought there was some way back to being the happy, loving couple they'd been before. By the time Nico reached Brighton he was fired up and ready to see Storm. As there was no parking outside her home, he left his car near the seafront and walked along the promenade, the brisk air helping to calm his nerves. Turning into Storm's road, he took a deep breath and walked towards her flat, only to see her in the street talking to someone.

Getting closer, he realised the man could only be Dermot Whelan. Nico recognised him from the dossier his lawyers had compiled, and unless he was very much mistaken, it looked as though their conversation was getting intimate. Nico's mind went into overdrive as he tried to work out why on earth Storm could be talking to her ex. After all, he had set her up and betrayed her just as badly as he had Nico. Suddenly his heart was in his mouth as he saw Dermot get down on one knee, reach into his pocket for a tiny box and hold it aloft. Storm looked shocked, he noticed, before she broke into what he could only assume were peals of delighted laughter.

A mixture of shock, anger and nausea washed over Nico as all the pieces of the jigsaw slotted into place. More deception. Storm hadn't had her phone hacked, she'd obviously been in on the whole thing with that scumbag of an ex. Except it was now very clear to Nico, that Dermot was not her ex. Dermot was very clearly her future. How could he have been so stupid as not to see this coming?

He turned on his heel and stomped back towards his car in the freezing cold. He'd seen all he needed to see and wasn't going to hang around. When would he realise Storm had never been interested in him, that she had been playing him for a fool all along? Carly, the stupid bitch, had probably been in on it too. Getting their agent to set up a meeting to tell even more lies . . . It was sick. But what had been the point of it? To set him up for an even bigger story? To make more money out of him? Well, forget it. Storm wouldn't make a fool out of him twice.

God, she was a piece of work, he had to give her that. Cunning and clever. He thought back to just a couple of hours ago when he'd dreamed of the two of them spending Christmas together. What a joke! No, he was better off alone, sitting in his beloved kitchen, dreaming up new recipes for his restaurant.

Shaking his head in sorrow, Nico hurried back to his car and clambered inside. Letting out a howl of despair, he thumped the steering wheel over and over again, repeatedly cursing his own stupidity. He swore there was no way he would ever allow Storm back into his life again.

Chapter Twenty

Christmas Eve

'Oh my god, babe! This is gorgeous,' exclaimed Storm, unwrapping a beautiful black, sequin-encrusted designer dress.

Storm and Carly had decided to get into the Christmas spirit by treating themselves to lunch in the pub near Storm's home. It had become quite the local for the girls since they'd made up, and they had spent many a happy night there swapping stories about their days over a bottle of wine.

'I feel so bad now. I only got you that rucksack,' Storm sighed.

'Are you kidding me?' beamed Carly, who knew Storm was struggling to make ends meet. 'That rucksack's just what I need for my adventures next month.'

'I still can't believe you're going.'

'Neither can I.' Carly grinned at her. 'I wanted to go with

Ed for the whole year, but *Morning Cuppa* refused to hold my job open for me, and much as I love him, experience has taught me not to give everything up for a man.'

'So you're only going to Australia for a month then?' Storm confirmed.

'Yeah. I think a few weeks of living out of a backpack will make me more than ready to come home.' She shuddered at the thought. 'But I'll be with Ed, and that's all that matters.'

'So what will you do after that?' asked Storm, nibbling on a plate of chips. 'Ed's going to be gone for six months, do you think you'll cope?'

'We've both compromised,' explained Carly. 'He wanted to go for a year, but doesn't want to be without me, and I've said I'll come out for a fortnight in April when I can take more time off. It won't be that long.'

Storm looked at her admiringly. Since Carly and Ed had started dating, she'd really blossomed. She'd gone back to being the confident, sassy, gorgeous girl Storm had known and loved. The romance was going well and Storm couldn't have been more pleased for her friend.

'Still, you're in for a hectic few weeks travelling across the globe.' Storm smiled. 'Flying out to Val d'Isère this afternoon, then off to Melbourne the day after you get back from ski-ing. When will I see you?'

'It is going to be hectic,' agreed Carly. 'But, hey, life's short. So screw it, why not? As for you and me, no doubt I'll be Skyping you constantly about the tortures of slumming it in a youth hostel with no access to any of my designer toiletries.'

'You'd better,' Storm urged, mopping up a mound of tomato ketchup with her last chip.

'Anyway, more importantly, have you decided what you're going to do now?'

Storm sighed. 'I think so. I did offer to run the café for Ed while he was away, but he seemed adamant about selling it.'

'It hasn't been doing very well,' Carly admitted. 'Despite your best efforts to turn things around. So he's just going to keep the one in St Ives open, which is a little gold mine apparently.'

'I know. It's a shame. He never told me how bad things were and I'm really sad today's my last day,' sighed Storm. 'Then tomorrow I'll be home alone, watching box sets and eating mince pies.'

Carly reached across the table and squeezed her friend's arm. She had never told Storm she had gone to visit Nico, convinced that hearing how much he hated her would only halt her friend's healing process. 'Are you sure you're OK with spending Christmas on your own? Because, honestly, if you want, I'll fork out for you to come ski-ing?'

'Don't be daft, babe. A last-minute ticket would cost a fortune. Honestly, I'm fine. You know Christmas doesn't bother me.' She shrugged.

Carly eyed Storm thoughtfully as she took a sip of her wine and changed the subject. 'So what are you going to do next? Any more news on your case against the *Herald*?'

'Yes. My solicitor is working on an out-of-court settlement with Miles. I'm not sure what Nico and Francesca are doing, I think they're planning on taking their case all the way to court as they want to make a point. Unlike me. I've had enough of being in the spotlight and my solicitor reckons Miles will make sure the settlement is quite generous so that should mean that in the New Year I'll be able to put a deposit down on a flat.'

'That's brilliant news, babe. It seems like it's all happening for you! Let's hope next year's better than this one.'

'For both of us,' Storm agreed.

'And what about work? Are you going to accept Chelsea's offer?'

'No. I thought about it, but it doesn't feel right.'

'And is she OK with that?' Carly asked.

Storm nodded. Chelsea had rung her the week before and told her that she was moving to LA permanently and Adam had offered her enough cash to start up her own luxury travel magazine. As a result Chelsea had offered Storm a job travelling around the world, writing about gorgeous hotels.

'Babe, just think how glamorous life will be as you jet from country to country, staying in the best hotels in the world!'

Storm had paused before answering. 'I know you're going to think this is mad, Chelsea, but actually I think I'd rather stay in Brighton. Now I've made up with Carly and established a new relationship with Mum, I want to focus on what I've got at home rather than travel halfway around the world looking for glamour. I've realised that all the time I was chasing a glam, party lifestyle, all I really wanted was my family – I've got that now.'

'Oh, Storm,' Chelsea replied tearfully. 'I don't think that's mad, I think that's beautiful. I completely understand. But any time you fancy a holiday, I insist you come to stay with me. Let me give you a glam life for at least a couple of weeks.'

Storm grinned. 'I can't think of anything I'd like more.'

'So does that mean you'll be taking Ron up on his offer then?' Carly asked.

Storm nodded. 'Yes. As of next month I'll be the *Post*'s chief crime reporter, and you know what? I can't wait. I've actually really missed journalism, something I never thought I'd say, and this job will be brilliant as I'll be based mainly in court and will be able to talk to many of the victims of crime as well.'

'No more boring council meetings for you then?'

'No! And no more showbiz stories either. Ron has promised me there won't be a celebrity in sight.'

Carly raised a glass to her friend. 'Well, I'm really proud of you. You were wasting your talents making coffee. You're a brilliant journalist, Storm, and you should never have turned your back on it.'

She grinned as she clinked her glass against Carly's. 'Maybe that's why Ed's business wasn't doing well. I probably spilled more coffee than I served!'

Glancing at the clock above the bar, Storm groaned as she realised she'd taken well over her allotted hour and was a little bit tipsy to boot.

'I'd better be getting back,' she said. 'Ed wants to get on the road back to Cornwall, and I promised him I'd lock up.'

'Poor old Ed,' Carly said, draining her glass and getting to her feet. 'I know he's going to be devastated to say goodbye to the business here.'

'That's why I offered to lock up for him one last time,' Storm replied. 'Goodbyes are tough, and he's got enough on his plate organising this trip to Australia.'

'You're too generous.'

'I know.' Storm shrugged. 'Perhaps I'll put this lovely new dress on for my last afternoon at the café. Say goodbye in style.'

'You'd better not, Storm Saunders,' Carly warned. 'That dress is designer and meant for pulling only!'

'Fine,' she groaned, as they left the pub and braced themselves against the cold sea air. 'But I hope you realise that means this beautiful dress will more than likely remain in the back of my wardrobe for ever. The first of my New Year's resolutions is to avoid men and falling in love.'

Nico slammed his foot down angrily on the brakes as the car in front stopped suddenly. It was always this way at Christmas, he fumed. The roads were full of Sunday drivers and he needed this like a hole in the head.

Earlier that morning the chef at his Brighton restaurant had called to tell him he had to leave work immediately. There'd been some kind of family emergency and the chef couldn't work Christmas Day as planned. Was there any way Nico could find someone else to cover his shift? Nico had felt like screaming. Of course there wasn't anyone else who could work Christmas at short notice – Nico would have to do it himself.

Ungraciously, he'd told his chef not to worry. After paying through the nose for the last remaining room at the Hotel du Vin, he got in his car. It was just as well he didn't have any plans of his own other than sitting alone eating turkey sandwiches. Francesca had been sweet when she'd learned he would be alone for Christmas and had invited him to go away with her and Paula, but he'd refused.

'Why don't you go to your own family's then?' she had suggested. 'I hate to think of you here all by yourself at this time of year.'

'Please,' Nico had scoffed. 'You know how *Mamma* has been since the newspaper article. She can't wait to sit me down, find out all the details, and talk to me about settling down with a nice Italian girl. Much as I love her, her fussing is the last thing I need right now. I'd rather be here, trust me.'

'If you're sure?' Francesca had said.

Nico was sure. In truth, he couldn't wait to spend some time alone and get his head around everything that had happened over the past year. It had been a horrible few months, and much as he hated to admit it to himself his heart was still broken. He'd done everything he could to get over the woman who'd betrayed him, including dating another woman, but it had been a disaster. Despite his best efforts to forget Storm, his new girlfriend had seen straight through him and recognised he was on the rebound, breaking up with him immediately. Nico wasn't bothered, but he was determined to get his life back on track. He intended to spend Christmas coming up with new ideas for the restaurants and for making his career bigger and better than ever. Thankfully, the public had been sympathetic after the story about him and Francesca was published and business had boomed, but he was still keenly ambitious.

Funnily enough, though, driving to Brighton on Christmas Eve and working in his restaurant there hadn't been part of his master plan. Once again he cursed his bad luck, along with the traffic, for another hour as he finally crawled past Preston Park and into Brighton itself. Spotting a space near the Pier he slung his car into the spot, not caring if he was parking on private property or if he would get towed. He'd made it, that was all that mattered.

He wandered along the seafront towards his restaurant. Brighton really was pretty at this time of year, he thought. Although the sea was grey and the sky cloudy, the promenade was illuminated with beautiful twinkling lights, while everyone around him seemed happy and excited about the fact that Christmas Day was less than twenty-four hours away. Kids clung excitedly to parents' hands, groups of lads were dressed as Santa, in the mood to party, while loved up couples snogged in shop doorways, ready to celebrate the romance of the season.

Nico looked around him and found the atmosphere was rubbing off on him. Passing a seafront coffee shop, he decided to get into the Christmas spirit by treating himself to a mince pie and an espresso.

Pushing the door open, he saw a young woman balancing on a stool while reaching for a box at the back of the store. 'Be with you in a minute,' she called.

'No rush,' he said, looking around him. There were boxes everywhere, he noticed, and all the tables and chairs looked as though they were being stacked ready to store. On the counter he noticed a large sign pointing to cakes and a small array of sandwiches. *Closing down. Everything must go!* it said. Nico felt sad. Too many small businesses were being forced to shut these days. It was a worrying sign of the times. He watched the woman get down from the stool.

'What can I get you?' she said, turning round to face him.

'Storm!' he spluttered, coming face to face with his ex. 'What are you doing here?'

Her pulse raced as she drank in the sight of Nico. She'd thought she'd never see him again, and yet here he was in the flesh, still as handsome as ever. His brown hair was ruffled, but his skin glowed and his eyes sparkled. With a start, she realised the single life must be suiting him.

'I work here,' she said quietly.

'Pah! Is this another career you're pretending to have, like being an air stewardess or a hospitality student?'

Storm sighed and rested her hands on the counter. She knew Nico's anger was justified, but it seemed especially cruel to have to deal with it now on Christmas Eve.

'Yes, I was a showbiz reporter but I handed in my notice the day you left for Italy. I'd intended to transfer out of showbiz and into another department, but when you ditched me I realised I didn't want to work there at all.'

'So you came back to Brighton?'

'That's right. I had no job, no home, nothing, but I knew I couldn't be in London any more. It seemed too hard to stay in the place where you and I had been so happy. I made up with Sally, got a job here, moved into a studio flat and sorted things out with Carly.'

'Sounds like everything's worked out for you,' he said quietly.

Storm looked him in the eye. He seemed consumed with pain and anger, and she felt terrible, knowing she was the one who had caused him so much sorrow.

'I know I hurt you, Nico,' she said softly. 'And I cannot apologise enough for all the lies, but I had good reason. It was stupid of me to go along with the air stewardess joke that Jez came up with but I couldn't seem to find the right time to tell you the truth about what I really did. Then you and I agreed we'd never see each other again, and it seemed pointless to confess.'

'Until you decided to set me up for a story in your paper,' Nico pointed out, leaning closer to her, his face twisted with rage.

'I didn't set you up, Nico. You have to believe me, I had no choice. Dermot had got hold of that pap shot of us. He threatened to publish it unless I agreed to take part in a honey trap. I told him I'd do it, but really I was protecting you. I knew if I didn't go through with it, then they'd just get another reporter. When I left, he wanted revenge and hacked my phone, which is how he got the story about us. The last thing I have ever wanted to do, Nico, is hurt you. You have to believe me.'

'Why would I believe anything you say? Even now you're telling me a pack of lies. Dermot never set you up, you were in it together. Or why would you be marrying him?'

'What? I'm not marrying Dermot.'

351

Nico ran a hand through his hair and sighed. 'Storm, you have to stop lying. There's no point any more. I saw you, OK? And I saw Dermot the other week, down on one knee in the street, and you giggling excitedly as you saw the ring.'

Storm couldn't help herself. Great waves of laughter rose within her as she realised how badly wrong Nico had got things.

'Why are you laughing again, Storm?' he snarled. 'This isn't funny.'

'But it is!' she giggled. 'You obviously didn't hang around otherwise you would have seen me send Dermot packing, with the threat of a restraining order if he ever bothered me again. He and I have been over for a year. I never loved him, Nico, not like I love you. You're all I've ever wanted.'

Storm felt she had nothing to lose by speaking so bluntly; after all, she'd probably never see Nico again after this. At least by telling the truth there was a possibility she could set the record straight. Looking at him now, his mouth set in a grim line, his eyes filled with hatred, Storm felt a sharp stab of pain in her heart. She would never get him to forgive her. She had to accept that. The two of them stood in silence in the empty coffee shop for what felt like hours until he spoke.

'Did you know Carly came to see me?'

'No,' replied Storm, stunned. 'When?'

'About three weeks ago. She told me you were working here and living in a studio flat. She told me everything, in fact. Why you entrapped me, how you gave up your job, how Dermot had betrayed you. She even gave me your address, urging me to come and see you.'

Storm was astonished. 'I had nothing to do with that, honestly, she never told me anything about it. I wouldn't have encouraged her.'

'She gave me a few things to think about actually,' Nico confessed. 'Asked me if the real reason I disliked journalists so much was because I had something to hide. She had a point. It was something I'd never considered before, but she was right, that *was* why I hated journalists, so I decided to come and see you. Talk to you, see if there was some way we could work things out.'

Storm looked him in the eye. 'And?' she whispered.

'And I saw that bastard propose to you, Storm. It felt like my whole world had come crashing down around my ears again. To see you getting engaged to another man . . . it felt like someone had taken out my heart and shredded it into tiny pieces.'

Storm's eyes filled with tears as she saw the strength of his emotion. 'But, Nico, I didn't say yes to Dermot. I was as surprised to see him as you must have been and I certainly didn't want him around. The guy ruined my life, he ruined my relationship with you,' she cried. 'That's something I have to live with for the rest of my life, knowing how close I was to finding true happiness.'

To her surprise, Nico walked around the counter towards her. 'Please,' she continued. 'I never meant for any of this to happen. At the very least, please don't walk away from here hating me. I was set up and I made some bad choices for the right reasons, but Carly was telling the truth.'

'I know that now, Storm. I can see that everything she told me is true,' Nico said, reaching for her hands.

She shuddered with delight as that tell-tale charge of electricity and desire shot down her spine at his touch.

'I'm the one who should be apologising. I leaped to so many conclusions. I never gave you the chance to explain when I should have done. If I had, maybe we could have avoided all this pain. All these months of misery, being without each other.'

As Nico locked eyes with Storm, he bent down to kiss her and she felt her body melt into his. No kiss had ever tasted so sweet or felt so right. It was time to forget the past and look to the future. It had only just begun.

'Wow, you look gorgeous!' Nico breathed as Storm sashayed into his restaurant.

'Thanks.' She smiled, silencing his compliments by kissing him full on the mouth.

When Nico had invited her that evening to a private dinner for two after the restaurant closed, she had known exactly what to wear. As she'd hoped, Carly's present fitted her like a glove, and Storm couldn't resist texting her friend a selfie.

Who are you wearing that for? Carly had texted back immediately.

Nico, Storm had replied.

Unsurprisingly, Carly had rung from Gatwick airport straightaway, desperate for the details.

'What's going on?' she squealed.

Storm had quickly filled her in, telling her how Nico

354

had found her at the coffee shop and it was there they had kissed and made up.

'So does that mean you're back together then?' Carly asked.

'Yes,' Storm replied happily.

But Storm didn't tell her everything. For example, she didn't tell her that after Nico had kissed her and kissed her, she had walked over to the door, turned the open sign to closed then turned the key in the lock. Behind the counter they'd made love, each so desperate to hold, touch and feel the other that they couldn't wait to make up for lost time. She also didn't bother to explain to Carly how, after they'd made love, they'd talked and talked, about the past and the future. Storm had told him how much she wanted to be a part of his life, and how much she'd missed him, but that she was planning on returning to journalism. She told Nico she'd understand if that would be too much for him to cope with, but after everything that had happened she knew she had to be honest.

Incredibly, he had been more than understanding. He knew what it was like to feel driven in a career, and to feel real passion for work.

'No more honey traps or kiss and tells, though,' he said warningly. 'Deal?'

'Deal,' agreed Storm happily.

Now, she couldn't help noticing how beautiful the place looked. Every table was lined with crackers, table decorations and gorgeous little gifts for all the customers Nico would be cooking Christmas lunch for the following day.

'I've got a confession to make,' he said as he led her by the hand through the restaurant.

'Oh, yes?'

'I'm afraid I haven't got you a present. This all happened so suddenly . . .' He broke off.

'What!' Storm teased. 'You cheapskate.'

'I was going to suggest you come back with me to my hotel tonight,' he whispered, nuzzling her neck. 'And I was going to suggest waking up together on Christmas morning and enjoying breakfast in bed.'

'Sounds good,' Storm purred. 'How about I lie in bed naked all day, so I'm ready and waiting for you when you finish work.'

'Now that would be the perfect Christmas present,' he agreed. 'In the meantime, though, I can offer you this.'

As he led her to a table that was laden with roast turkey, potatoes, and all the trimmings, she wondered when on earth Nico would have had time to pull off something so elaborate, not realising he had made one phone call to his sous-chef and asked him to organise something before he left for the day. One thing Storm couldn't help noticing was the fact that the table Nico had chosen for them was behind a large pillar towards the back of the restaurant.

'Why are we here? I thought you might like us to sit near the kitchen or by the window.'

'Because . . .' He smiled, reaching for her hand and bringing it to his lips. 'It was at this very spot you spilled wine all over me and our story began.'

'I can't believe you remembered.'

'I remember everything about that night. I remember

356

you looked gorgeous in your navy dress, how you spent most of the night consoling your friend Carly, and how your smile lit up the room. I looked at you, Storm, and I knew then what I know now: that I want to spend the rest of my life with you.'

She looked at him in shock. 'Are you asking me to marry you?'

Nodding, Nico stared into her eyes. 'I don't have a ring, Storm, but I do have a heart filled with love all for you, if you'll have me?'

'Yes.' She smiled and wrapped her arms around him. 'Yes, I'll marry you.'

Storm wiped the tears from her eyes as Nico reached for the champagne bottle.

'You didn't ask me to marry you to get out of buying me a present, did you?' she asked cheekily. 'Because FYI, a marriage proposal is *not* a Christmas present.'

Laughing, Nico popped the cork and filled their glasses.

'You mean, I have to get you an engagement ring *and* a gift?'

'Afraid so!' Storm teased.

Nico groaned. 'I knew getting married was expensive but this is taking the piss!'

Handing her a glass, he kissed her lightly on the mouth and proposed a toast.

'To us.'

'To us,' Storm whispered. 'And to years of very Merry Christmases together.'

He's the One

Katie Price

Can you ever forget your first love?

Liberty Evans hasn't. She has a beautiful daughter, a successful career as an actress, and she's married to one of Hollywood's most powerful directors.

But behind the glamour, things are not what they seem. Her daughter Brooke is turning into a spoiled teenager, her husband controls everything she does, and Liberty longs for Cory, the man she loved before she became famous.

Unable to live a lie any longer, Liberty returns to England with a reluctant Brooke to start a new life. While her daughter has to cope with a massive lifestyle change, Liberty finds that she cannot get Cory out of her head.

'Glam, glitz, gorgeous people... so Jordan!' *Woman*

'A real insight into the celebrity world' *OK!*

'Brilliantly bitchy' *New!*

arrow books

Santa Baby

Katie Price

'I thought Tiffany should know that she has a half sister. She's Angel Summer – the famous model.'

With these words from the mother who gave her away, Tiffany Taylor's life is turned upside down.

To Tiff's surprise, Angel welcomes her with open arms and suddenly Tiffany has gone from being a waitress to working as a stylist on Angel's TV show.

If only Angel's seriously sexy bodyguard Sean could be as welcoming. But with the threat of kidnap hanging over Angel and her daughter Honey, he has to stay vigilant.

Then, as everyone gathers at Angel and Cal's mansion for a big Christmas celebration, Sean's defences finally drop. But as he relaxes, the danger moves closer, and Tiffany finds herself in serious trouble

'Glam, glitz, gorgeous people... so Jordan!' *Woman*

'A real insight into the celebrity world' *OK!*

'Brilliantly bitchy' *New!*

arrow books

In the Name of Love

By Katie Price

On a sun drenched beach in Barbados, feisty sports presenter Charlie meets the irresistibly gorgeous Felipe Castillo. Instantly attracted to each other, they have a passionate affair, until he walks out, leaving her heartbroken.

It is only then that she discovers that Felipe is related to the Spanish royal family, is a brilliant rider and the lynchpin of the Spanish Eventing team.

But just when Charlie thinks she's managed to put her heartbreak behind her, Felipe returns, and she falls in love all over again. Soon they are the golden couple of sport, followed by the press wherever they go.

But as the pressure on the couple mounts, a dark shadow from Charlie's past comes back to haunt her.

'Glam, glitz, gorgeous people... so Jordan!' *Woman*

'A real insight into the celebrity world' *OK!*

'Brilliantly bitchy' *New!*

arrow books

The Comeback Girl

By Katie Price

Once upon a time, Eden had it all; she was one of the most successful young singers in the UK, and the darling of the pop industry. Life couldn't have been better. But just two years after a sell-out tour, Eden is regarded as a has-been, better known for her drinking and the kiss-and-tell stories that a string of men have sold to the papers.

Desperate to get back in the big time, Eden begins recording a new album with songwriter Jack Steele, a man who drives her crazy for all the wrong reasons. But when she's asked to be a judge on the TV talent show *Band Ambition*, it's just the break she needs, and she's determined not to mess it up. So falling in love with Stevie, a contestant on the show, is probably not a very good idea. But Eden has always followed her heart, and she is sure that Stevie is 'the one'.

But is Eden setting herself up for another fall?

'Glam, glitz, gorgeous people . . . so Jordan!' *Woman*

'A real insight into the celebrity world' *OK!*

'Brilliantly bitchy' *New!*

arrow books